SECRETS IN THE SHADOWS

D1388487

Virginia
ANDREWS

SECRETS IN THE
SHADOWS

POCKET
BOOKS

LONDON • SYDNEY • NEW YORK • TORONTO

First published in the US by Pocket Books, 2008
A division of Simon and Schuster Inc.
First published in Great Britain by Simon & Schuster UK Ltd, 2010
This edition published by Pocket Books, 2010
An imprint of Simon and Schuster UK Ltd
A CBS COMPANY

Copyright © the Vanda General Partnership, 2008

This book is copyright under the Berne Convention.
No reproduction without permission.
® and © 1997 Simon & Schuster Inc. All rights reserved.
Pocket Books & Design is a registered trademark of Simon &
Schuster Inc.

The right of Virginia Andrews® to be identified as author of this
work has been asserted in accordance with sections 77 and 78 of the
Copyright, Designs and Patents Act, 1988.

1 3 5 7 9 10 8 6 4 2

Simon & Schuster UK Ltd
1st Floor
222 Gray's Inn Road
London WC1X 8HB

www.simonandschuster.co.uk

Simon & Schuster Australia
Sydney

A CIP catalogue record for this book is
available from the British Library

ISBN: 978-1-47113-249-0

This book is a work of fiction. Names, characters,
places and incidents are either a product of the author's imagination
or are used fictitiously. Any resemblance to actual people living
or dead, events or locales is entirely coincidental.

Printed and bound by CPI Group (UK) Ltd, Croydon, CR0 4YY

SECRETS IN THE
SHADOWS

Prologue

Imagine you're a sixteen-year-old girl growing up in a small community where everyone you knew and who knew you was aware that your mother had murdered someone when she was your age and was now and has been in a mental institution ever since.

Imagine knowing that whenever people were looking at you and whispering, they were probably wondering if you had inherited sin and madness so that eventually you would do something terrible, too.

Imagine wondering about it yourself every time you looked at yourself in a mirror.

Imagine trying to have a best friend, to be accepted and trusted, but never succeeding because everyone's parents were afraid you would somehow contaminate their children.

Imagine waiting, like someone listening to a time bomb ticking away inside you, waiting for the explosion, when suddenly, without any sort of warning, the evil genes inside you finally joined into some genetic whip and snapped, sending you out in the night to do something horrendous, and in doing so confirming what everyone had thought—that despite all the warmth and love you were given, you could not deny being your mother's daughter. You could not deny yourself and your own destiny.

If you can imagine all that, you might be able to understand who I was and who I tried to be.

And why it took me so long to grow my own wings and fly away.

1

My Mother's Daughter

I sit by the window in the attic that looks out on the wooded area behind the Doral House, just the way I imagined my mother had done more than sixteen years ago when she was about my age. This year heavy March and early April rains had turned the trees and foliage so plush and thick in upstate New York that sunlight was barely able to reach the forest floor. While I sit here, I try to envision and understand what it was like to feel like a bird in a cage, especially a bird that had flown into the cage deliberately and then locked the door behind her, for that was what my mother had done. However, unlike a bird, she couldn't sing or flutter about too noisily.

My mother had turned herself into a silent prisoner, mute and ghostly, and even though I was created up in this attic, fathered by my grandparents' son, Jesse, while he and my aunt Zipporah hid my mother in this attic after she had killed her stepfather, Harry Pearson, I was, for all practical purposes, born without parents.

Almost from the first day I was nurtured and began my relationship with the people caring for me, the people who were supposed to love me and whom I was supposed to love, I understood them to be Grandma and Grandpa, not Mommy and Daddy.

Neither pretended to be anything more.

Of course, I can't remember exactly when I heard the words *Mama* and *Papa, Mother* and *Father, Mommy* and *Daddy.* Maybe I first heard them watching television, watching other little girls and boys my age being cared for by younger people. Even then I began to feel I was different and began to understand that someone else, someone very important, was missing from my world, my life. Now, years later, I still feel like someone who had part of herself amputated even before she was born.

I imagine a child psychologist would have a field day with all this. He or she might even decide to do an article about me for some therapy magazine. My classmates—and even my teachers—would not be surprised if my picture appeared on the front page of *Child Psychology* or some such publication. I'm sure I don't do myself any good or change their minds either by keeping so much to myself or, especially, by the way I dress. I can't help being drawn to darker colors and blouses, skirts and shoes that detract from my appearance. I wear clothing usually a size or two too big, things women my grandmother's age would wear. In fact the other girls call my wardrobe Granny clothes. They bob their heads and cluck like hens about me whenever I walk by in the school hallways.

I've always deliberately kept my hair cut a little too short, and, unlike most girls my age, I never wore lipstick, trimmed my eyebrows or used any makeup. I had no mother or older sister to show me how, and my grandmother has never offered to do so, but I'm sure

I've refrained from doing any of those things for other reasons, too.

I readily admit one reason to myself. I am fully aware that I have made choices that will keep boys from noticing me or caring about me, including deliberately wearing clothing that makes me uninteresting. The reason is simply that I wish I really was invisible or at least slowly disappearing, and being ignored helps me feel as if I am. I know all this contributes toward why people think me somewhat weird, so in a real sense, I suppose I am at fault. I am a bit mad.

And it isn't just my fellow students who remark about me. Over the past sixteen years, I probably heard some adult whisper something like *"That girl should see a psychiatrist"* a dozen times if I heard it once, and even if people didn't say it, they surely thought it. I could see it in their eyes as they followed me along while I walked with my head down, skulking through the village of Sandburg or to the Doral House.

It was interesting to me that I could not refer to where I lived as home. To this day I call it the Doral House, as if I knew instinctively that I was living in a place that was as temporary for me as the various small hotels and tourist houses in this New York mountain area were for vacationers.

Other girls and boys my age would say they had to get home, whereas I would say, "I have to get back to the Doral House." I made it sound like a safe haven, like my private embassy where I had diplomatic privileges and immunities. Once I was shut up inside it, no one could bother me, no one could send any accusatory darts from his or her eyes, and none of their dark whispers could penetrate the walls.

In a very true sense, then, my mother, the woman I had yet to meet, had turned me into a prisoner as well. That was why it wasn't all that difficult for me to spend so much time alone up here and why I would sit by this attic window for hours looking out at the world the way she had. The questions I would ask myself from the moment I understood the story, as well as the questions I knew to be on everyone else's minds, were, What else did she pass on to me? What similar demon hovered under my breast? What would I become? Would I end up in an attic of my own making?

As I imagined her doing, I would sprawl and put my ear to the floor to listen to the muffled sounds and voices below to try to picture what everyone was doing. I wanted to feel exactly the way she had felt. For most of her day, this was her only contact with anyone. I thought the loneliness would have been enough to drive her mad, even if she had come up here in a clearly sane state of mind.

The only pictures I have of my mother were the pictures my aunt Zipporah had of the two of them. If looking at these pictures could wear the image down, they would have disappeared long ago. It was like studying the Mona Lisa to see what clues I could find in that smile, those eyes, the turn of her mouth, the way she held her head. I even studied how my mother cupped her fingers against her hip in one picture. Did she always do that? Did it mean she was always tense, afraid? Who was she? What was her voice like? Was mine at all similar? What about her laugh? Was it short and insecure like mine, or was she totally uninhibited?

Babies cling so firmly to all those magical little

things about their mothers. They are reassured by their mothers' smiles. Their mothers' love and the melodic flow of their mothers' praises help them feel safe, comforted, but, most important, never alone. I had to imagine all that, pretend I had heard it. Was it part of my madness that I thought I could hear her whispering up here or thought I had caught a glimpse of her dressed in a shadow's movement caused by the sun and clouds and especially the moon? Or was it all just my desperate need to know?

I could see the unhappiness on my grandparents' faces whenever I had the courage to ask about my mother, and I especially could see the fear in my grandmother's eyes. It was like asking about the devil. It was better not to ask, not to be curious, but what child would not want to know? It was what drove orphans to pursue their origins, for to know as much as you could about your parents meant you would know so much more about yourself.

It was in fact the way to find the answer to the haunting question we all ask about ourselves, perhaps all our lives. Who am I? And not just who am I to other people, but who am I to myself?

For me the answer was buried in the twisted and crooked way my history was entwined. To discover the answer, I had to unravel it.

At first it was all told to me in simple ways, like my grandmother explaining what a grandmother was really supposed to be and what she was now. Whether she intended to do it or not, she made it clear to me that even though she was doing what a mother should be doing, she could never fully fill a mother's shoes. Of course, as soon as I understood, I wanted to know why I didn't have a mother or a father with whom I lived just as other girls and boys my age did.

"The reason you don't have a mother and a father is because people are supposed to get married first and plan when to have their children so they could take care of them properly," she said. "Yours didn't."

She didn't come right out and call me a mistake. She told me I was as unexpected as a sudden summer thunderstorm. I actually used to think I fell out of the sky, came floating down like a leaf from a tree to settle at their front door. Sometimes, I wished it was true, wished that I had been left on their doorstep. It was all so much easier to accept when you believed a stork brought you to your family. That way a baby was his or her own little person and arrived without any baggage, and especially without any dark past. Stork babies were truly like Adam and Eve, original, born with no past, only a future.

However, at an earlier age than most of the girls around me, I learned the so-called Facts of Life, and so the stork, like so many of the fantasies other girls were being told, was swept outside my door. It was too dangerous for me especially not to know the hard, cold realities as soon as possible. According to my grandmother, who still worked as a special-duty nurse at the hospital, teenage pregnancy was practically a raging plague, and after all, wasn't that what happened in this very house? The chance of that happening again was greater for me because of who my mother was. No one came right out and said so, but I could hear it whispered in every dark corner. I could feel it. It was palpable in every fearful glance. As Karen Stoker's daughter, I was more susceptible to weakness and lust than most girls my age would be. I must be aware of that at all times and therefore be extra cautious.

Maybe that was an even more important reason why I did everything I could to keep boys from noticing me. I was afraid it was true, afraid of myself. "Stay out of the water and you can't drown," I told myself. For a long time, it wasn't all that difficult for me to do. Boys didn't look at me with desire, only amusement.

Being she was a nurse, my grandmother was always good about explaining the mechanics of sex. She made it sound as impersonal as the workings of a car engine, maybe to keep me from being at all intrigued or interested. Until I reached puberty, her efforts were successful. I found her lectures dry and boring and wondered what all the excitement was about.

"However," she told me in a veiled warning, "even if you explain it all clearly to your son or to your daughter, there's nothing you can do if he or she permits his or her body to take control of his or her mind. There's nothing you can do," she said, her voice drifting off under the pressure of the heavy regret. I knew she felt like a policewoman whose son had become a bank robber. I didn't know whether to hate him or not for causing me to be born. I saw him so rarely and had little opportunity to think of him as my father. I really had no clear understanding of how much of him was in me.

I winced every time I heard someone refer to another girl or boy my age to be so much like his or her father or mother that they were like two peas in a pod.

Whoever said it in my presence usually said it loud enough for me to hear. Of course, I suspected this person was thinking my mother and I were two peas in a pod and not my father and I. My grandparents had told me so little. How was I to know if it was true or not?

Actually, I had learned the most about my mother and the tragic events from my aunt Zipporah, who had been my mother's best friend at the time of the tragedy, and against my grandmother's wishes had given me those pictures of the two of them. It was from Aunt Zipporah that I learned that before anything terrible had occurred, she and my mother had turned the attic into their private imaginary world. I would never have known otherwise, because neither my grandmother nor my grandfather would talk about it and because my grandfather and my father had emptied it of all that had been in it and remodeled it. I suppose it was their attempt to erase the past. However, Aunt Zipporah helped me understand why and how it had been their playground before it had become a prison.

She described how they fantasized up here, pretending the sofa was a car taking them on cross-country trips. She told me about the old clothing they had found in old chests, and how they dressed in them and put on the heavy shoes, clumping about pretending to be this one or that one. They made up stories to fit the pictures of former residents they had discovered in dresser drawers, in boxes and cartons.

"We were surprised at how much the former residents had left behind. Your mother called the attic a 'nest of orphans.' She was so good at imagining what their lives had been like. She spun tales of love and deceit, loss and joy, adventure and romance on a magical loom. The attic walls are full of our laughter and pretended sobs and wails. For us it was way more fun than watching television or going to a movie."

I clung to every word she used to describe my mother. I was truly like a starving person treasuring crumbs. The stories she told about the two of them filled me with such warmth and pleasure. I couldn't help wishing that I had a friend that close who would do similar things with me, a friend whose parents weren't afraid of her coming here to spend time with me and share intimate feelings and thoughts. How wonderful it must have been for both of them to have someone each could trust, have someone who brought her joy and happiness.

Aunt Zipporah described how inventive, imaginative and unpredictable my mother had been even outside of the attic, and how that had given her so much pleasure.

"If it weren't for your mother, life in this small town would have been boring for me. We had moved up from a far more urban area close to New York City, where there was so much more to do, but your mother made sure that nothing was ever what it was in reality. Karen cast her imagination at homes, people, even dogs and cats and turned them into fantasies. People used to say we walked on air and bounced about as if we had swallowed helium. In those early days, they were always smiling at us, shaking their heads and laughing at our boundless energy. They enjoyed us."

She said other girls were jealous of their relationship.

"They stared at us with half smiles, wishing we would let them into our world," she told me, a half smile on her face as well.

It filled her with such pleasure to remember, but she was also so saddened by the way it had all turned out.

When she relived all that, her smile would evaporate and be replaced with a pained expression that made it look like she was having a severe headache. I couldn't help feeling that she had felt betrayed, that her trust and love were things she should have been more careful about spending, especially when you realize how her and my mother's tale had ended.

Finishing high school here had been difficult for Aunt Zipporah afterward, but she had recuperated enough to do well and go on to college in New Paltz, where she had met and married Tyler James, a young man who had inherited his own café in the city where the state college was located. She earned her degree, but she didn't go on to be a teacher as she had intended. Instead, she worked in their café, and over the past two summers, I spent time there working as a busgirl, clearing off tables and sometimes helping with the hostess duties. I was happier there because I was away from my mother's history, which remained like some ugly stain, not only on me but also on the very streets and buildings.

Even people who were too new to the community or too young to have known my mother and my maternal grandmother, Darlene Pearson, knew the story. It was the most infamous tale in the community. The drugstore my mother's stepfather owned, Pearsons Drug Store, was practically a historic landmark because of what had happened. Nothing different had been done to the front of it and very little to the inside, from what I was told.

Not long after I had been born, Darlene Pearson (I can think of her only as Darlene Pearson), my maternal grandmother, sold the store, and it had been sold again since. She moved away, or, as I had heard many times, she fled, literally packing up and driving off in the middle of the night. No one, not even my grandparents, knew where she had eventually gone. Her real estate agent had been sworn to secrecy and handled all the paperwork between herself and the buyer, the Harrison family, who owned the lumber and hardware company in Sandburg. As far as I knew, my grandparents had never received a phone call or any written inquiry from Darlene Pearson asking about me.

Neither she nor my real mother had anything to do with naming me, nor, as far as I knew, did my real father. When I asked why my mother had no interest, my grandmother told me she didn't know I existed.

"How can she not know that?" I asked. "Surely, she knew she was pregnant and knew she had given birth to me."

"I'm only telling you what I've been told by the doctors at the clinic. Your mother is not in her right mind. She has blocked out any memory of you. It's better if we don't talk about it. It makes me just as upset as it does you," she said and snapped her hand in the air between us as if that would send all the questions and all the answers out of the house.

No matter what she told me, I couldn't imagine not remembering you were pregnant and had given birth. She must be pretending she can't remember, I thought. According to my aunt Zipporah, my mother was so good at pretending that I imagined she could even fool brilliant doctors.

My grandmother decided to call me Alice. When I once asked her why, she said, "Because maybe like Alice, you'll fall into a Wonderland someday."

Consequently, *Alice in Wonderland* was one of the first books I ever read and soon after, escaping into another world became my dream. I couldn't help feeling that no one, not even my aunt Zipporah, was all that happy to see me in this one. Darlene Pearson was certainly not happy about it. It was the final straw, sending her fleeing into the night.

Of course, I wondered almost as much about my maternal grandmother as I did about my mother. How could she have no interest at all in her own flesh and blood? How could she not have at least some curiosity? Later, when I was older, it gave me pause to wonder if the details of my mother's tragic story were true after all. Perhaps she wasn't so crazy when she killed Harry Pearson and the things she had claimed he had done to her were really done to her. I didn't know specific details, but I knew it had to do with sexual abuse. Perhaps Darlene Pearson was running away from that as much as running away from anything because she felt responsible, guilty since it happened in her home to her daughter.

Of course, I had a selfish reason to hope this was possible. If it had all happened as my mother had first alleged, I wouldn't have evil to inherit. I'd be the daughter of a victim not a mad person, and people would owe me sympathy, not disdain. They could be cordial, not fearful. I'd have lots of friends. I'd be invited to parties and sleepovers, and the gloomy cloud that hovered always over my head would be blown away. I would walk in sunshine. I could smile and laugh and, most important, not be so afraid of the shadows that spilled out of the moonlight and edged farther and farther, closer and closer toward the Doral

House and toward me. When they arrived, I'd be like Dr. Jekyll and turn into Mr. Hyde, unless I really was the victim's daughter.

But without ever meeting my mother or my grandmother, how would I ever know what was true and what was not? It was truly as if I had no maternal family. I knew only the relatives on my father's side, and even they were distant and impersonal. Because I saw him from time to time, I at least knew something about my father. I snuck peeks at his high school and college yearbooks, and there were all the pictures in my grandfather's office, of course.

I knew my father was bright and handsome and had once been a very good athlete, a college baseball star, but he moved away after he achieved his law degree, and my contact with him became infrequent. I understood that my grandfather and my father had dreamed of opening their own law firm here in upstate New York someday but the events that led to my birth pretty much made that impossible. A so-called wise business decision was made and my father took the California state bar exam and put as much distance between himself and the past, which included me, as possible.

Not long after that, he had married Rachel Petersen, another attorney in the firm he had joined in Los Angeles, and she had given birth to twin boys, Justin and Austin, who were now five. They were my half brothers, of course, but to keep peace in his marriage and new family, my father and my grandparents, as well as Rachel, had decided that in front of the twins, they would treat me as if I were my grandparents' child. Otherwise, they would be just too confused. Justin and Austin were growing up believing I was their aunt.

They lived far enough away and were never exposed to the truth.

When I was older, I understood the fabrication was created more for Rachel than it was for the twins. My father's wife didn't want to think about him having had a child with a woman out of wedlock, a woman who had committed murder and had gone into a mental institution. Of course, none of their friends or business associates back in California had any idea. She was adamant about keeping the secret buried.

"I don't ever want Jesse to think of you as his daughter," Rachel told me on one of their recent visits when we were alone. "It's better for all of us if we continue forever to pretend what happened never happened, better especially for my children."

"I know. I just appeared magically," I told her. "One day my mother had a headache and then I popped out of her head, just like Athena popped out of Zeus's head." I had just read the myth in English class.

She wasn't looking at me when she had spoken, but her head sure snapped around when I replied. I had never taken that tone with her. Her eyes were wide with both anger and fear. My stepmother, which was who she really was even though she never acknowledged it, always was uncomfortable around me. I once overheard her tell my father that she thought I stared at her in a very unnatural way because of how I narrowed my eyes and stiffened my lips.

"I feel her resentment," she told him.

"That's silly, Rachel. How could she? She doesn't understand all this."

I was only about five then myself, not that it mattered to her. I could have been two. She wanted me to be unnatural; she wanted me to be weird.

"Oh yes, she does," she insisted. "Yes, she does."

I thought that if anyone believed I inherited evil, it was Rachel.

She was a tall, thin, dark brunette with hazel eyes and that light toast California complexion. I could see why she would be a successful attorney. She had a careful exactness about everything, as if she had a built-in editing machine to trim her dialogue so as never to waste words. No one had to wonder what she meant when she spoke. She was even that way with the twins, and especially with my father.

I wondered if they had fallen in love or simply fallen into marriage.

It was easy to see that he was at a disadvantage every time they visited us. I was sure that before they arrived, all sorts of promises had been made, stipulations, as she might refer to them. It wasn't difficult for me to imagine what they were. In my mind, my father practically had them printed on his forehead or had agreed to them by signing in blood. Even before they arrived, I heard them whispered in the wind.

Don't spend very much time alone with Alice, time without the boys, too.

Don't show any more interest in her than you do in them.

Don't permit them to call her anything but Aunt Alice and don't let them spend too much time alone with her either.

Don't ever take the twins up to the attic.

Don't ever ask any questions about Karen Stoker or her mother in front of me or the boys.

And remember, we don't stay too long and we must never, ever give Alice even the slightest reason to hope that she might come to live with us someday.

It occurred to me that my father would never stop paying for his sins. It also occurred to me that he deliberately married a woman who would see to that because he never wanted to stop punishing himself for disappointing his own parents.

At least I had a purpose. I made my father's pain everlasting.

How would you like that to be your reason for being born?

2

Tell Me Everything

I turned from the window when I heard voices and laughter, and the squeals of delight from the twins below. I was sure my grandfather had swept them both up in his arms and was bouncing them about, pretending to decide which one weighed more and then playfully squeezing their biceps to see who looked to be stronger. Against my grandmother's wishes, he always teased them to make them competitive with each other. I knew he was afraid that Rachel was making them too docile; sometimes he went so far as to accuse them of being little spoiled princes without a castle or a kingdom.

"They'll be at a disadvantage if they're too soft," he said when Rachel complained.

"They need to compete with other people, not each other," Rachel countered. She wasn't afraid to challenge anyone, which was a strength I admired in her and wished for myself, but I once overheard my grandfather tell my grandmother, "That woman never shows any weakness, never cries. She has no tear ducts."

"You train at home for the wars to come," Grandfather told Rachel. "And believe me, they will come." He never backed away from an argument either.

Rachel got along better with my grandmother, which I thought was odd since both Rachel and my grandfather were attorneys. Anyone would think they would have more in common, more to share. Lately, however, I began to suspect he was not happy with the way she treated me. He was far more protective of me than my own father was.

But then again, except for the biological reasons, he might as well be my father. The twins could go on believing it forever, for all I cared.

Of course, I knew they were all coming during the spring holiday break. Their visit had been planned for months. I just didn't know that there would be a bigger reason for their coming than just another family visit and that reason had to do with me. Although I heard them below, I didn't rush right down to greet them. I liked the twins, but because of Rachel, and because of my father, I was always on pins and needles, afraid I might say something to them or do something that would bring a cascading waterfall of criticism and reprimand.

I knew that the arrival of my father and his family was supposed to be a time to celebrate and do fun things, but the truth was that as soon as I had heard they were coming to visit, I went into a deeper withdrawal and spent more time in the attic. Whenever they were here, I sought every opportunity I could to avoid spending time with them. I could tell that my grandmother, who was always more nervous when they came, wasn't terribly unhappy about that, but my grandfather sensed it and usually insisted I was included in everything possible, sometimes when it wasn't even necessary, simply to make a point.

"She has just as much right to be here as any of us," he muttered.

To make sure further that I wasn't ignored, he usually paraded whatever of my achievements he could, starting with my report card and then going to the latest pictures I had painted. When I was twelve, and he was told by the art teacher in school about my artistic ability, he immediately went out and bought materials and easels and then, without my grandmother's blessing, turned the attic into a makeshift art studio for me, even improving the lighting.

"She spends too much time up there as it is, Michael," my grandmother complained.

"Why waste the space? Besides, up there she can have the privacy an artist needs to create," he insisted.

"Yes, we know too well about that sort of privacy and the creative things that went on up there," she replied.

She was far less forgiving, but my grandfather ignored her and went ahead anyway. He even bought me an artist's smock and a French artist's hat. Sometimes, I thought he was more excited about it all than I was. I know that often I tried harder because of him, because I wanted to please him. I knew that he wanted me to be good and successful in anything I attempted as a way to ease his own conscience. Good came from bad. Parents, no matter what, blame themselves for the actions of their children.

I began with simple watercolors of the scenery around us and then one day decided to try to do a painting of the Doral House itself. Early on, I understood the difference between a photograph and a painting. I never simply tried to put a picture on a canvas. I let whatever was at work in me at the time turn the lines, add the shadows and the light. In the picture I did of the Doral House, I had a shadow in the attic window that was unmistakably in the shape of a girl looking out. My grandmother was very unnerved by it. She made sure I didn't bring it down from the attic. She referred to the picture as proof as to why my grandfather shouldn't have made the attic my studio.

"There's just something about that attic," she insisted, making it sound truly supernatural.

He thought that was ridiculous. However, I couldn't help feeling my grandmother wasn't all wrong. Whatever connection I felt with my mother, I felt more vividly up here. Something lingered. Something lived on in these attic walls.

"Alice!" I heard my grandfather calling to me. "Come on down. Everyone's here."

I took a deep breath as if whenever I left the attic and went downstairs, I was going under water. It was only up here that I could breathe and think freely. Did that make me more like my mother, too?

Despite my attempts to make things easier for my father by trying to remain as indifferent to him as I could, I couldn't help but steal glances, wondering what it was of him I had inherited. My hair was more the light brown I saw in the pictures of my mother, but I had my father's blue eyes. We both had high cheekbones, too. And we had the same-shaped ears.

Actually, I was more interested in knowing if he

was at all curious about me. Did he ask my grandfather questions about me when they could talk to each
other without Rachel knowing? Had he kept up on my
schoolwork, my interests? Was he at all worried about
me? Would he ever, ever take me aside to tell me about
my mother and him, especially how it had all begun?
In short, would he ever, even for fifteen minutes, be
my father?

Rachel was taking the twins to their bedroom for a
nap as I came down the stairway. The drive up from
the airport had tired them out, and when they were
tired, they were usually cranky and restless. Putting
them to sleep was always her method of reprimand-
ing them. They hated taking naps and whined and
shrieked all the way down the hall, pausing only
to look up at me as I descended. I knew they were
hoping that my entrance would somehow put off
their banishment, but Rachel was relentless about
something whenever she had made up her mind to
do it. She practically lifted them off their feet as she
dragged them by the hand. I imagined she was a formidable advocate in any courtroom. For me she was
precisely the sort of person I admired and disliked
simultaneously.

And I knew she knew it, too.

"Hello, Alice," she said. "I'll be out after I put the
two terrors to sleep for a while."

I nodded and continued to the living room, where
my father sat with my grandmother and my grandfather. For as long as I could remember, I was always
shy about going to my father to give him a kiss, and
he, especially in front of my grandmother, was as
shy about kissing me as well. Our compromise was

usually his hugging me hello and brushing my cheek with his lips. This time, he didn't even do that. He remained sitting, smiled and said, "How you doing, Alice?"

"Okay."

"You're a few inches taller than you were the last time I was here."

"She's not at all taller," my grandmother said. Despite the resemblances between my father and myself, she liked to emphasize and stress the ones between me and my mother, as if she was trying to convince herself I was cloned and her son didn't have anything to do with the sinful mess that followed. Height was one of the characteristics I shared with my mother, and from what I could tell from the pictures, I was molding into a figure similar to hers as well.

"Well," my father said, "she must be thinner then or something. She looks taller."

"She's lost any traces of baby fat; that's for sure," my grandfather said, smiling.

"Ridiculous," my grandmother muttered. "A girl this age is not supposed to have any baby fat, Michael. She's over sixteen."

"Precisely. A young lady," my grandfather replied, nodding. "Working on a new painting?" he asked quickly, knowing I had been up in the attic all day. "She's doing some remarkable work," he told my father, who flashed a smile.

How sad, I thought, to think that a smile was such a risk. I wondered if Rachel counted how many times he did smile at me while he was here, as well as how many times he touched me. She surely counted any kisses, lip brushes included.

"You'll have to show everyone the one you did of the tree in the meadow. I swear. Every time I look at it, it seems to have changed. It's almost alive on the canvas!" my grandfather said.

I could see from the expression on my grandmother's face that she didn't like to hear him talk about my art like that. She actually looked a little frightened, as if my art was some sort of witchcraft. Did she really believe my mother was speaking through me in my art? I wondered myself if that was at all possible.

"Well, you couldn't have a better public relations man, Alice. I guess I'll have to see it then," my father said.

"See what?" Rachel asked, coming into the living room.

"Dad was just telling me about one of Alice's new pictures and how wonderful he thinks it is."

She smirked. "They put up a fuss, but the moment both hit the bed, they closed their eyes and were out," she told my grandparents, as if nothing had been said about me. Then she turned to my father. "Are you taking me to the drugstore now, Jesse, or what?"

"We just got here," he protested.

"I'd like to go while they're asleep," she said, "and I don't want the store to close. I need my things."

"Well, okay, I guess," he said, rising. Was he reluctant to take her because he was taking her to what had once been my mother's stepfather's drugstore? Rachel was either unaware of it or simply didn't care.

"They should sleep a while," she told my grandmother, "but if they wake up . . ."

"Don't worry about them. I'll listen for them," my grandmother said.

My father glanced at me.

"I'll see your picture later, Alice."

I shrugged and turned away until they left. For a moment it was as if all the air had gone out of the room with them.

"I'll look in on the twins," my grandmother said, rose and went off toward the guests' bedrooms.

Why had I bothered coming down?

My grandfather was staring at me, a very thoughtful, if not painful, look on his face. He slapped his knees and rose.

"Come take a walk with me, Alice," he said.

"A walk? Where?"

The Doral House was on a nearly deserted rural road with the next property being a good half mile or so east of us.

"Just a walk. It's a rather nice day and you haven't been out to enjoy any of it," he said. "Come on. You'll get an idea for a new painting perhaps. I do my best thinking when I'm just walking."

I followed him out of the living room and then out of the house.

"I didn't think we'd stay here this long," he said, pausing on the porch and gazing at the road. He was still a very handsome, physically fit man and looked years younger than he was. He loved golf but had taken up racquet ball to keep his weight in check. He told me most of the attorneys he knew were overweight. "Too many free lunches," he said. "And martinis."

"Why not?" I asked.

"Oh, I don't know. After both kids were off, Elaine talked about us moving to Monticello into one of those town houses. She'd be closer to the hospital and I'd be closer to the office and the courthouse, being that's the county seat. We wouldn't have to worry about maintenance."

"Why didn't you move then?"

"Can't say. The idea just sort of drifted away, and she had done so much to improve the property. I suppose neither of us wanted to desert it."

"But it has such bad memories," I dared mention.

"Naw. You can't blame the house. It's just a house," he said, smiling. "You haven't seen any of those ghosts people think dwell here, have you?"

"No. I wouldn't be afraid of them if I did," I added, and he laughed.

"I bet you wouldn't."

I wouldn't, I thought. Ghosts were probably as lonely as I was, trapped between two worlds.

He started down the walk to the driveway and then to the road. I followed along. He looked back and gestured with his head for me to catch up. I did, and we started to stroll down the street, walking along quietly. It was a nice day with the sort of sky that seems to be a faded blue, dabbed with starch white puffs of clouds that looked more like smoke from steam. When I was little, my grandfather called those clouds God's breath, comparing them to the little puffs we saw of our own breath on very cold winter days and nights.

We continued walking. The warm breeze stirred the trees, causing the branches to shudder rather than rustle. A small black bird did a little dance on the road and then lifted off and into the forest to disappear in the pockets of darkness. Occasionally, I would see a deer on this road looking bewildered about the strip of macadam in the midst of its natural habitat. There were always lots of rabbits hurrying along as if they were late for a very important date. Once I saw a fox, and my grandfather swore he saw a bobcat. He was walking with his head down now, but he suddenly paused and took a deep breath before looking at me and smiling.

"I wasn't just kidding back there about you losing your baby fat, Alice," he said. "Sometimes, a girl—or a boy, for that matter—grows up overnight. At least it seems that way. Elaine's afraid to see it happening. That's natural for mothers and grandmothers, I suppose. She was the same with Zipporah."

"Why?"

"Oh, I suppose they don't want to see their children and grandchildren have to face all the problems they know come with it."

"Like what?"

"Boys, for one thing," he said, widening his smile. "Worrying about relationships, looks, the whole ball of wax, as they say. You ever hear the expression 'Little kids, little problems, big kids, bigger problems'?"

"No. Where would I hear it?"

"Right. Where would you? Which is something I wanted to talk to you about, Alice."

He continued walking.

"What is?"

"You should try to do more with your opportunities at school. You're spending too much time alone.

Join clubs, teams, whatever, anything that will help you get out more. Despite how protective and worried she seems sometimes, I'm sure your grandmother would like to see that, like to see you do more social activities. It's not good to spend so much time by yourself at your age."

I felt tears coming to my eyes. Did he think all this was my fault?

He glanced at me because I was so silent.

"I'm not complaining or criticizing you, honey. I just want you to be happier. You should do fun things kids your age are doing. I mean, I love your paintings and I think you might just make something of your art, but you want to also do things that enable you to be with other kids your age."

"It's not because I don't want to," I said, which was at least a half-truth.

"Oh?"

Surely he had noticed my isolation before this, I thought. This was just his way of investigating.

"The school is full of cliques. I don't exactly fit in with most of them."

"Nonsense. Tell me the truth. Have you turned down invitations to things, Alice, because . . ."

"No," I said sharply.

"Well, sometimes you have to go halfway. It's hard to find a perfect friend or friends. You have to forgive them for their failures. Why don't you just join something? Isn't there any club, activity that interests you besides your art? Once you're in something, you'll see how much easier it is to make friends, because you'll have common interests."

I didn't say anything. We walked on.

"It's just a suggestion," he said. "I want you to be happier."

He paused and looked out over a field of high, wild grass.

"I was thinking of buying this property once," he said. "Developing some modest housing. It's going to happen soon. People from New York are thinking more and more of this area for second homes. I might still do it. I've sent out some feelers through a real estate agent."

He glanced at me.

I didn't have much interest in any of that and he knew it. *He's just trying to change the subject,* I thought.

"No one's made fun of you lately, have they, Alice?" he asked sharply.

Last April there was a very bad incident. Two of the girls in my class, Peggy Okun and Mindy Taylor, were slipping nasty notes into my hall locker, asking things like, How can you sleep there? Do you hear the moans of Brandon Doral? (Brandon was supposedly murdered by his wife and buried on the property.) The worst note was, Who's hiding in your attic now? Is your mother back?

I didn't tell anyone about it, but one afternoon, after I had come home, one of the notes fell out of the math book in which I had put it, and my grandmother found it near the front door. She showed it to my grandfather and he went ballistic. I had to tell him it had been going on for some time. At his insistence, the principal put the dean of students on the case. Through observation, they discovered who had been doing it by catching them in the act. The hullabaloo it created was more disturbing for me than the notes had been. Both Mindy and Peggy were suspended for two days and then had a week's detention, but all that did was bring them more sympathy and make me look more terrible.

"No," I said.

"You'd tell me if they were, right?"

"Yes," I said, but not with any enthusiasm. He knew I wouldn't.

"Maybe we should have moved away," he muttered. I didn't think he meant for me to hear it.

He snapped out of his dark mood quickly, however, and talked about taking the family to a fun new restaurant in Middletown tomorrow night.

"Your grandmother made sure she had time off while Jesse and the kids are here."

"Isn't Aunt Zipporah coming to visit?"

"Oh, sure. She'll be here tomorrow morning," he said. "But Tyler will have to stay at the café. She'll be with us for a couple of days."

"That's good," I said. I so looked forward to seeing Aunt Zipporah, especially when my father and Rachel had come.

We turned back toward the house.

"Well," my grandfather said, "I suppose I should seriously consider resurfacing the driveway. I've resisted all these years, but your grandmother says it's embarrassing. I imagine the birds have been saying nasty things about us," he joked. "I can't think of anyone else who would care. The rabbits don't seem to mind, right?"

I smiled. It was so much easier to be with him than it was to be with my grandmother. Why wasn't he as worried about what I might have inherited and what I hadn't as she was? I wondered. Did he see or know something I didn't? Did he know the truth all these years?

"Can I ask you something, Grandpa?"

"Sure. Anything," he said. "Just don't ask me to be late for dinner."

"I'm serious," I said.

"Oh, no. When one of these Stein women gets serious, I'm in deep trouble." He paused. "What is it, Alice?"

"Were you absolutely positive that the things my mother claimed Harry Pearson had done to her were never done to her?"

He glanced at the house as if he wanted to be absolutely positive we were too far from it for my grandmother to overhear the conversation.

"I really wish you wouldn't be thinking about that so much, honey."

"I can't help it," I said.

He nodded.

"Well, I'm sorry to say there was never any doubt that she was a very disturbed person."

He looked like he was going to tell me more. I waited, holding my breath.

"Her story was quite fantastic, and there just wasn't any concrete evidence to support any of it. Could it somehow still have been true? Well, I suppose we should never absolutely discount anything. It's so long ago and so much damage has been done to the truth, whatever it is, that it's impossible to make any firm conclusions that will satisfy you—or me, for that matter. It won't change anything now."

"It would for me," I said.

"I meant for your mother." He turned to me. His face darkened with the shadow of his deep thoughts. "I don't know how you can do it or if you ever will, but somehow, I wish you could let it all go, Alice. Be your own person and put it away."

"I don't know who I am, Grandpa. I don't know how to be my own person."

"You will," he said and put his arm around me to squeeze me to him. "Someday, you will. I'm confident."

We saw the car my father and Rachel had rented coming down the road toward the house.

"Why does Rachel hate me?" I dared ask.

We watched my father turn into the driveway.

"She doesn't hate you, Alice," my grandfather said in a tired, frustrated voice. "She's threatened by you. I think you're old enough to understand. You're a part of Jesse that she doesn't want to admit exists. In time, she'll get more comfortable with you, especially when you come into your own. Until then, treat her like thin ice. Don't worry. I'll always be there," he added.

Even if my father isn't, I wanted to add but didn't.

"Hey," my father called to us when he stepped out of the car. "You know how big the potholes are in this driveway already?"

"Really? I never noticed," my grandfather said and winked at me.

I smiled, and we walked back to join them. Rachel walked faster into the house.

"Where you guys been?" my father asked.

"I took Alice over to look at the Bedik property.

Still thinking about buying it all for development. As an artist, Alice could envision it all better than I can."

My father looked at me.

"So what do you think, Alice?" he asked. "Is your grandfather crazy?"

"No."

"And even if I were, she wouldn't say so," Grandpa told him. They laughed.

"I'd like to see that painting we were talking about before I left," my father told me. "Where is it?"

"In the attic," I said. He flashed a look at my grandfather and then at me, his eyes at first full of trepidation and then, suddenly, brightening with excitement.

"Okay. Let's go take a look."

He had never, ever been up there with me alone. My heart didn't pound; it twittered and then filled me with an electric excitement that streamed down my body as we all headed for the front door.

Rachel had gone to put away whatever she had gotten at the drugstore. My grandmother was in the kitchen, and the twins were still fast asleep.

"I have to make a few calls," my grandfather said. He glanced at me. I think he wanted to make it possible for my father to be alone with me.

My father nodded. He looked a little nervous but started up the stairway. I looked down the hallway to see if Rachel was coming back, and then I hurried up after him. When we reached the second landing and the short stairway to the attic door, he stepped aside to let me go first.

My eyes were practically glued to him when he

came into the attic behind me. Of course, he knew how it had been changed, but still, coming up here had to have a special meaning for him. As he panned the room, I could almost see him turn back into the boy he had been years ago. Memories were surely flashing across his eyes in snapshot fashion. Self-conscious at how he was behaving, he quickly turned to me.

"Dad's improved the lighting up here, I see." He nodded at the rows of lights in the ceiling. "Where's the new painting?"

I stepped up to an easel and uncovered the picture. He approached and studied it as if he were truly an art critic, nodding and smiling.

"I see what Dad means. It's very good, Alice. You've really blended those colors well, and I love the sort of kinetic energy you have in the turn of the leaves. Is this any particular tree on the property?"

"Yes," I said, moving toward the windows that faced the rear of the house.

He stepped alongside.

"See across the field to the left?"

"Oh yes."

"When I'm up here for a while, looking out the window, concentrating, I see things that would ordinarily be missed," I told him.

"Really? Like what?"

"Things," I said. I took a breath. "Things I imagine my mother must have seen spending hours and hours alone, looking at the same scene."

He was silent.

Had I violated some unwritten rule by mentioning her? Was this the end of our special time together?

"Actually," he said, "I'd like to talk to you about all that."

Was I hearing correctly? I dared not utter a word, a syllable, even breathe.

"Dad . . . and Mom are worried about you, Alice. It's part of why I worked out this short holiday for Rachel, the boys and myself."

"What is?"

"You," he said.

"What do you mean, me?"

"You have to start thinking about your future. Even if you want to become an artist, you've got to expand. Any artist, writer, songwriter, anyone in the creative fields has to have real experiences from which he or she can draw to create."

"Emily Dickinson didn't," I said. "She was like a hermit. She wrote poems on pillowcases."

"But think of what she might have achieved if she had gone out among people, events, activities."

"She's in our English literature book. She's that important to our literature. She didn't need real experiences. She invented them, imagined them."

"You're a pretty smart girl, Alice, a lot smarter than I was at your age, I'm sure, but believe me, you have a great deal to give to other people and draw from other people. You've got to let yourself go. Join things. Dive into it."

"That's what Grandpa was just telling me," I said. I nodded to myself. *This is a conspiracy, all right.*

"You should listen to him. He never gave me bad advice."

The entire time we spoke to each other, my father and I looked out the window and not at each other. We rarely looked at each other directly.

"I know it's been hard for you," he continued. "You inherited a lot of baggage, but you have to step out of it."

"Like you did?" I asked and turned to see his reaction.

For a moment his lips trembled and I thought he was going to be angry, but then his face softened and he nodded.

"Yes," he said. "I was selfish, but you do selfish things to survive sometimes. What I owe you, I can't even begin to pay back. Your grandparents stepped up to the plate on my behalf, pinched hit. They've done a better job than I could have. That's for sure, but they're both very worried about you, as I said, and it's time I stepped in, too."

"To do what?"

"Help you in any way I can, Alice."

"Any way?"

"I'll do whatever I can," he said, which I knew meant whatever Rachel permitted. "I mean, I want to give you advice, guidance, be a sounding board. I hope it's not too little too late, but . . . well, you see what I'm trying to say, don't you?"

I turned away and looked out the window again. I did, but I wasn't sure that what he was offering was anywhere nearly enough.

"Dad's right," he continued. "You have to let go of the darkness, Alice."

"You want to help me do that?"

"Yes. Very much," he said. "If I can."

"Okay," I said and slowly turned to look at him, blue eyes to blue eyes. "If you really mean that, then tell me everything," I said.

"Everything?"

"Tell me exactly who she was and tell me what happened up here."

3

Take a Chance

Of course, I expected my father to shake his head, mumble some excuses and flee the attic, but instead, he walked back to the small settee my grandfather had put up here and sat. I didn't move from the window.

"When I see you standing there by that window, Alice, with the afternoon light playing around you like that, you really do remind me of her. There is a remarkable resemblance. I used to think that was lucky for me. No one would look at you and think there's Jesse Stein's daughter. I could continue to pretend I wasn't responsible. I was very immature then."

"I'm about the same age she was when she was up here, right?"

"Yes, but of course, I knew her before all that. The truth is, and your aunt Zipporah doesn't even know the true extent of this to this day, I had seen your mother secretly a few times before she was up here. I knew how close your aunt and your mother were, and I thought your aunt would be quite upset about it."

"Then you didn't think she was crazy all the time

or else you wouldn't have been seeing her, right?"

"No, I didn't think that," he said and smiled. "She was pretty unusual, unpredictable, however. You'd never know what she would do or say. She could change moods in an instant and loved doing and saying things that had shock value. I had never met another girl like her and haven't since. She was like a wild mare you wanted to corral but never could. She couldn't stand any sort of confinement, whether it was physical or mental or emotional, which was why I'm sure she hated being up here."

He laughed.

"Why is that funny?"

"That isn't, but she once told me she'd never fall in love because falling in love turned you into a slave, took away your independence. She said she'd rather fall in and out of love continuously, even with the same person, which is what I think she did with me."

"Why did you want to help her? Why did you keep her secretly up here after you learned what she had done?"

He looked away, and he was quiet so long, I thought that was that. He had told me as much as he ever would or could. I gazed out the window, then looked at him again.

"It was selfish," he finally said.

"Selfish? How?"

"I had found a way to control her, to keep her under my power. She needed me, depended on me. The short time we had up here before it all fell apart was ironically the happiest time I had with her. We pretended we were married and in our own home.

Actually, pretending anything made her comfortable.

"It was very wrong and later, it was very painful. I had betrayed the people who loved, trusted and believed in me the most. For that reason alone, nobody wanted Karen to be telling the truth about what had been going on in her home more than I did. It wouldn't completely excuse what I had done, but it would help explain it and in some ways rationalize it. No one was more disappointed than I was the night your aunt and I discovered that the story your mother was spinning was a total fabrication."

"Total?"

"It was just too fantastic, bizarre. She had depicted her stepfather to be some Norman Bates character from *Psycho*. She told both Zipporah and me some things going on at her house that we found not to be true. All the stories about a separate apartment for Harry Pearson's mother proved false, for example, and therefore all the things she claimed had gone on in there were obviously just as false."

"But why would she do something so terrible to her stepfather then?"

"As I said, she was a very complicated person. Something just cracked inside her, I suppose. That's something people trained and educated in psychology will have to answer or maybe have already."

"You don't know?"

He shook his head, a look of shame washing over his face.

"No, I didn't keep up with her situation."

"Did you ever tell her that you knew what she had told you and Aunt Zipporah was all untrue?"

"Yes, of course. Right in this attic," he said, looking around. "Matter of fact, she stood by that window when we told her."

"What did she say?"

"She said her mother was lying, the police were lying, everyone was lying but her."

"Then what did she do?"

"She just walked out and went home, or tried to. Your aunt and I called your grandfather, and he called the police. They picked her up strolling down the street as if nothing was wrong, nothing had happened. I suppose she was in some state of shock. From there, she went to a mental clinic where they diagnosed her as delusional and, well, you know the rest of it."

"No, I don't. Talking about my mother is practically forbidden in this house. Grandma gets so upset at the mention of her name, she practically faints. Didn't you ever go to see her? Ever?"

He stared at me, and then I saw him glance at the attic door.

"You did, didn't you?" I pounced.

"No one knows," he said almost in a whisper. "Not even your grandfather." He thought for a moment and then said, "Maybe keeping it secret doesn't matter anymore."

"Tell me about her. Please," I begged and inched closer to him. "What was she like when you visited her?"

"She was Karen again," he began. "Doing what she does so well to cope with the reality she hated."

"What do you mean?"

"She had created a whole new scenario to explain where she was and why she was there. She didn't act at all like a patient in a clinic. It was as if the whole thing, everyone working there, was at her beck and call, there solely for her.

"First, she looked absolutely beautiful—radiant, in fact. I had been expecting to find a defeated, mousy young woman, wrapped up in her own madness, impenetrable, shut up tightly. I feared that not only would she ignore me, but she might turn on me, be enraged."

"And?"

"She was the complete opposite, buoyant, cheerful, back to the way she had been when Zipporah first had met her. She came rushing out of her room into the hallway to greet me. Her hair was longer and she had done something clever with her bangs. She extended her hand and, I'll never forget, said, 'Jesse, how sweet of you to make the trip to see me. How are your parents and your sister? You must fill me in on everything you've been doing. Don't leave out a single thing.'

"I glanced at the nurse who had escorted me down the corridor and saw she was smiling. Later, I found out everyone there enjoyed your mother. Contrary to what I had expected, she was not only not depressing, but she cheered up other patients and made the staff comfortable as well. It was remarkable. I felt as if a coat made of iron guilt had been lifted off me. I couldn't help but laugh myself."

"When was this? I mean, had I been born?"

"Yes. It was nearly a year later."

I hesitated to ask and then blurted, "Did she remember giving birth to me?"

"She never mentioned it and I was afraid to say a word until she did."

"Then she never asked about me?"

"No," he said. "I'm sorry, Alice. I'm sure it had to do with her mental condition."

I nodded. My grandmother had told me the truth, but that didn't make me feel any better. If anything, I felt even more alone now, even more lost.

I sat on the settee.

"That seems so incredible," I muttered in disappointment.

"Psychiatrists attribute it to the brain's defense mechanisms. It was too difficult for her to face it, admit to it, whatever. Selective amnesia, I once heard it called. We all do some of that."

"Well, what did she remember then?"

"Seemingly most everything else, but nothing specific about the events relating to Harry Pearson. She went around ugly things, babbled about the village, the people, laughed about things she had done with Zipporah. After a while I realized she was talking incessantly partly to keep me from talking, from asking anything, I think."

"How did she explain being where she was?"

"That was what I was referring to. She told me she was being studied by some of the world's most renowned psychotherapists, and had agreed to it to do something worthwhile in her life. She told me as a result she was treated like some sort of princess and everything I saw, all these people, were at her disposal. She could order anything she wanted to eat. She had her own television set, clothes, magazines, books, anything. 'I merely ask and it is done,' she told me. She assured me I would be reading about her someday in magazines and books.

"She acted as if the clinic were a palace, her palace. She showed me about the place and introduced me to everyone, telling them I was her first high school crush. The way some of the staff members reacted to her made me think that they thought she was telling the truth. She was there because she had volunteered to be there. She did appear to have the run of the place without any restrictions.

"Toward the end of my visit, she asked me if I didn't think she had been so lucky to get out of our sleepy village and do something interesting with her life. Of course, I said yes and she told me not to worry. I'd surely find my way out as well and do something worthwhile.

"I asked her if there was anything she needed, anything she wanted. She smiled and countered with, 'But Jesse, what could I possibly want that I don't have?'

"I kissed her on the cheek and started out. Before I reached the door, she was talking and laughing with some of the staff as if my visit were nothing more than a slight interruption, as if what she had said was true, I was a young girl's infatuation, some memory pasted in an old album and basically forgotten.

"It did me a lot of good to make that visit, however. As I said, it relieved me of guilt. Maybe she knew what she was doing. Maybe that was her gift to me. I never went back, never wrote to her or called. That's why I don't know anything about her condition now. I'm sorry," he added, seeing how silent I was, "sorry that I don't have anything to tell you that would help you understand more."

"Jesse!" we heard Rachel calling.

He looked at me.

I had to get it out quickly, get out what gnawed at my heart, my very soul.

"If the only explanation for what she did is madness," I said, "then I'm afraid whatever that madness was will someday awaken in me, too."

I didn't think he had ever thought I had that fear. He looked a bit shocked for a moment.

"Jesse!" Rachel called again.

"Coming!"

He stood up. "The wonder of the genetic pool is that we're all different, Alice," he said gently. "You look like her, but you're not her, and besides, you're growing up under different circumstances, different conditions. That plays a role in things as well."

He looked at the door.

"We'll talk about it some more when we can, but what you're feeling and thinking is what's worrying Grandma and Grandpa, Alice. You've got to break out of this. Get into the stream of things so you can develop all your potential."

"I know," I said. "Join clubs, make friends."

"There's nothing wrong with being happy," he said, starting away.

"Unless it's all pretend," I tossed at him. He paused at the doorway.

"It won't be for you," he said. "Give yourself a chance." He nodded toward the painting I had done of the tree. "That is a remarkable piece of work for someone as young and as untrained as you are. Grandpa is right: you're going to do something with your art."

He left the door open and descended. I looked at

the window again. Using my memory from the pictures, I imagined my mother standing there and listening to my father and my aunt reveal that they had determined she had fabricated the whole story and therefore had done a terrible, terrible thing. The two people she had trusted and depended upon were casting her out to sea in a small boat. She would soon be at the mercy of whatever winds occurred, tossed and thrown every which way, and no one would be there to rescue her, not even her own mother. No wonder she had wandered off in a daze.

I had never met my mother, but I could cry for her, because in my mind and heart, I was crying for myself.

I rose and walked out of the attic, closing the door softly behind me. I could hear the twins below. They had wakened and were running through the house, playing some sort of hide-and-seek game with my grandfather. I quickly realized my father and Rachel were in their bedroom with the door closed. Was he already paying the price for being my father for fifteen minutes?

When he came out, I saw that the tips of his ears were crimson. Whatever had been said in privacy had stung him. It was easy to envision Rachel as a bee or a hornet. There was a sharpness to her every move and gesture, a biting precision to her words. I went right to work to help my grandmother with the evening meal and avoided Rachel for as long as I could.

It wasn't the most pleasant dinner we had with all of us. Nothing the twins did at the table pleased Rachel, and soon it felt as if we were all on edge. My father's eyes were full of apologies. I saw how unhappy my grandfather was becoming, too. I was glad when we were finished with our dessert and I could help my grandmother in the kitchen and get away for a while. While I was helping her, I realized just how well planned the conspiracy was. She surprised me with her new offer.

"How would you like to do a little shopping with Rachel, Zipporah and me tomorrow? Zipporah should be here by late morning. We thought we'd all go to lunch and hit some of the department stores."

"What sort of shopping?"

"You need some new clothes, Alice."

"Rachel wants to go, too?"

"Yes. You see how fashionable Rachel is. She keeps up on it all better than either Zipporah or I do. Your grandfather and Jesse are taking the twins to the fun park. Okay?"

I shrugged.

"I don't care," I said.

"You'll feel better about yourself when you have new things, Alice. I know I do. Sometimes, nice clothing gives us more self-confidence."

"Changing clothes isn't going to win me new friends, Grandma," I said.

She slapped the kitchen counter so hard, I was sure she hurt her hand.

"Do you have to always be so negative, Alice? Do you have to bite every hand that tries to feed you?"

I didn't respond, but I felt the tears burning under my eyelids.

She turned to me.

"We're all going to enjoy ourselves," she said firmly, "whether we like it or not."

I nearly smiled.

"Okay, Grandma," I said. "I'm sorry."

"Good. I'll finish here. Go spend some time with the twins," she told me.

They were lying against and over Grandpa Michael in the den and watching television as if he was a big human pillow. The moment they saw me, however, they practically leaped up to play the mechanical bowling game my grandfather had in his den.

"Thank God! Reinforcements," my grandfather cried.

I didn't mind spending time with the twins. Despite Rachel's continually complaining about their behavior, I found them to be very intelligent and very perceptive. Of course, I wondered what, if anything, we shared because we shared a father. Their outgoing, buoyant personalities were so different from mine. Someday, I thought, they would learn I was not their aunt; I was their half sister. How would they react, feel? Would that make them think of me as weird? Would they then not want to have much to do with me? The lines that tied me to family were so fragile that I was sure it wouldn't take much to shatter them.

That night I went to sleep thinking about all the things my father had finally told me. I wondered if this meant that other doors would open, that Aunt Zipporah would be more forthcoming as well. Of everyone, she had been the least reluctant to talk about my mother, but I always felt she held back things nevertheless. Maybe, just maybe, they had all discussed me and had decided I was now old enough to know whatever they knew. Once again, I felt this wasn't just another family gathering. This was the beginning of some new day, and I couldn't wait to see what exactly it would bring and what it would change inside me.

Fortunately, Aunt Zipporah arrived even before the day had begun, so I didn't have to contend with the heaviness from the night before. By the time I descended to have breakfast, she was in the kitchen with my grandmother, stringing one story after another, summarizing everything that had happened at the café. I couldn't help but be jealous of their relationship. Even with my small experience concerning other mothers and daughters, I could see and understand that Aunt Zipporah and my grandmother had a special connection. In fact, they seemed more like sisters at times, laughing and talking, sharing their experiences as if they were contemporaries. Sometimes, I enjoyed just sitting on the sidelines and listening to them talk, imagining what it would have been like for me if I had been brought up by my mother. Would my relationship with her have been this special?

"Alice!" Aunt Zipporah cried as soon as she saw me. She rushed to hug and kiss me. No one greeted me with as much warmth and happiness. There was nothing insincere about that greeting, either. I often wondered if that was because she saw so much of my mother in me and had been so fond of her.

She took me by the hand and pulled me to sit beside her at the kitchen table.

"Tell me everything that's going on in your life. I don't care how small it seems to you."

"Nothing's going on, Aunt Zipporah. Nothing's

different," I said, and she turned her face into an exaggerated mask of disappointment.

"Can't be. Not at your age."

I shrugged.

"I'm boring," I said.

"That you can never be," she suggested. I saw my grandmother smirking and shaking her head as she prepared our breakfast. "Really, honey? There's no one on the horizon?" she asked, her eyes turning. I couldn't help but laugh. "C'mon."

"No one. I've been too busy," I offered as an excuse.

"With what?"

"My art," I said.

She looked at my grandmother.

"She's not lying about that. She's up in that attic more than she is anywhere else."

"Oh, Alice. You have to—"

"What?" I asked, waiting. Her face softened.

"Take a chance," she said.

"That's what we're all trying to tell her," my grandmother echoed.

"We're all afraid of being hurt, rejected, but even if that happens, you survive it, Alice. It happened a lot to me, believe me," she said.

"I'm not afraid of being rejected," I told her. "In fact, I'm used to it."

"Oh, Alice."

She stared at me a moment. Aunt Zipporah didn't resemble her mother as much as I apparently resembled mine. She had my grandfather's face, with his narrower cheeks and sharper jaw, but her features were small and I always thought she had perfectly shaped ears. She kept her dark-brown hair very long now, a good two inches below her wing bone. Grandfather Michael called her his personal hippie because she always wore a tie-dyed headband and Indian jewelry, the turquoise necklaces and earrings, bracelets and rings, lots of rings. Usually, she didn't have a bare finger.

From what I understood of her life after my mother, what was sometimes referred to as AK, After Karen, Aunt Zipporah went into a deep depression and then gradually emerged with a different attitude about herself and the world. She was more cynical and for a while was a great worry for my grandparents. Eventually, she found herself, but that discovery was one that led her to lean more toward the rebels—the oddballs, as Grandfather Michael liked to call them. It was as if she had to carry on my mother's legacy and be as outrageous as she could be. I was told that she almost flunked out of college at one point, but then got hold of herself and ended up doing well.

I knew that her not going on to become a teacher was a great disappointment to my grandparents, but they had come to like Tyler, a hardworking young businessman who ironically proved to be a stabling influence on Aunt Zipporah. The only mystery I had yet to solve was why they never had any children of their own, or hadn't yet. She was still young enough. Her stock answer to me was, "I'm not ready yet." If she and Tyler had arguments about it, they were well hidden. Never during the times I spent with them did I ever see them have any sort of serious fight. Tyler, if he disagreed with her, would just shake his head and smile as if he knew she would eventually come around to his way of thinking. Most of the time, that was just what she did.

What amused me more was the way she treated—or, I should say, handled—Rachel. Although it was difficult for most people to read Aunt Zipporah, I had no problem. Just as she had a special relationship with her mother, she had a similarly special relationship with my father, her brother. Whenever they were together, they were always up and happy, laughing and joking. It was nearly impossible to say or do anything serious when they were together. I knew that bothered Rachel. She was jealous, but no matter what Rachel said to her or how she treated her, Aunt Zipporah was always very pleasant. I would smile to myself because I could see she was humoring her, treating her as if she were the one who needed tender loving care and not me, or Jesse, or herself.

When it came to meeting someone head on, Rachel was surely a formidable opponent. She simply wasn't prepared for gentle, nonviolent reactions and would either retreat or sigh with frustration and go on to something else. I knew my father was amused by it as much as I was at times.

Rachel would be aggressive and say something like, "You really look ridiculous in that dress with so much jewelry, Zipporah, especially at your age."

Aunt Zipporah would nod and smile and reply, "Yes, I know, but most people look ridiculous where I am, so no one really notices or cares, but thanks for worrying about me."

How do you fight someone like that? If only I could be the same way, I thought, but what was in me wanted to come out scratching and kicking like a wildcat and not gentle and pleasant like a female Gandhi.

"Hey!" my father said, coming into the kitchen. They immediately hugged and kissed. "What did you do, leave at the crack of dawn?"

"I thought I'd better get started before Tyler came up with something for me to do. Where are the twins?"

"Rachel is getting them dressed. Morning, Mom, Alice. Where's Dad?"

"He went for some fresh bagels."

"He won't let me bring any from New Paltz," Aunt Zipporah said, "just because they come pink, blue and green."

Our laughter drew the twins to the kitchen, and Aunt Zipporah made a big deal over them. She had brought them flutes someone made and sold on the street back in New Paltz.

"I don't want them putting those things in their mouths before they're washed," Rachel said and made a face at my father.

"Hi, Rachel," Aunt Zipporah cried and gave her a big hug.

Rachel shook her head. "You know, Zipporah, if you wear one thing, dress one way forever, it starts to look like a uniform," she said.

"I know. We have our own little army up there. Actually, no one knows this because it's a top secret, but we're part of the National Guard."

Jesse laughed.

Rachel shook her head again and sat the twins at the table, ordering them to behave or she would see to it that they didn't go to the fun park. My grandfather returned with the fresh bagels, and our breakfast reunion began. Aunt Zipporah and my father dominated the conversation, she telling story after story about people, college students and the café, and he remembering things they had done together when they were not much older than the twins. Every story brought more laughter. Even the twins were intrigued.

Finally, my grandmother announced we would clean up and get ready to go. I was nervous about the shopping expedition we women were preparing to make. I didn't like being the sole reason for it, but I didn't say a word. Finally, Rachel would be able to speak and take some control, for my grandmother was determined to defer to her advice when it came to my new wardrobe.

"I want her to look fashionable and yet like girls her age," she prescribed.

"I know exactly what you mean," Rachel told her.

"That's what I'm afraid of," Aunt Zipporah whispered, and I smiled. "But cooperate. Mom wants you to look nice, Alice. I promised I'd be on their side."

The conspiracy grows, I thought and got ready for our trip.

During the ride to the shopping centers, Rachel talked about clothes, but she really talked about herself more than I had heard her. Aunt Zipporah and I sat in the rear and listened as what Rachel began as a lecture gradually turned into the most revealing anecdotes about herself.

"I wanted to be rebellious and dress outlandishly, too, when I was your age, Alice, and even when I was older. Not as old as Zipporah, however. I had grown out of it by then, but I had this aunt who was a real socialite, Aunt Dorothea. We could never call her Aunt Dorothy. It had to be Dorothea, and God forbid anyone dared call her Dot. For the most part, I thought her stuffy and snobbish, but when I permitted myself to listen to her, I realized she had something to offer."

"And what was that?" Aunt Zipporah asked.

Rachel turned around.

"Something Alice can appreciate, being an artist. Just like a painting can be enhanced by a beautiful frame, so can a woman be enhanced by beautiful, well-fitted clothes. Aunt Dorothea was a very classy woman." She looked at me intently. "You're very pretty, Alice, beautiful, in fact."

It was the first real compliment she had ever given me. It nearly stole my breath away.

"Thank you," I said, glancing at Aunt Zipporah, who was now smiling widely.

"It's almost sinful not to frame yourself properly, however," she added. "You wouldn't detract from a beautiful painting by framing it in something very inferior, would you?" She threw a disapproving look at Aunt Zipporah.

"Well, we're going to correct that today," my grandmother said. I saw her look up at the rearview mirror to see my reaction. "We're going to correct a lot of things," she muttered.

Aunt Zipporah reached over the seat to take my hand and squeeze it.

As long as she was at my side, I wasn't afraid. It was the closest thing to having my mother there, I thought.

Later, when I tried on a pair of designer slacks and a matching blouse, Aunt Zipporah dared whisper in my ear, "You are beautiful, Alice, as beautiful as she was. Rachel's right. It's time for you to take center stage."

And do what? I wondered.

I was having trouble being in the wings, let alone take center stage.

It wasn't going to be much longer before the curtain opened and I would find out.

4

Craig Harrison

Despite how much I knew it pleased everyone in my family, I couldn't help feeling like a fraud in my new clothing. The brighter colors, form-fitting, expensive garments and new shoes were a radical change for me. Part of me had to admit that I did look more attractive, but as before, that thought, that possibility, made me nervous, even frightened. I knew what was going to happen the moment the spring break was over and I stepped onto the school bus and then into the building. Everyone's eyes would be drawn to me, and who knew what terrible things they would come up with now? It would be impossible for me not to be very self-conscious.

I did wear my new clothes to every restaurant, and I even wore something new for our dinners at home. As if she had been a bull and I had been wearing red all this time, Rachel did seem to become friendlier and less concerned about me after I dressed in my new, brighter and less baggy clothing. It was more like I had come over to her side, the side where a woman's femininity mattered the most. I was surprised and even a bit shocked one night when she came up to my room with her makeup kit and offered to show me how to highlight my good features.

"Now that you're dressing better, there are other things you should do. It's important that you complement one advantage with another and keep it all well balanced," she said, standing there just inside my doorway.

For a moment I didn't know what to say. Was this the same woman who seemingly couldn't stand my shadow nearby, much less my actual person? Was this the same woman who seemed to ration every look at me, every word spoken to me? Why would anything involving me suddenly become important to her? Of course, my mind flailed about, searching for some ulterior evil motive.

Maybe she wanted to turn me into a promiscuous young girl so she could say, *"See, I told you so."*

Maybe she hoped I would get into trouble like my mother had and be taken away or sent away.

Maybe this was all being done against my father's wishes and my compliance would do more to turn him against me, which was what she always wanted.

Maybe she hoped I would reject her so that she could then say, *"I tried to be decent to her, but she's too far gone."*

I didn't see that I had much choice.

"Thank you," I told her, and she came in and set up her makeup kit on my vanity table, first clearing away the books. I had never really used the table for anything more than a place to do my homework. Unlike most of the girls at school, I ran a brush through my hair in less than a minute and more than one time started out for school with remnants of breakfast at the corners of my mouth or on my chin.

"Sit here," she told me, pulling out the chair.

I did, and for a few seconds she stared at me in the mirror. From the expression on her face, I thought she might just close the makeup kit and say, *"There's not much we can do."* Instead, she played with my hair, then picked up the brush and changed the way the strands lay. It was mostly haphazard, but she gave it some style with only a few firm strokes.

"You see what I'm doing here?" she asked.

"Yes."

"Just let it grow for a while, but keep this style. It suits your shaped face. You look a lot like an actress we know in Los Angeles, a young actress."

No one had ever compared me to an actress or a model, not even my grandfather.

"There are some very basic things about makeup that you should know," she continued and began to show them to me. She demonstrated how I should highlight my eyes. At that point came the most shocking thing of all. "You have Jesse's eyes," she admitted.

She didn't sound upset about it, and it wasn't said in anger. She was very matter-of-fact.

"He has beautiful eyes," she continued.

I don't think I moved a muscle or took a breath. My heart might have actually paused, every part of me, every organ in my body waiting for some second shoe to drop, some horrid afterthought, but none came.

"That's what attracted me to him first," she added. "Now then," she continued, "because you spend so much time indoors, you're a little pale, so some of this on your cheeks can't hurt."

She showed me how to brush in the makeup, blending it, and then she went on to lipstick. I did have some, but it was dry and she said the color not only didn't do anything for me but it actually detracted from my looks.

"You don't want to turn your lips into a headlight. Subtlety is the key to everything, Alice. All a face like yours needs are some suggestions here and there. Think of everything like a finger pointing out this aspect or that and nothing more. Most girls your age overdo it. Their faces shout, and just like you don't want to be in a room with someone shouting at you, you don't want to be looking at them as if you were looking into a spotlight."

She stepped back to look at me.

"Well?" she asked me. "What do you think of yourself now?"

"I . . . it's nice," I offered, and she laughed.

"No, Alice, it's not nice. It's beautiful. Jesse is always looking at this girl or that one in California and saying things like, 'She's so beautiful, she should have to register like someone has to register a firearm.' He's going to say that about you, too."

I stared at her through the mirror. Was this a dream? Or a trap? She was treating me with such kindness and talking to me as if she were my older sister. I really was at a loss for words. My thoughts were spinning on a merry-go-round in my head. I even felt a little dizzy.

"Where did you learn all this?" I finally managed.

She laughed.

"Are you kidding? In my family the women were determined to be on the covers of magazines. I had aunts who went into mental depressions so deeply over a new wrinkle, they were nearly committed. In my family we put aside money for plastic surgery the way other people put aside money for life and fire insurance. Growing old, losing your looks was as horrible a conceit as watching your home burn to the ground. That was the world in which I was raised."

"But you don't seem that way now," I told her, not sure if that was the right thing to tell her. She liked it; she smiled.

"For some stupid reason I can't fathom, most of the women I know think they have to make a choice between brains and looks. I know other female attorneys who deliberately dress as masculinely as they can before they go to court. They think it matters. Maybe it does, but I won't ever give into that. I have to have the judge, the jury and my witnesses not see me only as a woman but as an advocate equal to any other in the courtroom. You should never give into that sort of narrow thinking," she added. "You're a full person. Don't let anyone put you into a comfortable stereotype. I never did."

I just sat there listening. She saw the look of amazement on my face.

"Sorry," she said. "I don't mean to lecture, but it's one of my pet peeves. Do you think you can handle this by yourself from now on?" she asked, nodding at me in the mirror.

"Yes."

"Good. Don't forget. Let your hair fill out and see about using a conditioner from now on as well," she added, fingering some strands. "You could soften it a bit. How often do you wash your hair?" she asked.

"Not very," I said.

"Change that to very. You know, I have a pair of emerald earrings that will look good on you. I'll leave them for you," she said. They were going back to California in the morning.

"Thank you."

"You're welcome," she said and turned to leave.

"Oh, your makeup kit," I called to her when she reached the doorway.

She turned and shook her head.

"No, that's your makeup kit now. I bought it for you the other day when we were all shopping."

My jaw seemed to lock at the hinges. She didn't smile. She nodded and walked out.

I turned and looked at myself in the mirror. It was as if someone else sleeping inside me had been awakened. I could almost hear her say, *"Hello. Let me introduce myself."* Only it was my mother and not me.

"I'm Karen Stoker."

I pushed myself back from the table and seized the sponge to bring it to my face so I could wipe away all the makeup, but something stronger seized my wrist and kept me from doing so. I sat there staring at myself for nearly a full minute before putting down the sponge and closing the makeup kit. Then I rose and went downstairs, walking as if in a trance.

Aunt Zipporah had returned to New Paltz two days after she had come because she was worried about leaving Tyler at the café so long. Of course, I promised to call her more often. I didn't know what new headlines she expected, but I could see she was hoping for some.

Rachel was putting the twins to bed, but my grandparents and my father were in the living room, talking softly, when I descended. They paused and looked up with surprise as I entered. I was most interested in my father's reaction. His eyes widened, and then he smiled. If I did look like my mother, it didn't frighten him or put him off.

"Well, who's this?" my grandfather joked. "I didn't know we were having guests tonight."

"You look terrific, Alice," my father said. "Rachel knows her stuff, huh, Mom?"

"Yes, she does. Very nice. It's not too much and it's not too little."

"Maybe you should have Rachel give you a lesson, too, Elaine," my grandfather said. The second he said it, we could all feel what he felt. He had put his foot squarely in his mouth.

I couldn't recall Grandmother Elaine's face that deep a shade of crimson. I was sure I saw two puffs of smoke emerge from each ear. My grandfather threw himself to the floor and pleaded for forgiveness. He started to kiss her feet.

"I was kidding. I was joking."

"Get up, you idiot," she told him.

My father was laughing hysterically. Even I started to laugh, and for a moment, a long and precious moment, we were all truly like a family, enjoying each other for our weaknesses, our foolishness and our love.

I waited until the last possible moment before washing away my makeup that night. I was now afraid that I wouldn't be able to duplicate what Rachel had done for me, but she reassured me that it wasn't hard.

"It's not brain surgery," she said, "although the way most girls your age use their makeup, you'd think they had lobotomies."

Everyone laughed at that as well. For the first time

I could remember, I was actually sorry to see Rachel, my father and the twins leave. I felt as if I had just begun a journey with them and it had come to an end too quickly.

In the morning we all stood outside in the driveway as my father packed the rented car. There wasn't a cloud in the sky, and the breeze was now riding on a wave of late-spring warmth announcing the oncoming summer. I still had nearly two months of school left for my junior year, but as I had for the past two summers, I would go to New Paltz and work at Aunt Zipporah and Uncle Tyler's café. This summer I would be graduated to a waitress.

Before I went down for breakfast, I redid my makeup so Rachel could check me out once before she left. She told me I had done it perfectly.

"You're fine," she said. "You'll be fine."

We had a big breakfast again, delaying the end of it for as long as we could, but finally, their flight schedule dictated that they get started for the airport.

The twins didn't want to leave and whined and pleaded to stay longer. They were somewhat placated by the promise of return and the suggestion that they might even be able to stay without their parents for a while. It was clear they knew they would get away with tons if it were just their grandparents caring for them.

I hugged them both, then my grandfather chased them around the car a few times with the expectation it would wear them out and keep them quiet for the ride to the airport. As usual, he misread their energy compared to his own, and they begged him to keep chasing them.

"Get them out of here before they kill me!" he cried, breathing hard.

He and my father hugged and my father embraced my grandmother and they kissed and held each other a little longer. Rachel hugged and kissed my grandfather and grandmother and then took my hand to pull me a little to the side.

"Think of your life as a courtroom argument," she said. "Be careful about how you lay the foundation, and then argue vigorously for yourself. The rest of the world is the jury, and they have one clear ability. They can see insincerity, of course, but they can see a lack of self-confidence even easier. Good luck, Alice."

She didn't actually hug me. She held my shoulders for a moment, then she turned to get the twins into the car.

"Hey," my father said. He looked at my grandparents, and then he took my hand and we walked down the driveway.

"I hope our coming did some good for you, Alice. I'm glad we had a chance to have that conversation in the attic, and we shared some very personal secrets."

"Me, too."

"I guess you know now that your grandparents put out an SOS on you. No one can blame them for asking for help, least of all me. They paid their parent dues when they brought up me and Zipporah. I guess all anyone wants for you is for you to give yourself a chance. Take a chance on yourself. Go out there and compete. You're too young to go into retreat. You have no reason to hide from anyone or anything.

"I know it's easy for me to tell you all this. I have no right to tell you anything. I went into hiding in a sense and left you behind, but I'm trying to make up for it as much as I can. I promise I'll keep trying."

"Why was Rachel so nice to me this time?" I asked, looking back at the car. "I thought she was mad at you for spending time with me in the attic."

"She was at first, but . . . can you keep a secret?"

I laughed at that and so did he.

"Your grandmother and I used a little psychology on her. We went to her for help with you, and there's nothing Rachel likes more than responsibility. She's a bit of a control freak, but another secret is I need her to be. I'm not stupid. I recognize what her strengths are and how that helps us both be successful. Once you became her project, too, it put a new light on everything.

"So," he concluded, "you better not disappoint her. She's tough."

"Okay," I said.

"I have never really told you, Alice," he said, "but I love you and want only happiness for you."

I nodded, now squeezing my eyes to keep the tears imprisoned under the lids. They were determined to break free any moment.

He kissed me on the cheek and then hurried to the car.

My tears escaped.

He waved. They backed out, waved from the windows, and drove off, disappearing the way a dream might, the images of them lingering for a few moments, ghost memories, soon caught in the breeze and carried off, leaving us with empty eyes.

My grandfather put his arm around my grandmother, and she put her head on his shoulder and they

started back to the house. In that moment I truly understood how hard it was to be a parent and a grandparent
and put another good-bye in your pocket. Even though
they had each other, they couldn't fill the emptiness in
their hearts. It was at once the curse and the blessing
such love brought with it.

Instead of following them into the house, I started
a walk toward the village. I hadn't intended to go the
whole way, but I was in such deep thought about everything that I wasn't paying attention to time and distance and suddenly realized that I had reached town.

I rarely went to the village alone. There wasn't
much for me to do there, and I was especially uncomfortable under the gaze of some of the older residents
who knew everything about my story. Some spoke to
me, asking me how my grandparents were. Maybe it
was all my imagination, but I sensed they were asking
how they were holding up, having a granddaughter
like me living with them. One of the houses in which
I couldn't help but have interest was the one that had
been my mother's. The people who lived in it now,
the Harrisons, had owned the lumber company for
generations. Recently, they had expanded it into a
hardware supermarket as well. Now they were one of
the wealthiest families not only in the community but
in the entire county as well. Of course, even if they
hadn't lived here, the Harrisons had to know the history of the house. I understood from my grandfather
that the death of Harry Pearson had to be in the disclosure any real estate agent offered to a prospective
buyer.

The house was a rich-looking home with brick sid-
ing and perfectly manicured hedges. My grandfather

said Dan Harrison was obsessive about his lawn and insisted on having the greenest, richest grass in the community. His lawn did stay green longer than anyone else's. They made some changes in the windows, redid the roof and added a flagpole, but other than that, the house, at least on the outside, remained as it had been when my mother and my grandmother Darlene Pearson lived there with Harry. I couldn't help but wonder what it looked like inside and especially what my mother's old room was like. I had this overwhelming need to stand in that room and look out the same windows. That was my obsession.

The Harrisons' son Craig was a junior in my school and one of the most popular boys. In fact, he was currently president of our class, the captain of the baseball team, and one of the starting five on the basketball team. He was one of those people who seemed to have been blessed with everything. He was bright, good-looking and from a wealthy family. I couldn't help but wonder what it was that determined he would be born into the world he was in and I would be born into mine. Were we sinners before we were born? Or was that biblical phrase I heard true: the sins of the fathers would be visited on the heads of the sons, but in my case, the sins of the mother would be visited on the head of her daughter?

I sauntered up the sidewalk and paused in front of the Harrisons' house. I don't think I ever walked or rode past it without looking at it and thinking about it. The flag flapped and snapped in the breeze. I saw the lawn sprinklers go on and begin saturating some of the new seeds and the blades that were already starting the spring grasses. Mrs. Harrison had a row of multicolored flowers in front of the porch. It all looked picture perfect, belonging on some house and garden magazine. There was nothing to suggest its sordid past.

I started to turn away when I heard someone ask, "Is that you?"

I turned more to my left and saw Craig Harrison step out from behind a hedge. He had a pair of hedge cutters in his hands. He wore a very tight T-shirt, which emphasized his sculptured muscularity, a baseball cap on backwards and jeans. Some strands of his light-brown hair stuck out of the sides of his cap, and his bangs seemed to float over his forehead, not touching his skin. His eyes were light green, but in sunlight they became a richer emerald. At six feet two, with his broad shoulders and narrow waist, he looked like a prime candidate for Mr. Teen America. I always thought there was something impish about his tight smile. Although I tried to ignore most of the boys at school, especially the ones who leered and whispered when I passed by, I couldn't help but cast a glance at Craig.

"No," I said. "It's someone else."

I started to walk away.

"Hey, wait a minute," he cried and came hurrying around the hedges to the sidewalk. "What's the rush?"

"I have a dental appointment," I said.

"Huh?" He stared at me a moment, and then he laughed. "Okay. Sorry. I just didn't recognize you. Nice outfit," he said, letting his eyes move slowly up from my feet to my head, as if he had to capture me in some memory bank forever and ever. "I knew there was a pretty girl in those potato sacks you wear."

"They're not potato sacks."

"Whatever." He drew closer. "Never saw you wearing lipstick and stuff. What's up? You have a birthday or something?"

"No. Why would that matter anyway?" I asked, smirking at him.

He shrugged. "I heard some mothers don't let their daughters wear makeup until they're a certain age."

I didn't want to point out that I didn't live with my mother, but I could see the thought registering in his mind.

"Or grandmothers," he quickly added.

"No. I just decided myself," I said.

"Good decision. So what are you up to?"

"Nothing. I just took a walk."

He nodded, glanced at his house and then at me.

"I've seen you looking at the house before, you know."

"Great. Have a nice day," I said and continued down the sidewalk. He quickly caught up.

"Take it easy," he said. "I wasn't complaining about it."

"I don't care if you were."

"Jeez."

"What?" I said, spinning on him.

"I heard you could be pretty nasty for no reason."

"I'm not pretty nasty."

He laughed. "If you're not nasty now, I'd hate to see you when you are."

I stared at him a moment. "Okay," I said. "I'll admit it. So I have looked at your house before."

"It's only natural you'd be curious about the place. I was when we first bought it. You ever been inside?"

"No."

"Would you like to go inside?"

"What do you think?" I fired back at him. I imagined he was teasing me and having some fun that he would brag about later, but I didn't really care.

"I think yes. I have to warn you, though. It's nothing like it was when we first bought it. My mother redid it from top to bottom. She even changed the kitchen, ripped out counters, expanded it, put in new cabinets. We didn't move in for nearly eight months after we bought it."

I didn't know what to say. I did think anyone would have changed it. That was no surprise.

"There was nothing left in it that belonged to your mother and grandmother," he continued. "Don't think I didn't look in closets and cabinets."

"What did you expect to find?" I was going to add *"dead bodies"* but didn't.

"I don't know. Hey," he said, "we have something in common."

"And what would that be?"

"We both live in houses where a murder took place."

I didn't respond. He was right, if the legendary story about the Dorals was right.

"So?" I finally replied.

"So nothing. C'mon. I'll show you the place."

"Maybe your parents wouldn't like it," I said, hesitating. Now that he was really inviting me, I felt nervous and even a bit afraid.

"They're not here. They're in New York seeing a show. I've been left to do chores. C'mon. Don't worry about it."

He started away, expecting me to follow. After another moment, I did. He waited at the entrance to the walk, and then we started for the front door together.

"You sure?" I asked when he opened the door.

"What's the big deal? You're not going to do something evil to me, are you?" he joked.

"I haven't decided yet," I told him, and he laughed.

"You know, I've always wanted to talk to you, but to be honest, I thought you'd insult me or embarrass me," he said.

I smirked skeptically and pulled my head back.

"No, I'm serious," he continued. "I mean it. I came close to starting a conversation with you a few times in the hallway when I thought you looked my way, but I wasn't sure if you were looking at me with interest or disdain."

The way he was still standing in the doorway made me think that my answer would determine whether or not he would let me in.

"I don't know you well enough to dislike you," I said. The answer pleased him. He smiled and stepped back.

"Come in."

I walked in slowly, pausing in the entryway. The floor had a very pretty cocoa tile, and there were mahogany coat hooks and a hat rack on both sides. There was a rich-looking wood floor down the hallway, and the stairway was carpeted with a thick dark brown to match the balustrade. Everything looked brand new, spotless and immaculate. Right above the entryway hung a chandelier with teardrop crystals.

"The kitchen and dining room are to the left," Craig said. "This is the living room," he said and continued walking down the hallway. I gazed in at the furniture, paintings, beautiful marble fireplace and mantel.

"What kind of furniture is this?" I asked. I hadn't been in many houses other than my own, but I had never seen such elegant sofas, chairs, tables and lamps.

"It's all imported from France," he said. "That took almost a year, too, but it was what my mother wanted. Their bedroom is the same furniture style. Mine's a lot different, but the guest rooms are the same decor, as are the dining room and my father's office, which is really our den. As you can see, there's no television set in the living room. I've got my own set, and so do my parents, but our biggest screen is in the den. That's where Dad and I watch all the sports. It's also the only room in the house where my mother permits smoking. I don't smoke, do you?"

"No."

"I mean cigarettes," he said, smiling wryly.

"I don't smoke anything," I emphasized. I knew what he meant. He shrugged.

"Ever try it?" he asked.

"I don't care to."

"You don't know what you're missing if you don't try it."

"I don't care."

He laughed and then turned serious.

"You know my bedroom was supposedly your mother's, don't you?"

"No, how would I know that?"

"I thought you might. You want to see it?"

A part of me wanted to simply turn and run out of the house, but a stronger part of me was drawn to those stairs. I glanced at them.

"C'mon," he said, not waiting for my answer.

Under the rug were the steps upon which my mother had walked many times. It was down these steps that she'd fled. I could almost feel myself falling back through time, watching her rush out of the house and into the darkness that would surround me as well.

He paused on the stairway and leaned toward me.

"I know all about the murder," he said. "I know exactly where they found Harry Pearson's body and exactly how it looked when they found it."

He continued up.

My feet felt frozen to the step. I thought there was something terribly morbid about the casual way he talked about it all, but something fascinating as well.

"Hey," he said, stopping again to turn back to me. "I just realized something. You know what's amazing, incredible about your coming here, in fact?"

I shook my head. Suddenly, because I was here and literally a few feet from my mother's room, I felt too weak to even speak.

"Today. The date. Don't you get it?"

"No."

"It's the date of the murder!"

5

The Scene of the Murder

I suddenly completely understood the concept of selective amnesia.

Of course, I knew the date of Harry Pearson's death, but neither my grandmother nor my grandfather, no one in the family, as a matter of fact, ever mentioned it or acknowledged it in any way. Maybe they had selective amnesia as well, or maybe they just thought it was wise never to mention it, even to themselves. I had heard that when I was very young, not more than three perhaps, one of the local newspapers did a column on the murder and that had revived interest, but nothing had been written about it ever since.

"I thought that was why you had come around today," Craig said.

I shook my head. He looked skeptical.

"Are you telling me you didn't know what had happened today?"

"I forgot," I said.

"Wow. Interesting. Well, it is the date anyway. C'mon up. We'll be like historical detectives or something."

I continued up the stairs slowly, stairs my mother

had climbed many times, my legs feeling heavier. It was as if I were dragging my grandmother behind me because she had seized me at the waist and was trying to prevent me from going any farther. I knew she would be upset to know I was in this house.

"Everything's changed up here as well," Craig explained when I reached the landing. "My mother put in all new lighting, including those chandeliers," he said, pointing to the two in the upstairs hallway. "She redid the flooring, covered the walls with this wallpaper, had doors replaced and redid the fixtures in the bathrooms as well. My room was changed from top to bottom, including the fixtures and the closet. She ripped out part of a wall to expand it. Then, she had the wall on the opposite side torn out and had a bathroom put in for me. That was a very big job. My father complained that it was costing as much to redo the house as it was to have bought it.

"But, being we could get all the materials wholesale and great deals on the labor, he didn't stand a chance." He leaned toward me to whisper, as if there were others in the house. "The truth was my mother wouldn't have moved in here if he didn't go along with all her changes. A dead body in your house is a dead body. For most people it would give them the creeps, but this was too good a house to pass up, especially for the price."

"I understand," I said. "Your parents were smart to buy it, I'm sure."

He nodded.

"My dad's a good businessman. It's supposed to run in the family, so there's high hopes for me."

He went to his right and opened his bedroom door.

Then he spread out his arms and cried, "Ta-da. Here it is. The scene of the crime."

He stepped back. I hesitated. How many times had I imagined myself here, dreamed of looking into the room and envisioning Harry Pearson's body on this floor, my mother standing over him? It was the meat to fatten the bones of my worst nightmare.

"Harry Pearson's body was sprawled on the floor just inside the door. He was lying facedown, both arms out above his head." Craig looked down as if the body was really there. It gave me a surge of ice along my spine, and I actually shuddered. He turned to me. "You know how she did it, right?"

I nodded even though I really didn't know any of the gruesome details. I felt as if I had a heavy stone on my tongue.

"She stabbed him in the throat," he told me.

I didn't need to hear it. I didn't want to hear those details, and yet I did. I was caught in the web of that horrible contradiction. I was like a moth drawn to a flame. Get too close and you set yourself on fire. Craig smiled.

"I know the whole story, of course. I couldn't help but be curious about something like that happening in the house we had bought and were going to live in and especially the bedroom I would sleep in," he added, as if he had to provide me with an excuse.

I nodded, but I couldn't get my gaze off the floor where Harry Pearson's body supposedly had been found.

"He wasn't half in and half out. He was fully in the room."

I looked up at him.

"So?"

"There were no pictures of your mother in the papers," he continued, ignoring my question. "She was still considered a juvenile, but I found her picture in one of the old yearbooks in the school library. You ever go in there to look at those?"

"No."

Since my father had graduated from a high school in Yonkers, New York, looking at his yearbook wouldn't have provided my mother's picture, and Aunt Zipporah had never shown me my mother's picture in a yearbook.

"There's just pictures of her with her class, and her face is so small you need a magnifying glass. She was very pretty," he told me. "Now that I see you out of a shell, you're very pretty yourself, and you do bear a strong resemblance."

"I wasn't in any shell."

"You weren't?" He smiled.

"I wasn't."

"All right. You weren't. Anyway," he said, turning back to his room, "I think my bed is where her bed had been, between those two windows. My mother had the panes replaced with more efficient ones, but that's where the windows were then and that's where they are now."

I walked in slowly and looked around. It was difficult now to envision this room ever being my mother's or any girl's room, for that matter. The furniture was heavy-looking dark oak. He had a set of dumbbells on a stand in the corner. Over the headboard of the bed was a school banner celebrating the basketball championship last year. On the top of his bookcase, he had trophies as well.

I thought the most interesting thing was an oil painting of a baseball player swinging his bat. The artist captured his movement and the tension in his forearms, neck and shoulders. There was just enough of his profile to show his intensity.

"That's very nice," I said, nodding at it. "It has great detail."

"Yeah. I saw it in a gallery in New York and my father bought it for me. It's called *Hitter's Dream*. I heard you paint, too."

"Heard?"

"Dicky Steigman is in your art class. Mr. Longo's pretty impressed with what you do. I agree with him. I saw one of your paintings."

"When?"

Nothing I had ever done was put on display.

"Oh, one day when no one was in the room. I went in on my own and found it on Longo's desk. It was the one you did of a hawk or some large bird sailing over a pond."

"That's sneaky," I said.

He shrugged.

"Would you have shown it to me if I had asked?"

"Probably not," I confessed. The last thing I needed was for the other students to start poking fun at my art.

"Case closed."

I turned away and looked out the window. It looked down on the front of the house, but from this vantage point, I could see the street and some of the village as well. Had my mother felt as trapped up here as she had back in our attic? It was a good-size room, but nowhere near the size of the attic.

"What exactly do you know about the Pearson case?" he asked.

"Not that much. My grandparents don't like to talk about it," I said.

He was just staring at me now, wearing the expression of someone who wasn't sure he should say anything else.

"What?" I urged.

"As I said, because I'm living in the house and sleeping in her room, I couldn't help but have some curiosity about it. However, my parents don't even know how much I've learned. It's better that way. They accused me of having a macabre curiosity, and my mother hates to hear about it."

"What did you learn?"

"I know what she claimed was happening to her and how in the end no one believed her because she made so much stuff up. Some of it was quite off the wall. Actually, I suppose most of it was."

"I think I better go," I said. Talking about my mother as if she was someone else was starting to bother me, and I was afraid of what else he might say. "I didn't tell my grandparents I was going for a walk."

"Take it easy," he said. "I'll drive you home. You might be interested in what I think about it all."

"I'm not," I said, starting out.

"Why not?"

"I'm tired of people making fun of me, for one thing," I said, pausing. "Slipping notes in my locker, whispering behind my back. Spying on my art," I added.

"Wait a minute," he said as I walked out. He followed me to the stairway. "I'm not making fun of you and I don't whisper behind your back. I'm not going to say I haven't heard other girls making fun of you, but they're idiots."

"Exactly what do you want?" I asked, turning at the top of the stairs.

"I just wanted to share my ideas with you, that's all."

"What ideas?"

"About your mother, the case. I told you why it intrigued me, and it has nothing to do with making fun of you. Not everything has to be about you. That's what my mother's always telling me about myself," he added, smiling.

"Okay, what?" I said, folding my arms under my breasts and shifting my weight to my right leg. Aunt Zipporah told me my mother used to do the same thing when she was a little annoyed.

"Come on back to my room for a few minutes. I have something to show you," he said and turned and walked back as if there was no doubt I would, too.

He's pretty damn sure of himself, I thought, but instead of concluding he was simply another arrogant boy, I envied him for his self-confidence and followed. He was sitting at his desk.

"Come on in," he said. "I won't bite."

"Aren't you worried that I might?"

He laughed. "I might enjoy it."

"Very funny. What do you want to show me?" I asked, stepping over to him. He reached down and opened the drawer on his right to pluck out a folder. Then he put it on his desk and opened it. The top page was a copy of a news story about the Pearson murder. I thought the headline was gruesomely tongue-in-cheek:

"Prescription for Death, Druggist Murdered in Sandburg."

"You ever see this stuff?"

I shook my head.

"I duplicated as much as I could at the public library. Here," he said, standing. "Sit down and read it. There's more in the folder. You'll even find the police report."

I looked at him, surprised.

"How did you get that?"

"Someone at the police department has a brother working for us at the lumberyard and did me a favor. Do you know, were you aware of the fact that your grandfather worked for my grandfather at the lumberyard?"

I shook my head.

"Yes, it's true. He died young. You knew that, right?"

I was ashamed to admit how little I knew about my mother's family, so I didn't respond.

"Go ahead. Read some of it. You want something to drink? A soda, juice?"

"Just some cold water," I said, staring down at the papers on the desk. It was truly like a magnet drawing my eyes. I slowly lowered myself to the chair.

"I'll be right back. Take your time."

I could see how excited he was that I was going to read all this. I heard him charge down the stairs to get my water and get back. I smiled to myself, and then I began to read what was in the folder. It was truly like opening a forbidden door.

The first story told about the discovery of Harry's body and then the search for my mother. There were follow-up stories about the continual search, each story repeating the gruesome details. From the dates on the paper, it looked like not a day had gone by without something being written about the case. The reporter who was writing the stories made reference to the Doral case, as if somehow they could be related. It was the only other famous murder in the village, and here I was living in the Doral House, ironically touched by both crimes.

My aunt Zipporah was never mentioned by name, but references were made to a "close friend" who claimed this and claimed that. It was obvious to me who that was. There were many quotes attributed to Darlene Pearson, who was in and out of a state of shock, according to the reporter. In every instance, she had no explanation. According to her, it had all come as a big surprise. For a while at the very beginning, she even doubted my mother had done it and was worried that maybe she had been kidnaped by whoever had. That idea quickly disappeared when someone leaked the information that my mother had fled to New York City.

And then finally there was the story of the police picking her up. Someone in the police department, quoted as an anonymous source, revealed that she had been hiding in the attic of the Doral House, and once again, the possible murder of Brandon Doral was discussed as if there was some direct tie-in to the Pearson case.

Craig had everything, including the follow-up stories about the court procedures and my mother eventually being remanded to a mental institution.

"What do you think?" he asked, handing me a glass of water.

I took it and sipped some. "What do you mean?"

"Anything you didn't know?"

How would I explain that most of it I didn't know?

"No."

"Did you read the police report?"

"Not yet."

Actually, I was shying away from it. I imagined the gory details. He picked it up and looked at it.

"Harry Pearson wasn't a small man, you know. He was six feet two inches and weighed close to two hundred and ten pounds. Your mother was about your height, five feet four inches. I'm six feet one."

"So?"

"So stand up," he said.

"Why?"

"Just do it."

I did. He reached out for my shoulders and turned me to face him directly.

"Okay. Here," he said, putting a pen in my right hand. "Pretend that's a knife. Swing it at my neck. Stab me in the neck."

"What?"

"Do it. Don't worry. Do it hard, fast. Do it!" he nearly screamed.

Here I was, standing in what had been my mother's room, reenacting the crime she had committed, acting out a nightmare. Was he getting some sick pleasure out of this? Would he brag to his friends and make me even more of a target in school?

"I'm trying to show you something. Please, just do it."

I started to shake my head and then, I can't explain why, I did it. I raised my hand and swung it at him, and he easily blocked it. He held my wrist and smiled.

"That doesn't prove anything," I said. "He could have been looking away, never expecting it."

"Looking away?"

"Yes. Let go."

He did, and I put the pen down.

"Why did you swing at me with your right hand?" he asked.

"What do you mean? You put the pen in it and you told me to do it."

"Are you right-handed?"

"No."

"Do you know where the wound was?"

"I told you. I didn't get to the police report."

"It was on Harry Pearson's left side."

"So?"

"So, she had to have the knife in her right hand. That's why I told you to do it."

"Terrific," I said. All I wanted to do now was run out of his room and the house. I started to walk out.

"Wait. Like you, your mother was left-handed, and I wasn't there telling her to put the knife in her right hand. C'mon. Read this," he urged, shoving the police report at me.

I stared at him a moment and then slowly backed up and lowered myself to the chair. He handed me the police report, and I read it quickly. Then I looked up at him.

"Are you saying you don't think she did it?"

"No. She probably did it, but not with careful, well-thought-out premeditation like the stories implied. When you're in a panic or under some threat or struggle, you would do whatever you can. Actually, I think Harry was on the floor already when she stabbed him in a panic."

"On the floor already?"

"Maybe in a struggle with her and she reached for the knife. That's why he had his arms out." He shrugged. "My theory."

"Why wouldn't the police consider that, think about her being left-handed and wonder about it like you did?"

"It wasn't important to them. They knew she had killed Harry. She was telling a story that was so off-the-wall that they discounted everything. There was no reason to believe any of what she said, no evidence, no one who said a bad thing about Harry Pearson. And besides, police like to close cases, make it easy. She had been diagnosed and sent to a mental clinic. What difference did anything else make? From what I can tell, it's as if her attorney fell asleep in the courtroom."

I looked at the report again and at some of the headlines on the stories. Could he be right? If he was . . . It made me dizzy, and I put my hand on the desk to keep the room from spinning. Then I took a deep breath.

"Are you all right?"

"Yes," I said quickly. "Thank you," I said and stood.

"Hey, no problem. I'm happy to talk about it with someone, especially you. I haven't looked at that stuff for some time, but I've thought about it often."

"I've got to go."

"C'mon," he said. "I said I would drive you home."

"You don't have to."

"I know I don't have to. I'm an American citizen," he said, laughing. "I have the freedom of choice, but I would like to, okay? So don't take away my fundamental rights."

uld I dare tell them I had been in my mother's
and even in her room? Should I dare tell them
the research Craig Harrison had done? I had to at
ell them about him. He was coming for me in the
ng, or said he was. Maybe he wouldn't show up.
s. I met Craig Harrison," I said. "And then he
me home."

ally?" I heard my grandfather say. He came to
ving room doorway. He looked down the hall
grandmother and then back at me. "We didn't
you were friendly with him."

wasn't until today," I said. "He wants to pick me
the morning for school. I said okay. Is that all
"

ure," my grandfather said quickly. Then he
d at my grandmother. "Right, Elaine?"

suppose so," she said. She looked nervous. "Es-
ly since you jumped in so quickly to say it was."

ey," he told her. "You're the one who had Rachel
er into Miss America."

did not. Anyway, what are you implying, Michael
?"

laughed and then winked at me.

ll be right down to help with dinner," I told my
mother.

here's nothing to help with. I was just cleaning
it. Your grandfather is taking us to have Chinese
n Monticello. We'll leave about five-thirty."

kay," I said and hurried up the stairs to the attic.
enly, I felt I had to be up there. It was the only
where I could think clearly and be comforted.
nind was reeling with a kaleidoscope of mixed
ons. The girl in me was excited and even fasci-

I had to laugh, too. After all the heavy reading, it
was a relief to laugh about something.

"Okay," I said. "I don't want to be accused of being
a bad citizen." We started out.

I glanced back at the room and the hallway before I
followed him down the stairs.

"This way," he said and took me through the kitchen
to the door that opened to their garage, where he had
his car.

"When we bought the house, there was an area behind the garage where construction had begun to turn
it into what my mother thought was a maid's quarters.
She didn't like the idea of having a maid live with us,
so she let my father turn it into a small workshop for
himself. He put a television set in there and uses it as
a hideaway," Craig added, smiling. "Although he pretends to be working on his little projects."

We backed out of the garage.

"I've got to tell you," he said after turning onto
the street, "that I've always been curious about you.
Not," he added quickly, "like some of the others in our
school. I know what Mindy and Peggy did, and I've
always thought they were air heads."

"What are you curious about?"

"Why you keep to yourself so much, for one thing.
Where do you go in the summer, for another."

"I haven't found anyone I'd like to pal around
with," I said.

He smiled. "C'mon. You really don't even try, Alice.
You don't belong to anything, any club, any team. You
don't go out for plays, chorus, whatever."

"You sound like my grandparents. If you know so
much about me, why ask?"

"I don't know so much about you. That's the point. The other point," he said, looking at me again, "especially after seeing you dolled up, is I'd liked to."

I didn't say anything. I could feel the heat come into my face, and I didn't want him to see me blush, so I turned to look out the window.

"I go to my aunt's café in New Paltz every summer and work."

"Oh. And you stay there all summer?"

"Yes."

"You're going to do that this summer, too?"

"Yes. I'm going to be a waitress."

"Well, that's not too far."

I looked at him.

"Too far for what?"

"A visit or two or three," he said.

If there ever was such a thing as a magical, winning smile, Craig Harrison had it, I thought. It made me want to dive into his face. Again, I felt the heat rise up through my neck.

"You like riding the bus to school?" he asked.

"I don't mind. I get some reading done."

"How about I pick you up tomorrow?" he asked as we drew closer to the Doral House.

"Why do you want to do that? It's out of your way."

"That depends on what my way is," he said, smiling again. "I'll be here at seven a.m. The bus doesn't come by until about seven-fifteen, right?"

"Yes, that's right."

He pulled into our driveway and looked up at the Doral House.

"Your house is the most interesting in the area. I think, anyway. You ever go up to the attic?"

"Of course. That's where I do m

"Oh. Well, how about quid pro q that is?"

"Yes. Tit for tat," I said, and he l

"So? Do I get to see it?"

"Not right now, but maybe," I sai

"I'd even volunteer to be a mode smiling impishly.

"I bet you would. Thanks. For ev and got out.

"See you in the morning."

He waved and backed out. I watcl Why was he doing this? Was he re me, or was he going to use me to ar his friends? How do you know when especially someone like him, who, as cerned, could choose any girl in the s

It was nice of him to think that m as terrible as she had been made out had to wonder if he was saying all t me all that just to win my trust. My I thought, I needed to get out and wouldn't be so naive and helpless wh cializing, especially with boys.

"That you, Alice?" I heard my gra entered the house. He was in the livi My grandmother was in the kitchen. moving about and then saw her peer

"Yes, Grandpa."

"Where were you?" my grandm didn't know you were still outside."

"I went for a walk and ended up ii

"Oh?"

I had to laugh, too. After all the heavy reading, it was a relief to laugh about something.

"Okay," I said. "I don't want to be accused of being a bad citizen." We started out.

I glanced back at the room and the hallway before I followed him down the stairs.

"This way," he said and took me through the kitchen to the door that opened to their garage, where he had his car.

"When we bought the house, there was an area behind the garage where construction had begun to turn it into what my mother thought was a maid's quarters. She didn't like the idea of having a maid live with us, so she let my father turn it into a small workshop for himself. He put a television set in there and uses it as a hideaway," Craig added, smiling. "Although he pretends to be working on his little projects."

We backed out of the garage.

"I've got to tell you," he said after turning onto the street, "that I've always been curious about you. Not," he added quickly, "like some of the others in our school. I know what Mindy and Peggy did, and I've always thought they were air heads."

"What are you curious about?"

"Why you keep to yourself so much, for one thing. Where do you go in the summer, for another."

"I haven't found anyone I'd like to pal around with," I said.

He smiled. "C'mon. You really don't even try, Alice. You don't belong to anything, any club, any team. You don't go out for plays, chorus, whatever."

"You sound like my grandparents. If you know so much about me, why ask?"

"I don't know so much about you. That's the point. The other point," he said, looking at me again, "especially after seeing you dolled up, is I'd liked to."

I didn't say anything. I could feel the heat come into my face, and I didn't want him to see me blush, so I turned to look out the window.

"I go to my aunt's café in New Paltz every summer and work."

"Oh. And you stay there all summer?"

"Yes."

"You're going to do that this summer, too?"

"Yes. I'm going to be a waitress."

"Well, that's not too far."

I looked at him.

"Too far for what?"

"A visit or two or three," he said.

If there ever was such a thing as a magical, winning smile, Craig Harrison had it, I thought. It made me want to dive into his face. Again, I felt the heat rise up through my neck.

"You like riding the bus to school?" he asked.

"I don't mind. I get some reading done."

"How about I pick you up tomorrow?" he asked as we drew closer to the Doral House.

"Why do you want to do that? It's out of your way."

"That depends on what my way is," he said, smiling again. "I'll be here at seven a.m. The bus doesn't come by until about seven-fifteen, right?"

"Yes, that's right."

He pulled into our driveway and looked up at the Doral House.

"Your house is the most interesting in the area. I think, anyway. You ever go up to the attic?"

"Of course. That's where I do my artwork," I said.

"Oh. Well, how about quid pro quo? You know what that is?"

"Yes. Tit for tat," I said, and he laughed.

"So? Do I get to see it?"

"Not right now, but maybe," I said.

"I'd even volunteer to be a model," he added, now smiling impishly.

"I bet you would. Thanks. For everything," I added and got out.

"See you in the morning."

He waved and backed out. I watched him drive off. Why was he doing this? Was he really interested in me, or was he going to use me to amuse himself and his friends? How do you know when to trust someone, especially someone like him, who, as far as I was concerned, could choose any girl in the school?

It was nice of him to think that my mother wasn't as terrible as she had been made out to be, and yet I had to wonder if he was saying all that and showing me all that just to win my trust. My family was right, I thought, I needed to get out and about more so I wouldn't be so naive and helpless when it came to socializing, especially with boys.

"That you, Alice?" I heard my grandfather call as I entered the house. He was in the living room, reading. My grandmother was in the kitchen. I could hear her moving about and then saw her peer out to see me.

"Yes, Grandpa."

"Where were you?" my grandmother asked. "We didn't know you were still outside."

"I went for a walk and ended up in the village."

"Oh?"

Should I dare tell them I had been in my mother's home and even in her room? Should I dare tell them about the research Craig Harrison had done? I had to at least tell them about him. He was coming for me in the morning, or said he was. Maybe he wouldn't show up.

"Yes. I met Craig Harrison," I said. "And then he drove me home."

"Really?" I heard my grandfather say. He came to the living room doorway. He looked down the hall at my grandmother and then back at me. "We didn't know you were friendly with him."

"I wasn't until today," I said. "He wants to pick me up in the morning for school. I said okay. Is that all right?"

"Sure," my grandfather said quickly. Then he looked at my grandmother. "Right, Elaine?"

"I suppose so," she said. She looked nervous. "Especially since you jumped in so quickly to say it was."

"Hey," he told her. "You're the one who had Rachel turn her into Miss America."

"I did not. Anyway, what are you implying, Michael Stern?"

He laughed and then winked at me.

"I'll be right down to help with dinner," I told my grandmother.

"There's nothing to help with. I was just cleaning up a bit. Your grandfather is taking us to have Chinese food in Monticello. We'll leave about five-thirty."

"Okay," I said and hurried up the stairs to the attic. Suddenly, I felt I had to be up there. It was the only place where I could think clearly and be comforted. My mind was reeling with a kaleidoscope of mixed emotions. The girl in me was excited and even fascinated with the way Craig Harrison spoke to me and smiled at me. I had no idea he had been watching me, thinking about me all this time. And of course, I had no idea he had developed such interest in my mother's story and secretly done so much in the way of research.

When I had first seen it, I was bothered by what he had done. I thought, just as his mother accused, that he might have a macabre fascination with it all, but he seemed so sincere when I spoke with him. It was not only comforting but intriguing as well. After all, what if his theory was right?

Isn't that what I had wished for so long?

His explanation as to why no one would believe anything she had said made sense, too. I had no trouble considering the possibility that my mother had exaggerated and created so much more in her story than what might have been. Craig didn't hear my aunt Zipporah speak about her. He didn't understand how much she depended upon and used her imagination.

But that didn't mean it was all untrue necessarily.

Did it?

Would there ever come a time when I could confront her and win her trust enough to ask her?

And if I did and she told me her side of it all, would I believe her?

I'd be predisposed to do so. I couldn't be objective—or could I?

I sat on the sofa, where my father had sat when he was up here with me, and I looked at the window and tried with all my imaginative powers to see her standing there the way he obviously had. I envisioned her turning to me and smiling.

"I knew you would come up here," she would say. "I always had faith that someday you would come to my defense, my only real ally, my daughter. You'll find a way to show them all. You'll set me free so I can walk out of here and outside again. I'll leave the attic.

"Finally, we'll be together, mother and daughter, walking and talking and laughing about everything that happens to you as you grow up. I'll be there at your side when you fall in love and get married and have children of your own.

"And then I'll make sure that you never, ever get trapped in any attic."

Tears streamed down my cheeks when she turned away. I had lost her so quickly again.

What could I do to bring her back?

I looked around the attic and at the picture of the tree both my grandfather and my father so admired, and then it came to me. Maybe it came from her.

I would paint her standing there by that window. I wouldn't let my grandparents, Zipporah, my father, anyone know until the picture was finished.

That way, I would lock her forever and ever in my eyes, my mind and my heart.

And she would never disappear again.

6

Showing Craig the Attic

I had just finished outlining the picture when my grandmother called up to tell me to get ready to go to dinner. I hated leaving the work, but I knew it would be exactly the wrong sort of message to send if I told them I'd rather stay home to paint. They were so determined to get me out of this house, and specifically out of this attic, more.

On the way to the restaurant, my grandfather teased me about Craig Harrison until my grandmother gave him those big eyes of hers, a look that usually froze him in place. He told me even the big-shot doctors at the hospital fled from her when she did that to them.

In the back of my mind, I was still unsure about Craig's motives anyway. I was terrified of being deceived and made the object of even more ridicule at school. My new fashionable appearance was bound to create enough chatter as it was; adding Craig's driving me to school would surely make me topic number one on the chatterbox network. Disappearing in the rear of everyone else's thoughts was soon to be impossible.

The following morning, as I stood outside where I normally waited for the school bus, I almost hoped

Craig wouldn't show up, but he appeared just a few seconds after 7:00 a.m. I glanced back at the windows in front of the house and was positive I saw my grandmother sneaking a peek through the curtains as he pulled into the driveway, backed out and right up to me standing on the side of the road.

"Forget the school bus. Your chariot has arrived, madam," he said, and then he leaped out and went around to open the car door for me. He did a silly, sweeping bow and I got in. "You look great," he told me as soon as he got in and started away.

"Thank you."

"So what really made you change? I mean, your clothes, your hair and makeup, if I might be so bold to ask."

"Let's just say it was either this or banishment."

He laughed. "And here I thought it was all to win my heart."

I glanced at him. "You mean your heart is that easily won?"

"Whoa," he said. "I'd better bring in reinforcements quickly. You're not going to be easy."

"You mean as easy as the others were?"

"The others? Another false accusation?"

He pretended to be wounded and then lose control of the car.

I screamed and he laughed.

Then I saw him turn serious.

"You know when you first really caught my attention?" he asked.

"How would I know that? I didn't even know I had."

"It was in English class when Mr. Feldman pushed

you to give your interpretation of why Frost repeated the last line in his poem 'Stopping by Woods on a Snowy Evening.' You know the line I mean: 'And I have promises to keep and miles to go before I sleep.' Everyone else was saying or would say he repeated it because he wanted to emphasize his responsibilities, but you said because he was insecure about what he had to do. He had to talk himself into it with the repetition. When you added the words 'like most of us,' I went, Wow. This is a girl I'd like to know."

"That was months ago," I said. "What happened since?"

"What can I say? I'm shy."

I looked at him skeptically.

"I am! I'm the basic example of someone who tries to overcompensate to cure his shyness. Besides, as I told you, I did look at you, smile at you, even nod at you, but you looked like you were looking right through me, so I thought, forget it. She's not interested."

Could that be true? I wondered.

"I'm not blaming you. You probably thought I was like the others, just playing with you."

"Maybe that's what you're doing right now," I said, and he pretended to be wounded again, this time coming so close to the right shoulder of the road that I was positive we would go into the ditch.

"Reinforcements! Reinforcements!" he shouted, and I screamed again.

By the time we pulled into the school parking lot and he parked beside another student's car, we were both laughing. That alone stopped some of the girls entering the building. They stared in utter disbelief.

"What'cha doing, catching flies?" Craig asked them as we walked by and saw their mouths still open.

I smiled to myself.

Maybe, I thought, just maybe, I might enjoy being in school for once. But that made the possibility of being disappointed and deceived even more terrifying for me. I felt like holding my breath all day and tiptoe-ing my way from classroom to classroom, fearing that if I moved too quickly, I might shatter the illusion of happiness and bring the world of hope crashing down around me in sharp shards of betrayal.

It wasn't that way. Craig was truly like my body-guard, fending off any teasing comments his friends threw in my direction.

"Who's the new girl?" was the top ten remark.

"Wouldn't you like to know," was Craig's defense, and then he would scoop his arm through mine and direct me away, talking and laughing as if we had been together for months and months and not just hours.

"How about coming to baseball practice today to watch me show off?" he asked me at lunch. "I'll take you home right afterward."

I had never even gone to a game, much less a prac-tice, where, I knew, the girlfriends of other players hung out to watch. I could easily use the excuse that my grandmother would worry if I didn't step off the school bus or show up after school. Craig wouldn't know she was going to do an afternoon into the eve-ning shift at the hospital and wouldn't be home. My grandfather would be at the office until late in the afternoon. Our dinner would simply have to be heated up, and either I would do it or he would because I was so involved in my work in the attic.

My hesitation in replying concerned him.

"I'll do better if you're there," he said, "and so the team will benefit. You'd be helping your school."

"Yeah, right."

"You'll see," he said. "What do you say?"

I'm getting in deeper and deeper, I thought, *but isn't that what I really want?*

"Maybe," I gave him, and that was enough.

When the bell for the end of the final class of the day rang, I had still not really decided. My heart was racing. I went to my locker and found myself moving exaggeratedly slowly. If I missed the bus, I would have to attend the baseball practice. Maybe it was the coward's way to decide, but that's exactly what I did. I missed the bus.

At the end of the day, the school always cleared out so quickly that it looked like a deserted sinking ship. Doors slammed closed, and except for some students who were in detention or doing some extra help session with their teachers, no one was around. I made my way through the corridor to the doorway that led out to the ballfields. The girlfriends and those interested in becoming girlfriends of players were already getting into the stands to watch the practice. Of those who were there, there was no one with whom I had much contact in school. I barely had spoken to most of them, even though some were in my classes.

The ballplayers came charging out of their locker room entrance with the coach and his two student assistants trailing behind. When Craig saw me walking toward the bleachers, he stopped to wave, and I waved back. It drew the immediate interest of all the girls already seated. They watched me approach, but no one called to me to sit beside her. I sat a good two levels behind and above them all and set my books down. Whether it came from my nervousness or somewhere else I wasn't sure, but I opened my sketch pad and at first pretended I was doing some sort of drawing related to the baseball practice. I knew that all the girls were turned to look at me. They were buzzing away like a mad hive of hornets. Mindy and Peggy were there among them, so I didn't expect I was getting any flattering compliments.

Nevertheless, one of the African American girls, Charlene Lewis, stepped away from the pack and headed in my direction. She was a very tall, pretty girl with very light brown eyes and probably the most attractive figure of any girl in the school. I knew she was going steady with a senior, Bobby Robinson, the baseball team's best pitcher. I overheard enough in the hallways and cafeteria to know he'd been offered a scholarship, like my father, to play baseball at a prestigious Midwestern college.

"Hey," Charlene said as she approached. "Why are you sitting way up here?"

"Better view," I said and continued to sketch some lines.

"That the only reason you came to the practice?" she asked, nodding at my pad and smiling.

I looked up at her.

"Maybe."

"Sure," she said, laughing. She slipped onto the bench and looked at my preliminary sketching. It was a random view of the field. I hadn't yet drawn any players. "You know you and Craig were the biggest topic of discussion today?"

"I can't imagine why," I said, and she laughed.

"I like your outfit. Where'd you get those jeans?"

"I think the place was called Bottoms Up, something like that, in Middletown."

"You think? You don't remember the store?"

"We were in and out of so many. It's a blur."

She pulled her head back.

"Girl, you sure surprising everyone 'round here."

"I can't imagine why," I said, and she laughed again. I stopped drawing for a moment and looked at her. "You know, if you form stereotyped opinions of someone, you get surprised when they do something different. Whose fault is that? I think you would know something about people forming stereotyped opinions. I think you would understand better than any of them why that's so distasteful and hurtful," I added, nodding at the pack of girls below us.

Her expression changed so fast I was sure she was going to jump up, say something nasty and go off, but instead, she nodded, smiled again and relaxed.

"I've been looking for an excuse to get away from those pack rats. Glad you came," she said.

We watched the players start their batting practice. Her boyfriend was on the mound pitching.

"Bobby is really graceful out there. Watching him wind up and throw is like watching a ballet sometimes," she said.

I studied her boyfriend and agreed.

"So, all kidding aside, how come you changed your style, and how did you hook up with Craig Harrison so fast? No one even saw you two talking before today."

"All kidding aside," I replied, "were you sent over here to find out?"

She laughed. "Sorta."

I liked the fact that she was honest.

"Well, I sorta decided to try new clothes, and then I put a spell on Craig and seduced him," I told her. "I've been studying witchcraft in the basement. You had better warn them. I can cast spells and turn girls into houseflies."

"Girl, you are something else," she said, laughing.

"We're all something else, Charlene. That's the point."

She nodded. "You two go out over the holidays?"

"Not really. I had a lot of family visiting."

"Here he goes," she said, nodding at the ballfield. Craig was at bat. "Bobby says he's the only one he can't figure out. They're always competing with each other."

I leaned forward.

Bobby's first pitch seemed to go right through Craig's bat.

"He's too anxious to show off because of you," Charlene said. "Bobby's going to get him."

Already someone's mistakes are being blamed on me, I thought. *That didn't take long.*

Craig swung and missed the next pitch, too.

He paused, stepped away from the plate, looked down at the ground and seemed to say a prayer or something. Then he returned. Bobby Robinson was all business, intent. He went through his windup and hurled what looked like another strike, only Craig timed it just right. The ball came sailing toward the bleachers in a high arc and fell near the pack of girls, who shrieked and leaped in every direction.

"That boy's definitely in love," Charlene said. "No other explanation Bobby gonna accept."

She laughed, squeezed my arm gently and returned to the pack.

The contest sparked an idea for me, and I began to work madly on a new drawing, concentrating on it so hard that I had no idea how much time had gone by or that I had worked to the point where the coach had blown his whistle and declared the practice had ended. The pack of girls exploded in every direction, each catching up with one of the players. Craig came sauntering out toward me and waited while I finished a line. Before he could speak, I turned it so he could see it.

It was a picture of him, swinging hard, his whole body in movement, but as the ball came off his bat, it turned into a bird.

"Wow," he said, taking it to look closer. "Can I have this?"

"Sure," I said.

He handed it back. "Sign your name. Someday it's going to be worth a ton."

I laughed and wrote my name in the bottom right corner.

"See," he said, "I knew you'd have a good time coming to practice. What did you think of my first hit?"

"It looked like you were aiming for those girls."

"I was," he said, holding his hand out for me.

I took it and we started back toward the school building.

"Give me fifteen to take a shower and dress and I'll be out to drive you home."

"Okay," I said. Before he turned to go in, he leaned over and kissed me softly on the lips.

"In baseball," he said, his lips still close to mine, "we call that getting to first base. Did I get on with a hit, a walk or an error?"

"Felt like a hit," I said. He beamed, kissed me again and hurried into the building.

Oh please, please, I prayed, *let this not be deception.*

While I waited for him, I gazed back at the ballfield and wondered why my aunt Zipporah never spoke about her or my mother having any boyfriends at school. Didn't anyone ever ask either of them out? Didn't they watch boyfriends at basketball or baseball practice? Why weren't they in the school plays? Surely, they could have met boys there. They were as void of any school activities as I was. Could that possibly have had something to do with what had been going on and what had occurred later?

It seemed that whenever I went into deep thought about my mother, I left time and place and had no concept of where I was or how long I had been there. The next thing I heard was Craig calling to me. Finally, I felt him nudge me.

"Hey, what's with you? I was shouting like crazy," he said.

"Oh. Sorry. I was just thinking about things."

"That deeply? I hope it involved me," he said, reaching for my hand.

"In a way it did."

"Great. I'll take anything. Even 'in a way,' " he said, and we headed around the building toward the parking lot. Just about everyone had already dressed and gone. There were only a half dozen cars left, including his.

"I saw you were talking to Charlene Lewis in the stands," he said as we approached his car.

"You weren't concentrating on your practice?"

He laughed. "No, but I did finally. She's a nice girl. I like Bobby, too. Maybe we'll go on a double date with them."

I didn't say anything. He opened the car door for me, and I got in.

"You didn't say anything when I mentioned a double date," he said after we drove out of the lot.

"What should I say?"

"You'd like it or not, for one thing."

"I don't know. I've never been on a double date. I've never been on a date," I added unashamed.

"No secret romances?" he kidded.

"If there were, they were so secret, even I didn't know," I told him, and he laughed.

"You know you're a pretty interesting girl, Alice. As I told you, what I like about you is I can't tell what you're going to do or say. Most of the other girls here are carbon copies, almost mass produced. I was thinking about them when Kasofsky was describing Henry Ford's creation of the assembly line the other day, and then I looked at you and I thought, unique, custom made from the bottom up."

"Not weird?"

"No," he said and then smiled at me and added, "well, maybe a little."

I laughed.

"But I like it," he said.

I said nothing. *Am I being seduced? Am I hearing what I want to hear? How cautious should I be? How trusting? How truthful? What are the rules, the guide-*

lines? How much do you rely on your own instincts? Does it boil down to how much you can trust yourself? And what am I risking anyway? My virtue, my virginity, my reputation? What does that amount to here? Or is it something that will change me so much, I will hate myself, never mind what others think?

"You get into your thoughts so deeply again, Alice, that I feel like you're gone every once in a while. Does anyone else tell you that?" he asked.

"Sometimes my grandparents do."

"Maybe that's the way all artists, creative people are. You're the first girl I knew who does anything creatively, seriously creative, I mean. I'm sorry. I don't mean to be so personal."

"Yes, you do," I said. Then I smiled when he thought I was angry. "It's all right. I can't answer everything about myself because I don't know the answers yet myself."

His eyebrows rose, and he nodded.

"I like that," he said. "I think that's pretty smart. I think it's true for me as well. Maybe it's not as true as it is for you, but nevertheless, I like the idea that we're still making discoveries about our own identities. We get so much pressure on us at our age, don't we? What do you want to be? What do you like? Why are you interested in this or that? It's almost as if we should have our whole lives laid out like . . . like that damn assembly line. I know my parents have plans for me that might not exactly be my own."

Speaking of his parents, I wondered what they would say to him when they found out he had been seeing me, especially his mother, who had been so unnerved and disturbed about what my mother had done in her house. Wouldn't she think I'm bringing all that back?

I suppose I'll find out soon enough, I thought as we pulled into the Doral House driveway.

"Thanks for the ride home," I said.

He looked up at the house.

"What about your promise?"

"What promise?"

"To show me the attic, your art studio?"

"You really want to see that?"

"Very much," he said.

"Okay."

He shut off the engine and followed me into the house.

"My grandmother is still at work," I said. "My grandfather won't be home for another hour probably," I added, and he looked like that relaxed him.

I watched him take in everything.

"I knew this house would be interesting. The ceilings aren't that high, but the rooms are big. They didn't make ceilings high in those days because it was hard and expensive to heat the rooms," he explained. "Wow, that fireplace looks like it goes back a century," he muttered when he looked into the living room. "This is really a historical property."

I had to laugh at his enthusiasm. "You're not too far off. Sometimes my grandmother treats it as if it was a museum," I told him. "This way."

I led him up the stairs to the short stairway to the attic. Before I opened the door, I hesitated. For a moment I felt as if I were possibly betraying someone, betraying a secret to be kept under lock and key. I hardly knew Craig really, but something in me was so eager for his companionship and affection that I was willing to do it. Was that selfish? Would I be punished?

"Something wrong?" he asked, seeing my hesitation.

I shook my head and opened the door.

"Pretty nice," he said as soon as he entered. "I guess it's been changed a lot." He sounded a little disappointed about that. Was he expecting to find it exactly as it had been when my mother hid out here?

"Yes, completely," I said.

He walked about, looking at my pictures and then pausing at the one I had started depicting my mother at the window.

"Is this a self-portrait?"

"No," I said. He studied what lines were there and looked at me and then at the window.

"It's supposed to be your mother? Up here?"

"Yes," I admitted. I actually looked about, studying the corners, thinking I was being watched, heard, revealing a secret.

"I can't wait to see it when it's done. I like the stuff you've done, Alice, as much of it as I've seen, I mean."

He sat on the sofa and nodded as he looked around. "I can believe someone could have hidden up here for some time. Not without help, of course," he added.

"It wasn't always that. My aunt and my mother used it as their sort of clubhouse."

"Oh yeah? Why not? I would have." He smiled. "I would now," he said.

"That wasn't the exact sofa, but there was one here and they used it to pretend they were in a car, traveling, seeing America."

"Would you like to do that?"

"Pretend?"

"No, silly. See America?"

"Why not? Who wouldn't?"

"Right. I've been to a few places for vacations," he said, leaning back. I drew closer, envious.

"Where have you been?"

"We've spent part of the summer up at Cape Cod. We've gone to the Finger Lakes, once to Wyoming and lots of times to Florida during the winter break, of course. My mother wanted to see Nashville, and once we visited some relatives in Chicago. How about you?"

I shook my head.

"Not anywhere as much as that. New York City."

"That's it?"

"And my aunt's place in New Paltz."

"No wonder you sit on the sofa."

"I didn't say I do that. I said my aunt and my mother did," I said sharply.

"Wouldn't be terrible if you had," he replied, undisturbed by my reaction. "C'mon," he said, patting the spot beside him. "I'll take you for a ride."

I hesitated.

"Just for fun. Remember, I don't bite."

"I don't think so," I said, shaking my head.

"Stop being so afraid of everything," he warned. "You'll never get those answers about yourself you're looking to get if you remain so timid and afraid."

I had heard that before—and recently, too. He was truly like a marksman hitting the bull's-eyes, I thought. Again I wondered if it was all part of a clever seduction. I inched closer, then he reached up for my hand

and I sat beside him. He put his arm around my shoulders, drew me closer and kissed my cheek and then my lips before leaning back and pretending to have one hand on a steering wheel.

"Okay," he said, "we're entering Provincetown, Cape Cod. It's at the very tip of the cape. You look to your left and right and you see the dunes . . . it looks like desert going on and on to the ocean. Now there are houses and soon we're entering the village. Smell the sea?" He took a deep breath. "Do you?" He looked at me, and I laughed.

Was this exactly what my mother and Aunt Zipporah had done sixteen years ago?

"Isn't it breathtaking? We're going to eat fresh lobster tonight. Look up at the sign above that restaurant . . . The Lobster You Eat Today Last Night Swam in Cape Cod Bay."

I laughed again and again he kissed me, only this time it was a longer kiss, one that drew me into him, one that relaxed my shoulders and softened me enough to turn. His hand went down my back. He pulled away to kiss my nose, my closed eyes, and then my lips again.

"Alice," he said, but he wasn't just saying my name. He was calling to me, calling to something deep inside me, to a longing, awakening the sleeping curiosity that came in dreams and quiet moments, the curiosity about my own body and the way it struggled to discover and find answers about itself.

His hands were at my waist, moving under my blouse, gliding over my ribs to my tightly held breasts clamoring to be free. He fidgeted only for a moment behind my back to undo the bra, and then I moaned under the first touch of his fingers over my breasts and nipples. I closed my eyes as if I couldn't watch because if I did, I would stop him from lifting my blouse away, from bringing his lips to my breasts, from letting him take off my blouse and my bra and then from feeling his lips working a path of kisses down to my waist as he unzipped my skirt.

I felt as if I were lowering myself into a warm, erotic bath of pleasure. His mouth followed the downward movement of my skirt and panties. My arms and hands were above me. It was as if I was holding onto a bar to keep myself from going too deeply and I was losing the grip on the bar, sliding, sliding . . .

"Alice," he said again. "You're beautiful."

All my grandmother's admonitions about sexual promiscuity rang in my head like distant church bells sounded to send out alarms and warnings, but I wasn't heeding them even though just below the cacophony of bongs and cries, I could hear him undoing his own pants, preparing . . .

And then, like some Lone Ranger, some great comic hero arriving at the last possible moment to save the day, we heard my grandfather call up to us.

An icy sheet of reality froze us both. The sensual fingers that had so gripped me inside and out released me. Craig sat up quickly and straightened himself. I rushed to do the same.

"Alice? Are you upstairs?"

"Yes, Grandpa," I called back as I fixed my bra and blouse. Craig leaped off the sofa and brushed back his hair. When we heard my grandfather's footsteps on the attic stairway, Craig went to one of my paintings and stared at it as if he had come here to consider making a purchase.

I sat back on the sofa and waited. My grandfather stepped in and looked about the attic.

"Oh. I wondered whose car that was in the driveway."

"Oh, I'm sorry, Mr. Stein. Did I block you?"

"No problem," my grandfather said. He looked at me, his eyes full of questions.

"Craig wanted to see where I worked and some of my paintings."

"They're really good," Craig followed quickly.

Anyone, even a complete idiot, I thought, could see how nervous we were. My grandfather smiled softly and nodded.

"Yeah. She's good. Well, I'm just going to get out of my lawyer's uniform," my grandfather said. "You want to stay for dinner, Craig?"

"Oh, no, thanks. I've got to get home. My parents were in the city and came back this morning after I had already left for school, so I had better get my rear end moving," Craig replied.

"Sure," my grandfather said, nodded at me and left.

Craig and I looked at each other. Then he walked over as I stood up.

"This is a magical place," he said. Then he kissed me softly and walked to the door. "I'll call you later. And I'll pick you up for school tomorrow." He nodded toward the window. "Finish that," he said and left.

My heart was pounding so hard and fast that I felt faint for a moment. I closed my eyes, took a deep breath and started out of the attic, too. When I reached the door, I thought I heard the sound of two girls giggling. I turned and looked back at the sofa and envisioned my aunt and my mother, sitting there and conjuring the scene I had just played.

"She's just like me, Zipporah," I could hear her say. "See? She's just like me after all."

I fled down the stairs, exactly how someone running from herself might, regretting both what I had done and what I had not, for a part of me was happy I was saved, and a part of me was not.

Am I really so much different from any other girl my age then? I wondered.

Or am I simply traveling a longer, more convoluted route to the same answers, driven by the same questions.

Who am I?

What do I want?

Where am I going?

When will I know if I'm home?

7

A Date to the Prom

I warmed the dinner for my grandfather and myself and set the table. He came out of his den when I called for him. I was holding my breath, waiting for his comments about finding Craig and me in the attic. For a while, I thought he wasn't going to say anything about it. He talked about some case he was on and about some ideas he had for fixing the front of the house, but then he put his fork down and clasped his hands and looked at me with those intense eyes he could switch on whenever he was ready to say or do something very serious and important.

"I'm glad you've a friend, Alice. Whether you put *boy* in front of *friend* now or soon is no problem either. And I won't give you any of the lectures your grandmother is fond of giving. All the advice I'll give you is centered on two words."

"What two words?" I asked when he paused too long for my patience.

"*Go slowly.* Like anything, most things in life, if you take your time, you're usually better off. Some of those old adages are so true. Fools rush in where angels fear to tread. An ounce of prevention is worth a pound of cure. You know what I mean. I'm sure. That's it. That's my fatherly or grandfatherly advice. The rest is up to you. Enjoy yourself. Have a good time. Goodness knows, we're always worrying you won't. I don't want to put the wrong interpretation on anything and put you back in some cage. Just know I trust you will always make the right decisions."

"Why do you trust me?" I challenged.

"I just do," he said.

"You mean you just hope," I countered, and he laughed.

"That's why I trust and not just hope," he said.

"Why?"

"You're pretty smart. You've got something special. You have that artist's insight, that third eye."

I didn't have his confidence in me. I didn't know why he should have any. I had no doubt I would have gone too far with Craig if my grandfather hadn't arrived when he had and I couldn't claim I was happy that we had stopped. I was at least a little disappointed. What did that say about me?

My grandfather either couldn't or wouldn't see that in me. In the end, everyone sees and believes what they want to see and believe, I thought. Maybe my mother wasn't so different from everyone else after all. She just had a different shade of rose-colored glasses.

Craig called after my grandmother had come home from work at the hospital. Her face was a movie marquee full of questions about him and me. She came at them indirectly by asking, How was school? What did I do after school? I knew my grandfather had told her Craig had been up in the attic with me. They never kept secrets from each other. Because my answers were so simple, she finally asked about him, and I said he was very nice and was going to take me to school again in the morning. She didn't approve or disapprove. She simply nodded, and I went up to do my homework. That was when he called.

"Is everything all right at home?" he asked. He was sure my grandfather was at least suspicious.

"Yes."

I could almost feel his relief through the phone.

"Good. Listen," he said, "I know you might think I'm moving too fast, but I was never one to procrastinate."

"You don't have to convince me of that," I said, and he laughed.

"I never know what you're going to do or say," he told me. It was becoming a chant. "But I love it," he quickly added.

Was it his way of dealing with my cold truthfulness, or was I really like that? Was I spontaneous and unpredictable, the very words Aunt Zipporah had used to describe my mother?

"Anyway," he continued, "I've been thinking about you all night and wondered if you would go with me to the prom."

"The prom?"

"It's not quite a month off, but I know a girl needs time to prepare. You probably heard that we're having it at the Cherry Hill Hotel this year. As a community service, the hotel owners donated their ballroom. You know how we all hate to go to dances at the school. You're there all day. Who wants to return at night for a dance? This is more like a night out. It's going to be great, probably the best prom the school's ever had."

I didn't know how to react. One of the most popular boys at school was asking me to be his prom date. Because I didn't say anything quickly, he kept talking.

"They've got this four-piece band that's supposed to be terrific, and the hotel's providing the food. Some of the guys want to rent a limousine, but I haven't decided whether or not to join them. We could just go ourselves, of course. It's up to you. We don't have to make that decision right away.

"It's traditional for us to stay out all night," he continued without pausing to take a breath. "The next day we drive to Bear Mountain and have a picnic. It's the boys' responsibility to get the food and drinks. We throw out blankets and listen to music, do some barbecuing. I'm babbling," he finally said.

I smiled to myself. Then I thought about his parents and how they would react. Would it spook them to hear that their son was going out with the daughter of the woman who committed a murder in their home?

"Are you sure you want me to be your prom date?" I asked.

"About as sure as anything I've ever done or wanted to do. What do you say?"

"All right," I said. "Yes."

"Good. I'll stop holding my breath."

I laughed, and then we talked about his baseball schedule, the away games, which was specifically to let me know when he could and could not take me home after school. Finally, before we ended the call, I asked him if his parents knew he was picking me up for school and that he was asking me to the prom.

"They'll know soon," he said. "Don't worry about

it," he added, but I was sure I felt and heard some note of nervousness in his voice.

"Okay. I have to finish my homework. See you in the morning."

"Absolutely," he said. "Good night, Alice, and . . ."

"Yes?"

"I'm looking forward to another ride on the sofa in the attic." He laughed, but I felt a sharp, electric chill both of excitement and fear.

How did he see me? What did he really think of me? Was my inexperience showing, and did it put me at a big disadvantage? Should I have accepted the prom invitation so quickly, or should I have said, *"Let me think about it"*? Should I go slowly as my grandfather had advised? Only a short while after he had given me advice, I had ignored it. Some third eye, I thought. Even if I had that magical vision, I was asleep when I should have been the most awake.

I decided to take my time telling my grandparents about Craig's invitation to the prom. After all, I wasn't sure I wasn't going to change my mind about it. As he had pointed out, it was nearly a month off. What if I decided I didn't like him after all? And yet I couldn't keep it secret too much longer. Craig was right about that as well. I needed to think about my dress, my hair, all of it.

I knew Aunt Zipporah would be excited for me. I wondered how Rachel and my father would react to the news. Would she think or say my new romantic success was all because of her contributions? Helping to decide my new wardrobe? Helping me put on makeup? Maybe that would be good; maybe she wouldn't want me out of their lives so much.

Craig was there right on time the next morning. Amazingly, his first question for me was, What did my grandparents think of his asking me to the prom? I countered with, What did his parents think of it?

"I didn't get a chance to talk to them about it all yet," he said diplomatically.

"Neither did I," I told him, and he looked at me, surprised, and then smiled.

"What do we care what adults think of it anyway? It's our decision, right?"

"Right."

However, in the small community in which we both lived, our seeing each other wasn't going to be unnoticed and unreported long. I was sure he knew that even better than I did. He was more in the thick of it all. We were spending every free moment we had in school together, whether it was moving from class to class or our lunch period. On Thursday, he had an important away game, and I went home on the bus. It was the first time all week we were separated. I could feel the eyes and the attention on me all the time.

Some of the other girls besides Charlene Lewis began to talk to me as well. It was mostly friendly banter about something I was wearing, some lipstick or some homework. Sprinkled in their conversation were comments about Craig. I could see the envy on the faces of some of the girls and how some still couldn't understand his attraction to me. In every way they could, they tried to learn how I could win the attention of one of the school's most popular boys. I know I frustrated them with my silence or cryptic short replies. However, for the most part, when I wasn't with Craig, I tried to stay to myself. I didn't trust them, didn't even trust Charlene enough to reveal any of my feelings or thoughts about Craig.

Word got out before the end of the week that he had asked me to be his prom date, and that started a whole new wave of conversations in the girls' room or physical education class. Suddenly, it was important for them to know what I planned on wearing, where we planned to go right afterward and whether or not we were going to go in the limousine. They all wanted very much to know if I would be permitted to be out all night and go to the picnic the next day. I didn't want to tell them that I was actually still thinking about going at all. I had yet to tell my grandmother and grandfather, so I didn't have any answers for them.

"I'm not sure yet," was my stock reply.

Craig asked me to go for pizza and a movie with him on Friday. It would be our first formal date. I decided that if all went well, I would tell my grandparents about the prom the following morning. The team had won its away game, which meant our school was in the play-offs for the league title. Everyone was in a mood to celebrate. I didn't know what we would really be doing Friday night until Craig picked me up and told me that our plans had changed.

"Mickey Lesman's having an open house to celebrate the play-offs," he told me as soon as I got into his car. "Most of the team's going. His parents are off on a holiday, and his little sister's sleeping over at a friend's house. You cool with it?"

I shrugged. How could I tell him I didn't know what to expect? This would be the first open house party I ever attended.

"We could still go for pizza and a movie, if you

want," he said. "Or we go to the party and if we don't like it, we could always leave," he added.

I knew it was what he wanted to do, and my own curiosity about it was strong enough not to say no.

"It's fine," I said.

Mickey Lesman's house was a sprawling, modern, ranch-style, rich-looking home outside of the hamlet of Hurleyville, which wasn't much bigger than Sandburg, where I lived. Like most country roads, Mickey's road had no streetlights, and the houses were well spaced apart, some home owners having ten or so acres. Mickey's father was the owner of a major department store. By the time we arrived, there were at least two dozen cars parked in front of the house. The moment we stepped out of Craig's car, we could hear the loud music. I felt the ground rumbling beneath my feet with the vibrations from his big outside speakers. It was lucky the neighbors were far away, I thought.

Whenever my grandfather and I rode these back roads and saw these homes at nighttime, I often thought about the similarities with the way we lived, especially how I lived. To me people wrapped their homes around themselves and, like the citizens of a fortress town in the Middle Ages, pulled up their drawbridges. Instead of looking out of the windows at the world and imagining all sorts of things going on outside in the darkness, they sat around television sets and looked at what someone else had imagined for them.

My grandfather told me that when he was young, a few years younger than I was, he and his family listened to the radio and had to create their own pictures in their own minds from the words and sounds they heard.

"People," he said, "used to sit around campfires before that and tell each other stories. Nothing's changed except the delivery system. What's important, what seems to matter the most, is not being alone in the dark."

I listened and looked at him and thought, *But Grandpa, that's where I've been most of my life, alone in the dark.*

I so wanted not to be alone anymore. Maybe I wanted it so much that finally I was willing to take risks, and maybe, just maybe that was what happened to my mother. She had been alone and she had put her trust in someone, and she had been betrayed. Why else would she have been so creative and dependent on that imagination of hers? It was all she had. It was her personal fortress, and when she pretended, imagined, created, she pulled up her drawbridge and felt safe.

"You look worried," Craig told me as we stepped into the glow of the house lights. "Don't be. They're just a bunch of stupid kids like us."

"I'm not worried about them," I said. "And I'm not a stupid kid."

He laughed and put his arm around my shoulders just before we entered the house.

The sight of us seemed to stop people in mid-sentence, or mid-laugh, or even in the middle of a kiss. There was a pause and then some cheers.

The girls gathered around me when Craig went to talk to his teammates, everyone talking at once. Suddenly, everyone wanted to be my friend, to give me advice about dating, about clothes and about boys in general. I felt like a foreign exchange student who was finally being accepted. With an amused smile painted on my lips, I listened and nodded but said little. One girl, Marlene Ross, either jealous of the attention I was getting or simply frustrated by my noncommittal nods and smiles, burst out with, "So why don't you tell us what finally brought you into the twenty-first century?"

Everyone was quiet, waiting for my response.

"Probably the same thing that brought you, Marlene, the union of a sperm and an egg. Don't you know about that stuff yet?"

There was a pause, as if everyone had and was still holding her breath, and then a roar of laughter that sent Marlene and her red face off to pout. Craig and his friends heard the commotion, and he came hurrying back to me.

"What's up?"

"Nothing. Just girl chatter," I said, suddenly full of self-confidence.

He raised his eyebrows, glanced at the other girls and then put his arm around my waist.

"Let's get something to eat and drink," he said.

A few dozen assorted pizzas had been delivered, and everyone flocked to the table. The boys were drinking beer mostly, but some had harder alcohol and the party began to expand out of the house, to the backyard where the Lesmans had their pool, now all lit. It wasn't really warm enough to swim, but I could see that before the night ended, a few would be pushed in or even jump in. There was already some horseplay going on with just that purpose in mind.

Craig and I stayed off to the side to watch, as if we had been sent by some newspaper to report on the behavior of some primitive tribe. The music was piped out to the backyard, too, so that the partygoers were dancing on the patio. I was nervous again when Craig asked me to dance. By myself, sometimes up in the attic, I played tapes and danced in front of the mirror there, but I wasn't confident about my moves and rhythm. I knew we were still the center of attention, me especially, and it was impossible not to be self-conscious.

"You need to relax, Alice," he told me. "You're too stiff, uptight."

He suggested I drink some vodka and orange juice that had been prepared.

"Just a little can't hurt us," he said. "They're called screwdrivers. There's nothing like a nice buzz."

Except for the glasses of wine I had at dinner with my grandparents from time to time, my experience with alcohol was nonexistent. My grandfather urged my grandmother to let me taste the wine so I would learn my own boundaries in the house, rather than on the streets, as he put it, and she agreed. I enjoyed some of it but far from craved it.

The vodka was so well disguised in the orange juice that I was actually disappointed. Fooled, I drank more, and, after a while, I did loosen up, laughed more and got into the music. I remember thinking, *I'm having fun. Finally, I'm having fun.*

When the first boy was heaved into the pool, Craig looked at me and whispered, "Maybe we should make a graceful, quiet exit. The natives are getting restless."

A part of me wanted to stay and see the silly behavior, but I knew he was being responsible and protective. I nodded, and we slowly slipped around the now boisterous crowd of partygoers and through a side door that led us out of the house. He took my hand, and we hurried through the shadows down to his car.

"Are you all right to drive?" I asked him. I was feeling a little dizzy, and I thought he had drunk the same number of glasses of vodka and orange juice that I had.

"Sure. I'm fine," he said. "The drinks weren't really that strong. I'm not that crazy about drinking too much anyway. I hate hangovers, don't you?"

"I never had one," I said. "I hope I don't have one tomorrow either."

"I doubt it. You didn't drink that much," he assured me.

We drove off. It wasn't that late yet, but even though my grandfather hadn't set down a specific time for me to be home, I knew he and my grandmother would be waiting up for me.

"Are you taking me home?"

"This early? It's not even eleven-thirty," he said. "Besides, I want to show you one of my favorite places," he added, making a turn and then speeding up. A little while after that, he turned into a driveway in the woods and we bounced over a dirt road.

"Where are we going?" I cried, laughing.

"Just a little bit farther," he said, and we came out on the edge of a lake. The sliver of moonlight from a quarter moon threaded through some clouds and sliced the top of the still water, drawing a gold line from one side of the lake to the other. He shut off the engine and nodded at the scene. "Well? Am I right or am I right?"

"It's pretty, Craig. What's out there on the water?" I asked, squinting at some dark blobs gently rising and falling.

"Ducks, I expect, maybe geese."

"How did you find this spot? Anyone else would not have noticed that driveway."

"I went fishing here a few times with my father. We have a boat we pull on a trailer hitch."

"Are you very close with your father?"

"Yeah, sorta," he said. "He's a workaholic, so whenever he wants to take off some time, I go. He hasn't been but to one baseball game this year, however. My mother never comes," he said. "She doesn't like the dust and sitting on the hard wooden bleachers. Dainty. Are you dainty?" he asked, turning to me.

"Hardly," I said. "Maybe I should be," I added, and he laughed.

"You realize that now we're really in a car. No pretending on a sofa in an attic. This is the real thing. Does that make any difference?"

"Why should it?" I asked. What was he getting at? I wondered.

"I just want you to be as comfortable with me here as you are up in the attic," he said.

"I'm absolutely fine," I said. Even though I knew he was just teasing me, I didn't like the implication that I had to live in my imagination to be comfortable. I wasn't even sure he knew what he was implying.

"Let's see," he challenged and leaned over to kiss me. His lips moved quickly over my cheek and down to my neck. I felt his hands travel up under my blouse, over my back to my bra clip to unfasten it and then he lifted my blouse. I started to turn away.

"Hey, c'mon," he said. "I hit a real triple this time."

My head was spinning a little more, and suddenly I felt a churning in my stomach. I was uncomfortable as well because of the way he was twisting and turning over me. I had an acidic burn in my throat and then suddenly gagged.

"Are you all right?"

"No," I said and reached quickly for the door handle. I nearly fell out when the door opened, but I got my feet down quickly and put my hand out to rest my palm against the car so I could steady myself. I couldn't help it. I began to throw up. He leaped out of the car and came around to hold me.

"Oh damn," he said. "We ate and drank too quickly maybe."

I shook my head and threw up some more. My stomach ached. It wasn't the speed of drinking; it was how much, I thought. Finally, I settled down and he sat me back in the car.

"How are you doing?"

"I'm okay. Sorry," I said.

"That's all right. I hate booze actually. I'll have something better next time," he said.

I wasn't listening closely. I was trying to get my head from turning like a top. I closed my eyes and lay back on the seat.

"We'll ride around a while until you feel better," he said. "Keep the window down to get fresh air. I don't want to deliver you home like this. Your grandfather will have me strung up or something."

I didn't say anything. He was right, of course. I couldn't walk into the house looking like a mess. We drove out and cruised very slowly back toward Sandburg. After a while, I felt my stomach settle down and my head clear. I fixed my clothing, and then we stopped and I got out and walked a bit.

"I'm okay," I announced. "Really, I'm fine."

"The good thing about vodka," he said, "is you don't reek from it. But that's a no-no from now on," he added. "I have to take care of you. No booze. We have a pretty heavy date coming up."

I got back into the car and he drove me home, apologizing continually.

"It wasn't your fault, Craig. I didn't have to keep drinking that stuff."

"Naw, I should have paid more attention to you instead of the idiots around us," he insisted. "Are you sure you're all right now?"

"Yes. Sorry," I said.

"Nothing to be sorry about. I enjoyed being with you."

He kissed me good night when we pulled into the driveway, and then he backed out and I walked slowly to the front door, hoping that my grandparents were at least waiting up in their bedroom so I wouldn't come under close scrutiny. I still had a little headache, and my stomach felt very weak.

I was lucky. My grandfather called to me from the bedroom as I climbed the stairway.

"How was the movie?" he asked. I paused at their door and looked in. Both of them had been reading in bed, probably to keep their minds from dwelling on me.

I saw no reason to lie.

"We didn't go to a movie. One of Craig's team-mates had a party to celebrate the team getting into the play-offs."

"Who's that?" he asked.

"Mickey Lesman."

"Oh yeah. First baseman, right?"

"How do you know that?" I asked, amazed.

"I follow the team in the papers. Nice party?"

"It was okay. They started to get a little wild, throwing each other into the pool, so Craig decided it was time for us to go."

That was all true.

"Really? Very mature of him. Good," my grandfather said.

My grandmother was just listening to us, looking at me.

I decided to give them everything.

"Craig asked me to be his prom date. I said yes," I told them.

"Prom date, huh? Well now, that's something, right, Elaine?"

"Yes," she said. "That's very nice, Alice. I'll help you find a nice gown. When is it?" she asked, and I gave her the date.

"We're all going to stay out all night and then go to a picnic at Bear Mountain."

"All night?"

"Now Elaine, kids can do that. We did, remember?"

She was quiet.

"I'd just like to know all the details," she said.

"I'm sure we will," he told her. "Right, Alice?"

"Yes," I said.

"Prom, huh?" my grandfather said. "I remember I looked like a penguin in my tuxedo. I was so stiff in it that I could have been mistaken for a storefront mannequin. I'm sure Craig will look a lot better," he added.

I said good night and went to my bedroom. I didn't realize how tired I was until I lowered my head to the pillow. I barely closed my eyes before I fell asleep. I woke once in the night because of a nightmare in which I heard footsteps above me, and then I slept later than usual the following morning. When I did wake up, I had a dull headache and did the best I could to hide it from my grandparents.

My grandmother was excited about my going to the prom now and talked to me at breakfast about the various dress stores she wanted us to try. Since she had the weekend off, I couldn't very well postpone a shopping safari, even though I felt I could easily sleep away the day. I was more than grateful now to Rachel for showing me how to brighten up my face. It surely needed the makeup, lipstick and eyeliner. My grandfather was going to spend part of his Saturday catching up at his office, so for the first time in a long while, it was going to be only my grandmother and myself.

She couldn't wait to call Aunt Zipporah and give her the news about the prom, however. Before we left, I spoke to her on the phone.

"I never heard Mom so excited for you, Alice."

"I think she's more nervous about it all than excited."

"She's both. That's her job. Is he a nice boy?"

"Yes," I said. "I think so, but I'm not exactly the one to ask about dates and dating."

"Yes, but you have good instincts, Alice."

"I don't know why everyone thinks that," I replied.

"Don't be down on yourself, honey," she warned me. "One thing about your mother was she never let anyone look down at her. She could stand up to the best of them. In fact, I used to depend on her to protect me most of the time."

"Did she date much before . . . before it all happened?"

"Not much," she said. I thought she sounded as if she was withholding information, however. "We weren't much older than you are. I'm sure she would have been queen of the hop if . . . if things had been different."

"Was she planning on going to college?"

"Oh yes, we talked about it. We decided we would apply to the same schools and neither of us would go to any school that didn't accept us both. We took an oath, remember?"

"The birds of a feather oath," I recited.

"Yes," she said with sadness.

"How did that go again?"

"We'll be friends forever and ever and we swear to protect and help each other as much as we would help ourselves."

"That's a nice pledge," I said. "I hope I find someone who will take it with me."

"You have," she said.

"Who?"

"Me," she said. "Always."

I thanked her, and we talked for a little while about the upcoming summer and some of the plans she and Tyler had for the café. They were going to develop a new summer menu. My grandmother called for me to get ready for our shopping trip, and I had to hang up.

"I wish I was there with you. It's so exciting," Aunt Zipporah said.

I was excited but also still very unsure about it. I

knew I would be on an even bigger stage soon, and I couldn't help worrying about it.

On the way to the stores, my grandmother talked about her first prom. I was keen on listening to her description of her boyfriend and asked her how much she had liked him.

"Oh, when you're your age, Alice, you're always in love."

"How are you supposed to know whether it's more than just a crush or not?"

She nodded. "It's a good question. I suppose the answer lies in the idea that love is more substantial, more complex. You're not only physically attracted to someone but you can see yourself spending forever with him, day and night. That's a bigger thing."

"So maybe people do have to live with each other first," I muttered.

"Well, I wouldn't advocate that."

"Why not?" I pursued, suddenly sounding more like Rachel than myself.

"The more of a commitment you make to someone, the harder it becomes to back away. You have to—"

"I know, go slowly."

"Exactly," she said. "Go slowly."

"Did you?" I dared ask, again with Rachel's tone.

She glanced at me. "You didn't ask your grandfather that, did you?"

"No. Why?"

"He'd tell you something like I went so slowly in our relationship, he was having breakfast while I was still having dinner."

She laughed, and I smiled and thought, *This is wonderful.* For the first time, I really did feel like her granddaughter. She wasn't afraid to share intimate things with me. Getting out and casting off the dark shadows I had become too comfortable wearing was the best thing I had done after all.

For the remainder of our day together, we were truly more like mother and daughter, even like two sisters, just the way she was with my aunt Zipporah, laughing at some of the dresses I tried on and consulting closely on every possible aspect of my complete prom outfit. She described her own prom gown to me and even went into details about the evening and how exciting it had been for her.

"Of course, we didn't stay out all night, despite what your grandfather might imply about how we were when we were your age. But I suppose we have to bend a little with the times," she added. "Just be sure I know where you'll be and when, okay?"

"Yes," I promised.

Some of the dresses we considered were very expensive, I thought, but she didn't seem to care about price. In the end both of us liked a peacock gown with a strapless sweetheart neckline and a layered split tiered tulle ball gown skirt with beads.

"I have the perfect necklace to go with it," my grandmother said, "and matching earrings."

I looked at myself in the full-length mirror and bemoaned my short hair, because the picture we saw in the magazine of gowns in the store had a girl wearing it and the girl had her hair beautifully done up with a bun at the top and strings down the side.

"I have an idea," my grandmother said, seeing my unhappiness over my hair. "Don't worry. Let's get your shoes first."

After that, she drove me to a hair salon, where they had hair pieces that would match my color. The stylist she knew sat me in a chair and worked on it until I was amazed at the difference in my appearance.

"Now you're truly complete," my grandmother said. "You make me wish I was your age again."

She hugged me and I thanked her.

How perfect the world suddenly seemed.

It truly made me feel as if I had found a safe place, a fortress of happiness. Slowly, with less and less hesitation, I was lowering the drawbridge, unfolding my arms and holding them out to welcome the world, to invite it to come in.

And then those angry shadows that had followed at my heels all my life pushed everything else aside and galloped over the bridge to sack and pillage my joy and delight and get themselves some sweet revenge.

8

Nothing Will Change

Some alterations were made on my prom gown, and it was delivered by the end of the week. Craig was occupied with the baseball play-offs that were going to be held on Friday at a neutral field. He had picked me up for school every day but was unable to take me home any day during the week. I felt he was quite distracted and less talkative, but it wasn't until Friday morning that I discovered the reason.

This particular morning he was acting even more withdrawn. At first I thought it might be because he was nervous about the game, but after a few moments I realized it was something more serious. I knew him well enough by now to understand when he was very upset. If he fell into any dark mood, he usually shook it off the moment he saw me and was sweet and funny almost instantly. He was always making a big effort to snap me out of any depression or unhappiness.

"The last thing I want to see," he told me more than once, "is for you to return to that withdrawn, frightened little mouse you were. You're too beautiful, and you have too much to offer to be hidden away in some attic, Alice. I won't let it happen," he told me.

But now, just as I had always wondered, what could he do to stop it if the shadows were too thick and powerful and wanted me back? I could see on his face that he couldn't avoid bringing me bad news.

"I've got a small problem," he began, "but before I tell you about it, I want to assure you that nothing will change."

"What is it?"

"Nothing will change."

"Okay, Craig. What?"

"My mother is a snob. She's always been a snob. Even before she married my father, she had money and thought she was some kind of royalty. Her father was a very successful business attorney, and she and my uncle Steve, her younger brother, were always spoiled. My dad's the first to say so, too. I mean, I love my mother, as you'd expect, and I love my uncle, too, but I'm not blind and stupid about it all."

"What is this all leading to, Craig?"

"I should have told her I had asked you to the prom and that we've been seeing each other. She found out from one of her gossips at the beauty parlor and first was angry that I had not told her."

"Well, she's right to be angry. Why didn't you tell her?"

"Because I knew exactly how she would react. I wanted to hold off telling her until it was absolutely too late for her to say or do anything about it."

"What do you mean? What did she say and what can she do about it?"

He was quiet as we drove on to school. I sat patiently waiting. *If anyone should know how difficult it was to explain, rationalize and cover for the words and actions of our parents, it was surely I*, I thought.

"I wasn't exactly truthful and accurate about everything I've told you," he continued.

"Like what?"

"The reason I started to research and investigate the Pearson murder in our house. It didn't bother me at all that we were moving into that house, and I didn't think much about your mother until—"

"Until what?"

"Until I started thinking about you. You intrigued me for some time, Alice. I wasn't kidding about looking at you all the time and hoping you would show some interest in me. It was not because of the house and what happened in it that I tried to learn everything I could about your mother; it was because of you. I thought that someday, I'd be able to discuss it intelligently with you and win your interest in me."

"Isn't that what happened?" I asked, now feeling like I had been manipulated after all. He heard the note of annoyance in my voice.

"Yes, but I was and have been very interested in you for some time," he quickly replied. "Anyway, my mother found out about the research, as I said, and was angry about it and said all sorts of nasty things to me. All the rest I told you was true: how she fixed up the house to erase the event and the history and ignore any references to it."

"And then you start to go out with me and ask me to the prom," I said, understanding. He didn't reply, so I turned on him. "She thinks that's sick, right? She thinks I'm sick, as sick as my mother, and she doesn't want you to have anything to do with me, especially go out with me and ask me to the prom."

He didn't try to deny it.

"What she thinks and what she wants doesn't matter to me," he said. "She's not going to run my life."

"Great," I said, turning away and pouting. "What am I supposed to do?"

"Nothing. Like I said at the start, nothing will change between us."

"What about your father? What does he say?"

"My father's always taken the easiest way out. He gives her what she wants and does his own thing."

"What does that mean exactly, Craig?"

"Well, I can't bring you to the house anymore. I wanted you to understand why not."

"And? C'mon, what else?" I demanded.

"My father's threatening to take away my car and my allowance. But," he added quickly, "I've got my own money. I've put away a ton, and they can't do anything about that. I could easily rent a car for the night of the prom, or we could go with the others in the limousine."

I felt my insides tighten like a fist. It made it hard for me to breathe. I was like a leper in this village. He wasn't wrong to say that nothing had changed. Nothing had. Despite my changing appearance and more socializing, I was still considered an undesirable in this village.

"I'm not proud of my parents," he continued. "The truth is, Alice, I can't wait to leave home, go to college, and start my own life. So don't you dare think that anything I do or say now is your fault."

"It doesn't make me feel too good, Craig."

"We'll just ignore it," he said. "Just forget about them. It's not your problem anyway. It's mine, and I'll handle it. The only reason I'm telling you now is because I thought you might not understand why I wasn't bringing you around to meet my parents, or just in case—"

"What?"

"The gossip spreads and your grandparents hear about it. My mother can be very vicious when she doesn't get what she wants."

"Great. Just what I need, another dog yapping at my heels in this community," I muttered.

"Listen to me, Alice," he said, slowing down and pulling to the side of the road so he could turn to me to speak. "I'm telling you that if the choice is between you and my parents, my mother especially, I'm choosing you."

"I appreciate that, Craig. I just hate being the cause of anyone else's unhappiness," I said.

"You're not the cause!" he cried, the frustration building in his face, his eyes. "She's the cause of her own unhappiness. And my father's. And mine!"

He looked like he was going to burst a blood vessel in his temple.

"Okay, okay."

"If you back out of our prom date because of this, I'll be far more miserable, Alice."

I nodded.

"I'm sorry," he said. "But we're going to have a good time anyway, the best time, and if she wants to eat her own heart out over it, let her."

I took a deep breath. Was life always going to this way for me, dramatic ups and dramatic downs? My grandmother and I were so happy while I was going for my gown. Everyone in my family was happy. When or if they learned about this, it would be devastating to them, too. They would be angry and miserable for me. Maybe, somehow, we could keep it from them.

I'll be like my mother, I thought. *I'll pretend. I'll imagine. I'll make up stories. I'll do anything to keep the darkness out of our fortress.*

"Okay," I said, nodding. "We'll ignore them. Whatever you work out will be fine with me."

He smiled. "Great. I knew you'd rise to the occasion. That's why I wasn't afraid to tell you the truth."

"Just do that always, Craig, tell me the truth from now on, no matter what it is. If anyone can handle it, I can," I said.

He laughed and leaned over to kiss me. "If I didn't have the first game of the baseball play-offs today, I'd ask you to cut school with me and we'd go off for a long ride, maybe even into New York City."

"And get us both into more trouble? Let's not do anything to throw any more wood on the fire," I said.

"Yeah, you're right. Besides, I can't risk doing anything that would get me suspended and thrown off the team now."

"So, finally, we know what's most important to you," I teased, and he laughed.

He started away again. "You know what I did after she and I had this argument yesterday?"

"I can't imagine," I said.

"I pinned the picture you drew of me at bat on my wall. She nearly had a heart attack."

That's all I need, I thought to myself, *to cause another death in that house.*

Craig was true to his word. After we parked in the school lot, he made me promise that I would never ask about the problem or bring it up. He swore that he wouldn't either. The chatter in the school was all about the baseball game anyway. We were playing against a school nearly twice our size, a school that had won the championship four times. We had yet to win it once. Almost all our teachers ended their classes with good luck wishes for the team.

Craig wasn't able to take me to the game. His coach insisted he ride on the team bus, but he gave his car to one of his closer friends, Gerry Martin, specifically to drive me to the game. I was sure I was as nervous as any of the ballplayers. Most of our senior high was in attendance.

It was a hard-fought pitching match. According to Gerry, Bobby Robinson was pitching as well as, if not better than, he ever had, but the opponent had a pitcher of equal talent, and both teams were held to two hits by the time the ninth inning began. Mickey Lesman made an error that put one of their players on base to start the inning, and then a deep fly ball advanced him to second. They got their third hit after that and scored a run. Bobby struck out the next two players, but we were down to three outs. One of the opportunities for us was Craig. He had grounded out, popped out and been called out on strikes. When he got up this time, we already had one out. Everyone from our school was holding his and her breath. I saw some of the girls look my way.

Craig took his time, measured each pitch, and worked it to a full count. Unfortunately, he went for a bad pitch then and struck out. I could feel the hope go out of our side. It was like a punctured tire. When our last player popped out, the game ended and we were out of the play-off.

There was a funeral atmosphere immediately. As Gerry and I walked to the car, I felt as if some of the other students, especially the girls, were looking at me as if I were somehow to blame for Craig's failure at bat. In a way I thought I might have been, because I knew that although he was acting indifferent to his troubles at home, it had to be eating away at him.

He refused to talk about it. He blamed himself and his eagerness. I didn't dare suggest it had anything to do with our problem with his parents or, more specifically, his problem. I knew what he wanted: It was to be like it didn't exist, and although I couldn't stop thinking about it, we didn't discuss it directly. The only thing he did say over the weekend was there wasn't exactly a truce at his house, just a quiet lull. His father had laid down the threats, and he and his mother were simply doing a minimum of talking to each other. It was one of those situations where each side was waiting for the other side to blink.

The week of the prom, however, Craig's father lowered the boom on his privileges because of his continued defiance. He took away Craig's car so he couldn't pick me up for school or take me home. He didn't have to ride the bus himself. He could have gone with one of his teammates to school and even had him pick me up, but instead, as an act of further defiance, he got onto the same bus I got on and we sat together. It amplified the chatter about us and, because I was no longer being picked up, brought the news home to my grandparents.

We had almost made it without their finding out about the turmoil, but my grandmother just happened to be home the first morning I had to ride the bus, and I could see in her face that she was already full of questions because of that. The community gossip lines began ringing, so that by the time I was home from school, she and my grandfather had their ears stuffed. Like usual, they saved the discussion for dinner.

"Is there a problem between you and Craig, Alice?" my grandfather began. I could see from the look on my grandmother's face that they had discussed how to deal with me and Craig. They'd developed a strategy. My grandfather was, after all, a lawyer.

"Not between us, no," I said.

"Why isn't he picking you up for school then?"

"His father took away his car privileges," I said. I wasn't going to lie; I just wasn't going to spill it all out at once.

"And why is that?"

I put my fork down and folded my hands.

"Craig's mother is upset that he's seeing me," I began. "And especially upset that he asked me to be his prom date."

"I knew it," my grandmother said, slamming her palm down on the table and making the dishes and silverware jump. "I just knew it. That woman—"

"Easy," my grandfather told her. He put her on pause. She barely blinked an eye. "Did Craig tell you why she's upset?"

"It's because of my mother, because of what happened in their house, because she thinks I've inherited evil or something," I said. "She's redone the house from top to bottom inside to erase the possibility that there is anything in it that my mother might have touched or walked upon or even seen."

"Yes, we knew the Harrisons had done that," my grandfather said.

"You were in the house then?" my grandmother asked.

"Just once. That day Craig and I met in town and he took me home. His parents weren't there," I quickly added. I wondered if I should tell them about the research he had done on the Pearson murder. Something told me to hold back on that.

"You saw the whole house?" she asked.

"No."

She was quiet. I could see she'd rather not know anything more about it.

"So what's Craig going to do? Has he decided against taking you to the prom?" my grandfather asked.

"No. He's taking me."

"The Harrisons can't be pleased," my grandmother told my grandfather. "It doesn't make for a pleasant experience, Michael. Maybe you should have a word with Tom Harrison."

"And say what? They have a right to control what their own son does, Elaine."

"We're going to the prom," I emphasized. "We've already decided. Craig has the money he needs, and he has access to another automobile, or we could join two other couples and go in a limousine."

"Not very pleasant," my grandmother muttered, shaking her head. "Damn that woman."

"Elaine."

"It's not fair to Alice," she said, gesturing at me as if my grandfather had to be told where and who I was. "If I hear that she is spreading any stories . . ."

"I doubt that she's doing that," my grandfather said, but not with confidence.

"I'm sorry, honey," my grandmother said. "If you feel you don't want to go to the prom with Craig now, don't worry about it. You'll have other uses for that gown. I'm sure."

"Oh no, we're going," I said. I had worked on my self-confidence and built my indifference and determination along with Craig. This was no time to retreat. "I'm not going to let someone tell me I'm not good enough."

"Good for you," my grandfather said, smiling. "I'm sure Greta Harrison will realize how foolish she's being."

"Don't count on it. If she had her nose any higher, she'd be on oxygen," my grandmother said, and they both laughed.

I smiled. Craig's mother did look like someone who thought she walked constantly on a red carpet. The few times I had seen her since Craig and I had been going out, I couldn't help but stare and even study her. Parents, after all, at minimum, were the pool from which we drew our own characteristics. What, if anything, had Craig drawn from such a woman? Was it her arrogance that he toned down to strong self-confidence? Everyone needed that; that was good. He had some of her good physical characteristics, her hair, eyes. I imagined that so much more of him, however, had come from his father, who was as strong and handsome looking. Between the lines and small references, I understood that his father had a good sense of humor and was liked by most people. Craig said he was a perfect politician, especially in regards to his mother.

"Well, you just let us know if anything nasty happens, Alice," my grandmother said. "And if there's anything you two need. Maybe you can lend him your car, Michael," she suggested.

He shook his head.

"That's a little too much involvement, Elaine."

"You're thinking more like an attorney and less like a grandfather," she countered. His face immediately turned a little crimson. "But you're probably right," she added quickly. "Just let us know, Alice," she concluded.

I nodded, and we finished our dinner talking about other things.

As prom night drew closer, the excitement in the school was palpable. There was truly an electricity in the air, spurts of laughter and giggling, smiles flashing, everyone assuring and promising everyone else that the night would be very special. I began to feel sorry for those girls who had not been asked. Their faces looked pale and forlorn. It was almost as if they were watching their youth pass them by, leaving them lost and alone on some street corner, at some bus stop where no bus ever came.

My grandparents kept asking about how we would spend the time between the prom and the picnic the next morning. I finally found out that a group of us was going to spend the night at Ruth Gibson's house. Her parents had to attend her father's brother's twenty-fifth anniversary affair in Dover, Maryland, so she had the house to herself, and they had given her permission to have some friends over. It was one of the bigger homes in Centerville, the nearby village. Being so close to our hamlet gave my grandparents some comfort, although my grandmother wasn't happy about there not being any older person to chaperone.

"Let them take on their own responsibilities," my grandfather said. "Alice is a pretty levelheaded kid."

She gave in, but she wasn't as confident about me as he was, and besides, she said, pointedly directing herself at me, "Sometimes, it's not you but your friends who get you into trouble."

"You toss the dice from the moment you drop them off at kindergarten on," my grandfather muttered.

Because I had imposed such a restricted, introverted, almost hermetic existence on myself, they were caught in a conflict. They had done what they could to get me to be more social, and now that I was, they didn't know how restrictive they should be without turning me back to the person I had been. I couldn't give them any clue. I was in uncharted waters myself. I would either drown or sail on. Grandfather Michael was probably right—you just toss the dice and pray.

Now that everything was laid out, our evening began to fall into place. Craig informed me Friday night that we were definitely not going in the limousine, however.

"First, I don't need to hear or to have them question me as to why I don't have my car," he said, "and second, I don't intend on sharing my time with you, not even a few minutes."

"What will we do?"

"Don't worry. I'm working on something very special," he told me and winked.

The night before the prom, I had this terrible nightmare in which I discovered that Craig's parents had decided to have him locked away so as to prevent him from taking me. He was chained to some wall, crying and screaming. Now I was like those other girls, the ones without a date, watching her youth float away unexplored. I actually woke in a sweat and found my heart thumping. Nothing pleased me as much as seeing the sunlight come pouring through my windows, cutting the darkness into shreds.

He called me twice that day, both times to reassure me that all was fine.

"My mother decided to go on a full-day shopping spree. It's her way of getting back at both me and my father, mostly him, because she's probably going to spend a ton of money on unnecessary things."

"What is your father saying?"

"Nothing. He just looks at me and shakes his head. I don't respond. They'll get over it," he said. "She'll have her tantrum and that will be that. Now be sure you take a nap like the young women did in *Gone with the Wind*," he said, laughing.

"Like I could fall asleep."

He laughed, and then he told me his special secret about our transportation. He had rented Harold Echert's '57 Ford Thunderbird, a restored classic automobile.

"As it turns out, we're going to arrive at the prom in the most striking automobile."

"He let you rent it?"

The car was always parked in front of the Echert garage and drew the attention and admiration of tourists and locals alike. It was always kept washed and shined. There was a story about a movie company that had even used it in a film. It was fire engine red with those big white wall tires.

"Let? I gave him a pretty big chunk of change. It has that tuck and roll interior. I took it for a ride yesterday to be sure it was in tip-top condition. What power it has. Wait until I pick you up," he said. "My father did me a favor taking my car away."

"Okay," I said, laughing. "We'll send him a thank-you card."

His excitement was infectious.

Later in the day he called again to make sure I had rested and was ready for what he described as a life experience. I began to prepare myself nearly two hours before he was to come by. My grandmother was in and out of my room the whole time, fidgeting with my gown, my shoes, checking on my makeup and my hair, acting more nervous about the prom than I was. My grandfather finally told her to leave me be.

"You're driving her crazy," he said.

"I just want her to be—"

"She'll be; she'll be. Relax, Elaine," he said, and finally she retreated to sit with him to wait for me to descend.

I did the best I could to stuff my own nervousness deep down inside me. Before I left my room, Aunt Zipporah called to hear how I looked in my gown and wish me a good time.

"I almost drove over to see you off, but Tyler said I would make you nervous."

"You would," I said, and she laughed.

"Make sure I get a picture."

"Okay."

"Have a great time, honey."

"Okay," I said as if it was all up to me.

Finally, I started down. Craig was due any minute. My grandparents, both pretending to be interested in what they were reading, nearly leaped out of their chairs. My grandmother couldn't help herself. She had to get up to fix one or two strands of my hair that had come loose from my hairpiece.

"You look fantastic, Alice," my grandfather said. "It's like a real princess came downstairs."

I smiled at him. If only I could find someone to love me half as much as he did, I'd be fine, I thought. We heard the doorbell ring. My grandmother gave my grandfather a look, and he hurried to get their camera. Then she let Craig in.

He looked so handsome in his tuxedo. His face was beaming with excitement, and when he saw me, he looked like he had lost his breath.

"Wow," he declared. "I've got the prom queen for sure. Do I know talent, or do I know talent?"

"Oh, shut up. And stop congratulating yourself so much," I said.

He laughed and produced my corsage. As he pinned it on me, my grandfather started to take pictures. We posed for a few, and then my grandparents followed us out to look at the car.

"A beaut," my grandfather said. "I've been envious of the Echerts for years because of that car."

"She rides like a dream," Craig told him. My grandfather looked in the window at the seats and dashboard and whistled.

"Brings back memories," he said. "Nights in the drive-in, cruising . . ."

"Keep those memories to yourself, if you don't mind," my grandmother told him, and they laughed.

Then they both hugged me, and Craig ran around to open the door for me.

"Have a wonderful time, you two," my grandfather said.

"Call us in the morning," my grandmother said. "Please. And be careful."

"We will," Craig said.

He started the engine, nodded at them and then we drove off. I thought I had been holding my breath the whole time, waiting to see if I would wake up and discover it had all been a dream. Craig reached over to squeeze my hand gently.

"We did it," he said. "And you are beautiful, Alice. You're truly like a discovery, a treasure, someone who has been hidden away too long." He laughed. "If we were real socialites, this would be your coming out party, like some debutante."

I smiled and thought, *It's true. It is an emergence of sorts. I'm breaking out of the attic.* The shadows were in flight. The brightness from our happiness was too strong for them.

We floated off like two meteors side by side on the way to another universe, one where darkness and unhappiness didn't exist. Neither of us spoke. It was as if we needed only to think at each other and look at each other to know the contents of our hearts.

"I've always been afraid to be this happy," I said in a loud whisper.

He turned and smiled at me.

"Why?"

"I don't know. It's like . . ."

"Like you're letting go of all the bad stuff?"

"Yes."

"And that makes you feel guilty?"

"Yes."

"Then let's both feel guilty," he said, "like Adam and Eve. We'll both break the rules."

He laughed.

But was it funny? Should we laugh and be happy? After all, they lost paradise.

9

The Accident

The Cherry Hill was one of the most glamorous and well-known hotels in the upstate resort area. It was a large, sprawling property with its own golf course, Olympic-size pool, nightclub and indoor skating rink. Normally, the students who went there for any reason were excited about it, but tonight we were given the golf club to use as our private dance hall and party room, and that made it even more exciting.

The hotel provided valet parking and had spotlights set up so it looked like celebrities were arriving. There was even a red carpet for us. When we drove up in the classic automobile, the students who had already arrived came to the door to look, and those who had just arrived ahead of us stood by to watch us pull up. There was even some applause. The class had hired a photographer to take the prom pictures, and he was clicking away madly as Craig and I stepped out of the car, his flash popping. The music was piped into some outside speakers so that it felt as if the party began the moment I stepped out of the car. Showing off for his friends, Craig took me in his arms and spun us around like two professional dancers on the red carpet. There was laughter and applause.

Craig's face seemed to absorb the brightness from the flashbulbs. His shoulders rose, and he swelled with pride. Right from the moment he had picked me up, I had been wondering if his parents' anger and attitude about his taking me would somehow seep into the evening and ruin our night. I was sure it was on his mind as well.

"I knew I asked the right girl to the prom. I told you that you would be the prom queen," he whispered as he took my arm and continued to lead me down the red carpet.

Craig's buddies wanted to know how he had managed to get the car. No one asked why he had done it; they all just assumed he wanted something special. Everyone was shaking his hand and patting him on the back as if he had hit a home run at the play-off game and not struck out.

I felt as if I had been lifted off earth in a rocket ship. Just a few weeks ago, before the spring break, I had been less than a shadow in the school—and a passing one at that. Now, I was the absolute center of attention with a ring of envious girls circling me, trying to get me to talk to them. Girls like Mindy Taylor and Peggy Okun, who had once tried to hurt me, were now relegated to the dark corners of the room. Amazed at my turnaround, they had sour faces and looked like they had been shrunken. I was sure they were in just as much a daze over all this as I was, only they weren't enjoying any of it.

Craig and I went out to the dance floor immediately, and so did the others around us. In fact, it seemed as if we were leading most of the prom attendees about on a leash, doing whatever we decided to do. When we went to the punch bowl, others did. When we had some snacks, they did. When we danced, they danced, and when we stood around to talk, the crowd gathered to hear every word.

What would my mother's life have been like if she had experienced these things? I wondered. Would it have changed her, helped her, kept her from disaster? If ever there was such a thing as an injection of self-confidence, this was it. I could now tell myself that there wasn't anyone who intimidated me, who danced much better than I danced, or looked much better than I looked. Suddenly competing with girls my age in this world didn't seem all that difficult. I truly felt as if Craig and I glowed on that dance floor, and it wasn't only because of the car and our clothes.

Craig was already a big shot in the school, being the class president and an athletic hero. Our stunning, dramatic appearance and the energy we radiated simply enhanced it all. Now that I was here, I did feel like I had been discovered, and deservedly so. I soaked up the attention from other boys and the girls willingly. I know I was far more talkative than ever, laughed more than I had ever laughed, and simply enjoyed myself for myself. I had never really taken pleasure in who I was, but I did this night and thought perhaps I would from now on. We had both made good decisions for ourselves when we remained determined to stay together and attend the prom.

"I can't believe how pretty you look. You're like an actress or something," Marsha Green told me. I just smiled at her. I didn't know what to say to someone gushing at me like that, especially her. She sat next to me in math class and hadn't so much as yawned in my direction before this.

A little while later, Craig pulled me aside and took the glass of punch out of my hands.

"I just found out that someone poured vodka in it," he said.

"Really? I didn't taste it."

"That's the idea. It's well disguised, but I don't want a replay from Mickey's party. I have something else for us that's better," he told me and patted his jacket.

Before I could ask him what that was, he was pulled away by Bobby Robinson to hear a joke. Even though all the boys had dates to attend to, they still liked to clump together and pass stories among themselves. Why were only girls considered gossips? I wondered and laughed to myself. I was making so many new and wonderful discoveries about the world I was in and the people I knew.

Moments later, the band, who was given the task of choosing the prom king and queen, stopped playing to announce whom they had selected. My heart began to pound. I could see from the way most of the others were looking at Craig and me that they expected we would be crowned. Nevertheless, when the band leader said our names in the microphone, I felt my legs nearly turn to jelly.

"C'mon," Craig urged. "Let's get those crowns before they decide they made a mistake."

I was in such a state of shock that I'm sure I looked like someone sleepwalking to the stage. I was to be the prom queen? Me? The town leper?

In a mock ceremony with lots of pomp and circumstance, trumpet and drum roll, we were coronated, and the others cheered and clapped. The photographer was snapping his pictures from all angles, and some of the other students who had brought cameras were doing the same. I even saw one of our chaperones, Mr. Kasofsky, taking pictures.

After the crowning, we had to dance by ourselves, like a bride and groom at a wedding, while a small spotlight followed us about the floor. I was terrified I would stumble or somehow look silly and awkward, but in Craig's strong embrace, I felt secure. He moved me about gracefully.

"I was afraid they'd choose Bobby and Charlene," Craig whispered. "They were our only real competition."

I glanced at Charlene. Although she had a soft smile on her face, I was sure she was disappointed. I felt sorry for her. In my mind she was really the most beautiful girl in the school, and Bobby cut a handsome figure, too.

"I guess in the end we were just too much for them," Craig added.

I looked up at him. Self-confidence was slipping quickly into arrogance, I thought. Maybe his mother was coming through, after all.

"I don't feel right about it," I said. "Charlene certainly dances better than I do, and she's prettier."

"The band didn't think so, and that's what matters most," he replied. "Don't be silly. Enjoy it," Craig said.

He was certainly basking in the attention.

"Won't my parents be speechless when they find out?" he muttered. "Dad's customers will be congratulating him, and he'll have to smile and thank them. I know my mother will permit herself to bask in the glory, even though she'll never admit she was wrong. Serves them both right. I hope they find it difficult eating crow."

I wished he wasn't so bitter about his own mother and father. It still bothered me that I was partly, if not wholly, to blame, and it made me feel funny to see him happier about making his parents uncomfortable than enjoying our moment for what it truly was.

The attention we received on first arriving was compounded by the coronation. Everyone wanted to know what our plans were for after the prom and the next day. An invitation to Ruth Gibson's house quickly became as valuable as an invitation to the White House. I was surprised by the girls who came to me to ask if I could get them and their dates invited.

"It's not my house and not my party," I said, blowing the ingratiating smiles off their faces.

"How quickly someone can become stuck up," Jennifer Todd muttered loudly enough for the other girls nearby to hear. Heads were nodding, and my welcome mat was quickly pulled out from under my feet and rolled up again.

Envy has a way of turning into resentment, I thought and wished we had made far less of a spectacular appearance. I had wanted only to have a good time, to have something to remember forever, a cherished remembrance to press into a photo album. I wasn't looking to conquer the school and become Miss Popularity.

Soon after, the group that was going to Ruth's house decided it might be time to leave. Some of them asked Craig, and he told them yes. The prom had run out of speed, especially for him. What else was there to do here after you had been crowned king?

"Now the real partying begins," he whispered to me as we left. "We're going to have a good time," he chanted. "My parents have failed to spoil this night for me. We've shown them."

That sounded that earlier sour note. I certainly didn't want us to have a good time in order to spite anyone. I wanted it to be our good time for ourselves, pleasing only ourselves, but Craig was on a tear about it now. During the last hour at the prom, I noticed he was behaving differently anyway. He kept leaving me to join his buddies around the punch bowl, which I knew had vodka in it. There was no smoking permitted inside the club, so those who wanted to smoke had to go outside. Craig joined them even though he didn't smoke. He left me alone for a good ten or so minutes, and when he returned, he was more hyper and excited. It was soon after that when the decision to leave was made.

We got into the car quickly and followed the line of cars off the hotel grounds, heading for Ruth Gibson's home. We were still wearing our crowns. I thought it was silly to keep them on, but Craig insisted.

"We have to wear them all night, even sleep in them," he joked.

It was just past midnight. The party at Ruth's house consisted of ten couples, but only three were going to sleep over. We were all taking one of the back roads, a shortcut that would get us there faster. With only our car headlights and the taillights of the cars ahead of us to illuminate the way through these secondary roads slicing through wooded areas, I suddenly felt as if I were in an eerie procession. It made me nervous.

"Here," Craig said, taking his hand off the steering wheel to hand me a dark cigarette. "Light one of these."

"I don't smoke, and I thought you didn't," I said.

"It's not a cigarette, Alice. Don't you know what it is?"

I shook my head but smelled it.

"Is it . . . pot?" I asked.

"Yes," he said, laughing. "It won't make you sick, and you'll relax quickly." He reached for the cigarette lighter and held it toward me. I hesitated. "C'mon, hurry up. I want some, too. We have a right to celebrate. We're royalty."

Even more nervous now, I lit the joint and took a puff, blowing it out quickly and coughing. He laughed at me again.

"You have to hold it in," he said and took it from me to show me how to smoke pot.

"Here, try it again."

"I'd rather not," I said.

"C'mon, Alice. Loosen up. We have a great night ahead of us."

"That's the way I want to keep it," I said.

"Wow."

He shook his head in disappointment, but he didn't argue. I could see he was very annoyed with me, but he didn't say anything nasty. Instead, he smoked faster and held the smoke in his nostrils longer. "You don't know what you're missing," he sang and bounced about in the seat, leaning over to kiss me and then offer me the joint again and again.

I tried to ignore him. Finally, he turned up the radio and laughed.

"Look how fast Jack Montgomery is going," he said, nodding at one of the cars quite ahead of us. "I know what's on his mind. He wants the best guest room for him and Brenda. That creep.

"Wait a minute," he said. "We're the king and the queen of the night. We shouldn't be following them. They should be following us."

With that, he pulled out and accelerated, passing two of the cars ahead of us and leaning on his horn. They did the same. Jack Montgomery's car was the last one ahead of us. Craig sounded his horn, but Jack refused to move to the right. Craig drove up to his bumper, practically colliding, and tapped the horn continually. Jack only accelerated.

"The bastard," Craig said and accelerated too.

"You're going too fast," I said. "It doesn't matter, Craig. Let him go."

"It matters," he said. "Everyone is trying to box me in. It's like my mother is in that car," he muttered.

"What?"

What a strange thing to say, I thought.

He didn't respond. He drove faster.

The back roads were far more narrow than the main roads in our area. Some of them hadn't been attended to for years and were broken up. The shoulders of the roads were soft, and on both sides there was deep ditching, but because the ditches hadn't been cleaned out for some time, they were disguised with mud, leaves and dead branches.

Craig drove with the joint dangling from the corner of his mouth like any ordinary cigarette. When he took a deep and hard draw on it, the smoke streamed out of his nostrils, making him look like a mad bull.

Gradually, he caught up to Jack's car again, only this time, instead of trying to get him to pull to the right, he swerved radically to the left and began to pass him. We were side by side, and when I looked over, Jack was laughing, but his girlfriend Brenda was just as terrified as I was, and she was pounding him on the shoulder to get him to slow down. I saw him turn to push her away, and when he did, he jerked his car dangerously close to ours. Craig compensated by moving to the left, only our front left wheel fell into the ditch.

It was as if someone, some great invisible giant, had reached through the darkness and taken our car into his huge hand, spinning it around. The wheels froze on the macadam, and the car literally lifted off the ground and turned over, crashing into the large oak and hickory trees. I screamed. I heard the sound of glass and metal smashing and felt myself being lifted and thrown about. My eyes were closed. I never felt any pain when we stopped thrashing about. I was simply in the darkness.

When I opened my eyes again, I was looking at a white ceiling, and I heard the sound of some sort of beeping. Slowly, I began to focus, but with it came a surge of pain along my left side, up my leg and into my hip. I groaned. When I turned my head, I saw my grandfather sitting near me in what was obviously a hospital room. He had his head lowered so his chin nearly rested on his chest. I closed and opened my eyes and then called to him. At first I thought I was in a dream and calling in my sleep, because he didn't respond. Then he raised his head slowly and looked at me.

He looked exhausted, looked like someone who had been up for days and days. His face was unshaven and his eyes drooped, but he managed a smile and stood up slowly to come to the bed and take my hand.

"Hey, princess, how are you doing?" he asked.

"Where am I?"

"You're in the county hospital. You've been in and out of a coma for two days. Your grandmother is out in the hallway speaking with the doctor," he said.

"What happened?"

"Don't you remember?"

I shook my head. Was this that famous selective amnesia again?

"You were in a very bad car accident, Alice. Very bad. We're lucky to still have you. Don't you remember any of it?"

I stared at him. The pain seemed dull now. I noticed for the first time that something was stuck in my arm, and I followed the tube up to a bag hanging on a stand. I wanted to ask about it, but I felt my eyelids closing, and my effort to keep them open was futile. In moments I was asleep again.

When I woke this time, my grandmother was standing there with the doctor. My grandfather walked into the room and joined them.

"Alice," my grandmother said. "Alice, do you hear me? Alice?" She turned to the doctor. "She's looking at me, but she doesn't seem to hear me or even see me."

"She's still in quite a daze," he said.

Was I dreaming? I seemed to be looking at them through a thick fog. Slowly, it began to clear.

"What happened to me, Grandma?"

"You shattered your hip pretty badly," she said. "You're going to need an operation to see what can be done. You have a concussion, but the doctor says it's not life threatening. You have trauma all over your body, Alice. It's amazing you don't have even more serious injuries."

As she spoke, I looked at my grandfather and then the doctor. They weren't just watching my reactions. There was something else in their faces, something that frightened me. I closed my eyes and tried hard to remember everything. It was as if I were coming up from a pool of ink, slowly rising toward the light. A part of me wanted to keep from rising. I was shaking my head, pleading to stop going toward the light, but I couldn't prevent it.

I burst out, and the memories rushed at me like some sort of mad little animals, eager to take a bite out of me. I brought my left hand to my face and moaned.

"Easy," the doctor said.

"What . . . where's Craig?" I asked.

No one replied. They just looked at me. Then my grandmother looked to my grandfather and he stepped forward.

"Craig didn't make it, Alice."

"Didn't make what?"

"His injuries were far more severe."

I continued to stare at him, waiting for him to add, *"But he'll be all right."*

He didn't add anything. He lowered his eyes.

"You mean Craig's dead?"

"Oh God," my grandmother said. Her lips trembled.

It was as if her face was in an earthquake. Tears began to stream down her cheeks.

"He's dead?" I asked again.

"Yes, Alice. He's passed away," my grandfather said.

I closed my eyes, and then I fell back into the inky pool and began to descend.

When I woke up again, my aunt Zipporah was there. She was staring out the window.

"Aunt Zipporah?"

"Oh, Alice. I'm so glad you're awake. You poor kid."

"Where are Grandpa and Grandma?"

"They're having something to eat in the hospital cafeteria. How are you feeling?"

"Numb," I said. I thought for a moment. Had I been awake and had I spoken with my grandparents and did they really say what I thought they had said?

Aunt Zipporah pulled a chair close to the bed and took my left hand into her hands. She smiled at me.

"You'll be all right," she said. "Banged up, but you'll be all right."

"I was in a car accident."

"Terrible one. Your grandfather says anyone looking at the wreck would have a hard time believing you lived."

"But Craig . . ."

"I know. It's so sad. Can you remember what happened?"

I thought for a moment. Words and pictures seemed to jumble around like pieces of a jigsaw puzzle in my head. Slowly, some of them fit together.

"We were going to a house party."

"Yes, I understand," she said, nodding to urge me on. "It was after the prom."

"Craig wanted to be there first. We were crowned king and queen of the prom."

"I know," she said, smiling and rubbing my hand.

"He was going too fast and something happened . . . the car just flew."

"He lost control," she said. "Alice," she began. She looked at the doorway and then turned back to me. "Did you . . . were the two of you smoking pot?"

I stared at her. That was in the puzzle. Those pieces came together quickly, too. I nodded.

"He had it. I took only one puff and then he took it back."

"They found it, and I guess they could tell from the autopsy that he had been using it," she added.

"Do Grandpa and Grandma know?"

"Yes. But it's not your fault," she said quickly. "What happened is not your fault. Don't dare let anyone get you to think it was."

I studied her face. "Someone is saying it was?"

She didn't reply.

"Craig's mother?"

"You can't fault a mother for trying to understand and for being angry and trying to blame someone or something other than her own child, but we all know there was no way you could have had it. He had to be the one to get it," she said, but she said it with a lift in her voice, as if she was asking and not telling.

"Yes, he had it. I didn't even know until we were in the car and on our way to the party."

"Damn. Smoking grass while driving. That's a big no-no," she said.

My grandparents came back to my room. Grandpa smiled when he saw I was awake, but my grandmother looked terribly worried. She looked to Aunt Zipporah.

"It's true about the pot," she told my grandmother. "He had it," she emphasized.

"Oh Alice," my grandmother said.

"What could she do about it? He had it," Aunt Zipporah said.

"My God."

"There's no sense getting her more upset, Elaine," my grandfather said.

"She's blaming me? Craig's mother is blaming me?" I asked her.

"She's the sort that would never blame herself for anything, even if she were caught red-handed," my grandmother said.

"Don't think about any of that," my grandfather told me as he moved closer to the bed. "I want you to concentrate on getting better. Nothing else."

"As soon as you're well enough, they're going to fix your hip," my aunt Zipporah told me and smiled. "You'll be fine. You can't get out of working this summer, so don't even think about it."

I turned away.

All I could think about now was Craig's beaming smile at the prom and the great joy and excitement we both had felt. How quickly we had fallen from that cloud on which we had been sailing. It was truly as if it had all been a dream and now that dream had become a nightmare.

I didn't have to look at my grandparents' faces to know what awaited me out there. I could feel the gloom and doom coming toward me like rolling thunder. With Craig's mother finding ways to blame what happened on me, heads would bob in agreement and people in our community would say they always knew something like this would happen. They might as well hang a banner on Main Street that read THE APPLE DOESN'T FALL FAR FROM THE TREE.

I hoped I would die on the operating table and everyone's misery would end.

"We should let her rest," I heard my grandmother say.

"I'll bring you magazines, things to do, Alice," my grandfather promised. "Maybe, when you're able to sit up, they'll let me bring in some paintbrushes, paint and some art paper."

I turned sharply to him.

"I don't want to paint anymore," I said.

"What? Sure you do. You don't give up something like that, Alice."

"It's not important."

"Of course it's important."

"Don't think about it now. You're not in any state of mind to make decisions anyway," Aunt Zipporah said. "I know it might sound cruel to you, but in time, this will all pass and you'll go on. You can't change what happened, but if you let it destroy you, too, then everything anyone says bad about you will seem to be true."

She made sense. I was just not in the mood to acknowledge it. I closed my eyes instead. They all kissed me on the cheek before leaving, but I didn't open my eyes. I wished I could keep them closed forever.

A little while later the nurse came in to check on me, and then the surgeon who was going to do my operation arrived to talk to me about my injuries and describe what had to be done to my hip.

"Your hip-joint socket was broken in four places, Alice," he said. "It's going to be a long operation, but you won't notice because you'll be under anesthesia. To you it will seem like a few minutes," he said, smiling.

I wanted to ask him if he could put me under anesthesia now. I think he saw it in my face.

"Look, Alice, you're a very young girl. You'll recover from this and get strong again."

"The boy I was with will never recover."

"I'm sorry about that. Believe me, I wish I had a chance to try to make a difference for him, too. I have a son not much younger. But right now, we have to give you our attention. I want you to be stronger and have a good attitude about your healing," he said. "It helps."

"Okay. Thank you," I said. He patted my hand, checked my chart and left.

It's easier to say okay than to say anything else, I decided. People leave you be when you agree with them.

My operation was scheduled for a later date. Until then, I was left to heal and get stronger. Tyler sent me flowers and a box of candy. Aunt Zipporah visited me at least a half dozen times, and my grandmother was there every day. My father called, and then he and Rachel sent me flowers and candy as well, but he said nothing about coming to see me. He wished me good luck on my operation and promised to keep in touch and especially to keep in touch with my grandparents.

No one from my school came to see me or even called until two days after my operation.

I found out the operation took nearly ten hours—the hip joint was that shattered. I was told that we wouldn't know how successful it had been for a while and that I would need some physical therapy.

The day after I was returned to my own room, Charlene Lewis came to see me. My grandfather had gotten me my school assignments to work on as soon as I was able. I had done very little. In the back of my mind was the idea that maybe, just maybe, I would never return to school. I didn't know what I would do as an alternative, but I dreaded the day I would walk back into that building, so when Charlene appeared in my hospital room doorway, some of that dread came in with her.

"How are you?" she asked.

I shrugged.

"I don't know yet. I was operated on and we have to wait to see."

"Very little about you has trickled out, but we did hear that you had something seriously wrong with your hip," she said.

I nodded.

"If I can walk, I will probably have a bad limp. My dancing days were short-lived," I added.

She looked very unhappy for me. She and Bobby had been in one of the cars behind us, so they had seen the accident or come upon it first. I had also heard that they were the ones to get to a home and get the police and ambulance on its way.

"Nearly the entire senior high school attended Craig's funeral," she said. "The baseball team attended in uniform. Bobby and Mickey and two others were the pallbearers."

I didn't say anything. My grandparents—actually

my grandfather—had decided not to attend. My grandfather was afraid of a scene between Craig's mother
and my grandmother. He didn't come right out and say
that, but I knew it was what he was thinking.

"It's been horrible at school," Charlene continued.
"Girls break out in tears constantly. Bobby's so depressed. Everyone's depressed."

I pressed my lips together hard to keep myself from
crying.

"I suppose you heard that there was a police investi-
gation and they had found the pot in the car."

"Yes, I heard," I said.

"Most of us know, of course, that Craig had it. This
wasn't the first time, but his mother . . ."

"I know. She's telling everyone I brought it along,
right?"

Charlene nodded.

"Jennifer Todd's mother is one of Craig's mother's
best friends. She said Craig's mother had discovered a
lot of stuff about the murder your mother committed.
She said she had found it in the desk in his room and
she says you brought it to Craig to convince him your
mother didn't do it just so you could get him to be
your boyfriend."

"That's not true! He had it all there and showed it to
me. She knew that he had it before he even had spoken
to me. She knew!"

"She's telling her friends that you got him crazy
with it. She's making it sound like you put a spell on
him. Some of the girls, well, a few like Mindy and
Peggy, are telling people they saw you do witchcraft
stuff. Remember that day at the baseball practice
when you were kidding about it? I shouldn't have, but

I mentioned it. It gave them something else to make up about you. I'm sorry," she added quickly. "But it didn't really matter what I said and didn't say. You know how some people are. They enjoy listening to and telling stories about other people. It makes them feel popular."

"Why did you come here to tell me all this, Charlene?" I asked, my eyes narrow with suspicion.

She looked down and then up at me.

"I felt sorry for you, Alice. I know the accident wasn't your fault. Bobby was screaming at how crazy Craig was driving, and I don't believe any of that junk about witchcraft, of course. I just came here to make sure you knew about it."

"To warn me?"

"Yes," Charlene said.

"Don't worry about it. Tell everyone I'm not going back to school. They don't have to keep gossiping about me anymore. They've won. I'm gone," I said.

She looked surprised. "What do you mean? Where will you go?"

"Anywhere," I said, and I meant it. Then I turned back to her. "I wish you had been the one chosen prom queen. Craig might not have been so reckless, so swollen up with it all."

"You can't blame it all on that," she said, smiling.

"No? Did anyone, even Bobby, ever know that Craig's parents forbid him from taking me, that they had taken away his allowance and they had taken away his car?"

"They had?"

"He didn't rent that car to be a big deal, although it made him feel like one. He had to rent a car or join in with the limousine some were renting, and he didn't want to do that."

"I didn't know. No one did, I think."

"Yeah, well take that back to the gossip mill and have them churn it into something."

"I feel sorry for you, Alice. I really do."

"Oh yeah? Tell me, Charlene, if I do go back to school, will you be my best friend?"

"What?"

"Just what I said, will you?"

"I thought you said you're not coming back."

I smiled at her.

"I'm not," I said. "Now you can be the center of attention and tell them you saw me and heard everything firsthand. Make up whatever you want. Tell them I had candles burning in the room and I was chanting in a foreign language."

"I won't do that."

"Whatever. I'm tired. Thanks for stopping by."

She stared at me a moment and nodded. "I didn't mean to upset you. I'm sorry."

I grunted, and she turned to go. I did feel bad. Why take it out on her, the one girl who had cared enough to visit me?

"Charlene."

She turned back.

"I'm the one who's sorry. I didn't mean to sound so bitter. Thanks for coming to see me."

She smiled.

"One thing," I added. "Tell Bobby good luck on his college career and baseball career. If Craig were here, he would say that."

She widened her smile.

She really was beautiful. I wished that somehow things had been different and I could have been her best friend. We would have had a great senior year together. Maybe she and I would have become like my aunt and my mother had been.

"Good luck, Alice," she said and left.

The walls seemed to close in around me and shut out all noise, every peep, except the far-off sound of someone sobbing.

It took me a while to realize that the sobbing was my own.

10

A Fresh Start

The operation on my hip was not a total success. Even after I got over the pain, I was unable to walk without a pronounced limp. It made me feel as if I was walking on a tipped surface all the time. After nearly five weeks of care, surgery, postoperative care and therapy, I returned to the Doral House. My grandfather suggested I move to a downstairs bedroom for a while to avoid having to go up and down stairs, but the doctor had specifically said I should not avoid stairways.

"There's no reason why you can't climb a stairway. If you think of yourself as physically disabled, you'll be physically disabled," he told me with a smile.

I was easily able to rationalize and tell my grandparents that he was right. I could pretend my body wasn't that much different from the way it had been before the accident. I wasn't all that restricted in doing the things that were important to me. After all, I wasn't going to be a ballerina, was I? And I wasn't much of an athlete before the accident. However, pretending I wasn't any more disabled than I had been before the accident was just fooling myself, I decided. Nevertheless, I did reject Grandpa's suggestion to avoid the stairs. I remained in my own room.

During my recuperation period, I had done whatever schoolwork I had been given and was granted the right to finish with home study. My grandfather arranged for me to take my final exams after school when everyone else was gone. I didn't know exactly what he had told the administration and my teachers, but whatever he had said worked. He was good at convincing juries, so I had no reason to be surprised at his success in persuading the school authorities to treat me differently. I suspected he relied a great deal on my psychological trauma, which wasn't altogether a false argument.

I still had great difficulty recalling the exact details of the car accident. I had absolutely no memory of what had occurred immediately afterward. For a while I even had trouble recalling specifically how the accident evolved. The hospital assigned a therapist to speak with me, and together, she and I worked out the details until I felt it all come rushing back. She was surprised when I suggested Craig was reckless and practically suicidal because of his anger at his parents. However, after I detailed some of what he had said and what had led up to it all, she nodded at me with a look of appreciation.

"You're a pretty bright young lady," she said. "Don't sell your future short."

What future? I wanted to ask. Except for my art, I had never been ambitious about anything, and now it seemed to be impossible to envision myself passionate about any sort of career. As for my art, a very strange new fear came over me during my period of recuperation. For the first few weeks after my return from the hospital, I did not attempt to go up to the attic. My grandmother was not unhappy about it. She had looked for every opportunity to get me out of the attic as it was.

"I know what the doctor told you, but you don't have to go and climb another set of stairs every day," she said. "Your grandfather could bring all your art materials downstairs and set up a studio for you in the guest's bedroom. Why look for trouble? All you need, Alice, is to injure yourself before you're fully recuperated from the injuries you had."

"Fully?" I asked. "How can I ever recuperate fully, Grandma?"

She looked away rather than answer. No one seemed capable of coming right out and saying, *"Sorry, you're never going to walk right again. You'll always have this awkward gait, this pronounced limp."*

Hours and hours, days and days, weeks and weeks of therapy did little to change it. I was able to move faster afterward, but not eliminate the limp. I thought it made me look like an old lady suffering from arthritis, especially if anyone was looking at me from behind. Almost as an act of acceptance or, rather, an act of retreat, I returned to wearing the clothing I had worn before my seemingly overnight remaking. To my way of thinking, the so-called Granny Clothes my fellow students accused me of wearing were more appropriate for me now.

I know all this further depressed my grandparents, especially my grandfather. They saw it all to be a great setback, one disappointment piled upon another until the entire foundation for our family would collapse.

I knew that my grandmother blamed my grandfather somewhat for all that had occurred. I overheard them arguing about it one night. She accused him of pushing me too fast perhaps or being too permissive. I didn't know until I had overheard their conversation that she had wanted him to convince me to not go to the prom since Craig's parents were so against it.

"It was doomed from the start," she said. "That family was so divided, the poor boy couldn't enjoy himself no matter what he did, and Alice got caught in between. Think of where she'd be today if she hadn't gone. And perhaps that boy would still be alive, too."

I didn't think that was fair. My grandfather was no fortune-teller, and she wasn't totally free of blame either. She had encouraged me to become social, too. It all made me think that I really was the center of unhappiness in this house. I concluded that no matter what I did, it would always leave a dark, depressing mark on the heart of things. I imagined waking up one morning and finding the words *Doomed for Disaster* imprinted on my forehead, a different kind of mark of Cain, but one as infamous and devastating, nevertheless.

During these days and weeks, my grandfather appeared so defeated to me. He walked with more of a stoop, something I had never seen him do, and he was far less talkative, no longer excited about bringing home his legal war stories. Our dinners together became pantomimes, with the only sounds being the clink of dishes and glasses and silverware.

"Aren't you ever going back to your art?" my grandfather asked me one night.

I had taken to spending hours and hours lying on the sofa watching television, soaking myself in some-

one else's make-believe. Like some elderly lady con-
fined to her small world, I escaped only through the
famous boob tube.

"I don't know," I said.

"You haven't been up in the studio since you've
come back from the hospital?"

"No. Between going to therapy and resting, I
haven't had the time or the desire," I told him.

"Your art could become better therapy," he suggested.

I looked at him. He was so desperate for a glimmer
of happiness again, especially for me.

"To tell you the truth, Grandpa, I'm afraid of my art
now," I said. I had to tell someone about this new fear,
and he was the best one to tell.

"What?" He looked toward the door to be sure my
grandmother wasn't hearing this conversation. "Why
would you say such a thing?"

"I'm afraid of what I would draw, paint, what would
come out of me right now."

"Well, maybe that's a good thing, a good way to get
it out of you, Alice. Consider that," he said.

"Like the kind of art therapy mentally disturbed
people do in clinics, like what my mother is probably
doing?" I asked. It was mean, but I couldn't help it.

He didn't flinch. "If it works for them, it might
work for you. You've got to get back out in the world.
It's like falling off a bike, Alice. If you don't get right
back on, you might not ride again."

"What of it? Where am I going?" I muttered. "Who
else cares, anyway?"

"I wish you wouldn't think like that. You have to
stop blaming yourself for things. And," he added, lean-

ing toward me, his eyes almost flaming with the passion of his inner fury, "you've got to stop thinking you bring only bad luck to people. Don't tell me you don't, and don't let anyone ever convince you that you are."

I didn't want to say anything more about it. I especially didn't want to argue with him. I hated hurting him more than I hated hurting myself. It was better to be silent, to refer to that all-around perfect way out, the perfect word, the key to escape.

"Okay," I said.

He sat back and another day passed.

And another night. And another week, until finally, I was confident enough with my walking to go out, to take walks on the road, especially our road, a road with little traffic and people watching. In my own way I helped myself grow stronger until, one afternoon, I finally went up to the attic. It was truly like opening the door to another world, the famous escape to Wonderland my grandmother had ironically once hoped I would find.

There waiting for me was the picture of my mother at the window that I had started months ago now. I was drawn back to it to finish it. However, when I had done so and my grandfather, happy I had returned to my art, came upstairs the following Saturday morning to look at it, I knew I had driven a stake of deep sadness into his heart.

It was no longer my mother who was looking out the window, dreaming of escape.

It was pretty clearly I who stood there with that great need and desire. He wasn't going to recommend anyone else, least of all my grandmother, see the picture. He uttered a few words of praise and then said,

"Zipporah's arriving any moment. Come down soon."

He left. My aunt Zipporah was coming to see how I was doing and have lunch with us. She had tried to visit as much as she could, but the summer was beginning and with it all the new preparations for the café. I expected her to push for my going there to work and get my mind off the accident.

I sat on the sofa and remembered that first afternoon with Craig, those moments when I had almost given myself to him in order to answer the questions I had about my own craving, intimate needs. I had been created up in this attic, maybe on the sofa that had been here then. It seemed not only appropriate but also necessary for me to find the doorway to my own sexual identity and maturity here as well. In my heart of hearts, I believed it was almost something predestined.

For Aunt Zipporah and my mother, the sofa had been a sort of gateway, a place to find their escape. It gave them pictures, dreams, places, maybe even answers. Suddenly, as I sat there, it did so for me as well. It truly came like a revelation, a plan of action delivered from some spiritual energy or power I could connect with only up in the attic. I rose quickly and went downstairs, finally enthusiastic about something.

Aunt Zipporah arrived about twenty minutes later, gushing with exuberance, energy, happiness and excitement as always, but perhaps a little more so every time she came to the Doral House now. It was as if the three of us, my grandparents and I, were starving for joy and she was bringing us a Red Cross package full of delight and jubilation. I saw the way my grandmother fed off her cheerful laughter and smiles.

I could almost feel the transfusion of sunshine driving away the dark clouds, clouds I had brought.

She talked incessantly, refusing to permit any long moments of silence among us, filling them quickly with stories about the café, Tyler's new recipes, the characters who came in and the way the small city was preparing for the upcoming new college year. She had handicraft gifts from the artisans, jewelry, needlework, carved wooden figures, a bag of surprises with a story attached to almost everything.

The looks of joy and amusement I saw on my grandparents' faces convinced me that what I had envisioned upstairs in the attic while I sat on the sofa was right. I quickly decided that as soon as I had a chance to be alone with my aunt Zipporah, I would propose it. When she wanted to take a walk with me, I immediately agreed, because it would give me the opportunity to tell her my idea. I was afraid my grandfather would want to come along, but he saw us leaving as his opportunity to make some important phone calls, and my grandmother was preparing our lunch.

"You're walking so much better, I see," Aunt Zipporah told me as we started down the driveway. "No pain?"

"No, but I hate my limp. It makes me feel as if one leg is shorter than the other now."

"It's hardly noticeable."

"To the blind," I said, and she laughed.

"You never permit anyone to rationalize. You're more like your grandmother than you realize."

"Which is why I wanted to take this walk with you."

"I don't understand. What does that have to do with anything?" she asked.

"We should all face up to the truth, and the truth, Aunt Zipporah, is I really have never been a source of any happiness for Grandma and Grandpa," I began.

Of course, Aunt Zipporah tried to convince me otherwise. She had the verbal energy I dreamed of having. Immediately, she came at me with a barrage of arguments against my statement, describing the pleasure they took in my art, my good schoolwork, and simply my growing up under their protective wings.

"You made them feel young again when you gave them another bite of the apple," she concluded.

"Right now," I said calmly, "that's a bite of the forbidden fruit, Aunt Zipporah."

"What? Why, that's—"

"I'd like to do more than just go back with you and start working at the restaurant for the summer."

"More?"

"I'd like to come live with you," I blurted.

She stopped walking, finally speechless for a moment. Then she smiled and said, "Well, you are. You're coming for the summer, Alice."

"No. I want to register for school there and finish my senior year there. I don't want to return to this school, and I don't want to live in this town anymore. I can't."

"But . . ."

"If you don't want me, I'd understand," I said.

"Oh no, Alice. That's not it. Why, if I didn't want you, would I have you there for the summer?"

"This is different. It's longer, and Grandpa will be the first to warn you that you'll be responsible for me, my legal guardian or something. Maybe Tyler wouldn't want that. I wouldn't blame him. Who wants to be responsible for me?"

"Tyler? Tyler loves you. He's constantly inquiring after you. No, of course not. I just . . ."

"What?"

"I just don't know how Mom and Dad would take that, Alice. Right now, especially after all that happened, they might think you don't love them anymore or they've somehow failed you."

"It's just the other way around. I've failed them and will continue to fail them as long as I'm here. It's not their fault. It's not anyone's fault. It just is."

She nodded but still looked very troubled. We continued walking.

"Maybe you should just do as you've done, come for the summer and see how it goes. You might not want to stay much longer than that and—"

"I don't mean this as a threat, Aunt Zipporah, so please don't take it that way," I said interrupting, "but if I don't move away for my last high school year, I'll run away. Just like my mother," I added, and her eyes widened.

She shook her head. "Your mother never ran away, Alice. That's all a ruse."

"She came here to hide. That was the same thing, and both of you used to run away up in the attic."

"That was only two silly girls pretending."

"No. For my mother it wasn't pretending, just as it's not for me. I'm determined about this, Aunt Zipporah. You don't know, can't know, how I feel and how it will be for me returning to that school. I hate the idea of merely going into the village and facing people, especially with all that's been said about me and still being said about me."

She nodded. "I wouldn't tell your grandmother all

that exactly as you're stating it, Alice. If she knew exactly how you feel about this town, the people, she'd go after Mrs. Harrison with a meat cleaver."

"She knows. I don't have to spell it out for her, Aunt Zipporah. All that hangs in the air in this house. You don't live here and experience it as I do. It's so thick that you can feel it. It's not the Doral House anymore. It's the Gloom and Doom House."

We walked in silence again while she thought. "Okay," she said finally. "But let me be the one who brings it up first. In fact," she added, "let me pretend it was my idea from the start and I just told you out here while we were walking."

"No," I said a little too sharply. She stopped and winced.

"What? Why not?"

"I'm sorry, Aunt Zipporah, but I don't want to contribute to any lies or deception anymore in my life, no matter how small they seem to be. They're like cancer cells that eventually grow bigger and poison your body."

She smiled and raised her eyebrows.

"Maybe you're right," she said. "But there is such a thing as a little white lie, Alice, an attempt to keep someone you love or care about from suffering or feeling badly."

"In the end we're all better off with cold, hard truth. Maybe that would have been better for my mother."

"Your mother's situation was too complicated for any easy answers," she said. She paused and looked back at the house. "When do you want to talk about this with Grandpa and Grandma, Alice?"

"Before I do, are you absolutely sure it would be all right with you and Tyler?"

"Yes, I'm sure."

"Then right now," I said. "There's no point in putting it off until the last possible moment and springing it on them."

"How did you get so wise?"

"I'm not very wise," I said.

"You're wiser than I was at your age."

I looked back at the house. How could I tell her, explain that whatever insight I had came to me mysteriously up in the attic? She would surely think I was weirder than she could imagine, I thought. And then I thought maybe she won't. Maybe she once believed in the magic of the Doral House attic, too. I decided for now, however, to keep that secret to myself. I didn't want her to have any reason to fear my coming to live with her and Tyler.

I started back toward the house. She followed with her arms folded under her breasts, her head down. She looked very nervous, even a little afraid. It occurred to me that Aunt Zipporah might have rushed to move away for the very reasons I had. Her sense of guilt for contributing to what finally happened with my mother and its impact on her parents left her forever scarred and ashamed. Once, when I asked her why she had done it, why she had kept such a secret from her own parents, she thought a moment and said, "Misplaced loyalties. I should have had more faith in my parents."

I never forgot that, and now, recalling it again, it seemed even more appropriate that I should be with her, the two of us away from the people we loved the most and could hurt the most, both she and I now emotional refugees fleeing our own self-made wars.

Grandma had a nice lunch set out for us. All the

ingredients and condiments for a variety of sand-
wiches were placed on the kitchen counter. I saw my
grandfather chafing at the bit.

"I'm starving," he cried. "Where were you two? C'mon."

We all fixed our platters, then went into the dining
room. I decided to let everyone get into their food first,
and then, just before my grandmother started to talk
about dessert, I folded my hands in front of me and
said, "I would like to discuss something."

My grandparents looked at each other and then at
Aunt Zipporah, who shifted her eyes quickly in a vain
attempt to look completely innocent.

"What is it, Alice?" my grandfather asked.

"I'd like to move to New Paltz and live with Aunt
Zipporah and Uncle Tyler for my last high school
year," I said. "I'll help out in the café as much as they
want me to help."

"You mean move out of our house completely?" my
grandmother asked.

"For the year," I said, nodding. I paused a moment,
then added, "Maybe I'll go to college there, too."

The silence that fell around and about us was more
like a rainfall of ashes from a great fire. It was the sort
of silence and experience that steals away your heart
for a moment and leaves you speechless.

"You want to leave us then?" my grandmother finally asked.

"Not you. I'm not going to be happy at my school
here, Grandma. Grandpa knows that. He wouldn't
have worked so hard to get me out of having to attend
the last few weeks, and he made it possible for me to
take my exams separately. Nothing is going to change
dramatically over the summer."

She looked at my grandfather. He nodded slowly, then turned to Aunt Zipporah and did exactly what I told her he would.

"Are you for this, Zipporah?"

"If you two are. I have no problem with it. Neither will Tyler, I'm sure."

"You realize it means you'll have to take on the guardian responsibilities?"

"Yes, Dad. That doesn't worry me, won't worry us, but you two have to be in full agreement, other-wise—"

"Are you sure your heart is set on this, Alice?" my grandmother asked me. "Set on moving out?"

"I don't want to leave you two. I want to leave this town, this community. I'd like to have a fresh start."

"We did the best we could for you. We've always loved you as much as any parent could love his or her child," she said.

"I'm not saying no. Please understand, Grandma. There are too many ghosts in this town now," I added. Her eyes widened.

"Why don't you just do what you planned to do," my grandfather said in his calm, reasonable manner, "and if toward the end of the summer you're still of the same mind, Zipporah will register you at the high school and we'll bring up whatever else you want from the house. How's that?"

"It's just putting off the inevitable," I said with cold firmness.

My grandfather stared a moment, and then he smiled.

"She's your granddaughter all right, Elaine. No sugarcoating permitted."

"Whatever," my grandmother said, rising. I wasn't sure if she was simply angry or simply too exhausted to argue or care. "Anyone want a piece of apple pie? I have vanilla ice cream, too."

"I would," I said.

"Let me help you get it, Mom," Aunt Zipporah said, rising. I knew what she wanted was some private moments with my grandmother, so I sat.

My grandfather leaned forward.

"I'd be the last one to put obstacles in your path, Alice. You know that. And I appreciate all that you have endured because of some mean-hearted people. Maybe what you're proposing will be the best thing for you. I just want to warn you that sometimes what we think is an escape is simply a short diversion. Sometimes, running away doesn't work because you carry so much with you. It's better to face your demons head-on where they are."

"It's not worth it, Grandpa. Except for being with you and Grandma, there's nothing here I want to win or achieve."

"I'm only saying casting yourself out isn't as promising as you might think. We're all on rafts of one sort or another, and the only thing that gives us any stability, any hope, are the lines between us and the ones we love."

"I'm not breaking them. I'm only stretching them a bit," I said, and he laughed.

"Okay."

Moments later, Aunt Zipporah and Grandma brought in our dessert. My grandmother seemed more upbeat. I was confident Aunt Zipporah would quiet her fears and smooth it over for me. I suggested, of course, that I leave with Aunt Zipporah after lunch.

"Today? But if you're going for a longer period, your packing," my grandmother said. "And . . ."

"I don't need much right away."

"She's right. We'll bring the rest of her stuff a little at a time, Elaine. We'll take a ride next weekend," my grandfather said.

I could see the reality taking hold rapidly now in my grandmother's face. To talk about it was one thing, but to actually see it happening was another.

"I was going up there anyway within the week to work for the summer. What difference does a few more days make?" I asked.

She nodded. She knew that, but now that I had added the idea that I wouldn't be returning, she seemed frightened again.

"Don't worry about me, Grandma. I'm going to be all right," I said.

Afterward, Aunt Zipporah came up to my room to help me put my things together. My grandmother stopped in to be sure I was taking everything I would definitely need. "For a week or the rest of your life," she added, a little grumpy.

My grandfather stopped by to say he would bring up my art materials.

"I don't expect to have much free time for it," I said, but Aunt Zipporah disagreed.

"You'll have some wonderful scenic opportunities, Alice. Both Tyler and I will want you to continue your art. Maybe you'll do one for the café," she suggested. "And don't forget the studio we have behind the house." Her ability to be upbeat about everything was another reason I wanted to go back with her now and stay there.

"It's not a problem for me to bring the materials," my grandfather repeated.

"Okay. Thanks, Grandpa," I said.

Everyone helped pack the car.

"She's spent two summers with us already, Mom," Aunt Zipporah told my grandmother, who looked like she was about to burst into tears.

"I know, but all I seem to be doing these days is saying good-bye to everyone."

"It's not good-bye, Grandma. It's so long for now. I'll come see you if you don't come to see me," I promised.

"I've always done the best I could for you, Alice. Both of us have."

"I know, and I don't love either of you any less today than I did yesterday or I will tomorrow."

My grandfather stepped up to her and in a whisper loud enough for me to hear said, "Let her go, Elaine. Give her a chance."

She nodded, then stepped forward to hug me. She held onto me tightly a moment.

And then she said something to me that she had never said. "You're the rainbow after the storm, Alice. Always remember that."

She turned and started back to the house.

"Hey, call soon," my grandfather said and kissed me. He turned to quickly catch up with my grandmother to comfort her.

"C'mon, Miss Picasso," Aunt Zipporah said and got into her car.

I got in quickly. I wasn't going to look back at the

Doral House. I was going to be strong and just keep my gaze on what was ahead, but I couldn't help it. I turned around.

They were already inside. I did feel badly for them. Aunt Zipporah was right about creating some white lies and putting hard decisions off for as long as possible, I thought. I shouldn't have been so pigheaded about it.

"They'll be okay," she said as we continued down the road I had walked all my life. "It takes some getting used to, this living in a quieter house with just yourselves. But they've always been there for each other, so I'm sure they'll be fine."

"They've always been there for me, too."

"Sure, and for me and for Jesse. Dad was even there for your mother," she added.

When we entered the village, I looked hard at it all, and especially at the Harrisons' home. Their house was empty now, too. I gazed up at what had been Craig's room and, before that, my mother's. The curtains were closed, and it looked dark. In fact, despite the sunshine, the whole house looked imprisoned in shadows, trapped behind the bars of tragedy and sadness. No bright flower, no rich lawn and well-trimmed hedge could rescue it from what it was, what it had become and maybe would always be.

Now I truly wondered if anything could rescue me from who I was and what I was.

I gazed back as we left the village proper. Aunt Zipporah caught me saying my visual good-byes.

"It's funny how your mother and I used to make so much fun of the place. We had funny names for people and places, and she was great at imitating some of the village characters."

"Sometimes, you make it sound as if it was more fun than you thought."

"We did what we could. Your mother used to say Sandburg is so small the sign that says you're now entering Sandburg has you're now leaving Sandburg on the back," Aunt Zipporah told me and smiled.

"It's not small to me," I said. "It's been my whole world."

She nodded with understanding.

We were both silent then.

And as we drove on, I looked forward just like any explorer searching for signs of promise, for that Wonderland my name had promised.

11

A Home Away from Home

Any college town has a unique energy about it. The school, its students and faculty become the lifeblood. So many businesses cater to their needs and profit from their existence. There's also that constant sense of rejuvenation, new students flocking in and bringing with them their excitement and high expectations. I even felt it during the past summers, when the student population was smaller but nevertheless still a major presence. It was such a dramatic contrast to quiet, sedate life back in Sandburg that I always became optimistic almost the moment we drove into the city.

Aunt Zipporah and Uncle Tyler lived in a unique, Swiss-chalet style home approximately five miles out of the city and away from their café. Uncle Tyler had bought the home from a well-known sculptor, who eventually returned to Switzerland. To give himself a sense of his heritage and homeland while he lived and worked here, he had the house built in the Swiss style. Behind it was a small building he had constructed to serve as his studio. It would obviously serve as an ideal location for my studio as well. It had good lighting, some long, large wooden tables, an oversized sofa and a half dozen chairs. The bathroom had a small stall shower. He even had a smaller kitchen there so when he was very involved in his work, he didn't have to leave his studio. Other than that, it was a very unimpressive, basic structure with nothing done to dress it up or cause it to give much more value to the property. The walls within looked unfinished, the windows were curtainless and the floors were cracked concrete. Some of the electrical wiring still hung loosely from the ceiling. My uncle left the studio exterior just as it had been, a basic light gray stucco.

Uncle Tyler was someone who liked to step a little to the right or left of what would be known as mainstream, whether that was how he dressed, which was usually a black leather vest, jeans and Western-style boots with a tight-fitting, faded T-shirt and a baseball cap on backwards, or what he drove—a restored small English car called a Morris Minor. Instead of signal lights, it had signal flags that came out of the sides when he made a right or left turn. It had a very small backseat and a floor shift. The year before, he'd had it repainted an emerald green.

The house itself, which I did adore, had a low-pitched, front-gabled roof with wide eave overhangs. There was a second-story balcony with a flat patterned cutout balustrade and trim. The exterior walls were made up of a patterned stickwood decoration. The color of the home was a dark coffee. Again, Uncle Tyler had found a house painter who could repaint the home in the unique shade.

Set on a little more than two acres with the undeveloped backyard, the house had a small front lawn and a dirt driveway. Neither the previous owner nor Uncle Tyler wanted to put down a hard driveway. Uncle Tyler liked the rustic look and thought it actually added to the value of the property because the only people who would buy such a house were people who liked that style. When it came to those sorts of things, Aunt Zipporah went along with all his decisions.

The master bedroom in the house was upstairs. It had only that bedroom and a guest bedroom toward the rear of the downstairs. That was to become my bedroom, as it had been when I had visited the previous two summers. The guest bedroom had two windows that looked out on the forest and high grass. I could see the studio off to the left as well.

When I stayed here before, I often saw deer grazing with no concern or worry, occasionally lifting their heads to look at the house and listen. One afternoon, I walked out the back door and drew as close as ten feet or a little less to a doe before she bolted and glided gracefully into the safety of the woods and shadows.

Uncle Tyler swore to me that he had seen a bear come out of those woods, and he blamed the garbage cans being disturbed and subsequent messes on bears and raccoons, whom he would say jokingly "have no respect for other people's property." That was about as angry as he became over it.

In fact, I had yet to meet anyone with as calm and gentle a demeanor as my uncle Tyler. Aunt Zipporah told me his quiet manner and seemingly stoic acceptance of anything and everything was a result of his meditation and studies of Far Eastern religion and thought. He did have that soft, understanding smile that encompassed his light blue eyes and trickled down his cheeks to his lips.

Although he was a gentle man with a slim build who stood a shade less than five feet eleven, he did possess an inner strength and boundless energy. "You don't battle the current," he once told me. "You swim along with it and wait for your opportunity to step aside or perhaps divert it into a more favorable direction." He summed up that philosophy with the law of physics that said any action in one direction creates an action in the opposite. "Never go head-on into fights and battles," he told me. "Slip and slide around them, Alice."

He was especially like that with me, I thought— my life coach always coming up with some philosophical advice. He never tried to tell me what to do, however. He always suggested, and if I listened, fine. If not, he had that deep faith and self-confidence that comforted him in the belief that one of these days, I'd come around to his way of thinking, just as Aunt Zipporah often did.

I had come to realize that Aunt Zipporah was attracted to him for all these reasons. He wasn't the handsomest man in the world. His nose was a little too thin and long, and his ears were slightly more extended, but his inner peace was something she longed to have herself, especially after the dramatic tragedy of her time with my mother and the deep pain it had caused between her and my grandparents. Forgiveness didn't mean forgetting. In the end it meant accepting responsibility and guilt, but stains and scars were never completely out of sight and mind. They lingered under the soft places upon which her heart rested and beat. Tyler was someone who knew how to live with disappointments and defeats and yet maintain his strength. She fell in love with that part of him first, and the rest followed.

In almost the same way and for the same reasons, I was drawn to him and to the world they had created for themselves. There were no attics here, no hovering ghosts, no mean faces full of accusations. Maybe my grandfather was right. I was fleeing from things I could never escape, but at least for a while I could live in the illusion and maybe grow as strong as I had to grow in order to return and face the demons, as my grandfather had suggested.

Aunt Zipporah drove me to their house first to settle in. I did a little unpacking, getting my bathroom things laid out in the downstairs bathroom, and then the two of us set out for the café.

"We closed for a month during the semester break this year to break out the wall on the left side and expand the dining area, you know," she told me as we drove along the quiet, country road spotted here and there with modest houses, trim lawns and stone walls marking their property.

"I forgot you were going to do that."

"Well, we did, and we've added another ten tables, which meant we needed two additional waiters or waitresses during the busier season when the college kids return in force. Tyler occasionally pitched in as a waiter these past few weeks while you were recuperating just to be sure to save you the spot," she told me. "Yours truly became the chef from time to time."

Everyone was making sacrifices for me, I realized. When would I be able to reciprocate?

"That was really nice of him," I said. "I hope I can live up to his expectations, especially now." She knew what I meant.

"You don't have to run from table to table and to the kitchen, Alice. Your limp won't make a shade of difference, so don't beat yourself up about it. Besides, as Tyler is fond of saying, we are not a fast-food restaurant. Anyone who has those expectations should explore the quickest way out."

I laughed and then listened to her explanation of some of the new items on the menu. She then told me about the new band they had hired for the week-ends during the last college year—The Medicine Men—and how popular it had become. Besides the traditional rock fare, they were good at playing Cajun music called Zydeco, "which is so unique to our area. And we've got the only live band who can do it. It's been quite a hit. We've booked them to start again in September when everything gears up."

The more she talked about the café, the more excited and hopeful I became about my new life here.

"I never asked you before, Aunt Zipporah, but does anyone here yet know anything about the things that happened in Sandburg? I mean, with my mother?"

"Of course not. How would they? Why would they? It was so long ago. It's not exactly front-page news even back there. I certainly don't talk about any of it, and neither does Tyler, and neither," she said, making the point firmly, "will you."

I smiled. No, I thought. I didn't need any coaxing about it. Neither would I.

There was barely time for hellos and how are yous when we reached the restaurant. It was already jammed with customers, nearly every table full. Two waitresses, whom I had never met, were scurrying around to take orders. There were three busboys, one of whom was assigned the role of expediter. He brought the finished platters to the tables. All five were currently students at the state college, taking summer session courses. Their work schedules were constructed around their classes. All needed the money.

Mrs. Mallen, a woman in her fifties who was a sort of all-around employee, sometimes cashier, sometimes counter-girl and sometimes waitress, was there as well. She had been with Tyler and my aunt Zipporah for as long as I could remember. She lived in town in an apartment building only a block or so away, so she was often trusted with opening and closing the café as well. Childless and widowed for a little more than five years, she had adopted Tyler and Aunt Zipporah as her immediate family—or they had adopted her. I was never quite sure.

With curly charcoal gray hair, light brown eyes, and a plump what I called Mrs. Santa Claus face, stout at five feet four, she presented a jolly, pleasant figure who loved to mother the college student customers, telling them they smoked or ate or drank too much, advising them to wear warmer clothing in the winter, criticizing their bootless feet or poor eating habits, but doing it all in so friendly and caring a manner that no one objected and some even followed her suggestions.

Although she and I always got along, I could feel

her standing back a few extra feet, never sure how to approach me, how close to get, how intimate or interfering. Perhaps my aunt had warned her away, I thought, or maybe I just gave off those airs. After all, I lived in a place in which no one but my grandparents could be trusted. The one comment I recalled Mrs. Mallen making about me was, "Sometimes she looks like someone who has lived in a war zone."

Little did she know how right she was.

Aunt Zipporah grabbed two aprons, tossing one at me. Mrs. Mallen was at the cash register, and Uncle Tyler was working feverishly in the kitchen with his two kitchen helpers, a pair of brothers from the Philippines, Tony and Marco Aruego. Tony was twenty-five and Marco was twenty-two, but both looked like teenagers to me. They, too, performed a multitude of tasks at the café: dishwashers, janitors, at times short-order cooks and occasionally busboys when needed.

I had always found an atmosphere of comradery at the café. Uncle Tyler never treated anyone as lowly employees. The respect he gave them was mutual, and I couldn't imagine anyone who worked there doing anything to hurt the café or him, least of all stealing from him in any way.

"What?" I asked when I caught the apron.

"Grab a pad and help Missy Williams," she told me and nodded at the slimmer, more dainty looking of the two waitresses. She did seem a bit overwhelmed and confused, I thought.

"But I'm not that familiar with the menu yet."

"Get familiar," Aunt Zipporah said. "Quickly."

Quickly? It was like being tossed into the water

and told to learn to swim. I had never been a waitress before: I'd only bussed tables and helped at the counter.

"But—"

"Go on," she said, gesturing at the tables and customers.

She laughed. Uncle Tyler smiled at me and waved, but kept working. I grabbed a pad and went to the tables where the customers were holding the menus but obviously had not yet ordered. Before long, I was too busy to even wonder if anyone had noticed my inexperience and my pronounced limp. All these people really cared about was getting their food.

"See?" Aunt Zipporah said as I rushed back and forth with the other two, delivering the orders and helping our expediter serve the finished platters. "You're too busy here to have time to feel sorry for yourself."

She was right, of course. This early rush hour dinner left little time for anything but the work, and I did learn the menu rather quickly on the spot. Only a couple of customers even noticed how fresh on the job I was, or at least, that was what I thought. Missy appreciated my coming to her rescue and helped me along, too. The other waitress, a tall, strong-looking, short-haired blond girl with a take-no-prisoners expression on her face, barely paid me any attention and didn't introduce herself to me until a small lull in the action. Her name was Cassie Bernard, and she was a junior at the college.

"She's good," Aunt Zipporah whispered. "If people were patient, she could handle this entire café."

Missy's flighty, helpless look was a great contrast to Cassie's efficient and confident demeanor. I wondered whom I would look more like to the customers. During the dinner rush, I noticed that although Missy wasn't as good a waitress, the customers took more to her, however, maybe because they felt sorry for her or maybe because she was open enough for them to tease. The cynic in me wondered if some of it wasn't just an act on her part to win their sympathy and get away with some inefficiency.

Whatever it was, whatever anyone's real story here was, I realized there was enough human drama and activity to draw me away from thinking too much about myself, my grandparents and the world of tragedy I had just left. I felt like a little fish that had been alone in an aquarium, exposed to everyone's view, then was suddenly tossed into the ocean with schools of other fish, becoming too small and insignificant to even draw a passing glance. For that, I was truly grateful. If there was one thing I wasn't looking for, it was attention.

When the rush finally ended and the café thinned out, all the introductions were completed. Mrs. Mallen wanted to give me a welcome hug, but she just touched my shoulders and smiled. Uncle Tyler kissed and hugged me. I glanced at Aunt Zipporah. She hadn't yet told him about my request to come live with them and attend high school here. Despite what she had said about it and what I knew about Uncle Tyler, I was still nervously anticipating his reaction. The last thing I wanted to do was become the cause of anyone else's tension and unhappiness.

With the lull in business, we were able to eat a little dinner ourselves. Working this hard had taken away most of my appetite, but I especially loved Uncle Tyler's meat loaf, and it was still his signature dish. I sat at the rear of the new section in the restaurant to eat and talk with Uncle Tyler. He was very concerned about me and my reactions to the accident and Craig's death.

"It's not something you can ever get over or maybe should ever get over, but it's like most disappointments and hardships in our lives, something we have to learn how to live with, embrace. Yes," he said, nodding at my surprised expression. "We even have to embrace our unhappiness. It's part of the overall."

"Preaching your Far Eastern thinking again?" Aunt Zipporah asked him as she pulled up a chair with her platter of food.

"Preaching? Was I preaching, Alice?"

We all laughed. I looked at Aunt Zipporah. She knew why I had this look of expectation written across my face.

"Tyler, Alice asked me if she could do something. I told her how I felt about it, but she won't be comfortable about it until she hears your response directly from you."

"Oh? Okay. You can pierce your ears but not your nose," he said. I smiled, but he saw from both Aunt Zipporah's controlled reaction and my subdued one to his joke that this was far more intense. "What is it, Alice? What do you want?"

"I'd like to finish my high school education here, attend school here for my senior year."

He glanced at Aunt Zipporah and then turned back to me.

"You mean, you want to live here with us?"

"Yes," I said.

"What do your grandparents say about that?"

"They're not dancing in the streets, but they understand, I think."

"Zipporah?" he asked her.

"She's right. I couldn't have put it any better," she added, smiling at me.

"So you want to know if I mind?" He sat back, the fingers of his right hand grasping his chin. He squeezed and massaged and looked like he was in very deep thought. I knew he was putting on an act.

"A wise man once told me home is the place where when you go there, they have to take you in. Soooooo . . . welcome home, Alice," he said and slapped the table. "Free help forever!" he cried, laughing. "Sure, move in. I need someone who appreciates my jokes." He rose and kissed me on the cheek. "Whatever makes you happy, makes us happy, Alice. It's not a problem. Besides, Zipporah needs the practice. We're getting closer and closer to having our own child, right, Zipporah?"

"Closer," she said without fully committing. I wondered in what bed of doubt and insecurity her reluctance to have children lay. I couldn't help but puzzle over what she knew that I didn't and if it would lead me to be just as reluctant as she was.

"See?" Uncle Tyler said. "See why I need help?" He patted me on the shoulder and returned to the kitchen.

"I hope he's not putting on an act for me," I said immediately.

"You know him well enough by now to know that's not true, Alice."

"Are you really getting closer to having your own child?"

"We'll see," she said, shifting her gaze away as a way of telling me the topic was off the table. "I'd better go help him. We get a little play before we close this place, some latecomers, stragglers. Relax, finish eating," she said.

Missy had left, but Cassie remained, reading one of her textbooks and handling the occasional customers. Mrs. Mallen went home to do something but was returning to close, as usual. I remembered that during the summer hours especially the café really wasn't a bar hangout after dinner until the weekends, when there was music. I debated going over to talk more with Cassie and then thought she probably cherished the opportunities to grab some reading. It wouldn't be fair to steal some of that time for chitchat.

While I sat there, I gazed around the café, noting the changes and picturing where anything I painted could be hung. I was—perhaps because I felt so welcomed here—suddenly very eager to get back to my art and hoped my grandfather wouldn't forget to bring my things along when they came. I would finally make some use of that studio behind Aunt Zipporah and Uncle Tyler's house. Thinking about all that brought me to the phone.

"I'll call the Doral House," I told Aunt Zipporah, "and let them know I'm settled in."

"Good idea," she said.

My fingers trembled as I grasped the receiver and began the call. My grandmother answered so quickly that I could imagine she had been sitting on top of the phone, waiting.

"Hi, Grandma," I said when she answered. "We're here, and guess what?"

"What?"

"I had to get right to work. The café was packed and the waitresses needed help. I made forty-two dollars in tips."

"That's wonderful, Alice," she said, but not with a great deal of enthusiasm. I knew what she was waiting to hear. "How's Tyler?"

"He's great, as usual. They expanded the restaurant. I had forgotten."

"Oh, right."

"We just had a serious talk about it all, Grandma. Uncle Tyler isn't concerned about my staying with them and attending school here."

"Is that so?" she asked. There was disappointment in her voice, but also a sense of fatigue. I couldn't blame her for being tired of all my crises. It was time she and my grandfather enjoyed their lives again.

"Are you and Grandpa coming up next weekend?"

"That was the plan, yes."

"Well, you can tell him I would appreciate my art materials after all," I said. "I know I sounded unsure, but I'm not anymore."

"Really?"

"I don't know if I'll do anything good enough for it, but there is plenty of open space on the café walls for pictures."

"That will be something. I'm happy for you, Alice. Really, I am," she said.

"Thank you, Grandma. Where's Grandpa?"

"He went down to the grocery for me. We need some milk for the morning. Do you want him to call you when he comes home?"

"No, it's fine. Tell him hi and . . ."

"Yes?"

"That's all. I'll talk to you in a few days," I said. "Bye."

"Okay, Alice. Take care of yourself," she said, her voice drifting off, as if the phone line had been dying slowly or as if she'd been on a ship leaving port.

I'm the ship leaving port, I thought and hung up. Aunt Zipporah was watching me.

"Everything all right?"

"Yes," I said. "It's fine."

"Good."

She returned to work, helping to put away some things in the refrigerators.

I watched a dark-haired boy in jeans and a sweat-shirt with cutoff sleeves come in and deliberately choose a table in the far right corner of the café. He sat and started to read what looked like a notebook. I glanced at Cassie, who looked up at him and then back at her textbook.

How odd, I thought and walked over to her.

"Want me to take him?" I asked.

"Take him as far away as you can," she replied. "If he orders anything, it will only be a cup of coffee, and he'll spend an hour sipping it and sitting at the table. He'll leave you a dime."

She returned to her reading.

Everyone else was occupied, and there were no other customers in the café who needed attention at the moment. The boy, who looked old enough to be in college, didn't seem to care or mind that no one was hurrying to attend to him. He continued scribbling in his notebook, his head down. When I approached him, he didn't look up until I said, "Excuse me."

When he looked up, I was looking into what I thought were the deepest dark green eyes I had ever seen. He was good-looking, with a strong, firm mouth, nearly perfect nose and sharply cut jaw. He pushed back some strands of his hair and looked at me as if I had said the most unusual or weird thing.

"You're excused," he said and looked at his notebook again.

"I meant, can I help you?"

"Oh." He looked up at me again, this time more intently. "You're new here, huh?"

"No. I've been here summers for the past two years."

"Summers," he said disdainfully. "I've just started coming in here this past spring, so you're new to me."

"Whatever," I said. "Are you here for anything?"

He looked around as if this was the first time he was asked and wasn't sure what the café was or had to offer.

"Coffee," he said. "Black. Hot."

He returned to his notebook. I glanced at Cassie, who was watching, a wry smile on her face. She shrugged at me and returned to her textbook. I went to get the boy his coffee. He didn't look up as I returned or even when I put it on his table, but just as I turned to leave him, he asked, "Are you going to college here?"

"No. I'm going to start high school here in the fall, however."

He looked back at his notebook as though I held no more interest since I wasn't a college student.

"I'm going to live with my aunt and uncle, who

own this café," I added, feeling the need to impress him with something. He looked up with real interest.

"Where are your parents?"

"I don't have parents to take care of me," I replied.

He stared with his mouth slightly open. I waited another few moments, and then I went back to the counter. Mrs. Mallen had returned, and she began asking me questions about my grandparents, my school year. It was pretty obvious to me that Aunt Zipporah had told her nothing. She did express some concern about my limp.

"I don't recall your limping last summer."

"I was in an automobile accident," I said, "and had to have an operation. This is the best they could do for me."

"Oh my. I'm so sorry. You don't seem that disabled, however," she added quickly.

"No, I don't seem so," I said.

Some new customers arrived for a late dinner, and Cassie rose to take care of them. I glanced at the boy, whom I caught looking at me periodically now. Aunt Zipporah came out from the kitchen and asked me to accompany her to the grocery store.

"They won't need us here anymore tonight, and I have things I have to get for the house."

I nodded, made out the check for the boy in the corner and went to his table.

"Do you want anything else?" I asked him. He looked up.

"Yeah. World peace," he said.

"Very funny. I have to go. You can pay this at the cash register," I said and left the check.

"Wait a minute."

"Yes."

"You always have that limp?"

"No. I was in a car accident."

He nodded, as if he had expected that answer. *What a rude person,* I thought. *Most people wouldn't be so abrupt and direct when it came to someone who had a physical disability.*

"Were you the driver?"

"No."

"Did you sue?"

"No," I said, smirking. "The boy driving died."

"Really?"

"Yes really. Do you have enough yet for your news article?" I asked.

"Not yet, but I'll keep working on it."

"Work on your manners, too," I said and left him.

"What were you talking so much about with Duncan Winning?" my aunt asked after I took off my waitress apron and we started out of the café.

"He was being nosy, asking one question after another. You know him?"

"Know of him thanks to Mrs. Mallen, who knows all the local gossip and is better than the local newspaper. She says his mother is very involved with her church and pastor." She winked. "Maybe too involved, according to Mrs. Mallen."

"What happened to his father?"

"She says he ran off and left them when Duncan was ten or eleven."

"Does he attend college here?"

"No. He's still in high school. I hear he's a very bright boy, but very strange." She paused and, with a half smile, added, "Be careful, Alice. You don't need any more strange people in your life. We're enough."

I laughed, but when I looked back through the window at Duncan Winning, I saw he was looking after me.

And he was smiling.

12

A New Room

After I helped Aunt Zipporah get the things she needed for the house, I wanted to help her put things away, but she wouldn't hear of it.

"I can take care of it, Alice. You should rest, get yourself acclimated," she told me. "I rushed you out before to get to the restaurant."

"This isn't my first time staying here, Aunt Zipporah. I don't need to get acclimated."

"No, but you've been through a lot more than you might realize. And here you are putting down stakes in a new world. You deserve some time to yourself, honey. Besides, I want you to start thinking how you would fix up the room to your liking. Change anything you want and let me know what else you need, lamps, pillows, anything. The room is never used until you're here anyway. Tyler's parents are both gone, and his sister lives in Canada, as you know."

"I don't have to change anything," I said.

"You'll see. You're going to be living in that room for quite a while now," she said. "I don't want you just to be comfortable. I want you to like where you are," she added. It almost sounded like a warning.

"Okay, Aunt Zipporah."

She paused, put her hands on her hips and squinted at me with a half smile on her face.

"You know what, Alice. I know it's a sign of respect and everything, but you don't have to call me Aunt Zipporah all the time. You can just call me Zipporah. Besides, I'd like us to be friends more than relatives, if you know what I mean."

I smiled. "Yes, I do. Thanks."

"That's nice to see, Alice."

"What is?"

"Your smile," she said. She gave me a kiss on the cheek and I went to my room.

I finished unpacking what I had brought and thought about what Aunt Zipporah asked me to do. I knew that my grandmother was always itching to get her hands on the inside of this house. Whenever we had made a trip here and were heading home, she would rattle off a list of things she would do, from repainting rooms, to covering bare wood floors, as well as changing furniture, hanging pictures and certainly replacing the "old, tired window curtains that droop over those windows. I'm afraid my daughter was never much of a homebody," she told me. "Sometimes, I think she and Tyler could live well in a tent."

My grandfather always laughed about it. "They're ex-hippies, Elaine."

"Please, spare me."

"That's what makes for horse races," he would say. "Everyone's different."

My grandmother would just grunt.

She was right about the windows, however. The curtains—a sheer, faded white material that had long lost its shape—did seem to droop rather than hang. Years and years of sunlight had beaten them to nothing more than yellowing rag material. My grandmother was sure to be here soon. *Why not impress her by fixing up this room?* I thought. And then I realized what Aunt Zipporah was really after in asking me to do this. She wanted to be sure I was committed to living here and I wasn't only playing with the idea. When my grandmother saw the changes, she would be convinced of my intentions as well.

I started to make a mental list.

Besides the curtains, I thought we should put down some area rugs. The floor had grayed and aged, especially in the corners. I didn't feel right asking for a full carpet, but area rugs would help. I would get something happier for bedding. The drab light brown comforter added nothing to the queen-size bed. It had a blah headboard, just a smooth piece of wood and no footboard. It needed help. The room could use more lighting. A standing lamp at least, set up near the small desk in the corner, would work, especially when I was attending school and doing homework in here.

I looked at the large and smaller dresser. On both, the handles and the wood itself needed a good polishing. They looked like leftovers from a thrift shop somewhere. They probably were, I thought. While Aunt Zipporah tended to some other things around the house, I went down the hall to the pantry and located the cleaning materials, a pail, and a mop, and began working on the room. Because the curtains did little in the way of blocking the sunlight anyhow, I took them down and folded them. My cleaning and polishing didn't make a dramatic difference, but at least it made some difference.

Aunt Zipporah stopped in and looked around.

"So I see you took my advice and began. Good," she said. "What else would you do?"

I rattled off my mental list, and she agreed.

"All good ideas. Let's get on that in the morning. Tyler won't need us until just before lunch. It'll be fun," she added, nodding as she looked around the bedroom. "I haven't done anything with this house for some time. As I'm sure my mother has told you many times," she added, winking.

I laughed. There was no sense denying it. We both knew Grandma too well.

"I'm tired, and Tyler will be home any minute. I'm going up to do some reading. Do you need anything else?"

"No, I'm fine, Aun . . . Zipporah."

"That's it," she said. "Welcome back, honey. I hope it works for you. You deserve a break."

"Thanks," I said. She gave me a hug and went upstairs.

Although I had slept here so many times before, the realization that this was to be my home for at least a year, if not more, settled in. When I came here for the summers, it was more like an extended weekend. In the middle of both summers I returned to the Doral House for my grandfather's birthday. I never felt very far away or apart from either him or my grandmother, but after the accident and all that aftermath and now with my new plans unfolding, Aunt Zipporah was right: this did feel different.

For one thing, there was nothing here that in any

way attached me to or suggested my mother. Maybe my grandmother didn't understand, or maybe it was because she did understand that she was always so frightened about my wanting to be in the attic so much, but I wanted to be in there because it was there that I felt close to my mother. There I could imagine her, paint her, act as she might have acted and, in doing all that, keep myself close to her.

Sometimes, when I returned from school and went up to the attic, I imagined her waiting for me. She would, as any mother would, be full of questions about my schoolwork, my friends, my interests and activities. I pretended she was there, because even if it was only in my imagination, there was someone there to listen to my complaints.

Without the attic, there was no way to pretend here. I was really on my own finally, and that was good. I realized that without that independence, I would always be disabled in more than just the physical way.

I loved both my uncle and my aunt and really did enjoy being with them, but when I dressed for bed and turned off the lights, even the stars I saw through the window looked sad and alone, blinking away tears, crying for me. There was a different kind of silence here, too. This house didn't creak as much as the Doral House, and I was downstairs, not upstairs. Any sounds my aunt and uncle made were carried off in a different direction, except, of course, for their footsteps.

Once last summer, I woke in the middle of the night and heard their footsteps. I had forgotten where I was and I sat up, my heart pounding, because I thought I was back in the Doral House hearing my mother walking back and forth above me in the attic. I thought I wasn't imagining it. Then I realized I was at my uncle and aunt's home and it was the two of them walking. I relaxed, but I'll never forget the disappointment I felt, too.

Now I lay back on the pillow and listened with my eyes opened, and I thought that somewhere out there, somewhere far away, my mother was asleep or lying in bed as I was. Perhaps her eyes were opened too, and maybe, just maybe, she was remembering giving birth to me and wondering what I was like now, what I looked like, and thinking about what she would say to me if we ever met.

I felt sorrier for her than I did for myself.

Imagine not remembering you had lost something, someone, so precious, and then one day realizing it.

It would come like a hard blow from out of the blue. It had to be terribly frightening. How do you forget something so traumatic and important to you?

Maybe she began to shout and they had to give her something to keep her quiet.

And maybe that caused her to forget again, and just like a bubble popping, I was gone, lost to that place where everything forgotten and never retrieved is stored somewhere so deep down in the darkness that even God had forgotten it existed.

I shuddered and closed my eyes.

Sleep surprised me like raindrops surprised the surface of a lake.

Tyler was always up early, even before the sun had risen. Both summers I was here, I found he was as good as any alarm clock, because he was not light-footed and he had to have a cup of coffee before he left for the café. Aunt Zipporah told me he does it half out of a need to make our kitchen necessary. "He believes things are like people. If they're not needed or used, they fall apart faster."

The cacophony of sounds coming from the kitchen, cups clanking, cabinet doors banging, chairs screeching as they were glided over the floor, and the pot itself being rapped on the stove, would make anyone imagine a monkey had gotten loose in the house. Aunt Zipporah would chastise him, reminding him I was there, sleeping downstairs, and he always promised to take care next time to be quieter, but I think he was always too lost in his own thoughts to remember that sort of promise.

I saw no reason to stay in bed anyway, so I rose, washed and dressed before he left. He was sitting and sipping his coffee when I entered the kitchen. The sun had just begun to peek over the horizon, and early rays made the world look slightly tinted red. The sleeping birds began to stir, and I could hear them chirping just outside the opened front windows.

Uncle Tyler looked up, surprised.

"Hey. You're up? Oh no, I made too much noise."

"I'm glad you did," I said and poured myself a cup of coffee.

"Mornings are the best time of day for me," he said. "Zipporah likes to read herself to sleep and could be up into the wee hours. Me? I hit the pillow and I'm off. It gets her so annoyed. Sometimes, I try to stay awake just to make her happy, but my eyelids have a mind of their own."

I laughed and sat across from him.

"So," he said, "tell me. It was terrible for you, the accident, all of it, right? I imagine you don't want to relive those details."

"No, enough time's gone by." I explained about Craig's parents and how I thought that led him to be as reckless as he was.

"Whatever they did, they regret it now and will for the rest of their lives," Uncle Tyler said.

"That doesn't bring him back," I said.

"No. Sometimes I wonder if it all isn't just dumb luck. When I was your age, I did some pretty stupid things and came close. You know what they say, There but for the grace of God go I."

He studied me a moment, then put his cup down and ran his forefinger over the edge. I had long ago realized that was the preamble to some deep comment or very prodding question, so I braced myself.

"I couldn't be more pleased about your wanting to live with us for your senior year," he began and then looked up at me, "but I'd hate to think our agreeing to it was bringing your grandparents any pain."

"I know."

"And I'd hate to think you believe this is the total answer to everything. Those answers are inside you, Alice. It doesn't matter where you live."

I thought for a moment. He looked like he was holding his breath. I knew he didn't want to do or say anything that would upset Zipporah.

"I think it does in my case, Uncle Tyler. You see, where I live back in Sandburg my mother still lives. She haunts that village and those people. They won't let go of it, and that puts deep shadows inside me and prevents me from finding the answers you mentioned."

He nodded. "Very good," he said and slapped the table. Then he stood up. "Your uncle Tyler hereby swears to keep his big mouth shut and his philosophical muttering to himself."

"No, don't do that," I said, laughing. "I came here for those tidbits of wisdom."

He laughed and hugged me just as Aunt Zipporah appeared in the kitchen doorway, still in her nightgown, her eyes looking like they were filled with spiderwebs.

"What is going on here? It's still the middle of the night."

"Not quite, Zipporah. Alice and I are solving the world's problems. We thought if we could do that before breakfast, we'd enjoy lunch."

"Did he wake you up?"

"No, I was up," I said. She tilted her head. "Little white lie," I added. "I'm taking your advice," I said, and she brightened a bit.

"I'm going up to shower and dress. Since you've spoiled my night's sleep, I might as well start the day."

"See you two later," Uncle Tyler said, starting out.

"We're going to do a little shopping this morning. I told you, remember?" Aunt Zipporah called to him.

"Yes, no problem. We're fine. Take all the time you need," he said and left.

"I'll be right down," Aunt Zipporah said. "Eat something. Don't wait for me."

She hurried back upstairs.

After she had her coffee and some natural cereal, we set out for the department stores. Although it was fun shopping with her, it reminded me of when I had gone with her, my grandmother and Rachel to get my prom dress and shoes. That memory kept me from enjoying myself, and Aunt Zipporah was perceptive enough to see that something was bothering me. I told her what it was and she nodded.

"Alice, I didn't say anything when I went to Mom and Dad's and saw you had gone back to wearing these clothes and not doing anything with your hair and your face, but I'd like to see you try again."

I shrugged. "What difference will it make?"

"I think, just as before, it will help your self-image, but it will be good for the restaurant," she said, half-kidding.

"You think customers will be turned off by someone limping around and looking like I do?" I asked, maybe a little too sharply.

She held her gaze. And then she smiled.

"Tyler's not all wrong about some of the things he believes, Alice. He always says if you're not happy with yourself, you can't expect other people to be happy with you, right? That's not a mean thing to tell you, and I'm not saying we won't love and want you no matter what you decide, but will you at least think about it? I'd be more than happy to take you shopping for some clothes. Maybe I'll even buy something more up-to-date and get Rachel off my back," she added.

"If you do, I will," I challenged.

"It's a deal. Let's get all this back first, and on our way we can see how it's going at the café."

We started for home. About two miles out of the village, we saw the boy who had been in the café. He was walking with his head down. He carried that same notebook and—speaking of clothes—wore what looked like the exact same things he had worn the day before.

"That looks like Duncan Winning," Aunt Zipporah said and slowed down.

He looked up when we pulled alongside him.

"Hi, Duncan," she said. "Would you like a ride into town?"

He looked at me, then shook his head.

"No, thanks. I'm in no rush to get there," he said, lowered his head and kept walking.

"He's a strange duck," Aunt Zipporah said, "but I can't help feeling sorry for him. He looks so lost all the time."

"I'm sure people back home thought the same of me," I said.

"The difference is you really do have family who cares, Alice."

"I know."

Aunt Zipporah looked at Duncan. "Someone told me he writes poetry. Maybe it was Cassie who told me."

"Is that what he does sitting in the café?"

"I guess so. I just equaled all the words I've ever said to him and he's said to me," she told me.

"Doesn't he have any friends?"

"I've never seen him with anyone when I've seen him, but I don't know much more about him. His mother and he live out on what was once a chicken farm. Again, according to Mrs. Mallen, who knows a little about everyone's business, Duncan's mother had a little money after his father took off, and she does a mail out business from her home. Mostly religious material. They also sold off some of their land for development." She smiled. "Little cities, lots of gossip."

We started off again. I glanced at him as we passed

him by. He kept his head down, but when we were well beyond him, he looked up to watch us disappear around a turn.

"Does he get a job during the summer?"

"I don't know, honey. I don't imagine he would be easy to employ. Even Tyler, the master guru, would have trouble dealing with someone so introverted," she said, smiling.

I didn't smile. I thought to myself, *If it weren't for my uncle and aunt, I'd probably not have a job for the summer either.*

For some reason, the café wasn't as jammed for lunch as it had been the day before, so we were able to continue home to bring everything into my bedroom. After we put on the new bedding and set out the area rugs, hung the new curtains and placed the lamp, we stood back together and considered.

"You know what else you might think of doing?"

"What?"

"Painting these walls a happier color. Or papering them. Something. Maybe," she added, "if you brighten up the room, you'll brighten up yourself inside."

"Maybe." I relented, and we planned on when we would go look for some paint or wallpaper.

After we made ourselves some lunch and ate and talked, I revealed that I had brought along one of the more fashionable skirts and blouses I had bought during our shopping spree before the prom. After we ate, I put them on and she smiled.

"Now go fix your hair and put on a little lipstick, Alice."

I did, and then we left for the café to help with the after-lunch cleanup and preparations for the evening dinner. The crowd had thinned out to where there were just two tables of four. It was Missy's turn to stay on. Cassie had left, and Mrs. Mallen had gone to the bank to make a deposit for Uncle Tyler. As soon as we entered, I looked over at the corner table and sure enough, there he was, Duncan Winning, his head down, scribbling in his notebook, a cup of coffee on the table.

Aunt Zipporah raised her eyebrows and looked at me.

"He doesn't usually come in two days in a row," she said.

I pitched in with the cleanup and preparations but looked at him periodically. Aunt Zipporah again muttered something about feeling sorry for him. Finally, I approached him. I knew he saw me coming, but he didn't look up.

"What are you writing so intently?" I asked.

I thought he wasn't going to answer, but I didn't move. I wasn't going to let him ignore me.

He looked up slowly.

"I'm keeping a sort of journal," he said, "but I'm writing it in poetry."

"Really?"

"No, I'm making it up because I'm really a spy from another planet taking notes on human behavior. Which would you rather believe?"

"Very funny. How come you wouldn't accept my aunt's offer for a ride today?"

"I don't like being indebted to anyone for anything."

"A ride? What's the big deal?"

"You give in on the little things and before you know it . . ."

"What?"

"You give away your soul," he said. I know I was smirking. He shrugged. "You asked, so I told you. Since you're being so nosy, I'll ask you some questions."

"Go ahead."

"What did you mean when you said you don't have any parents to take care of you? Are they dead or not?"

"No, they're not dead," I replied but didn't add anything.

"I guess you're not going to tell me. That's all right. I'll live without the information," he said and turned a page in his notebook.

"My parents never married," I said. I wasn't sure why I should want to tell him anything, but I suddenly felt the need to do so. He was infuriating me, and it was like releasing some of the built-up steam. It was either do that or explode in his face.

"Ah, an unexpected bundle of joy, huh? How old were they?"

"In their teens."

"So who did you live with before you came here?"

"My father's parents."

"Oh. They took on the great responsibility. What, are they getting too old to handle you?"

"No, they're still very young."

"So why do you want to go to school here?"

"I need a change," I said. "Do you like going to school here?"

"I don't think about it. I just go."

"Do you have a job for the summer?"

"I do everything around our house. Maintain the

grounds, fix stuff. That keeps me busy. It's just my mother and me."

"What happened to your father?" I asked. I remembered what Aunt Zipporah had told me, but I wanted to see what he would say.

"I don't know. Maybe he was kidnaped by aliens."

"Very funny."

"Hysterical."

"Do you want any more coffee?"

"No." He closed his notebook and looked out the window. "So won't your boyfriend miss you?"

"I don't have a boyfriend, and before you ask, I don't have any friends who will miss me either."

"Why not?"

"I don't speak the same language," I said, and he finally smiled. He had a very nice smile, I thought. It was like a dash of light and warmth. I understood why my aunt wanted me to smile more.

"You working here tonight?"

"Yes."

"I'm fixing up my scooter. It's not much, but it gets me around. I'm going home with some parts, and I think it should be in working order in a few hours. If you need a ride home afterward . . ."

"You want me to accept a ride and risk giving away my soul?"

He actually laughed and then stood up.

"Okay," he said. "Touché." He started away.

"I'll tell you what," I said, and he paused and turned back to me.

"What?"

"I'll let you take me home if you'll let me read some of your poetry."

He considered.

"That way we're both taking a risk," I added, and he nodded.

"Okay. I'll be back about . . ."

"Nine-thirty," I said.

He nodded and walked out. Aunt Zipporah stepped up beside me quickly.

"Looks like you made something of a breakthrough. I don't recall anyone talking to him that long."

"He's not bad," I said. "Sorta interesting in a strange way."

"Strange?"

"Different." I looked at her. "Like me."

She smiled.

"He wants to give me a ride home later. I said he could come by at nine-thirty, okay?"

"He's got his own car? Why is he always walking everywhere?"

"He said he had a scooter he was fixing and it would be ready to go tonight."

She looked worried.

"If he goes fast, I'll make him stop and walk," I promised.

"Something happens to you here and I'm dog food," she said.

"Nothing will happen. Bad, that is."

"Okay. I guess I had better get used to having a teenager under my wing. Just like your grandfather warned."

"It'll be all right, Zipporah."

She hugged me.

"I know it will. Let's get back to work," she said.

I did, and with a new spurt of energy that surprised me the most.

Because we weren't that busy and I had time to loiter, I kept looking to see if Duncan had arrived early. I probably would have been thinking about him anyway. Aunt Zipporah caught me watching the front of the café and smiled to herself. Both she and Tyler had already discussed Duncan bringing me home, I was sure.

Just after nine, I saw him pull up on his scooter and park it outside the café, but he didn't come right in. He sat on it and folded his arms, looking off in the opposite direction as if he had no special reason to be here and couldn't care less if I came out or not.

"You can go now, Alice," Aunt Zipporah told me. "There's not much left to do. We'll be along in a couple of hours," she added.

"Okay."

"Please be careful," she said and then laughed. "Like I ever paid attention to that when my parents said it."

"I will," I told her with firmness. "Unfortunately, I know what it means not to be."

She nodded. "I guess you do."

I took off my apron and headed out. I knew he was watching for me out of the corner of his eye no matter how coolly indifferent he tried to look, because the moment I emerged, he turned.

"Released early for good behavior?"

"Something like that," I said. "You sure this thing is safe?"

It was a well-dented black scooter with some rust.

"It has a top speed of thirty-five miles an hour downhill. Don't worry," he said and sat. He waited. I looked back through the café window and saw my aunt watching with worry scribbled all over her face. Then I got behind Duncan on the scooter.

"You can hold on by putting your arms around me," he said and kicked the engine on. It sputtered. He turned back, smiling. "Look at that, you're making it stutter."

"Very funny."

We started away.

"How do you know where I live?" I asked as he headed out of the city.

"You're with your aunt and uncle, right?"

"Yes."

"Everyone knows that house. It's one of a kind around here."

Although we weren't going fast, the breeze slapped at my face enough for me to rest the left side of my head against his back. We were silent, moving through the darkness with just the rather dim illumination of the scooter's weak front light clearing away the night. There was no moonlight, and a mostly cloudy sky hid whatever starlight the celestial ceiling was willing to offer.

We didn't speak until we reached my aunt's home and he pulled into the driveway and stopped.

I got off. He remained seated, the engine running.

"I did my end of the bargain," I said. "Where are your poems?"

"You really want to read them?" he asked, his voice full of skepticism.

"That was the deal. Well?"

He shut off the engine and reached into his jacket to pull out the notebook.

"You might as well come inside," I said. "I can't read them in the dark."

He looked at the house as if something about it terrified him, and he did not make any effort to get off the scooter.

"What?"

"That's all right. I've got to get home."

"Really?"

"You can hold onto the notebook until tomorrow. I'll come by the café and pick them up."

He kick-started the scooter.

"I didn't mean to scare you off," I said dryly.

"You're not scaring me off. I just don't want to watch you reading my poems," he added with a note of belligerence.

I almost threw the notebook back at him.

"If I'm sitting there, you'll feel obligated to say nice things," he added with a little less anger in his voice.

"I would not. I would say what I believe."

"Fine. I'll hear it tomorrow then," he said and turned the scooter around.

He didn't even say good night. He shot off into the night, the tiny rear light of the scooter looking like a red eye that closed and was gone, leaving me fuming on the driveway.

He had to be the most infuriating, impolite, arrogant and annoying boy on the face of the planet, I thought, not to mention confusing. Why was it important to him to take me home and then ignore me?

Aunt Zipporah was right. I didn't need someone with just as many, if not more, emotional and psychological problems, I told myself. I'm dangling on my own high wire.

And yet it was just that danger and the danger that hovered about him that filled me with disappointment and frustration at his leaving me standing in the dark driveway.

I gazed at his notebook. No matter how he had behaved, I was filled with curiosity and interest in what he had written.

I'm no better than that perennial moth hovering about the candle flame, toying with setting myself on fire and going up in smoke, I told myself and went into the house to read his poetry.

13

My Deepest Darkest Secret

I took the notebook to my room and lay back on my bed. It was like opening a treasure chest and not knowing what you would find. His name, address and telephone number were on the inside of the front cover. Duncan's handwriting wasn't easy to decipher, but after a while, I understood how he made his letters and I was easily able to read what he had written.

Under his name, address and phone number, he wrote, *In the event that this book is found, please call or return. A substantial reward will be given. If you don't call or return, a substantial curse will fall on you and your family.*

I laughed to myself, turned the page and began to read.

Duncan hadn't been kidding when he had first told me that this notebook was his journal. It wasn't a day-to-day recording of his life as such, but it was about all his observations and things that happened to and around him. There were times when I had thought I would keep a journal, too, but not like this. He really was a poet. He didn't write verse. Nothing rhymed, but it was still very thoughtful poetry full of surprising ideas and thoughts and imagery. At times he sounded like someone who couldn't hate himself more, and then at times, he sounded like someone who thought he was above everyone else; everyone else was inferior. He compared most people around him to worker ants or drones, mindlessly doing their chores every day and never questioning why. He was especially critical of his fellow students, who, he said, had mirrors for faces.

I liked a lot of his ideas, but some things were disturbing, especially his views of his own parents. He never referred to them as *my mother* and *my father,* but it was obvious whom he meant.

On the first page, in fact, he wrote:

Like a bird she spreads her wings over me.
She wants to protect me from evil,
But she doesn't realize she is keeping me
  in the dark,
And she is smothering me with too much love.
Can I die happy that way?

Some of what he wrote nearly brought me to tears, but there were a few poems that brought smiles and laughter, too, like the one I assumed was about his English teacher.

Up and down the aisle she parades,
Unfolding her vowels and consonants
So sharply she cuts her own tongue.
If she could, she'd march us out before a firing
  squad

For misplacing a modifier or using the wrong tense.
I imagine the walls in her house
are covered with her husband's punishments.
A thousand times he wrote
I will not use ain't again.

And then about himself he wrote:

Too many nights I see stars backing into
  the darkness
And disappearing.
The birds keep their distance, too.
Even the rain drops avoid falling on me.
I live in my own shadow
And whenever I turn to see where I have been,
I discover I have not moved.
I'm caught in the web I spun around myself,
Trapped in my own name.

Was it possible to read someone's thoughts and feel as if you've known him all your life? Some of the things he wrote I had felt and thought, but not as strongly and as vividly. What I had whispered to myself, he was shouting at the world.

I was still reading when my uncle and aunt returned from the café. Aunt Zipporah stopped in to see me.

"I half expected to find Duncan here," she said.

"He is."

"What? Where?"

"Here," I said and held up the notebook.

"Is that the notebook he's always writing in at the café? His poetry?"

"Yes."

"Well, where is he?"

"He dropped me off and went home, I guess."

"I'm surprised he gave you that."

"We had a deal. I'd let him take me here if he let me read his poetry."

"That was it? All he wanted was to take you home?" she asked suspiciously.

I nodded and then shrugged, and she laughed.

"So how is his poetry?"

"Interesting."

She raised her eyebrows. "Uh-huh."

"No, I'm not trying to avoid saying whether it's good or bad. It really is interesting."

"Okay. Do you want me to read any?"

"No," I said quickly. "I don't think it would be right without his permission."

She smiled.

"You're right, Alice. See you in the morning when your uncle wakes you and me up again," she said and went upstairs, laughing to herself.

I finished his notebook before I went to sleep. At the end it left me feeling sad and depressed. I didn't think it possible to discover anyone who was sadder about his life, his family and his future than I was, but Duncan Winning took first prize when it came to that. A part of me wanted me to hand the notebook back to him and run as fast as I could in the opposite direction. In the state of mind I was in, someone as dark and depressing as he was could just push me over the edge. I should be surrounding myself with happy, contented people, young people my age who were more like Zipporah and Tyler. After all, this was supposed to be that time of our lives when we thought ourselves capable of doing anything and living forever, not dwelling on death, failure and disappointment.

But then I thought that giving up on him was surely the same as giving up on myself. Maybe the blind could lead the blind. Maybe we were allies fighting similar demons. Maybe I should be kinder, more understanding, and, in doing that, I would get him to treat me in a similar way.

I quickly learned that wasn't the way to win his confidence and friendship.

He showed up at the restaurant right after the lunch rush the next day and took his seat at what was rapidly becoming known as Duncan's table to Cassie and Missy. I went to the back of the restaurant, where I had hidden his notebook, and brought it to him.

"Some of this is truly wonderful," I said, handing it to him.

He took it without saying anything.

"A lot of it is sad," I continued. "There's funny stuff, but most of it is sad. I can understand why, but—"

"But there's a pot of gold at the end of the rainbow? Sunnier days are just ahead? There's always a silver lining? Which one are you going to give me?" he asked with a wry smile. "I've stored all the lines the way a squirrel stores acorns."

"I wasn't going to give you any line," I said. "I was just going to say that even though it's sad, it's good."

"Right, it's good."

"It is! Have you ever shown any of it to your teachers?"

He looked at me as if I was saying the dumbest thing. "What for?"

"I just think some of it should be published."

"It is. Right here," he said, holding up the note-book.

"But that's not publishing it. Publishing it is getting other people to read it."

"And get their dumb opinions? No thanks."

"Not everyone is dumb, Duncan."

"When it comes to me, they are," he said.

He put the notebook down and turned the pages slowly, inspecting every one.

"You don't have to worry. I didn't write in it or tear out any pages."

He continued to check. "A cup of coffee," he said without looking up at me. "Black."

I glared at him, then turned and went to the counter. Aunt Zipporah looked up from the counter in the kitchen. She watched me pour the cup of coffee.

"Something wrong?"

"No," I said, obviously too quickly. "Not with me," I added.

I brought the cup of coffee to him and slapped it down so hard on the table that some spilled into the saucer. He looked up.

"You're not the only one who feels these things," I said, "and expresses them in some artistic form or another."

"Oh really?"

"That's right, really. I'm not a poet, but I happen to paint, and that's where my feelings and deeper thoughts go. My grandparents are coming up this weekend and my grandfather is bringing my art sup-plies. I'm setting up the studio behind my aunt and uncle's house, the one the sculptor created."

His face softened with interest.

"Really?"

"Yes, really, Duncan, really. Maybe if you opened a window, some fresh air would go into your head," I told him and walked away to fume on the other side of the restaurant.

"How come you're spending so much time with him?" Missy asked me.

"I'm doing penance."

"What?"

"Penance. Don't you know what that means? I'm punishing myself to make up for my sins."

"Huh?"

The confusion twisted her face, making her lips look like thin pieces of rubber. I had to smile, which calmed me.

"Despite the way he talks to other people, he's an interesting boy, Missy. He's written some great poetry."

"You read it?"

"How else would I know it's good, Missy?"

She looked at him and then at me.

"But why bother with someone like him? Why spend the time?"

"I inherited a ton of it. I have lots to spend," I told her, and she gave me that quizzical look again.

"You sound nuttier than he is."

"So there you are. You've answered your own question. We're two peas in a pod. You want to come in, too?"

"No thanks. I'll stay in the sane world," she said.

"It's your loss," I called to her as she started away. She turned and smirked back at me before tending to a new table of customers.

Another half dozen customers sauntered in, and I took their orders and stayed busy for a while. I never noticed that Duncan had left, but when I did, I didn't have much time to think about it, because we started to prepare for the dinner crowd. It was Missy's night off, so she was gone after the lunch rush, and Cassie was off as well. Aunt Zipporah and I took on the full waitress responsibilities with Mrs. Mallen standing by to jump in if need be.

According to Tyler, we had a lively crowd for midweek. He was very happy about it. He had done a minimum of print advertising, so the café was building its following through the best way possible—word of mouth. When it came to food and where to go to eat, most people were heavily influenced by the opinions of others, even people they didn't really know.

"A satisfied customer is worth a ton of advertising," Tyler chanted periodically to his employees. "Keep that smile and give them good service. Make them feel special. The food will do the rest," he promised, and from what I could see during the few days I had returned, he was right. It felt good to be part of something successful.

I was pretty tired by the time the dinner crowd thinned out and we were dealing only with some stragglers. Everyone pitched in to help with the cleanup. Finally, close to nine-thirty, I had a chance to stand back and catch my breath. I didn't want to mention it, but my bad hip was aching. If my aunt and uncle weren't so busy, they surely would have seen how much more pronounced my limp had become.

However, from the look on Aunt Zipporah's face as she approached me sitting at the counter, I thought maybe she had noticed and was waiting until now to say something. I was preparing myself for her telling me I couldn't work this hard again.

"You didn't tell me he would be here again tonight, Alice?"

"What? Who?"

She nodded toward the front of the café. Sitting on his scooter and looking as nonchalant as he had the night before was Duncan Winning.

"I didn't know myself," I said.

"You sure you didn't agree to a few more trips on that thing in order to read his poems?" she asked, smiling.

"Yes," I said. "I'm sure. Believe me, I'm more surprised than you are, Zipporah."

"Well, you'd better see what that's about then," she added and returned to the kitchen.

I slid off the stool and walked out.

"What are you doing out here?" I asked him.

"Just hanging out to see if you needed another ride."

"You didn't tell me you would be back."

"I didn't know I would myself," he said. "It wasn't so bad last night, was it? I'm not reckless or anything."

"I didn't say you were."

"So?"

I looked back into the café. Although they were working at the cleanup, my uncle and aunt were watching us.

"I have to ask them if it's all right."

"If it was all right last night, why wouldn't it be tonight?"

"I'm not saying it won't be," I replied as sharply as he spoke to me. "I just said I have to ask. They are responsible for me now."

He shrugged and looked away.

Was I crazy? I should simply tell him to make like the wind and blow, but I didn't. I went inside and spoke to my aunt and uncle.

"And what are you getting for the ride this time?" Aunt Zipporah teased.

"A week's supply of single-syllable words," I told her, and she laughed.

"Be—"

"Careful. I know, I know," I said, taking off my apron. "See you later."

"Thanks, Alice. You did great work tonight," Uncle Tyler told me.

"I made more than seventy-five dollars," I bragged.

Duncan waited confidently on his scooter, never doubting I'd be out to ride with him. His shifting from arrogance to self-pity was driving me crazy.

"Do you have to be brought straight home?" he asked when I stepped out.

"Not straight home, but soon. Why?"

"I'd like to show you one of my favorite places around here. It's sort of on the way anyway."

"Okay," I said and got on behind him. He kick-started the engine and we took off.

Just as before, we didn't speak to each other much until he made a turn off the road I knew and followed another, more narrow road that eventually turned into pure gravel. After a dozen or so more yards, he stopped the scooter.

"Let's walk the rest of the way. It's safer than negotiating the gravel. It's just off to the left here," he said.

He shut off the engine and stabilized the scooter. Then he reached into his pocket and produced a small flashlight to show me how to move through some brush until we came out to a little clearing on the river. It was running so softly and silently that it was almost still.

"What river is this?"

"The Walkill. It meets up with the Rondout Creek and flows into the Hudson River at Kingston," he explained. "There are a number of spots like this around here, but this one is my private place. I actually came in here and cleared it and keep it cleared. I bring a blanket on summer nights and sprawl out, sometimes with something to drink. My mother doesn't know about that," he added quickly. "Years ago, I found where my father stashed his bottles in the basement of our house. The good thing about the whiskey is it's better when it's aged."

"Why do you need to drink anything? It's enough to look at this scenery," I said.

"Maybe. If you're not alone," he added. "A few times I caught some couples at it just down the bank a little ways," he said.

"At it?"

"Making love," he said with an underlying tone of disapproval, even disgust.

"How did you know that was what they were doing?"

"I saw them!"

"So you spied on them, invaded their privacy?"

"Not really. They invaded my privacy and silence with their laughter and moans. I threw some rocks into the water to spook them. Sometimes it worked and they left; sometimes they were so involved, I could have set off a bomb and they couldn't care less."

"I'd care," I said, "especially if I knew someone was watching."

"I wasn't exactly watching. I don't need to be watching," he said sharply. "When I saw what was going on, I turned away, in fact."

"Good," I said.

He looked at me, and for a while we stood there in silence, listening to the faint ripple of the water as it flowed over some rocks.

"What I like about the river is . . . ," he began.

"I know," I said quickly.

"Oh yeah? What?"

"The river's power comes from its movement. It never repeats itself. Like they say, you can't step into the same river twice. That's the way I wish our lives would be."

"You memorized that?"

"I told you. I liked a lot of your work. I wasn't just trying to be nice or anything."

I could feel his surprise even though I couldn't see his face that well.

"Why do you envy the river? Don't you think there's anything good to be said for staying in the same place for long periods of time, if not your whole life?" I asked him.

"A moving target's harder to hit," he replied.

"You don't have to always be a target, Duncan."

"In this world?" He laughed. "If it's not one thing, it's another, believe me. Look at you. You moved, didn't you? You didn't want to stay in the same place."

"That's different."

"Why? Why did you want to move? Why is it different?"

"It's complicated," I said.

"People always give you that answer whenever they don't want to answer something. It's an easy way out."

"Is that right, Mr. Know-it-all?"

He was silent.

I lowered myself to the grassy part of the clearing. He looked down at me and then did the same. We were silent again, both of us just staring out at the river.

"Look," I began, "all of us are born with a family history. Mine just happened to make it very hard for me to live in that village much longer."

I waited for him to ask why, but he just reached for a small stone and heaved it into the water. If I continued, I knew I would violate the agreement I had made with my aunt Zipporah. I would be telling the story, bringing it here with me. I'd be the snake smuggling sinful knowledge into paradise. Any place where my past was unknown was paradise to me, and I was about to ruin it.

"It's a very small village, maybe a street or two of this place."

"So everyone knows everyone's business," he concluded.

"That and more."

"So what's so terrible about that? Lots of people know about my family, know my father deserted us. It's not enough to send us packing. There are other things that might do that. Who cares what other people think anyway?"

I hesitated. Why I would even want to share my innermost secrets with him, I did not know. As strange as people like Missy and Cassie might think it was, I would say it was because of his poetry. I felt he had revealed the deepest and most intimate part of himself to me by letting me read the poems. Something permitted him to trust me that much. We had joked about taking risks. It was surely exactly that both for him and for me, for neither of us had much experience with strangers we could somehow believe in and rely upon. It was like that game friends play when someone stands behind you and you permit yourself to fall back in the expectation he will catch you before you hit the ground. We were both in the process of falling back.

I took a deep breath before continuing. In a real sense, I was coming out of the attic.

"More than sixteen years ago, my mother killed her stepfather."

He finally turned to me.

"Killed?"

"She claimed he was abusing her and her mother wasn't paying any attention. After she did it, she fled and hid in my grandparents' attic where she and my father, my aunt Zipporah's brother—"

"Created the wonder of you?"

"Something like that."

"What happened to your mother? Is she in jail?"

"No, she's in a clinic. She doesn't even remember she gave birth to me. At least, that's what I've been told."

"So you've never seen her?"

"Nor heard her voice, never." My voice cracked

with emotion, and my chest ached with my effort to keep my tears under lock and key.

He turned away, threw another stone and then lowered his head so that I almost didn't hear what he said.

"Thank you."

I had to ask him to repeat it to be sure I had heard him correctly.

"I said thank you. Thanks for trusting me with all that. I know how hard it is to tell anyone those things."

He leaned back on his hands. I liked what he had said. I liked the sympathy and sincerity in his voice.

"There's more," I said and told him about Craig's family, the house, the prom and some details about the accident.

"And therefore they blamed you and people in the town think the same thing," he concluded for me.

"Yes. You know how they say the apple doesn't fall far from the tree. I'm the apple back there."

"Funny how people always find ways to blame someone else. Parents blame their children, too. At least I know my mother does. She doesn't come right out and say it, but somehow, my very existence is the cause of her troubles."

"Why would she think that?"

"I'm not exactly sure, but I know it." He threw another rock. "She loves me and yet she . . ."

"Hates you?"

"No. Fears me or for me," he said.

"How could she be afraid of you?"

"Maybe I look too much like my father."

"You should know if you do or not."

"My looks changed since I was a child. I haven't seen him for some time—years, in fact."

"So? Don't you have any pictures of him?"

"No. She tore up all of them. She even tore up their wedding photo."

"Oh. I had never seen pictures of my mother until my aunt showed them to me. Your mother hates your father that much?"

He thought for a moment and stood up, as if he realized he had gone too far in telling me what he had already told me. "We'd better go. Your uncle and aunt are liable to be home and wonder if I kidnaped you or something."

"I doubt they got out that quickly," I said but stood up, too. "Thanks for bringing me here. It is beautiful. It was nice of you to think of it, to want to share it."

The wind above nudged the clouds, which seemed just at that moment to come apart and let the glow of a new moon slip through, its light reflecting off the surface of the river and softly illuminating his face and mine. He was staring at me with gentler eyes.

"Yeah, well, you're not only the first girl I brought here. You're the first person."

"I'm glad, Duncan."

He reached for my hand and then let go of it and moved his hand up my arm to my shoulder. He did the same thing with his other hand and suddenly like two statues who had come to life, we leaned toward each other until our lips met and we could kiss.

To me it felt like a seal of approval, a snap, a stamping to certify. He pulled back, but I didn't move, and after a moment, he kissed me again, this time embracing me, pressing himself gently but firmly to me. This kiss was passionate, hungry, and determined for both of us.

He pulled back.

"We'd better go," he said, sounding a warning as if he might lose control. He took my hand and slowly led us away from his private spot on the river, neither of us speaking until we reached the scooter.

"After your grandfather brings up your art materials, I'd be glad to help you set up your studio," he said, getting onto the scooter. Apparently, I didn't respond fast enough. "But I don't care if you don't need any help," he added, as if showing any interest in me was weakness.

"I'd like that. You know it was once a famous sculptor's studio?"

"Yeah, I heard all about it. Get on," he ordered, and I did. He started away slowly.

"How far is your home from where I'm at?"

"Far enough," he said, turned onto the macadam and sped up. We didn't speak again until we were at Aunt Zipporah's house.

"Thanks again for showing me your special place," I told him when I dismounted.

"It's anyone's special place really. It's a free country," he said.

All the warmth and sincerity I had heard before was gone from his voice. I felt the tension and frustration boiling out of me.

"What is your problem? Can't anyone be nice to you? And don't give me that junk about it means you'll be selling your soul."

"What soul?" he replied, turned his scooter around and started away. I watched him disappear into the darkness again.

He reminds me of a dog that's been kicked and

kicked until it growls whenever someone wants to pet it, I thought.

Just as I reached the door, however, I heard his scooter returning. I waited until he pulled into the driveway. He sat there, the scooter still going, looking like it was struggling for breath, the engine sputtering.

"Forget something?" I asked, moving toward him.

"Yeah."

"What?"

"I forgot to say good night," he said. "Sorry," he added.

"Don't tell me you're going to try to be human."

He laughed.

"No, I won't go that far."

He stared at me a moment and then he leaned over to kiss me, but he did so as if he was truly stealing a kiss. Then he turned the scooter around and took off. I watched him disappear again.

He is the reason for hot and cold water in any sink or tub or shower, I thought.

14

Children of Sin

During the next few days, I didn't see Duncan. He didn't come to the café or look for me at my aunt and uncle's home. He didn't even call me. I was disappointed, but I didn't try to call him. Because I turned so sharply in anticipation every time the café's front door was opened, my aunt Zipporah knew I was anticipating and hoping to see him, however.

"Things didn't go so well with you and Duncan?" she asked me with a wry smile.

"To tell you the truth, I'm not sure," I said, and she laughed. Mrs. Mallen overheard.

"Don't be surprised that boy's not coming around," Mrs. Mallen said. "He's very devoted to his mother. He's had to do a man's work around their property ever since he was ten. He's lost his whole youth."

"I don't care if he comes or not," I said, a little embarrassed my disappointment was that obvious to everyone in the café.

Aunt Zipporah smiled at me as if to say, *"Sure, sure."* Not another word was mentioned about him, however.

On the weekend, my grandparents arrived. My

grandfather had loaded up the trunk with as much of my art materials as he could fit into it. He began to take it all to the studio, while my grandmother came in to see the improvements in my bedroom. I had told her about them on the phone.

"Well now, this looks almost livable," she commented. Aunt Zipporah and I smiled at each other. "I brought most of your newer things, Alice, but if we need to get you more, we should do it while I'm here this time."

"I'm fine," I said.

"Those shoes you have are really not the best for being on your feet all day at a restaurant," she continued, looking down at my feet. She stopped just short of adding, *"for someone like you, someone with your injury."*

"I'm not having any problems. I'm not working that much," I said.

She looked at Aunt Zipporah for confirmation.

"If she shows any signs of fatigue, Mom, I'll be on it. I promise." She raised her right hand.

My grandmother grunted skeptically.

"Look, Grandma," I said, holding up a sheet with titles printed on it.

"What is that?"

"Aunt Zipporah went to the school and got the summer reading for those entering the senior year. I have one of the books already," I said.

She glanced at the list and handed it back to me before turning to my aunt.

"How far is the school from here? How are you going to manage getting her there and being at your café? Breakfast is a big deal for you and Tyler, isn't it? Don't you have to be there, too? Or will she ride a school bus? Has that all been looked into, Zipporah?"

"She doesn't have to ride a school bus. It's no problem. The school's not far from the café, and she has to be there early enough so it will work for me, Mom. She can even use my car lots of times, too."

"She hasn't driven very much since she got her license," Grandma said, making it sound like a complaint.

"So, she'll drive some here. Stop all this worrying."

My grandmother nodded and looked at me.

"Did your father call you?"

I shook my head but looked to Aunt Zipporah.

"He didn't call the restaurant," she said. "Jesse would know that's where we would be."

"He told me he was going to call you to discuss this decision you've made about your senior year," she said, anger and disappointment in her voice. I was disappointed, too. I wanted my father to have more and more interest in me and my future.

My grandfather stepped in behind us.

"That's a pretty nice studio, Zipporah. I never really looked at it before today. Airy and bright, and its own little kitchenette and bathroom. I bet that sculptor spent days in there without coming out."

"I hope that's not what Alice will do," my grandmother said sharply.

"Well, she'll have the privacy she needs," he said, smiling. "Isn't it time to get to the café? I'm looking forward to lunch," he said, rubbing his palms together. "What's that special I like, Zipporah? It's still there, isn't it?"

"Yes," Aunt Zipporah said, laughing. "It's Tyler's meat loaf, Dad."

"Right. Well?"

My grandmother shook her head and looked at me. I could see that she was half hoping I had changed my mind about everything, but the improvements in my bedroom and now my art supplies installed in what would be my studio drove home my determination.

"I'll be fine here, Grandma," I told her. "Next year I would be going off to college anyway," I said.

"Some birds throw their babies out of the nest," my grandfather said, smiling.

I quickly looked at Aunt Zipporah. She and I shared a secret. I knew that she and my mother had baptized the attic as Nest of Orphans, and ever since I learned that, I could never hear the word *nest* without thinking about it, thinking about the two of them treasuring their privacy, their imaginative world, their precious secrets.

"If you want to base your behavior on other animals and insects, Michael, female black widows kill their male mates, too," my grandmother threw back at him, and he roared with laughter.

We went to the café in two cars because my grandparents were going to leave right after lunch. Aunt Zipporah thought I should ride with them to spend as much time with them as possible. It also gave my grandmother one more chance to ask me questions that might annoy or embarrass Aunt Zipporah if she heard them.

"Are you sure Tyler is happy with this new arrangement, Alice?" she asked almost as soon as we started away. "That's not a very big house. You're probably stumbling over each other, and I'm sure they value their privacy."

"He seems very happy about it," I said. "They have their privacy, Grandma. I'm downstairs, and now I'll have the studio and be in their way even less."

"Besides, she'll make new friends and get into some new activities here," my grandfather said. "She'll have plenty to do outside of the house."

New friends? I thought. I didn't have any old ones.

"Zipporah and Tyler are very involved in that café of theirs. They're not going to be able to devote all that much time to you, Alice," my grandmother warned.

"I don't need a babysitter, Grandma. I'm nearly seventeen."

"She's right, Elaine. Stop bugging her."

"Are you feeling all right?" she asked me, ignoring him as usual. "No pains? No headaches?"

"I'm fine," I said. "If anything bothers me, you'll be the first to know."

Dissatisfied with my answers but unable to shake me out of my determination to remain, she settled back and finally relaxed. We had a great lunch together. I couldn't help looking to the door every time someone entered, as usual half expecting, and hoping, to see Duncan come in, especially today, so he could see and meet my grandparents, but he didn't come. At one point, Missy paused to whisper in my ear.

"Where's Mr. Weirdo these days? You give him his walking papers?"

"I don't know," I said.

"Lucky you," she replied, smiling.

Why did people take such pleasure in the unhappiness of others? I wondered. Was it simply because it wasn't their unhappiness, or were we all sadists deep down inside? Or could it be jealousy, too? From what I could gather, Missy didn't appear to have any boyfriend or even good friends.

This time the good-bye for my grandmother seemed to be even more difficult than the previous parting back at the Doral House. There, she had clung to the belief that I would come to my senses shortly after arriving here. I would see that it didn't matter where I was, and I would tell her that I would return after the summer. Now, she was really saying good-bye, and she knew it.

"We're taking a little summer vacation of our own, you know," my grandfather told Aunt Zipporah and me outside the café. "Next week we're heading up to Cape Cod for two weeks. We weren't sure about it until now, right, Elaine?" he asked pointedly.

It was obvious that she had been holding back her full agreement until she had seen for herself that I was doing fine and I was safe.

"Yes," she said. "But we'll be only a phone call away, of course," she added.

"Just enjoy yourselves, Mom," Aunt Zipporah told her. "Everything is good here. Alice will be very occupied between the restaurant and her art."

"Umm," my grandmother said. She looked at me. "Don't overdo it," she said.

"Okay," I told her and then hugged and kissed her.

My grandfather put his arm around my shoulders and slipped me five hundred dollars.

"Just in case the tips get a little low," he said. "I'm proud of you, honey. You've got grit. You're going to be fine."

He kissed me, then he and my grandmother got into their car and started away. We stood on the sidewalk and watched them make a turn and head home.

"Free at last! Free at last!" Aunt Zipporah said, laughing. She embraced me and shook me.

I smiled at her, but I kept my gaze on the corner around which they had disappeared. Despite my burning desire to find a new road and my independence, I missed them terribly. They were the shoulders to lean upon, the hands to reach for, the people in whom I found my safe haven. It wasn't easy cutting the ties and waving them off.

I was truly like the bird falling from the nest.

Would I fly?

Aunt Zipporah was confident I would. Nevertheless, she did her best to cheer me up the rest of the day, insisting that we go shop for those clothes we had promised each other. I had a fun time helping her find things in style to wear rather than wearing what my stepmother Rachel called "Zipporah's rebel uniforms." She even contemplated going to the beauty parlor and getting a different, more up-to-date hairstyle.

"You should," I said. Then, realizing I sounded like I was criticizing her in Rachel's style, I added, "I mean, it might make you feel better about yourself."

"Look at who's talking. I tell you what. If you'll go, I'll go," she added. "We'll do the whole enchilada—nails, pedicure, facials. What do you say?"

I laughed and nodded. The salon had openings immediately, so she made our appointments and we spoiled ourselves for the rest of the day. When we returned to the café, Tyler was amused and even impressed with Aunt Zipporah's and my new looks.

"I'm probably going to get new business because of you two," he told us. "Those truck drivers who think we're too sixties and distrust us will be coming in for sure now."

The three of us laughed. My uncle and aunt were truly an antidote for sadness. It was impossible to be either unhappy or depressed around them long. My grandmother's questions had put a little doubt in my mind, but this was a good move for me, I told myself.

We had a very busy Saturday night and I had little time to think about Duncan. I did look for him from time to time and thought it strange not to have seen him all day and now all night. All of us worked until closing, and when we went home, we went right to bed.

"Now, Alice," Tyler said on Sunday, "I want you to take Mondays and Tuesdays off completely to work on your art. Those are slow days for us in the café, and it would be a waste of your time to have you here standing around."

"Are you sure?"

"Absolutely. Missy and Cassie could use the extra money, too," he added.

"Besides," Aunt Zipporah said, "we're depending on you coming up with a great picture for the café."

"I'm not that good yet."

"We'll let the patrons decide. In fact, we'll put a

price on it and see if anyone buys it," Uncle Tyler said.

I couldn't deny that the prospect of my actually selling something I had painted was intriguing. Later that day, when things grew slow at the café, I agreed to take Aunt Zipporah's car and drive home so I could get started on setting up the studio.

"Don't forget to make yourself something for dinner. I'll check the kitchen to be sure you did," she warned.

As soon as I got there, I hurried back to the studio.

My grandfather hadn't known how I wanted anything set up, so he had placed everything in one corner. I wanted to be working as close as I could to the two windows on the east side of the building. They looked out at the forest and tall, wild grasses. It wasn't dissimilar from the view I had looking out of the Doral House attic windows.

I had some cleanup to do before I could get myself organized and actually get started. There was still some of the granite the sculptor had used and chips of stone all about the floor. I first had to sweep up all that. I brought over the brooms, mop, pail, rags and soaps, including the window cleaner. Since the studio hadn't been used for years, there were spiderwebs and, in some corners, tiny twigs and hay, where field mice and the like had established their homes. When I tried the lights, I realized some of the bulbs were missing and most were blown out. I'd have to tend to all that before it became too dark.

Although the kitchenette had running water and a working gas range, much of it was rusted and grimy.

I quickly realized it would take quite a while to get the studio livable. Now I appreciated the time off Uncle Tyler was giving to me. I got started as soon as I could and was so into the work, I didn't hear anything.

Suddenly, as if he'd been a ghost, I turned and saw Duncan standing in the doorway. He had his hands on his hips. He was wearing jeans, black boots and a tight, dark-blue short-sleeve shirt. He appeared taller, broader, more like a grown man than a teenage boy. He panned the studio and nodded.

"Nice," he said.

"How long have you been there?"

"Little while, not long."

"Where have you been?"

"I had work to do on the farm," he replied quickly. "I see you've changed your hair. It's nice."

"Thank you."

"It looks like you have a lot to do here," he said and walked over to my art materials. My grandfather had stacked some of my finished paintings against the wall. Duncan looked at them. "This is all your work?"

"Yes."

"It's very good," he said.

"Really?"

He smiled. "Okay. I'm no art expert, but they look good to me. Have you shown them to your art teacher?" he asked with a wry smile.

"Not those, but he's seen my work in school."

"Anyone else seen these?"

"No."

"They should be seen by the public. You know, like getting poems published?"

"All right. You've made your point, big shot."

He laughed and walked to the table, sorting through the cleaning materials.

"I'll start with the windows, inside and out," he said. "Okay?"

"Yes, thank you."

"Let's get going," he said and started to work.

We were both so into it that we barely spoke. Every once in a while, I glanced over at him and saw how intently he went at everything and with such confidence. After doing the windows, he found my uncle Tyler's tools in the toolshed, and he took the stove apart and cleaned it carefully. He replaced the dead bulbs, checked out all the electricity and opened and cleaned a drain in the sink. He had to readjust the inside of the toilet, because when the water valve was turned to on, it wouldn't stop running. He corrected a leak in the sink faucet as well.

"You're a plumber, an electrician and a carpenter built into one person," I said. "Have you done this kind of work for someone?"

"I told you. I take care of our property. I had to learn how to do all these things because my father left us. Some of it I did learn from plumbers and electricians who came around before I could handle things myself, and some of it I learned from manuals. Our property is one of the older ones in this area, so a lot breaks down."

"I was told it was once a chicken farm?"

"Not chickens, eggs," he said. "The coops are still standing, but we don't use them for anything. It's a big property on Dunn Road as soon as you make the turn off Stark. We just keep up the house."

"Well, that shouldn't be so much work."

He smiled. "Sometimes I think my mother breaks things deliberately so I'll have to stay around to fix them."

"Really? Why is she like that?"

"Maybe she's just lonely," he said.

"She has no friends of her own?"

"Just people involved with the church, but they aren't friends the way you and I would think of friends."

"She never met anyone else? Any other man?" I asked. I recalled what Aunt Zipporah had suggested about his mother and the pastor.

He shook his head. If it was true, he didn't want to admit to it, I thought.

"Maybe she will," I suggested.

"I doubt it. She should have been a nun. She lives like one anyway."

I wanted to say I was sorry, but I didn't know if that was right to say. When he talked about her, he didn't sound angry, just resigned. This was his mother; this was his life. There was nothing more to do about it.

I looked at the time and saw we had been working for hours and hours.

"I have to make something for dinner or my aunt will be angry. Can you stay for dinner?"

He looked at me with an expression of confusion, as if such a possibility not only never occurred to him but also didn't exist in the real world. He revealed why.

"I never ate in anyone else's home but my own."

"Never?"

"Well, no one else's except our pastor's, but when and if we're there, Mother does most of the cooking anyway. She doesn't like going to the homes of the other church people," he said. "My mother isn't comfortable eating at someone else's table, and she always complains about the way some of the other women cook and bake for the church."

"Well, do you want to have dinner with me?"

"Yes," he said. "Yes," he repeated more firmly, as if he had been arguing about it with himself. I had to laugh. "What?" he asked.

"You didn't even ask what we'll have to eat."

"Oh. What will we have to eat?"

"I don't know. Let's go look in the kitchen," I said, and we headed out and to the house.

We entered through the rear and I took him down the hallway, past my bedroom. The door was opened, so I paused.

"That's where I sleep," I said, nodding at the doorway.

He approached it and looked in, but he didn't go in. He leaned over to peer into it.

"It's a nice-size room."

"We added some things since I came and will be spending the next school year here. My aunt wants me to think about doing something with the walls, paint, wallpaper, making it brighter, happier."

He nodded. "Be easy to paint it."

"Would you help me do that?"

His eyes widened. "Paint your bedroom?"

"You just said it would be easy to do it, didn't you?"

"Yeah, but . . . it's your bedroom."

"So? I can't have anyone else work on it? That's stupid."

He looked in again, still keeping himself out of the room, even leaning more awkwardly to look to the right or left.

"You can go in if you want to and look around."

"Naw, I've seen enough," he said. He looked a little frightened.

"You think going into a girl's bedroom will somehow corrupt you?"

He spun on me as if I had slapped him. "You making fun of me?"

"No, but you're acting so—"

"Weird?" he said. "Right, I'm weird. I forgot." He started back toward the rear door.

"Duncan, stop it. I didn't say you were weird."

"It's all right. It doesn't matter. I just realized I can't stay for dinner anyway. My mother made a roast. See you," he said, and before I could say another word, he was out the door.

Nevertheless, I charged out after him. He practically ran to his scooter parked in front.

"Duncan," I called as he turned it around to head down and out the driveway. He kept going. "Thanks for helping me in the studio," I shouted.

He just lifted his hand to acknowledge and sped up.

"Damn you!" I screamed after him. "You took me to the river. You kissed me. If I thought you were that weird, why would I let you do that? Why are you running away now?"

Of course, he couldn't hear me. He was too far away, but I needed to shout it after him. I stood there long after he was gone, my head spinning because of his radical mood swings. After another moment, I went back into the house and paused at my bedroom door. *What could possibly have frightened him about this room so much?* I wondered and then saw a pair of my panties on the back of a chair and a bra dangling beside it. I had forgotten to put them into the laundry hamper. Aside from the dainty curtains, there was nothing else that really stamped this room a girl's room. I couldn't imagine why the sight of a pair of panties and a bra would put the shudders into a boy as old as Duncan anyway.

Suddenly, I realized how tired and grimy I felt from hours and hours of cleaning the studio. I needed a good shower, perhaps not so much because of all the work as because of the frustration I was feeling. There was something about warm water pounding down over my head and shoulders that was reviving. Afterward, I wrapped a towel around myself, then scrubbed my hair dry with another towel. I know I was muttering to myself aloud the whole time. Anyone who heard me would surely think I had gone mad. When I stepped out of the bathroom and walked back to my bedroom, I nearly jumped out of my skin.

There he was, sitting at my small desk, leaning over and staring down at the floor.

"Damn!" I screamed. "You frightened me, Duncan."

"I'm sorry," he said and slowly raised his head. The sight of me wrapped only in a big bath towel seized his full attention, but I didn't think about it. I was more angry now than anything.

"Why did you run out of here like a lunatic?" I said. He didn't respond. "It wasn't very nice to act like that. You're like a firecracker sometimes. I'm afraid to walk too fast around you, much less say anything. Well? Why did you run off?"

"I was afraid to stay any longer," he said, looking out the window.

"Why?"

"I was just afraid."

"You're not making any sense, Duncan. What were you afraid of? Me?"

"Not you so much as myself."

I stared at him a moment. What was he telling me? Was he capable of harming someone? Had he? I didn't recall anything in his poetry that suggested it.

"Can you explain that, please?"

"I told her I kissed you," he said, still looking out the window and not at me.

"What? You told who you kissed me? Your mother?"

He nodded, and I grimaced as if I had just swallowed sour milk.

"Why would you tell her that?"

"I've always told her what I do. Ever since . . ." He turned back to me, his face different, harder, more like the granite in the studio. "Sin doesn't just happen, you know. It has to fester inside you, grow, take hold. You've got to stop it when it's just starting, when it's a seedling inside your heart. The way to do that is to reveal it, confess it, expose it," he recited. "Once you do that, it loses its power, its hold over you."

He sounded like some hell and brimstone preacher.

"What are you saying? You think it was a sin to kiss me?"

"It could lead to a sin," he said.

"That's ridiculous. Looking at someone then could lead to a sin."

"It can," he said, nodding.

"Duncan, get real. All we did is kiss, and if two people feel something for each other, it's not a sin or even the start of one."

He stared at me. I tightened the towel around me.

"I wanted to do more than just kiss you," he said. "I still do. That's why I ran off."

"So? Big deal. If you didn't, I'd think you weren't interested in me, and if I didn't want you to, I'd let you know anyway. And fast," I added.

His eyes widened.

"Where are you getting these wacky ideas?"

"They're not wacky," he shot back.

"If you ask me," I continued, "your mother is driving you crazy. You already told me she deliberately finds ways to keep you at home. Wait a minute," I said, realizing something, "is that why I hadn't seen you for days? Because you told her you kissed me?"

He looked away quickly.

"That's sick, Duncan. You're old enough to know what you should and shouldn't do, and so am I. We're not children anymore. She shouldn't treat you like one."

"She doesn't treat me like a child."

"Really?"

"She doesn't mean to be mean to me. She's afraid."

"Why? I just don't understand it. Why is she so

afraid for you? Have you done something terrible?"
I asked.

"No. Not yet."

"Not yet?" I nearly laughed aloud. "Why do you
say that? Do you think you definitely will?"

"I'm . . ."

"What, Duncan? What are you?"

"I'm a child of sin," he said.

He looked down quickly. I stood there a moment,
and then I walked to my bed and sat.

"A child of sin?"

"Yes. It's why you were drawn to me and why I
was drawn to you and still am," he continued, as if he
had made an incredible discovery. "We're the same.
Don't you see?"

"I'm not getting it, Duncan," I said. "How are you
a child of sin, and how are we the same?"

He looked up at me.

"Just like your parents, my father and mother
weren't married when they made me. They didn't get
married until later. No one knows."

"And so that makes us children of sin?"

He nodded.

"Who told you this? Did your mother tell you
this? Well?"

"She's just trying to help me," he said defensively.
"She's devoted her whole life to me. She works for
God so God will have mercy on me."

"And you believe this? You believe because to
some people having a child out of wedlock makes
them sinners, the children are full of sin, too?"

"It's in Scripture. 'Those of you who are left will
waste away in the lands of their enemies because of

their sins; also, because of their father's sins they will waste away.' Leviticus 26:39."

"Is that something your mother made you memorize?"

"We read the Bible every night," he said. "Besides, you believe it yourself."

"I do not!"

"Yes, you do. That's when I knew you and I were so alike. When you told me how the people in your hometown saw you as evil, I knew you saw yourself the same way. You inherited it just like I did. You so much as told me that, didn't you? You shouldn't sit there with such a look of surprise on your face at why I think we're the same.

"And don't tell me you haven't thought about it. A lot," he added. "Don't tell me you look in the mirror and don't see what I see when I look in the mirror. Remember, you told me you had similar feelings and thoughts, similar to what you saw in my poems, and you said you expressed them through your art.

"You didn't say it, but you as much as told me that the tragedy you went through, the death of that boy, was in your mind as somehow your fault, that you will and would bring only trouble and pain to anyone who cares about you or gets involved with you. Well?" he asked sharply. "Well?" he nearly shouted.

I shuddered. He hadn't forgotten a word, not a syllable, and I couldn't deny it.

"Yes," I cried. "I have those thoughts."

He nodded, smiling.

"But the difference between us is I don't need to be reminded of them, especially by my family. Or by a parent!" I said.

"Like having a father who pretends he's not your father?" he asked smugly.

The tears that were coming from my eyes felt so hot that I thought they would scald my cheeks as they jerked down toward my chin.

"That's mean, Duncan."

He nodded. "I'm sorry. It is mean to say it, but it underscores how alike you and I really are."

I flicked the tears off my cheeks and sucked in my breath. "So why did you just come back if that's what you think? Why did you even come here today? Why be around another sinner or someone who could cause you to be a sinner?"

He took a while to respond. First he looked out the window again. Then he looked at his hands and the floor before he looked at me.

"Because like you, even though I say it, I don't want to believe all that and besides . . . I can't help wanting to be with you. Most of the time, as you know from my poem, I feel like I'm in a cage, but when I'm with you, I feel free, even if it's a reckless feeling, a reckless freedom, it's still . . . it feels good."

"Then it can't be bad, Duncan, and you can't let your mother or anyone else make you think it is. And don't whip yourself with Scripture either."

"I know," he said softly. "I know." He looked up at me again, and this time, I thought there were tears in his eyes, too. "Will you help me overcome this idea?"

"Yes," I said. "We'll help each other."

He smiled softly. I held out my hand, and he slowly reached for it. For a moment that was all we did, hold onto each other's hand. Then his grip grew stronger, and he rose to come to me. He knelt before me and lowered his head to my lap. I stroked his hair, and we were like that for a while, neither of us speaking.

He's right about us, I thought. *We are similar.* According to what he was telling me, he was afraid he would turn out to be his father, and I was running away from my grandparents and Sandburg because in my heart I was afraid I would turn out to be my mother. These thoughts drove us into the same dark corner, only at the moment he seemed more helpless, deeper driven. I was at least trying to escape from myself.

"Oh, Duncan," I moaned.

When he lifted his head this time and looked into my eyes, I couldn't help but lean toward him and draw his lips to mine. In a way we were both throwing each other a lifeline, pulling each other out of the darkness.

We kissed a soft, but long, kiss. I could feel him trembling, and it wasn't because I had excited him. He was trembling with fear. It both annoyed and angered me, and I was sure he saw that in my eyes.

"You're not going to go to hell because of how you feel about me, Duncan. I don't care what your mother or anyone has told you or how you have been made to interpret what you read in the Bible."

He looked a little ashamed that he was so easily read. I touched his cheek and smiled.

"Who knows? Maybe you'll find a little heaven with me," I said, and he smiled.

"You are good," he said with confidence. "I know you're good for me."

"We're good for each other."

"Yes, yes. You're right."

He kissed me again and I kept my hands around his shoulders, pulling him toward me until he was on the bed with me.

"Don't be afraid," I whispered to drive back his hesitation. "Not of me, not of yourself."

He looked down at me, and then, like a little boy opening a Christmas Day package, he began to undo my towel.

15

Two of a Kind

At first it seemed that all he would do is gaze upon me, feast with his eyes and then wrap me up again and run out. I anticipated it. I held my breath. Was it wrong for me to study his face while he looked at me? I was fascinated with how he reacted to me, to the power I seem to have over him. I could almost see the struggle inside him to look but not touch.

"I've never been like this with any other girl," he said in a hoarse whisper.

"You could have fooled me," I told him and then quicky smiled.

He lowered himself to kiss me again, to kiss my breasts and then gently lowered the side of his head to my body, just under my breasts.

"I can hear your heart pounding," he said.

"I can, too."

He kissed my stomach and I held my breath, waiting to see where he would bring his lips next, but he closed his eyes and turned over instead to lie beside me and look up at the ceiling. A part of me was disappointed, and a part of me was filled with curiosity. How could he pause, be so controlled?

"We can't go too far," he said. "What if we did exactly what our parents have done? I'm not . . . prepared to go any further," he said, sounding a little embarrassed.

I turned to him and reached out to turn his face to mine.

"You're right," I said. "You don't have to be ashamed of it either. It's not unmanly or stupid. I don't think any less of you. We're not going to inherit any sin," I added firmly, and he smiled.

He leaned over to kiss me, and we held each other.

"But that doesn't mean we can't want each other, need each other and love each other," I added.

He smiled and kissed me again before lying back to think. His gaze moved over the room slowly, as if he wanted to commit every inch of it and every second of us now to his memory forever.

"I've never been in any girl's room before," he told me.

"I've read that whomever you do the first things in your life with you never forget."

"I couldn't forget you no matter what."

"Does this mean you're going to help me paint it now?"

He laughed. "Okay, okay. I'm a dork."

"No, you're not, Duncan. And don't think I'm so much more advanced than you are when it comes to all this. I had one boyfriend for a split second."

"Split second?"

"That's how it seemed to me."

I brushed back his hair.

"Now I have two."

He laughed. "You're the first girl who constantly surprises me."

"Do you like that?"

"Yes, very much."

"Are you reconsidering having dinner with me?"

"She'll be mad at me, but that's okay," he said with a new determination.

"Good. I'm getting hungry. Go see what you can find in the kitchen while I finish getting dressed."

He kissed me again, and then he got up and walked out.

Was I mad to keep trying with him, to still want to be around him after what he had just revealed? I wondered as I dressed and fixed my hair. Was it arrogant of me to think I could help him when I had trouble finding ways to help myself? Really, how far could two emotional and psychological cripples go with each other? Which voice within me should I listen to more, the one that was telling me to run from him or the one that was telling me he and I needed each other?

"I can make the salad," he said when I entered the kitchen. He had a large bowl and ingredients spread over a counter. "There's some packages of pasta in the pantry, and in the refrigerator I saw what looks like some of the pasta sauce you have at the café and sell in jars. I've seen people gobbling it up at the café and raving about it."

I went to put that together while he worked on the salad. He was very good, very meticulous at cutting up vegetables and tomatoes and slicing onions. He even prepared a salad dressing out of oil and vinegar and some spices he had found. He caught me looking at him in amazement.

"What?" he asked, smiling.

"How do you know how much of each ingredient to use?"

"It takes years of experience." He paused and thought. "I suppose they'd call me a mama's boy because I work with her in the kitchen so often."

"My uncle's a great chef and no one's going to call him a mama's boy," I told him. That brought a smile to his face.

"Let's have the salad while the pasta cooks," he suggested, and we sat and began to eat. Aunt Zipporah had some of the café's special garlic rolls in the freezer. I had put them in the oven, so we had them as well.

"This is really looking like a feast," Duncan said.

As it turned out, he knew how long to cook the pasta better than I did, explaining that most people overcook it. He prepared that as well and mixed in the sauce.

"I should tell my uncle about you. Maybe you could work at the café part-time. You really are good at all this. You're the one who's full of surprises, Duncan, not me."

"I wouldn't have time even for a part-time job. I do a lot more than fix broken faucets at our home," he said. "My mother is very occupied with her mail-order work for the church and the like, so I often do all the house cleaning, make the beds, and I do most of our shopping, too, while she's at a church meeting or something. She won't let me take the car at any other time," he added. "She's very unhappy that I fixed up my scooter. She wouldn't give me the money for the insurance and registration. I had to scrounge that up myself."

"How did you get the scooter in the first place?"

"It was something my father had gotten from some job he was on and left in one of the coops."

"Exactly how long has your father been gone?" I asked him.

"Close to ten years."

"Did he just leave one day and not tell anyone?"

"That's what my mother says. I never saw a note, if that's what you mean."

"And he never called or sent a letter, nothing?"

He thought for a moment, ate some more and nodded.

"There were times when I was about eight or nine that I thought he did call to speak with her, but she never came out and said so and asking about him only drove her into a horrible rant. Sometimes, she became so enraged, I was terrified. Almost immediately after he left us, she changed her name back to her maiden name, Simon."

"How come your name wasn't changed, too?"

"It was, but I wouldn't accept it. It's the one defiant thing I've done. Up until now, that is," he added, smiling at me to clearly indicate I was the second defiant thing. "Thankfully, she's stopped harping on it, but she doesn't hesitate to correct anyone who calls her Edna Winning, and if someone refers to me as Duncan Winning, she'll correct him or her as well. It was a problem at school for a while, but it's not anymore. She doesn't have much to do with my schooling anyway. She never went to a parent-teacher conference, and my grades have been good enough to keep me from being of much concern."

"You've never been in trouble at school, given them a reason to call her?"

"You can't even begin to imagine what that would have done. I've always been conscious of her expectation that I would get into trouble, and I'm probably known as a goody-goody boy or something because of it. I'm the only one who calls his teachers sir and ma'am, if I don't call them Mr., Mrs., Miss. One of my teachers, Donna Balm, insists on being called Miz Balm. She won't let me call her ma'am either. She says, 'Ma'am is short for madam, and I'm no madam,'" he told me, obviously imitating her. I laughed.

He ate some more and then said, "You'll see when you go to our school."

"See what?"

"How the other students don't trust me, especially the other guys, because I won't smoke in the bathroom, do pot with them or take some of those pills they circulate sometimes. They think I'm some sort of spy for the administration or something. If you hang out with me, they'll treat you like a leper, too."

"I'm used to it," I said.

"Yeah, but you came here to get away from all that, didn't you? You think because no one knows you here, they'll accept you and you'll make friends. I can only make that harder for you."

"Let me decide whom I want and don't want for friends, Duncan."

"I'm just warning you."

Maybe he was, and maybe he was right. I shook the thought from my mind. After all, hadn't Craig faced the same problems and stood by me? Somehow, we had to find the strength to prevent other people from dictating our lives to us. He and I had the same challenges in a sense. We were truly alike. *Ironically, it's more often than not that people who are unlike each other end up together but don't find that out until it's too late,* I thought. His parents certainly fit that definition.

"Where did your father and mother meet?" I asked.

"She was going to a nearby all-girls prep school and he was a custodian, a handyman there. From the little she will tell me about that, about him, I understood that he was what she calls persuasive. That's the nicest word she'll use. Sometimes," he said, lowering his voice as if there were people nearby who could overhear us, "I believe she thinks he was the devil himself, seducing her. Anyway, after they did get married, they bought our property, and for a while it was a very successful egg farm. She said he began to drink heavily and that was when things got bad, so bad, she says, that he no longer cared about her or me."

He put his fork down and looked very pensive.

"What?"

"Maybe it was just wishful thinking, but there were times, not lately, but times when I had the feeling he was nearby, watching me. I used to dream about him coming by while I was walking to town or school. He would stop to offer me a lift and I would know it was my father immediately. It got so I studied every driver in every car that passed by me. Sometimes, I'd sit by my window and look out in anticipation of seeing him standing off to the side somewhere watching our house, anticipating me stepping out. I'd even go out and walk around aimlessly just in the hope that was true.

"My mother knew it. I could tell, and it made her furious. It got so I was afraid to even think about him in her presence, afraid she might see it in my face. She has a way of looking right through people and seeing their most inner thoughts and feelings."

"Oh, Duncan, I don't think she has such a power."

"No, it's true. Whenever we go to the church or she meets some of the people, she mutters about this one or that one, telling me things I have no idea how she could know."

"Maybe she's just assuming things, guessing."

"Believe me. She can do it," he insisted. "She's very strong in her own way. Other women would probably have folded up and gone running to their parents or family, begging to be taken in or something. She just seems to get stronger, harder with every hardship. She's always telling me that God tests us continually. I'm sure I'm being tested now."

"Because you're with me?"

"Yes, but I won't run from you again," he promised. "At least, I hope I won't."

"You better not. At least until you help me clean up here," I added, and he laughed.

"When she sees you, really gets to know you, she'll realize you're a good person, Alice."

"I hope so. I hope I am," I said.

"What about your parents? Your father?"

"He has another family and lives in California. I saw them recently, and he was the closest to me he's ever been. When he left, I had the feeling he would spend more time with me or care more about me, but that hasn't happened yet. His wife is very protective of their children, twin boys, and they've kept my existence, my relationship with him, a secret from the twins and from their friends."

"And you've really never seen your mother?"

"No. Someday, maybe," I said. "I often do what you said you do, imagine her around."

"Aren't we a pair of pathetic losers," he muttered.

"The jury's still out on that," I said, recalling one of my grandfather's favorite expressions. Duncan smiled.

I rose and began to clear the table, and he quickly joined in. Side by side, we washed and dried the dishes, bowls, silverware and then cleaned the counters and the table, putting everything in its proper place. By the time we were done, even Sherlock Holmes would have trouble proving anyone had eaten dinner here.

"My aunt's going to think I skipped dinner. I'm going to have to prove it to her," I said.

"You going to tell her I was here?"

"Why not?"

"Your uncle might not like it."

"They haven't told me not to have anyone here. They certainly know I'm seeing you. My aunt trusts me and wants me to be happy," I added, but I wondered if she might think I had been sneaky about it, pretended to have lost interest in him and hidden our secret meetings from her. I made up my mind to be sure to explain it all to her.

"They might forbid you to see me again. I can't blame them."

"Stop it, Duncan. My aunt knows who you are. She's never said anything like that to me."

He shrugged.

I recalled one of my uncle Tyler's favorite rhetorical, philosophical questions. "If you don't like yourself, Duncan, why should anyone else like you?"

"I don't know if I like myself or not," he said. He

looked at me intently, his eyes narrow, his face tight. "Like you, I'm still trying to find out who I am."

"Okay," I said. Whenever he became this intense, I felt myself tremble. "Let's just keep trying."

He said nothing.

I walked him out to his scooter. It was once again fully overcast. The air had the scent of impending rain. Way off in the distance, there was a flash of lightning.

"You'd better get home before it starts to pour," I said.

He nodded and got on his scooter.

"Any idea about what you're going to do for your first painting yet?"

I started to shake my head and then stopped.

"Yes, I think I do. It has something to do with a doe I once saw back there. I know that much, but not any more until I start."

"Sounds promising," he said and kick-started his scooter. I felt the first drop.

"It's starting, Duncan. How long will it take you to get home?"

"Twenty minutes at the most," he said. "I've ridden in the rain before. Don't worry."

"Not after being with me, though," I told him. It was almost a reflex to say it, and the words came out before I could stop them.

He stared and then nodded. "I thought you believed we both have to quit doing that," he said.

"What?"

He turned the scooter around.

"Thinking we're bad luck to everyone who has anything to do with us."

"You're right. I'm sorry. That was stupid."

"It's all right. Don't beat yourself up. You going to the café to work tomorrow?"

"No, I have the day off. My uncle wants me to get started on my art."

"Good."

He leaned forward to kiss me, and then he was off.

Like a curtain being lowered, the rain started to fall, the drops pounding on the leaves and the road as hard as the pounding in my heart. I hurried back into the house. Almost twenty minutes later, the phone rang. I lunged for it, hoping it was Duncan letting me know he was safe. Perhaps he had seen the concern in my face and heard it in my voice after all.

It wasn't Duncan. It was my father.

"Hey," he said. "How are you doing up there?"

"Good," I said. I wanted to ask him if Grandma had called him complaining that he hadn't called me, but I thought it wouldn't be nice. Also, he might be doing it on his own.

"Your grandmother told me your decision. Are you sure you're doing the right thing? Leaving school just at the start of your senior year to start in a new place—"

"I never felt like I belonged back there anyway," I said.

He was quiet a moment. "Yeah, I guess I understand that. Well, if you want to talk to anyone about it, don't hesitate to call me. I'll check on you from time to time."

"Okay."

"Tell Zipporah hello for me."

"I will," I said.

He wished me luck and said good-bye. I felt bad

about not being more talkative, but I couldn't help thinking about Duncan. I was sorry I didn't insist he call me when he got home. Finally, I decided I would call him. It took me a while to find his telephone number because his mother wasn't listed in the telephone book under Winning. I finally remembered he had told me she had changed her name back to her maiden name, Simon. I found the listing, but I hesitated to call.

Would I get him into some sort of trouble by calling? I tried to occupy myself with reading and with some television, but nothing worked.

The rain was really thumping on the roof by now, and I heard the thunder and saw some more lightning. It had been nearly an hour since he had left. I had to know he was safe. I wouldn't sleep. Memories of my car accident were flashing across my eyes, sending shivers up and down my spine. Would I cause someone else's death, someone else who dared to get close to me?

As I paced about, I thought that my limp was becoming more and more pronounced, as though it were meant to be another reminder—or maybe a prophecy. Soon I was envisioning him sprawled on some highway, the rain pummeling his face and his hand, his body twisted and broken, and then his mother arriving and screaming to the police and to the paramedics, "It's all because of her! My son is dead because he met her!"

Finally, I could contain myself no longer. With trembling fingers, I dialed the number. It barely rang once.

"I'm all right," I heard him say in a deep, hoarse

whisper and then hang up. He didn't even say hello; he was that sure he was getting a phone call from me. Or maybe, maybe his mother knew, could see through everything just as he had said. Maybe he had confessed again, told her every detail.

It was as if the lightning sizzling the air outside had shot through the window and sizzled my heart in half as well. I held the receiver and listened to the hum. Then I hung up slowly, just as my uncle and aunt arrived home from the café. I heard Aunt Zipporah call for me.

"Wow!" she exclaimed. "This is a real summer downpour," she said, shaking her hair.

"It's a good night for Macbeth's witches," Uncle Tyler added, laughing. "How are things going with the studio?"

"We got a lot done," I replied.

"We?" Aunt Zipporah asked, and I told her all about Duncan's surprise visit, helping me in the studio and then his helping prepare our dinner.

She and Uncle Tyler looked at each other with obvious surprise.

"I hope that was all right," I said quickly.

"Oh, sure it was," Aunt Zipporah replied.

"He got home ahead of this mess, I hope," Uncle Tyler said, indicating the rain.

"Just barely."

"Everything else all right?" Aunt Zipporah asked me, her voice ringing with curiosity and some suspicion.

"Far as I know," I replied.

"Well, this will be a good test of the repairs to the roof we did this year," Uncle Tyler said and started upstairs.

Aunt Zipporah lingered, fidgeting with things in the kitchen. I knew she was still concerned. She walked into the living room, where I was sitting and trying to read one of the books I knew I had to read for my upcoming senior year. My eyes continually moved off the page, and my thoughts drifted away from the story and characters so much that I couldn't remember what I had just read.

"So, now that you've spent more time with Duncan," she began, "what's he really like?"

I told her more details about the things he had done at the studio and how he had been so good at helping with dinner. The more I spoke, the wider her smile became.

"You sound like you like him very much, Alice."

"Yes, I do," I admitted.

"That's fine. I know his mother is pretty much to herself. I haven't seen her around, at any stores, shopping—"

"He does the shopping for them," I said quickly.

"Oh. I'm sure Mrs. Mallen is right. His youth has been stolen from him. It's not easy for him to make new friends."

"It's not that easy for me."

She thought a moment. I could almost see the thoughts and questions careening about in her mind.

"Well then, do you think he's the best young man for you at this time? I don't want to sound negative, but you and I know you have your own problems. Adding to your own burdens might not be wise."

"Did you think like that when you hung out with my mother?" I countered.

"It was different then, Alice. I had little or no baggage to carry, and Karen's mother and stepfather were in an active business in the community. There were people who thought her mother was a gold digger, but that was about as critical as anyone was about them. I'm just telling you to be careful, that's all. I don't want to stifle you or clip your wings, but I wouldn't be doing my duty if I didn't voice my concerns, right?"

"No," I said. "I understand. I appreciate it," I said. "I'm sorry. I didn't mean to snap at you. I really do appreciate your concern."

"Good. It's nice of you to care about him, Alice, but be careful," she said. And then, in order to explain what she meant, she added, "Sometimes, when you invest in someone, you're like a gambler who loses and keeps gambling to win it back but only loses more. I should know."

I thought for a moment. "You've told me how wonderful it was for you to become friends with my mother. Did she feel the same way about you?"

"I thought so. She didn't have all that many friends when I met her. Actually, she had no close friends, but I thought she was the most interesting and exciting girl I had ever met and didn't care if we had lots of friends or not. If nothing else, I was a great audience for her, and I made her feel good about herself."

"I guess in a way that's what I am for Duncan," I said.

She nodded. "Just be careful, honey. One of Tyler's favorite expressions is, Don't bite off more than you can chew. The great thing about all these adages is they hold up through time." She smiled and looked at my book. "Tyler loves this novel. When you're finished, he'll be happy to talk about it with you," she said.

"Great. I'd like that."

"I'm bushed. See you in the morning," she told me and left.

I sat there listening to the rain. It didn't seem to have let up a bit. I felt my eyelids growing heavy and decided to go to sleep myself. There was a lot on my mind, so many questions and thoughts because of the things my aunt Zipporah had said. I tossed and turned so much that I didn't really drift off until the wee hours.

I was so tired in the morning that I didn't get up when I heard Tyler moving about. I fell back to sleep. When I did get up finally, I found a note on the refrigerator for me. My aunt was reminding me that they wanted me to spend the day in my studio and not worry about working in the café.

I showered to help wake myself up and then made myself some breakfast. Aunt Zipporah called to be sure I had read her note and I was okay.

"I hope I didn't upset you last night, Alice."

"No. Stop worrying about it."

"Call the café if you need anything," she said.

I thanked her. Moments after I hung up, the phone rang again. This time it was Duncan, and he wasn't whispering.

"I'm sorry I was so abrupt last night when you called," he said, "but she was hovering right over me. She was very angry that I didn't call and tell her I wouldn't be home for dinner."

"Now she hates me, is that it?"

"No, she didn't even ask me why I didn't call or where I was. She's like that. She knows."

"Duncan—"

"No, she knows," he insisted. "Anyway, she's punishing me by not taking me along on her church trip today."

"That's a punishment?" I asked, laughing.

"She says I don't deserve God's grace until I show real remorse. She just left."

"Well, I don't think—"

"She'll be gone almost all day," he said, quickly interrupting. "I know you want to get into your painting, but maybe I'll see you later, if that's all right."

"Of course it's all right. You can make me a wonderful lunch."

He didn't laugh. He said nothing.

"Duncan?"

"I'll see. I have a few things I promised I'd get done around the house."

"I'm not going anywhere today," I said. He was silent again. "Are you okay?" I asked.

"Yes," he said. "I just . . . yes, I'm okay. Forget what I said. I'm sure I'll be tied up with all this. We have a serious plumbing problem. Our submersible well."

"Maybe you should call someone."

"I can handle it," he said defensively. "Forget I called. Sorry," he said and hung up.

"Duncan? Damn," I muttered and hung up the receiver. He was so complicated. One moment he was hot and then he was cold and it was almost impossible to anticipate when and why he would change. What's more, I had no idea what would make him change. It didn't have to have anything to do with me or what I said. He could be hearing voices only he heard. I should know about that.

I thought about my conversation with my aunt Zipporah. She was so right. I had to start thinking more about myself. I was getting in too deeply with someone who had as many, if not more, problems as I did.

Don't bite off more than you can chew.

It was good advice.

If you did bite off more than you could chew, you'd only choke.

And I didn't come here to choke.

I came here to be free and happy, to be that baby the stork left on the doorstep, to be my own person.

Maybe it was mean, but I was hoping he wouldn't come to see me.

To shove away my conscience, I dove headlong into my drawing and my painting. Happily, I quickly lost myself in my own imaginative world.

My grandmother didn't realize it when she gave me my name, but I was Alice and my art was truly my Wonderland.

16

Peeping Tom

Duncan didn't come around at lunchtime. In fact, I was so involved in my work that I forgot about lunch and didn't think about it at all until I had a bubbling in my stomach and realized that I was getting hungry and hadn't eaten. It was midafternoon by then. I paused to go into the house to get myself something to eat and decided that I would work on stocking my own little kitchen space in the studio to avoid long interruptions. I quickly ate half of a peanut butter sandwich and returned to the studio.

Because there was no phone in the studio, neither my aunt nor Duncan could speak with me. It didn't occur to my aunt until she started calling to see how I was doing, expecting that I would be in the kitchen around lunchtime. She drove Tyler so crazy with her concern that he finally sent her to the house to check up on me by late afternoon. When I heard footsteps behind me, I thought it was Duncan. I was sure anyone could read the disappointment in my face.

"Have you been at it all day?" she asked, smiling to hide her concern.

"Yes. I did eat something," I added quickly.

"Can I look at your work?"

"It's hardly anything yet," I said.

I stepped back from the easel, and she gazed at my work in progress.

"That's interesting, Alice. Your doe has an almost human face."

I looked at it myself. I hadn't realized it.

"It's going to be something," she said. She looked around. "You've been at this since you got up this morning?"

"Yes."

"Aren't you getting a little tired?"

"I guess. It's usually not until I stop that I realize it, however."

She laughed. "How about coming back to the café with me? You don't have to work, but Tyler's made this fantastic lasagna special, and you should have some before we sell out."

"Okay," I said and began putting things away.

"Has Duncan Winning been here today?" she finally asked. I knew she had been dying to do so.

"No. He called. His mother was angry at him for having dinner here last night." I described her punishment for him. "Isn't that odd? Why would she think that would upset him so much?"

"I'm sure it's difficult for him."

"He's so accomplished in so many ways," I said as we walked out. "Mechanically talented, poetic. Why can't his mother appreciate all that and let him be?"

"You remind me so much of your mother sometimes," she said. "She used to get so angry at the way some of the parents treated their children, but she would then just pretend she was a witch and put a spell on them."

"Maybe she put a spell on her own mother, too," I said, and Aunt Zipporah looked at me strangely. She said nothing else about it, however.

The café was as slow as Uncle Tyler had predicted it would be. Most of the time, I sat around talking either with Aunt Zipporah or Cassie, who was suddenly surprisingly open about herself, telling me about her social life and her on-and-off love affair with a boy named Johnny Skyler. She said that whenever he became too serious with her, he would pull back, fearing that he was missing out on something.

"He's so obvious about it, too. He's a terrible liar."

"Why do you stay with him?" I asked her. I didn't want to show how hungry I was for conversation with other girls near my age, but it was difficult for me not to cling to every word. I was very curious about the way other girls felt about their boyfriends and how they handled the conflicts and problems.

She shrugged, looking like I was the first one who had asked her that question.

"Amusement, I guess," she said.

"How can these feelings, these relationships, be just amusing?" I quickly followed, and she looked at me to be sure I was serious.

"What do you want, true love and marriage before you're eighteen? You can't date unless it's going to be forever? Maybe during your and my great-grandmothers' time, Alice, but haven't you heard, we're liberated. Girls can be just as casual about the boys they date as boys have always been," she said with some bitterness.

With that attitude, how will she ever find true love? I wondered. But then I thought, *Maybe she's right to be as she is.* Maybe that was how you never get hurt. I was in the mood to believe that. Duncan hadn't called, and even though I was conflicted about whether I should continue to care or not, I couldn't help looking at whoever came in, half expecting to see him outside with his scooter.

She caught my glances and maybe my disappointment.

"You've been seeing Duncan Winning?"

"Sorta," I said.

"Sorta?"

"We haven't gone on any formal date."

"What's a formal date?" she asked, laughing. "These days, it's meeting in the rear seat of someone's car."

"I meant we haven't done too many things together."

"You don't have to do too many things, just one thing," she teased. She was beginning to frustrate me. "Well, I have to admit there's something sexy about him. However, I don't think I could be with him," she added quickly.

He certainly couldn't be with you, I thought, but I didn't say anything. She gave me a knowing, licentious smile, as if we now shared intimate secrets about each other. Then she went to take care of some summer school college students, three boys and two girls, who had come in for something to eat. I sat back and watched them laughing and joking with each other. They seemed so carefree, loose and happy. What were their lives like? Their parents? Would I ever be like them?

I tried not to be too obvious listening in on their conversations. Just like Cassie, they struck me as young people unconcerned about tomorrow. Yes, they were saying, the future was out there with its responsibilities, but who needed that now? Listening to them talk and picking up some tidbits of information about each, I had the impression that if they could, they'd prolong their college educations for years and years. One boy even said he was thinking about cutting his final exam just to extend his college life. They were all critical of their parents for pressuring them to get on with their lives.

"You're only young forever once," a boy said, and they all laughed.

Watching and listening to them, I felt like the poor waif standing outside the restaurant window watching other people enjoy their food. I was so into their conversation that I didn't hear Aunt Zipporah call to me. She had to come over to nudge me to get my attention.

"Hey, I was calling you. Are you okay?"

"Oh, sorry. I was daydreaming."

"Let's go home early," Aunt Zipporah told me. "Tyler doesn't need us, and I feel like soaking in a hot bath and kicking back for a change."

"Okay."

We left and started for home. When we made the turn to start down the road my aunt and uncle's house was on, I was sure I saw Duncan off to the side, half in and out of the shadows, leaning on his scooter just the way he would outside the café. I didn't say anything, but my heart was pounding. Why was he out there? Why hadn't he called or come to the café?

I didn't say anything to my aunt, first, because I wasn't absolutely sure I had seen him, and second, because I didn't want to add any more strange behavior and get her to forbid me from spending any time with him.

"You sure you're okay?" Aunt Zipporah asked.

"Yes, I'm fine."

"You're so quiet," she said as we approached the house.

"Maybe I did work too hard on my painting today. I get so into it," I said, "I don't realize how much it can drain me emotionally."

She nodded. "I understand. I just get a little nervous. I was always afraid when your mother became too quiet."

"Why?"

"I felt as if she was lowering herself into some darkness from which she wouldn't emerge, retreating into herself, locking herself away. I'd do and say anything I could think of to get her into a jolly mood again. It was like throwing someone a lifeline."

"And you're afraid I've inherited that, right? You and my grandmother are both afraid of it. I know," I said before she could deny it. "I know depression can be inherited."

"You know too much for your own good," she said, laughing. "I can't even be subtle with you."

"You don't have to be, Zipporah. I can take the truth."

"I know you can, Alice, but I wish you couldn't."

"What? Why?"

"I wish you could yet be the young girl you've a right to be. I wish you were able to fall back on your

imagination and escape harsh realities the way your
mother and I were able to do."

"Yes," I said as the garage door went up, "so do I."

I anticipated Duncan's arrival any moment and was
surprised when he didn't come to knock on the door or
ring the doorbell. I sat waiting in the living room while
Aunt Zipporah took her bath. She lit some incense and
played one of Tyler's Latin chant recordings made by
monks. She wanted me to do the same thing, assuring
me it would help me sleep and feel so much better.
She was so good at describing the beneficial effects,
and she did look so relaxed afterward, that I took her
up on it and filled the tub, relit the candles and put on
the same music. I had given up on Duncan coming to
see me.

After I undressed, I looked at the scars around
my hip. Whenever I did, it seemed I was looking at
someone else's body, as if I had risen out of my own.
It was at this moment that I really wished I could do
what Aunt Zipporah had described she and my mother
could do. Perhaps then I could look at myself and not
see the damage. However, if ever I hoped and dreamed
that what had happened had been only a nightmare,
the scars were there to shout out the reality and keep
me from forgetting or ignoring the past. My imagination was just not up to the task.

Carefully, I lowered myself into the tub and closed
my eyes. The warm water felt like a glove around my
body. The chanting was as soothing as the water, and I
did like the scent of Aunt Zipporah's incense. If only I
could stay like this forever, I mused, living in a cocoon
woven out of the warmth of the water, the music and
the scent of the incense. I'd almost sell my soul for it,

I thought and then suddenly had the feeling I wasn't alone. I opened my eyes.

The door was closed. Aunt Zipporah had gone up to bed. There was no one in the bathroom. Nevertheless, the feeling persisted. I sat up then and looked up and into the window. Duncan's face was framed in it. He was staring in at me. He wasn't smiling. He actually looked like he was in pain.

"Duncan!" I called.

He blinked, and then he was gone so fast I wasn't sure I hadn't imagined it. After all, why would he suddenly become a Peeping Tom anyway? Why wouldn't he have just come to the front door? He had seen me undressed. We had kissed and been warm and intimate with each other. What possible satisfaction would there be for him to gape at me in the tub?

I got out quickly, put out the candles and turned off the music. Then, wrapping a bath towel around myself, I shoved my feet into my slippers and, still not dry, hurried out and to the front door. I opened it and stepped out, listening and looking through the darkness.

"Duncan!" I cried. "Are you out here? Duncan!"

There was no response. I waited, my hair dripping, and then I was sure I heard the sound of his scooter somewhere farther down the road. It quickly disappeared. *He was here,* I thought. *He was.*

The entire experience gave me the shivers, on top of the fact that I was dripping wet. I rubbed myself with the towel, then went back inside. Aunt Zipporah had heard me calling. She was at the top of the stairway.

"Alice? Is something wrong?"

"No," I said quickly. "I thought I heard someone at

the front door, that's all. There was no one," I added before she could ask.

"Oh. Were you finished with your bath already?"

"Just about," I lied. "It was as wonderful as you described. Thank you."

"Okay," she said, still not sounding convinced. "Good night."

"Night."

I returned to the bathroom and wiped up the trail I had dripped. Then I emptied and cleaned the tub before getting into my nightgown and going to my bedroom. I was still shivering a little. For a while I stood by the windows and looked out at the woods and field, wondering if he was still somewhere out there or if he had returned home. I felt certain I had seen him in the window and heard his scooter on the road. I thought I heard it again, but the sound died.

It was very disturbing.

I sat thinking about it for a while, and then I decided to call him to ask him if he'd been here and why he had done that. The phone rang and rang, and I was about to hang up when I realized someone had picked up the receiver.

"Hello?"

I waited but heard no one.

"Is Duncan at home, please?" I asked.

There was a long pause, and then in a voice that put daggers of ice in my chest, I heard someone in a coarse, raspy voice, a voice that sounded like someone struggling to breathe, say, "Get thee behind me, Satan."

The connection then went dead.

If I was on my way to enter a nightmare before, I was charging into it now. For a long moment, I couldn't move; I couldn't hang up. My fingers were locked around the receiver, as if I was holding onto it for dear life. After I did hang up, I stepped away from the phone so quickly that anyone watching would have thought I expected it to explode. Catching my breath, I retreated to my bedroom and sat, dazed and confused and still quite frightened. *That had to be his mother,* I thought. She had spoken in such a chilling, hateful voice. How did she know I was calling? I guessed I was the only girl who had ever called him.

I heard Tyler come home, and I went to my bedroom doorway. Just as he started for the stairway, he saw me.

"Hey, still up?"

It was on the tip of my tongue to pour everything out of me, accompanied by my sobs, but I swallowed it back and forced a smile.

"I'm just going to sleep now," I said.

"Me too. Sweet dreams," he said and went up the stairs.

I closed my door softly and, despite my effort not to, listened to my memory. Once again I heard the raspy whisper of Duncan's mother calling me the very thing I had feared all my life . . . evil.

Falling asleep was nearly impossible. Every time I did drift off, I woke with a start, expecting to see Duncan's face in one of the windows. I even dreamed I saw his mother's face in one as well. I had no idea what she looked like. When I thought about it, I realized the face I was imagining was that of Craig's mother, Mrs. Harrison.

After all, who else's face belonged in that nightmare? Who could possibly hate me more?

Had I found someone who could?

Despite my miserable night, I rose just about the same time Tyler did.

"Hey," he said when I entered the kitchen. He laughed when he looked up at me. "You sure you're not sleepwalking?"

"I couldn't sleep anymore," I said.

He nodded, concerned.

"Yeah, I know where you're coming from. You've got too much laying on your mind, Alice. I should give you some lessons in meditation."

"Maybe," I said, pouring myself a cup of coffee.

"I meant to ask you if you knew how to drive a stick shift?"

"No. I took driver's education class in school, and going for my driver's test was part of the final, but we always drove automatics. Actually, I haven't done all that much driving in any kind of car. Grandpa's always trying to get me to take the wheel, but I've never been that interested. Another thing that makes me weird to my schoolmates, I suppose," I added. "Grandpa would probably buy me my own car if I showed any interest."

"I saw how reluctant you were to take Zipporah's car the other day. It's because of the accident you were in, right?"

"Something like that."

"You know what they say. If you fall off a bike, you should get right back on. I'd be glad to give you some lessons on my stick shift. It's a fun car to drive."

"I don't have anywhere I'd like to go."

"Well, if you change your mind, let me know. My car isn't used all day and most of the night because

I'm chained to the café. With a few lessons, it could be your way of tooling around as well." He leaned toward me and whispered, "Zipporah hates driving it, so she'll be more reluctant to give up her car."

"Thanks for the offer," I said, smiling. "Maybe I will let you give me some lessons."

"That's the spirit. You're too young not to be eager to try new things." He sipped his coffee. "Zipporah was telling me about your painting. It sounds interesting."

"I don't know. I'm just tinkering with something."

"That's how most artists do it, I bet. Well, I'd better get going. Zipporah's still asleep," he whispered. "Something was bothering her last night. She tossed and turned so much, I thought she'd bounce me out of the bed."

"Oh?"

"I'm sure it's nothing serious," he quickly added. "She's had nights like that before. Don't worry about it," he told me, but I couldn't help wondering if she had seen or heard more than she had let on last night and she was worrying about me.

I didn't want to wake her, but I didn't go into the studio for a while, hoping she would come down. Finally, I went out and started to set up to continue my painting. I tried to get back into it, but there was just too much distracting me. I did very little before I heard Aunt Zipporah call from the doorway.

"Morning," I said.

"Morning. I don't want to bother you, but I'm heading out. I overslept. You going to be all right?"

"I'm fine," I said. "You sure I shouldn't go with you to the café?"

"Tyler is adamant that you have time for your art. We're so much busier on the weekends. Don't worry about it. Call me if you need anything, okay?"

"I will. Thanks," I shouted after her.

I went to the doorway and listened to her back out of the garage and then drive off. When I turned around again, Duncan was standing in the studio bathroom doorway. He looked like he had just woken up himself. His hair was disheveled, and his eyes were still sleepy. In fact, he looked dazed.

"How did you get in there?" I asked immediately. "How long have you been in there?"

He stared at me, then scrubbed his cheeks vigorously.

"I fell asleep on the floor," he replied.

"When?"

"Last night sometime."

"Why?"

He didn't say anything. He walked over to my painting and looked at it.

"Duncan? What are you doing? Why did you peep through our bathroom window last night?" I demanded, and he turned.

"Huh? I didn't do that," he said. "Don't say that."

"I saw you looking in at me."

He shook his head. "No. I didn't do that."

"You're scaring me, Duncan. I know it was you. I heard your scooter, too. I saw you waiting in the shadows when my aunt and I came home."

"That's not true. None of that is true." He pointed to my painting. "You're in this picture, you know. You're the doe and you don't even realize why," he said angrily and charged toward the doorway.

"Duncan!"

He turned. "I gotta go. I'm sorry I scared you, but I didn't want to go home last night. My mother is still very mad at me for eating dinner here the other night and not telling her where I was, and now she'll be even angrier that I returned and spent the night away from home."

"You're admitting you were here then. You're saying you were here?"

"I was in here. That's all. I told you. I had a bad argument with her and ran out of the house. I didn't have any other place to go. I fell asleep on the bathroom floor. That's all," he said and left.

I walked slowly to the doorway and watched him trekking across the field of high grass. He was marching with his head down, as if he had to get away as quickly as he could. *He's probably just ashamed of himself,* I thought, *but to be out all night just to avoid his mother* . . . I couldn't help but feel sorry for him.

Suddenly, before he reached the road, he stopped and stood there for a moment. Then he turned around, looked toward me and slowly made his way back. I folded my arms under my breasts and walked out to meet him.

"What are you doing, Duncan?"

He kept his head down.

"I'm sorry," he said in an entirely different sounding tone of voice. "I want to be . . . to be with you, but I'm afraid of what will happen."

"What will happen?"

He looked up, his eyes glassy, but said nothing.

"I thought we decided that wouldn't be the case

with us," I said. "I thought we decided we would fight it, fight the whole idea that we inherited sin."

"No, I was wrong. Something terrible is probably going to happen to either us or people we love or love us." He looked away.

"How can you tell that?"

He shook his head but avoided looking at me.

"Your mother is telling you that, right? She is the one saying all these things. I called your house last night after I was sure you were here."

He turned back quickly. "You spoke to her?"

"Sorta. I wouldn't call it speaking to her. I asked for you and she said something terrible to me."

"What?"

"She called me Satan."

"I'm sorry," he said.

"What's wrong with her? What's her problem? She doesn't know anything about me. How could she say such a terrible thing to me?"

He didn't answer my question. Instead, he looked at me intently and said, "I've never wanted to be with any girl as much as I want to be with you, Alice. I've looked at other girls and thought about them, but I've never been this close with any and I've never been thinking day and night about any like I do about you."

I smiled. "That's all good, Duncan. There's nothing terrible about that. Don't let her make you think there is."

His face softened, his eyes more relaxed.

"You're probably hungry," I said. "C'mon. I'll make you some breakfast."

"No, I don't think . . ."

"It's nothing. I'll put up some coffee. You want

scrambled eggs? I make great scrambled eggs. Even you won't be able to improve on them," I added.

He started to smile, then looked back at the field as if someone was waiting for him.

"You've been out all night, Duncan. What difference will another hour or so make?"

My logic got to him. He nodded and followed me back into the house. He sat in the kitchen while I poured him a glass of orange juice.

"What kind of eggs would you like?"

"I'll just have some coffee. Maybe some toast," he said.

I began to prepare the coffee. I could feel his eyes intently on me, on my every move. I could also feel a trembling inside myself. When I looked at him, he just stared back. He had barely touched his juice.

"Look, Duncan, I'm no one to be giving anyone advice about how he or she should live his or her life, but you can't let your mother do this to you. You're like someone walking around with invisible chains around his wrists and his legs."

"I know," he said. He looked away for a moment, and then he turned back, wearing a more confident—almost an angry confident—expression. "I'm sorry I lied before," he said. "I did look through your bathroom window. First, when I looked in, I saw your aunt."

"Oh, Duncan."

"So I ran away and then I returned and came to your front door to apologize and I saw you going into the bathroom. I went to the window of the bathroom intending to tap on it and get your attention, but—"

"But what?"

"I didn't want to stop looking at you. I wanted to see you undress and get into the bathtub. I wanted to watch you with your eyes closed, soaking there."

I was having the strangest reaction to his confession. A part of me wanted to be angry, enraged, scream at him and tell him to get out and stay away from me forever, but another part of me was titillated, excited and fascinated with his completely uninhibited disclosure. He was as naked with his feelings as I had been in the tub. Even now, I could see the erotic pleasure lingering on his face, in his eyes, in the memory of me.

"But . . . you didn't have to look at me through a window, Duncan. You were with me in my bedroom."

"It was the forbidden part of it, seeing you without you knowing I was seeing you. It was more exciting to me," he confessed. "And then, I knew it was wrong and I fled."

"But you didn't go home."

"No!" he said, his eyes wide. "I couldn't go home. The moment she set her eyes on me, she would have known what I had done. She would see how all the lust was festering inside me."

"Oh, Duncan, you make her sound as if—"

"She would have," he insisted. "So I went around to your studio and fell asleep on the floor in the bathroom. I heard you come into the studio and I was ashamed and didn't want you to know I was there. For a while I was unable to move, struggling to think of some explanation, and then your aunt came to say good-bye and I thought I had to get away.

"But I didn't want to get away," he quickly added.

He started to get up. "Now," he said, "I'm sure you

want me to leave and you want me to stay away from you. I don't blame you."

"No," I said firmly. "I don't. I wouldn't have invited you to stay if I felt that way."

He paused and looked at me, searching my face for signs of sincerity.

"I'm not mad at you, Duncan. I understand why you're so confused and troubled, why you question every feeling you have and everything you do." I smiled, remembering something. "We're birds of a feather."

His eyes lit with a brightness I had not seen. His smile deepened until he looked like he was smiling with every ounce of his being.

"I'm glad you said that, Alice. I don't know what love is exactly. I'm far from an expert when it comes to that," he said, "but I can't imagine feeling any stronger for any girl than I do for you."

"I don't know what it is either, Duncan, but I'm glad you feel that way about me."

He held his smile a moment longer, and then it started to wither. He looked like he was hearing someone talking and he was listening. For a moment I wondered if that was true. I listened hard myself, but I heard nothing.

"What's wrong?" I asked, seeing his eyes lower and his body soften.

"She won't like it, any of it."

"Why not? It's not normal for her to feel this way and to do this to you. You've got to get her to stop tormenting you. You've got to be firm, make a firm stand. Do you hear me, Duncan? Do you?"

He nodded. "Yes," he said. "I know exactly what I have to do. I've got to cross over."

"Cross over, do whatever you have to do to make her understand that you are your own person and you have a right to your own happiness."

"Exactly," he said. "I want to do it. I want to go too far to turn back, too far for her to turn me back."

"Good. Maybe then she'll stop tormenting you and blaming you for sins you haven't committed."

"Then you'll help me, want me, be with me?"

"Yes," I said. "We'll help each other. I've told you that before, Duncan."

He started to smile, stopped, and then wore the same expression he'd had when he'd looked at me through the bathroom window.

"What?" I asked when he didn't speak.

"This time I'm prepared," he said and reached into his pocket to show me.

For a moment I was stunned at what he had in the palm of his hand.

"No worries now," he said. "We won't make the same mistake our parents made. No accidents, no unwanted babies."

I looked up at him, truly speechless.

His smile returned. "Don't you see, Alice? It's how we'll both cross over," he said. "And when I do, I'll be too far for her to reach me. And," he added, "so will you. What?" he asked when I didn't respond.

"That's not the right reason to do this, Duncan. I didn't know that was what you meant by crossing over. I want to love you and be with you, but I want it to happen because we feel it and not as a trick to defeat your mother," I said.

He stared at me for a moment silently, his eyes turning glassy and tearful as his smile evaporated.

"Yeah, right," he said, shoving his protection back into his pocket.

"Please understand, Duncan. It makes it feel . . ."

"Wrong?" he asked, his new smile wry, crooked.

"Not wrong, mechanical, almost like a procedure rather than lovemaking," I said. "You don't want that either, right?" I asked him softly.

He nodded slowly and then looked away.

"I'm glad you're here," I said. "I want to see more of you. I want to see you every day, in fact," I added, but he didn't turn back to me.

Right now, he looked like he was in a sulk, I thought. He was like a little boy being denied something he had whined for.

"I gotta go," he said.

"But what about your breakfast?"

"I'll eat something later. I gotta get back. It'll only make things worse."

"Are you sure?"

"Yes."

"You're not mad at me, are you?"

Finally, he turned back to me.

"No," he said. He forced a softer smile. "No, I'm not mad at you. I'm mad at myself. I'm an idiot."

"No, you're not. You're one of the brightest, most accomplished boys I've met."

"I thought you haven't met many," he retorted instantly.

I smiled. "I haven't. Not the way you're suggesting, but I'm not a lump of coal, Duncan. I listen, see, understand who's around me. You're special," I told him.

He seemed to relax. "Okay," he said. "But I gotta go."

I walked him to the front door.

"Where's your scooter?"

"Just down the road. Not far," he said.

We stepped out together.

"You're absolutely sure you don't want anything to eat?"

"I'm fine. I'll try to see you later," he said.

"Good."

He hesitated, and then he kissed me. We held each other for a moment, but suddenly he pulled back and turned sharply, as if he had indeed heard something. I looked in the direction he was looking.

There, parked across the road from my uncle and aunt's home, was a woman in an older blue sedan. She was looking at us. I saw she wore a shawl. I could barely make out her features because she was parked in the shade of a sprawling oak tree. I did see her cross herself and then start the car and drive away.

He didn't have to tell me who it was.

17

Inheriting Evil

He started down the driveway.

I called to him.

He lifted his hand but didn't look back. I stood there and watched him turn at the bottom of the driveway, glance in the direction his mother had gone, and then turn and walk down the road to where he had parked his scooter.

"Call me later!" I shouted after him. "Duncan, did you hear me? Call!"

He didn't respond. I watched him walk until he disappeared around a bend in the road, never lifting his head, never looking back.

It was difficult for me to concentrate on anything the remainder of the day. I continually returned to the house to see if Duncan would call. I even moved one of the telephones as close to a window as I could and kept an ear out for the sound of it ringing.

I could only imagine what he was going through at home now. Was I once again the source of someone else's troubles, someone I cared about, got too close to? I couldn't help but wonder if all this did was prove I was the pariah I had always believed I was.

Memories of how the mothers of other girls and even boys my age would tighten their grip on the hands of their children whenever I was nearby returned to me. I could see the fear in their faces. It was almost medieval to see such abject terror, such a belief in evil looming in one as small and helpless as I was. Why shouldn't I have grown up thinking I could contaminate other children if adults believed it so intently? Why shouldn't that feeling linger under my heart? Repeatedly, I replayed the sight of Duncan's mother crossing herself, as if to protect herself from whatever darkness I could send her way and perhaps had already sent into her son.

When I stepped back and looked at the doe I was now fleshing out on my canvas, I did see myself. Duncan had been right. This was not a helpless, frightened doe. It was an angry little creature stepping out of the shadowy forest to challenge the world outside. There was actually a sneer on its lips and fire in its eyes. Its body was tight, poised, more the body of a small leopard than the body of an innocent little deer.

Disgusted, I shoved the painting off the easel. It bounced on the cement floor, a corner of it smashing as it fell over. I kicked it once, driving a hole into the center of it. I threw down my paintbrushes and left the studio. For a while I just hobbled about over the grounds, mumbling to myself. I was sure if anyone saw me, he or she would think I was some lunatic gone wild. I was waving my arms about as I limped along, but that was mainly to keep the gnats and mosquitos away from my neck and face.

I shouldn't have turned him away, I thought. I should have taken his hand and led him into my bedroom. That would fix her, fix all of them, every vicious, mean and insensitive parent who crossed herself or shifted her eyes quickly away whenever she confronted me near her child. I should have done exactly what Duncan wanted. I should have crossed over, gone too far and put on the clothes, the face, the very soul of the person they all accused me of being. Maybe then I would finally be comfortable in this world. Maybe I am the doe I painted. Maybe I shouldn't cast it aside anymore.

I stopped in front of the house. I was simply glaring at the road now, fuming, my eyes blazing at the place under the oak tree where his mother had parked and waited, confirming in her own mind that he had spent the night with me, sinning and selling his soul for lust and pleasure with this daughter of evil.

"You're just jealous!" I screamed at the shadow under the oak tree. "You're jealous because you're too twisted inside to love anyone or enjoy being with anyone now. You'll never admit you enjoyed making Duncan. You lie to yourself. I hate you and all who are like you. You have no right to look at me with eyes of accusation. Look at yourself. Hate yourself!"

Tears were streaming down my face. I held my clenched fists against my hips and found I was gasping for breath. Just then, the phone rang. I could hear it in the open window. I turned and hobbled my way back to the house as quickly as I could manage, hoping whoever it was would not hang up before I got to the receiver.

He didn't.

It was Duncan, but he sounded so strange.

"I told you," he said, speaking as if he was in a tunnel far away. "I told you she would know."

"Know what? We didn't do anything, Duncan."

He laughed. "She thinks we did. She knows what was in my heart, so it's the same thing. I can't tell you how many times in the past she has quoted from the Bible, telling me, 'For all that is in the world, the lust of the flesh, the lust of the eyes, and the pride of life, is not of the Father but is of the world.' "

"Duncan, she has no right to be doing this to you. Listen to me."

"No, no, that's good. Don't you see? At least in her mind I've crossed over. She thinks she can't control me anymore. She thinks it's too late and I'm forever lost. Maybe now she'll leave me be."

"Did she say that?"

"She didn't have to. I know it. She's upstairs, locked in her room surely asking for forgiveness, blaming herself, berating herself. Thank you," he said. "Thank you, thank you."

"For what, Duncan? We didn't do anything," I emphasized. "I didn't do anything. I don't understand this."

"Yes, we did," he said. "Yes. I'll see you later. I feel like someone who just got out of prison. I'm going off to write a poem about it. Thank you."

"Duncan."

He laughed and hung up.

I tried calling him back immediately. The phone rang and rang, but he didn't answer. It frightened me terribly. I retreated to my bedroom to lie down and think. Emotionally exhausted, I fell asleep and didn't awaken until the phone rang again. I hurried to answer.

"Hey," Aunt Zipporah said. "What are you doing?"

"I was just resting," I said, unable to hide the disappointment in my voice.

"Tired yourself out again?"

I hesitated, just barely holding back the flood of words and tears she would surely think was a mental breakdown. How would I even begin to explain it, explain Duncan peeping through the bathroom window at her as well as at me, sleeping in the studio all night and then being pursued by his mother, whom he now thought he had somehow defeated?

"Yes," was all I could manage.

"You want me to pick you up? There's a lull here. Mrs. Mallen and I are just sitting around."

I leaped at the offer. I didn't want to be alone.

"Okay, I'll be right along," she said in her happy, little voice, a voice I so wished was my own.

I went to the bathroom and fixed my hair and put on some makeup. Then I changed into one of my more attractive and brighter outfits and went out to wait for her. Of course, I wondered if Duncan would be calling again, perhaps making more sense this time, but I imagined when I didn't answer this late in the day he would figure out that I had gone to the café and would either call me there or come there.

As soon as I saw Aunt Zipporah drive in, I hurried out to get into her car.

"So how's your painting going?"

"It's not good," I said. "It's not coming out the way I want. I'll start again, maybe a new one, maybe an entirely new subject."

"Oh. Sorry," she said.

I was sure she thought my darker look and subdued manner were a result of my disappointment with my work. She immediately went into one story after another about the customers, Missy and Cassie, throwing every possible amusing incident out to distract me and cheer me up. By the time we pulled up in front of the café, she had managed to get me to laugh as well as smile. I felt guilty, however, for not telling her about Duncan and all that had happened.

Maybe I will later, I told myself and went into the café to enjoy being with her and Uncle Tyler. At least for a few hours I could put all the weirdness behind me, I thought. I certainly didn't want to dump any of it into their laps. They would surely regret permitting me to come live with them, and I couldn't blame them.

Aunt Zipporah did finally ask me about Duncan. She wondered why he wasn't coming around.

I hesitated a moment, and then thought she was the one who had put the idea and the need for occasional little white lies into my mind. This seemed like the right time for one.

"He called once. I happened to be in the house and heard the phone. He was very busy with chores."

She nodded, holding a half smile.

She knows I'm lying, I thought. *I'm not good at it. Grandpa use to tell me I was so used to telling the truth, telling exactly what I really thought, that a lie or even a half-truth would pop out like a pimple on my face. He was fond of saying I was my grandmother's granddaughter.*

"Lawyers are skilled at turning a phrase, concealing a fact, twisting reality to fit the brief, but nurses have a need to tell it like it is," he'd tell me.

"That's not true for Rachel," I told him. He laughed.

"Rachel is a different sort of lawyer. She should have been a surgeon instead. If you need your appendix taken out, she won't procrastinate or pretend otherwise. She'll take it out."

I'd rather be like Rachel, I thought and hated myself for not being that way now.

Duncan didn't call again that day, nor did he come to the café. I was troubled, but I swallowed it back as best I could and made every effort to hide it from my uncle and aunt, forcing smiles, talking with Mrs. Mallen, keeping busy. Even though I had little appetite, I ate more than I usually did. My cover-up seemed to work.

When we all went home after closing, I expected that Duncan might call. I kept listening for the phone, but it didn't ring, and I finally fell asleep. I didn't sleep well. I woke in the middle of the night and tossed and turned for hours, getting up and standing by my window to look out at the field and the studio, hoping to see him hovering in a shadow. I didn't and finally fell asleep again. I slept well into the morning, and when I did eventually awake, I found that my uncle and aunt had left me a note saying they were going to the café together earlier this morning and Aunt Zipporah was leaving her car for me to drive to the café when I was up and about.

I made myself some coffee and sat thinking, again wondering if Duncan would call. I decided to call him and tried, but the line was busy. I tried again and again, but all I got was a busy signal. Finally, I asked the operator to tell me if the line was out of order. She checked and returned to tell me it wasn't.

"Someone might have left the receiver off the

hook," she suggested. She said there was nothing she could do about it.

Would his mother deliberately do that? I wondered. *Doesn't anyone call her? Wouldn't she be afraid to leave it off the hook?*

When I went out to the car, I paused and looked down the road, thinking about Duncan and the strange things he had said to me on the phone. I made an impulsive decision, got into Aunt Zipporah's car, and drove off in the opposite direction from the café, following the memory of where Duncan had told me his home on the old egg farm was located. I recalled the cross streets, but I got lost looking for them and finally had to stop at a gas station and get directions. It wasn't that much farther.

There was no sign to indicate the property was Duncan's, but I saw a small statue of the Madonna just inside the driveway. The chicken coops were off to the right. They were long, gray buildings that looked dark and empty even from this distance. I saw a tractor parked beside one, but no one was around.

The house itself was a large, two-story Queen Anne with a turret roof on the lower porch and an upper porch just under the principal roofline. The exterior walls had patterned wood shingles, and the steeply pitched roof of irregular shape had a dominant front-facing gable. There was a short stairway leading up to the front porch. It was clearly a classic old house, and if it had some real money invested in it, it would surely be a prime property, I thought.

On first glance, it looked abandoned. All of the windows were dark. I drove a little further into the driveway, and when I leaned to the left, I could see a clothesline with sheets, shirts, skirts and dresses waving in the breeze just to the right of the rear of the house. The windows in the late morning sun glittered and reflected the blue sky.

I remained there, thinking and staring at the house. I saw Duncan's mother's car parked in front, but there was no sign of his scooter or of him. *Should I just drive up and knock on the door?* I wondered. *What could she do, shout at me, babble some biblical quotes? At least I would know he was all right.*

Yet I still hesitated. I had yet to see another car on this side road. Way off to the right, someone was developing the land. A bulldozer was parked there, but at the moment, there was no one working. I was hoping that at any moment I might see Duncan walking about the property, or at least he would see me parked out here and come to me, but nothing moved. Even the blades of wild grass off to the right and left seemed to have frozen.

I continued slowly down the gravel driveway, hearing only the crunch of tires and small stones. When I reached her car, I stopped and sat there for a few moments, now expecting that surely she or Duncan would step out on that porch. No one did. I turned off the engine and got out slowly, deliberately closing the door hard so someone would hear me. Again, I waited, watching the door. No one appeared.

A voice within me urged me to turn around, get back into the car and drive off. I seriously considered it until I heard what sounded like a woman's wail coming from somewhere inside the house. It sent my heart racing. I listened for it again, but heard nothing. Was it the wind? There was barely any breeze. Even the few clouds against the soft blue sky looked pasted, unmoving.

Why should I go forward? I asked myself. *Why should I care?* The debate raged inside me.

Finally, it wasn't only the similarities that I felt Duncan and I shared—this fear of inheriting evil, this self-defeating and depressing idea that no one would see anything good in us—that drove me to go to that front door. I had seen there was a softness in Duncan, a loving softness and a desperate need for real affection. In his eyes I saw the sincere affection he had for me. I had become his hope, his way back from the same twisted pathway I had been made to take. We could join hands. We could defeat the shadows and darkness. We could be something wonderful together.

Strengthened by my hope, I stepped forward and went up the short stairway. I barely heard my own footsteps and looked down to see if I was tiptoeing or walking on air. Moments later, I stood before the large, oak wood door and searched for a doorbell button. There was none, not even a knocker. Did no one ever come to this house? It made me think of a face without eyes.

I gazed around, looked back up the empty driveway at the quiet street, and then I knocked on the door and waited. I heard nothing, not a voice asking who's there or any footsteps from within. I knocked again, this time harder, and when I did, the door opened. It had not been closed tightly.

I didn't expect that, of course. For a moment it seemed as if some invisible person had opened it, some ghost. Surely, the sound of it opening would attract either Duncan or his mother, I thought, and I waited to hear footsteps or voices. There was nothing but the same deep, echoing silence.

"Duncan?" I called. "Are you home? It's me, Alice. Duncan?"

I waited and listened. At first I heard nothing and thought I should simply turn around and leave to go to the café. My aunt was probably wondering where I was by now. Suddenly though, I distinctly heard the sound of someone crying. It wasn't Duncan. It was a female, so I imagined it was his mother. Why was she crying?

I stepped a little farther into the house. Despite it being the late morning, it was very dark inside. All the shades were drawn closed on all the windows I could see, and there were no lights on anywhere inside. There was a sharp odor, the smell of strong disinfectants. From what I could see, there were no rugs or any carpets. The dull wood floors were surely the original, I thought. All the furniture I saw as I walked through the entryway and into the downstairs area looked as old as the house.

The loud gong of a grandfather's clock right beside me spun me around. I gasped and listened as it marked the hour and resonated throughout the house.

"Duncan?" I called again.

The sobbing was coming from upstairs.

I approached the stairway slowly. When I reached it, I heard this monotonous buzzing and looked down right to a small table in the hallway, where a phone sat, the receiver clearly off the hook.

"Hello?" I called up the stairway. "I'm looking for Duncan. Anyone here, please?"

The sobbing stopped. I waited, gazing back at the

still-opened front door to make sure I had a quick avenue of escape when and if I wanted it. I could hear the floorboards above me creaking. I held my breath and waited, and then she appeared at the top of the stairway.

Duncan's mother had her dark brown hair tightly tied in a bun at the back of her head. She wore a light blue bathrobe but was barefoot. She looked barely five feet three or four and quite petite in the robe, which appeared to be a size too big or perhaps even a man's robe. When she stepped forward, the dark shadow over her face lifted, as if she'd been removing a mask.

"What do you want?" she asked me.

"I'm looking for Duncan," I said. "My name is Alice—"

"I know who you are. You're related to the people who own that café in town, the one he goes to."

"Yes. Is he at home?"

"No," she said, wiping her cheeks with a tissue. She started down the stairs and paused about midway. "He's gone," she said.

I can imagine why, I thought, but I dared to ask anyway.

"Why?"

She smiled weakly.

Here it comes, I thought. *She's going to unload all the blame at me, send it cascading down the stairway in the hope it will drown me in guilt.*

"He blames me," she said instead.

"He should," I fired up at her. "Why did you make me seem so terrible? Why were you so cruel? You don't know anything about me."

She stared and then continued her descent. As she drew closer, I saw she had a pretty face with diminutive features that actually made her look very young. There was nothing hard or coarse in her eyes either. They were a soft hazel brown.

"I don't know what you mean," she said. "I wasn't happy with his staying out all night at your relatives' home without at least calling to tell me, but I was happy that he finally found a friend."

I recoiled as if she had spit at me.

"What?"

"For a long time I've been worried and terribly concerned about Duncan. I tried getting him to social-ize with young people at our church, but he refused. He wouldn't even talk to them, and he never wanted to do much with anyone at school. That's why I was so torn about his staying out all night and not calling to at least let me know where he was. I didn't want to discourage him from making a friend, but he shouldn't have done something so irresponsible.

"You're right. I don't know anything about you, but I know who your relatives are," she continued. "They're nice people, hardworking people."

I shook my head. What was she saying? "But when I called here for him the other day, you called me Satan. You said, 'Get thee behind me, Satan,' and you hung up on me," I said.

"Oh God have mercy," she said and choked back a sob. "I never spoke to you, young lady."

"You're lying. Didn't you . . . weren't you afraid he would be more likely to become a sinner if he was with me? Didn't you tell him that? Didn't you punish him for being with me, not take him on some church trip?"

"Oh God have mercy," she said once more. "Is that what he told you?"

I nodded.

Tears came into her eyes again. What was this act she was putting on for me? Did she hope to avoid being blamed?

"Why did he run away then?" I demanded. "It's because you made him feel terrible, right?"

She started to shake her head, but suddenly she represented all those people back in Sandburg who stood in judgment over me. I saw all the eyes glaring, heard all the whispers.

"What right did you have to do that? I know something about the Bible too. I remember something about 'He without sin cast the first stone.' "

She took another step toward me.

"He didn't run away because of me," she said firmly. "The only thing I did was forbid him to use my car."

"Then why did he go? Where is he?"

"He went to see his father," she said, then she wobbled weakly and took hold of the bannister as she lowered herself to the step and sat.

Her words flew like hard rain into my face.

"His father? But I thought . . . I thought he didn't know where his father was, hadn't seen him for years and years."

"He didn't. He hasn't seen him. Neither of us has, nor have we heard from him. That's all true. However, yesterday we received a call from a hospital in Albany. His father was brought there in an ambulance. From what I understood, he was found unconscious in whatever fleabag hovel he lived in. His drinking finally started the nails in his coffin," she said. "Somehow, on his deathbed, he was able to manage getting the information about us to the nurse or the doctor.

"Duncan was angry at me for not rushing out and up there. He was right to be angry. I should find forgiveness in my heart, but I just couldn't do it. God forgive me," she said. She looked down and then up at me again, her face riddled with concern.

"But he's not rushing up to him out of love or respect or a son's obligation. He's rushing up there because he's angry at him. He wants him to know it before he dies. He wanted me to stand beside him and both of us heap our rage on him. I told Duncan that was wrong, that it would be a dreadful thing to do, but he's very bitter about it.

"I told him it was wrong to keep blaming everything unpleasant or every one of his own mistakes and failings on his father. I tried to teach him to have responsibility for himself, to show him that if he shifts that to his father and never accepts responsibility for his actions or inactions, he will never improve. Without remorse, there's no forgiveness. That's what I taught him, but I never taught him to cast stones at anyone."

She took a deep breath. I could see how difficult it was for her to say all those things. She looked like her own words were poisoning her. They took my breath away.

"I'm sorry," I said. "I'm just so confused right now."

She nodded and wiped her eyes again with her tissue.

"I'm afraid for him," she said. "I never saw him like he was before he left. That was another reason why I tried to keep him from going. He sounded so mixed up, so confused himself, babbling about how he crossed over and how he was escaping. Escaping from where, from whom? I tried to understand, but he was in a frenzy and made no sense.

"I think," she said after a short pause and a sigh, "that he is escaping from himself. Only I don't know where that will take him, where he will go, or what he will do."

She continued to cry softly.

I leaned against the bannister.

"I'm sorry I said those things to you," I said.

She smiled weakly. "You're a pretty girl. I'm not surprised he wanted to be with you, and whatever he did say about you always sounded very flattering. You seemed to be someone he really trusted."

"He showed me his poems."

"Did he?" She shook her head. "He would never show them to me. I thought, okay, when he's good and ready he will."

I didn't want to tell her how much of his poetry was about his being in a cage, a cage he clearly made sound as if she had created.

"Can he really go all the way to Albany on that scooter?"

"I don't know," she said. "I was surprised he actually gave it any attention and brought it back to use."

"He said you wouldn't let him use your car."

"Well, we have only the one, so I did have to keep its use somewhat restricted. I never liked feeling helpless this far out with no close neighbors, but I was hoping to have enough money soon to buy him something used for himself."

"If he could have gotten a summer job at least . . ."

"Oh, I've tried to get him to do that, but he insists

on staying close to home. He does take good care of our property. I'm so worried for him now," she added. "So worried."

"What are you going to do?" I asked.

"I was just getting myself ready to drive up there, trying to find the strength. I thought maybe I would see him along the way if he is going all the way on that scooter. He might have gone to the bus depot in town, too," she suggested.

"I can check that if you like," I said. "I'm heading to the café, and I know the bus depot is nearby. If I see his scooter anywhere . . ."

"Oh, please. Call me if you see it. I'll wait so at least I'll know that."

"I will," I said. "The receiver is off the hook, so be sure to hang it up."

"It is?"

"Maybe he didn't want to speak to me. Maybe he was afraid I would react like you did and try to talk him out of going to the hospital to do a mean thing."

She smiled and stood up.

"You're such a mature young lady. I don't know many girls your age except the ones I meet at the church events, but you seem older to me."

"That's not always good," I said and started away. I knew that when she saw my limp, she would be curious. It was written in her gaze. "I was in a bad automobile accident this year," I told her when I reached the door.

"Oh, I'm sorry. Be careful," she added.

"I'll call you soon," I said and continued, but when I looked back at the phone in the hall, I saw a large framed photograph and paused to look.

"Is this . . . is this you and your husband?" I asked.

"Right after we were married," she said. "As you see, he was a very handsome man. Duncan looks a lot like him, don't you think?"

I was speechless for a moment.

"When . . . when was Duncan born?" I asked.

"Not for two years later. We were both worried about having enough to raise a family," she replied. "We had difficulty having another child. She died in childbirth. We don't talk about it, if you're wondering why Duncan might not have mentioned it."

"Yes," I said, nodding. Then I turned and walked out.

For a moment I stood on the porch looking out at the driveway. I was dizzy. All that she had told me, her whole demeanor, contradicted everything I had understood. Why had Duncan told me those things and not told me others? It filled me with a mixture of emotions—anger and disappointment, but also greater curiosity.

I got into my aunt's car and turned around to drive out and to town. I was in such a daze that I don't know how I got there without having an accident. Somehow, I made all the right turns and ended up in front of the bus depot. There was a parking lot nearby, and sure enough, I saw Duncan's scooter.

I went into the depot and asked the attendant when the last bus had gone to Albany. He told me it had left nearly two hours earlier and by now had arrived in Albany. Duncan was surely at the hospital, I thought.

As quickly as I could, I drove to the café. Without even saying hello to my aunt and uncle, I got to the phone and called Duncan's mother. She must have been hovering over it. I don't think it finished a first ring before she snatched up the receiver.

"His scooter was there. He's gone on the bus and it arrived a while ago. By now he's at the hospital," I told her.

"Thank you, dear," she said. "I'm on my way out. I'll bring him home," she said.

"I'll be at the café," I told her.

My aunt was standing nearby, a quizzical and troubled look on her face. For a moment I stood there silently after I hung up, and then I turned to her.

"I have to talk to you," I said.

She nodded and led me back to the pantry so we could have some privacy.

There I told her everything. She listened without interrupting me.

Then I burst into tears.

"I am a pariah," I said. "I do attract only dark and evil things."

"Alice."

"No. I am my mother's daughter. Grandpa was right. It doesn't matter where I go or what I do."

"That is utterly ridiculous, Alice," Aunt Zipporah told me. She embraced me. "Stop it. You can't take on everyone else's problems, and you can't blame yourself for any of it. There was obviously a whole history here before you arrived. You just happened to walk into it. That's all."

I shook my head. Nothing she could say would change my mind.

"Maybe you should go home," she said. "You're not emotionally strong enough to work today."

"No, please," I said. "I have to keep busy or I'll go

mad. And besides, I told Duncan's mother to call me here later."

"Okay, Alice. I'm sorry for all the trouble you've had so quickly here."

"Me, too."

"Should I call your grandparents?"

"No," I said. "Grandma will cancel their vacation and come running up here to get me to go home."

She nodded. "Probably would. We'll be fine. Give Missy some relief," she said and walked me out with her arm around my shoulders.

Tyler looked at us, concerned, but Aunt Zipporah gave him a look that comforted him and he continued working. The lunch crowd was building. I went for my apron and dove into the work, practically accosting the customers to please them.

Time flew by without my realizing it, which was a good thing. Hours later, Mrs. Mallen tapped me on the shoulder to tell me there was a phone call for me.

I looked at Aunt Zipporah. She was occupied with some short orders and hadn't heard. I picked up the receiver, my hand trembling.

"Yes, this is Alice," I said.

In a dry, dark voice, Duncan's mother said, "He died before Duncan got here."

"Oh, I'm sorry," I said. "How is Duncan?"

"He wasn't here when I arrived. The nurse on duty told me he was very, very upset and left quickly. I went to the bus station to see if I could catch him before the returning bus drove away, but he wasn't there and never appeared before the next bus left. He might be wandering about the city or anywhere," she said, her voice cracking now. "I have no choice but to start for home and hope he comes home soon."

"I'm sure he will," I said even though I had no confidence in anything I thought anymore.

"If he calls you, please, please let me know."

"I will," I said.

"Thank you, dear. Bless you," she said.

"Bless us all," I told her and hung up wondering if we weren't both making a phone call to God and getting the same busy signal.

18

Broken Promises

Despite how busy she was, Aunt Zipporah kept her eyes and ears on me. The first free moment she had, she came to me to ask about the phone call. After I told her what Duncan's mother had said, she advised me not to get too deeply involved.

"This problem is too complicated, Alice. Duncan and his mother have to work things out themselves. You're too fragile for something this heavy."

I nodded in agreement, but she wasn't convinced.

"Will you promise me not to do anything on your own? Will you?"

I hated promises. People made them to end arguments or to make themselves feel better, or, which is what often happened to me, to make someone else hopeful about something that looked pretty much impossible at the time. My whole life was built on a big promise, the promise that someday, somehow, I would finally understand who I was, that I would finally escape from all the shadows and secrets that hovered around me, invading my dreams and thoughts, that smiles and laughter were just around the corner. I was to be forever patient and optimistic and believe in the promise.

My grandparents, who had been seriously wounded emotionally, who had long ago had their own faith and optimism nearly fatally challenged, did their best to keep their own sadness and disappointment hidden, but I was unfortunately born with that third eye my grandfather described. I could see behind smiles and hear beneath words. I heard the gurgling stream of inky darkness running under our very feet. I knew instinctively that promises offered false avenues of escape.

Countries broke treaties, families broke loyalties, lovers broke sacred oaths, businesspeople broke contracts. Why was anything ever written or said to bind us to promises? We have been victims of them ever since the Garden of Eden. To me, for me, whenever anyone made a promise, he or she was lying to not only whoever had received the promise but also, more important, to himself or herself.

Both my father and my aunt broke the promise every child makes to his or her parents—the promise to be loyal and loving and to do nothing to hurt them. Both my father and my aunt broke their promise to my mother, the promise to protect and to help her. And my mother? Whether she was able to understand what she had done or not, she broke a mother's most important promise to her child—the promise to be her mother, to love and to cherish.

I shook my head. "There's no point in my promising anything, Zipporah," I told her. "I agree with you, but whether I write it in blood or ink, I can't tell you what will happen tomorrow."

"Oh Alice, I'm so sorry something like this happened so quickly to you here. I wanted you to get a

great start. I had a bad feeling about him. I warned
you. I told you to be careful."

"I won't let anyone blame you for anything," I told
her, which was the wrong thing to tell her. I saw the
pain in her face immediately.

"I'm not worried about that, Alice. That's not what
I meant at all. Do you think I would let my parents or
your father make me feel like that?"

"I'm sorry," I said, tears coming to my eyes. "I
didn't mean it to sound that way."

"I know you didn't." She put her arm around me
and pulled me closer to her. "You're very upset. I think
you should go home now, Alice. Get some rest. You
can't do any more anyway."

Just as she said that, a group of nearly a dozen summer college students came into the restaurant, talking
excitedly, laughing and teasing each other. They made
for the two long tables. *How do I become one of them?*
I wondered. *When do I live in a carefree manner and
wake up with a smile on my face and laughter on my
lips?*

Tyler looked up with surprise in the kitchen. We
were going to have a big day here in the café. Another,
smaller group followed the students in and sat at tables
close by. Missy looked overwhelmed immediately.
Cassie was busy with four tables of older people who
had come in for an early bird special.

"I should stay," I said.

"You look drained, honey. Go on home. I'll put on
an apron and take your place. Go ahead," she urged.

I glanced at the crowd building. My hip did ache,
and the thought of rushing about suddenly seemed
exhausting.

"Everything will look better tomorrow. You'll see," Aunt Zipporah said. "C'mon. Get your booty home."

I smiled and nodded as I undid my waitress apron. She took it from me quickly to be sure I didn't change my mind.

"Tyler's going to think I'm deserting you just at the wrong moment."

"Not Tyler," she said. "Maybe Cassie," she added, laughing.

I started toward the door and stopped.

"If I get a call—"

"I'll let you know," she said. "I promise."

The word fell like a bird that had a heart attack. I nodded anyway and continued out of the restaurant to her car to drive myself home, where I did hope I would lie down and get some sleep. I wasn't a bit hungry. I would go right to bed.

As I pulled away, I had a thought and took a quick turn down Main Street to the bus depot. When I looked at the parking lot, I saw that Duncan's scooter was gone. He had found a way home. *That's good,* I thought. *Maybe he and his mother would make peace and start anew.* Was that foolish even to consider? Maybe, maybe not. The discovery and death of his father had to have some serious effect on him. Maybe he would put some of his own demons to bed. I was even a little envious.

Of course, I wondered if he would be calling me. I hurried back to the house to wait. I feared that if he called the café first, Aunt Zipporah either wouldn't let me know or might even say something to him to discourage him from calling me here. I was on pins and needles about it and couldn't stop wondering. There was no point in trying to sleep. I nibbled on some bread and butter and tried watching television, but I neither heard nor saw what I was watching. My mind had truly left my body behind.

Finally, after nearly two hours of waiting, I ventured a call to the café. I could hear the commotion in the background when Mrs. Mallen answered. I was going to hang up, but Aunt Zipporah heard it was me and got on the phone.

"Are you all right?" she asked quickly.

"Yes. I hear you're really busy. That makes me feel bad."

"It's under control, Alice. Stop worrying about it."

"Okay." Dared I ask her? I couldn't help it. "Has anyone . . . have you heard anything . . ."

"He didn't call here for you, Alice. Get some sleep. Please," she begged.

"Right. I'll see you later."

"I hope not. I hope you'll be in a deep sleep," she said.

I had to laugh at that wishful thinking. I did start for bed after we spoke.

And then, as I brushed my teeth, I thought about Duncan's mother. Despite my near promise to Aunt Zipporah, I couldn't put his mother out of my mind. I did have some information for her. I knew he was back. By now she must be home, too, I thought. What harm could there be in a phone call letting her know I was thinking about her? And perhaps Duncan would answer. I wouldn't try to carry on a long conversation with him, but I'd want him to know I had a great deal of confusion about him and the things he had told me.

Twice I started for the phone, and twice I turned back.

This is stupid, I thought and seized the receiver with such force that the third time, I almost ripped the phone out of the wall. I dialed the number slowly, hesitating on the final digit, then closing my eyes and doing it.

It rang and rang. On the fourth ring, Duncan's mother answered.

"It's Alice," I said.

Before I could ask anything else, she asked, "Is he at your house now? Is he all right?"

"No, he's not here. Didn't he come home yet?"

"Yes," she said. "He came home. I told him you had come to the house and that you and I had a nice conversation and you were helping me, but that seemed to make him even more upset. I didn't know what to say. Where would he go?"

"I don't know," I said. "If he does come here, I'll make him go home."

"Yes, he should come home. Blessings, dear," she added and hung up quickly.

She probably didn't want to tie up her telephone line in case he did call her or someone did.

Someone like the police, I thought, and suddenly my memory of all of Craig's anger at his mother came rolling back in a thunderous replay. I was back in that car trying to get him to slow down and he was caught up in a bitter, self-destructive rage. He was in a place he would never have been in if he hadn't been involved with me.

Where was Duncan?

On what highway of bitterness and self-destruction

was he traveling? I stood there thinking about it and decided to go out to check the studio. After all, once before he had hidden himself there.

Because of the heavily overcast sky, it was pitch dark in the back now. The little illumination that spilled out of the rear windows outlined the studio, but if he was in there, he hadn't put on any lights. Nevertheless, I made my way to the studio door, opened it and then turned on the lights. Everything looked the way I had left it. My painting of the doe was still on the floor, facedown.

"Duncan?" I called, looking toward the bathroom. "Are you here?"

The sound of my own heart thumping was all that filled my ears. Nevertheless, I crossed the room to look into the bathroom. It was empty. I turned off the lights and returned to the house. Then I went out front and looked up and down the road that ran past us, listening for the sound of his scooter. The threat of oncoming rain rode on the shoulders of the wind building out of the southeast. It rustled leaves and whistled as it passed over and through the roof gutters that would soon carry the runoff down and away. The thick darkness and otherwise sense of emptiness reminded me of a line in a Shakespearean play—"when graveyards yawn."

I folded my arms around myself protectively. It was a good time for ghosts and spirits to emerge to visit the living and remind them of what awaited beyond the last heartbeat. It was not a time to be alone and deeply upset. Somewhere out there, Duncan Winning was deeply troubled and surely visited by the same feelings and forebodings I was sensing around me.

My anger and my curiosity gave way to sympathy, to compassion and understanding. After all, I couldn't stop thinking about all those nights I had spent alone out there, my mind reeling with confusion and pain, wondering why I had been brought into this world. Despite the lies he told and despite whatever reason he had for telling them, we were still in a real sense birds of a feather.

An idea came to me, a vision so clear and powerful that I had to wonder if it hadn't been delivered by some supernatural power. Still, I hesitated, reluctant to act because of the trust my aunt Zipporah had in me. She was relieved to know I was here and probably asleep, but I couldn't help myself in the end. I had to go. What was drawing me to do so was far more powerful than anything else. It had to be obeyed.

How vain and futile my promising not to get any more involved would have been!

I got back into her car, started the engine, thought about it once more and then backed out and drove off. I wasn't even sure I knew where I was going or if I would find what I hoped to find. I was truly like a blind person navigating in the darkness, guided only by her sense of purpose and her faith in the power that urged her forward.

I drove quickly and then very, very slowly, searching the side of the road, looking for that small, almost impossible-to-discover opening. Cars whizzed by me. Drivers behind me were annoyed with my pace and leaned on their horns, but I was determined. Finally, I found it and turned into the narrow road that, I recalled, led to a gravel one and then just bushes. Once I did, the night seemed to envelop me, even making my headlights appear dimmer and weaker. An inky octopus woven out of deep shadows wrapped itself snugly around my aunt's car. Panic seized me when I realized how difficult it would be to turn around and drive out again. I would have to back up very carefully, and if I got stuck out here, my uncle and aunt would be so upset when they heard my explanation.

I was about to give up and try backing out carefully when the headlights peeled away the darkness to reveal Duncan's scooter. A wave of delight and satisfaction rushed through me. Whatever it was that had brought me here—my intuition, third eye, spirit, whatever—had not disappointed me. I kept the engine running and the lights on and stepped out of the car.

"Duncan!" I shouted and waited. "It's Alice. Where are you? Duncan!"

Except for the sound of the car engine, I heard nothing. *He's sulking,* I thought. *He won't answer and after I went through all this trouble to find him.* It made me angry again.

"Duncan, damn it, answer me!"

I took a few steps toward the bushes and listened. I could hear the river working its way around rocks and boulders, sliding along the shoreline, but nothing else. *He heard me,* I thought. *He had to have heard me.* I considered returning to the car and keeping my hand on the horn until he stepped out of the bushes. When we had come here that first time, he'd had to use a flashlight to find his way between the bushes himself.

Listen, Alice, I told myself, *if he doesn't want to see you, he doesn't want to see you. Why push yourself on him? Let it go. Listen to your aunt's advice. Just make your way back and go to sleep. You have your own problems.*

I actually started to turn back to the car before I hesitated again to listen for him. I did hear something. *Was that a rustling in the bushes? Had he finally decided to confront me?* The sound weakened as it went off to the right. *It could have been some animal, a raccoon or something,* I thought.

Frustrated, I turned back to the bushes. Using whatever illumination spilled from the car's headlights, I located what I believed was the start of an opening in the heavy overgrowth. It wasn't until I stepped deeply in that I realized it was a false portal. The bushes were even thicker. The branches caught on my clothes and I felt one scratch my right forearm. I winced and cried out from the pain, now cursing and babbling my anger toward him.

"I'm not exactly a mountain climber or a hiker, Duncan. You're not being much of a gentleman leaving me out here like this. Where are you? I need you to show me the way. Duncan!"

Something did slither beneath my feet and I screamed. Were there bad snakes here?

I turned to go back and found that the bushes had closed around me. I wasn't sure now which way to head, and I was too far from the glow of the headlights to benefit from the illumination. I struggled as carefully and as gracefully as I could to separate branches to keep them from catching onto my clothing and scratching my arms, even my neck and face. The more I traveled, the more lost and trapped I became. I tried to keep myself calm. I knew that if I panicked in the darkness within these wild bushes, I would do more damage to myself and might even seriously entangle myself.

The rain began, very slowly at first, forming drops out of the mist and then becoming a slow drizzle. Lightning sliced the dark sky, and a roll of thunder echoed over the river. My hair quickly became drenched.

I asked myself how I had ended up in here. How had I been so pigheaded and stupid? *You deserve this,* I told myself. *Maybe you'll learn a good lesson.*

I continued to part the branches and find small openings in the bushes. I wasn't sure I was anywhere near the place Duncan had showed me when we came here, but I worked myself forward, until finally I realized I had come upon the border of the clearing he had made beside the river. I stepped out of the bushes, wiped the rain from my forehead and eyes and tried to see through the darkness, discover his silhouette somewhere.

I didn't see him, and I was struck by the possibility that while I'd been working my way through the heavy brush, he had picked up and left, not even caring that I had come here looking for him. Once again, I berated myself for being such a damn fool. I crossed the clearing and looked at the river. Raindrops were pounding away at the surface. Fortunately, it was a warm downpour, but I would soon be soaked to the skin.

"Duncan!" I called out. "Are you still here? Duncan?"

I listened and waited, now hearing the sound of the rain falling through the trees and over the water. I was about to turn to find my way back to the car when a sizzling flash of lightning, much closer to me, revealed someone in the water, someone who looked like Duncan. I gasped and walked closer to the river's edge.

Another shaft of lightning wiggled though the dark sky, and I could see him bobbing against some rocks a few feet off the shore.

"Duncan!" I screamed.

Blinded now by the heavier downpour, I waved my hands back and forth in front of my eyes like some sort of a human windshield washer. Not even bothering to take off my shoes, I stepped into the river and waded to the place where I had seen him bobbing among the rocks.

When I drew closer, I saw he was lying on his back, his head held out of the water because his body was jammed between some rocks. His lower legs and feet were under the water. His eyes were closed, but his mouth was slightly opened. I shuddered both from the cold water and the sight of him.

"Duncan!" I cried. I reached out to touch his face. The water made his skin feel icy.

Was he dead?

I positioned myself so I could put both my arms around his upper body, grasping him just under his arm. Then, with all my strength, I pulled him away from the rocks. He was so heavy, which surprised me, for I knew that when someone was in the water, the displacement made him or her much lighter. I struggled to move him along with me, barely able to keep him out of the water. His head lay against my shoulder and I began to back up as carefully as I could, afraid that if I stumbled and fell, he would go down and I wouldn't be able to bring him up.

The rain pummeled us both, but I concentrated on getting us to the shore of the river until I felt myself rising higher. When I stepped on the land, I pulled with all my strength and dragged him up and out with me. It was then that I finally permitted myself to fall back to rest.

My eyes had grown used to the darkness enough to see him well. His eyes were still closed. Gasping myself now, I lowered him gently to my lap. It was then that I saw it, and my heart surely stopped and started.

There, tied to his ankles, was a thick, heavy pipe obviously designed to keep him down under the water. The river current, however, had brought him to the rocks, where he had become embedded. I quickly searched his head to see if there was a bruise and felt the warm flow of blood.

I didn't hear him breathing, so I quickly moved to perform the CPR I had learned in my science class. I blew into his mouth twice and began pumping his chest quickly. I waited and then did it again. Nothing was happening. Was I too late? I tried one more time, and this time, I heard him choke up some water and then start to gasp.

Nature had saved him long enough for me to come along, I thought.

Death had sent him back.

I worked on the knot he had used to tie the pipe to his legs while he moaned and groaned and the rain fell harder and harder around us. I wanted to rush out and get some help, but I had this fear that if I left him and he discovered he was still alive and out of the water, he might very well go back in, and with the pipe still tied to him, he would surely drown this time. I continued to struggle with the knot. The water had made it almost impossible to get it loose. With the rain falling about me, Duncan's head bleeding, and my own body aching and screaming, I was quickly falling into a desperate panic.

Finally, I gave up on the knot and worked and worked at slipping the rope off his ankles, pushing and pulling until I managed to get it over and off, nearly exhausting myself completely with the effort. Nevertheless, I found the strength to drag the heavy pipe to the river and push it into the water so it would fall deeply enough not to be retrieved. In this inky darkness, he surely wouldn't find it anyway, I thought.

I went back to him. He was groaning, confused. I had to work on getting us help now. I surely couldn't carry him through these bushes to the car.

"I'll be right back, Duncan. Don't try to move or anything," I told him.

I was pretty sure, however, that he didn't hear me.

This time, I was able to find the pathway Duncan had cut for himself, where he'd taken me through the first time. My hip ached more than it had since I was in the hospital. I was sure all the strain and the cold water had aggravated the old injury. I swallowed back the pain and got to the car, which was still running. When I got in and shifted to reverse, however, I saw how difficult it was going to be to back out of the gravel road without going off into the brush. I couldn't see anything behind me. I opened the door and leaned out, trying to steer as I moved, but it was too hard for me to coordinate, and I did go off the gravel and into the brush. I felt the car sink on the right, and my heart sank with it. Sure enough, when I put it into drive and tried to pull forward, the wheels spun in mud. I was stuck.

Maybe death hadn't sent him back after all, I thought. *Maybe death was just playing, tormenting us.*

I got out of the car and started down the gravel road. The sound of the stones was enough to keep me on tracks, and finally I reached the harder pavement and could see an occasional vehicle on the main road ahead. Hobbling along as quickly as I could, I stepped out onto the road and waited for the next vehicle. Either the driver didn't see me or hear me or simply was too frightened to stop. The car whizzed by. Another car in the opposite direction did the same. I considered stepping onto the highway and holding out my arms. In this rain and on this slippery dark road that was very risky, especially for a girl with a bum leg, but I was desperate now. I had to do it.

The vehicle heading toward me was clearly a truck. As it drew closer, I screamed and waved and prayed. The driver hit his brakes, swerved away from me and managed to come to a stop not far ahead.

"What the hell are you doing?" I heard him scream back at me.

"Please, help us. Please!" I cried.

He put the truck in reverse and backed up to me.

"What are you doing out here? What's going on? Are you nuts?"

"My friend, he's injured badly down by the river. He nearly drowned. I can't get him out. Please help us."

"Huh? Where did you say?" He looked past me.

"I'll show you. Please," I said, backing up toward the side road. He watched me for a moment.

"Not me!" he screamed. "I know these tricks. You ain't robbin' me!" he shouted, put his truck in gear and started away.

"NOOOOO!" I screamed. I started after him. "It's not a trick. Please help us!"

I watched his taillights disappear around a turn.

The road was quiet again. The rain continued to pound the macadam and my face, the drops mixing in with my tears, making them indistinguishable. Hope seeped out of my body like blood from a fatal wound. I lowered my head.

Maybe this is the way we should both end up, I thought. *Maybe this is fate's final blow.*

The glow of oncoming headlights washed around me, but I didn't turn around. I stayed in the middle of the road, waiting, anticipating a car smashing into me. I heard the brakes and then the car come to a stop.

This time, when I turned around, I saw the bubble light on the roof spinning.

A highway patrolman stepped out. I nearly collapsed in his arms before I managed to explain enough to get him to put me into the car and start down the side road, radioing for an ambulance. He grabbed his oxygen tank and told me to just stay put. I smiled to myself. I doubted I could do much more anyway.

Duncan looked semiconscious when they carried him out on a stretcher. Moments afterward, my aunt and uncle showed up. I was wrapped in a heavy blanket the policeman had given me. The rain had slowed but was still coming down steadily. Uncle Tyler spoke to the policeman. A tow truck was ordered for Aunt Zipporah's car, and then they took me back home.

I kept apologizing to Aunt Zipporah. She was very

silent, which made me feel worse. Uncle Tyler wanted me to tell him everything, so I rattled it off as best I could.

"She saved his life, Zipporah," he told her after I had finished.

"I know," she said. "Let's get her warmed up and into bed," she added.

He drove faster, and as soon as we arrived at their house, Aunt Zipporah started a warm bath for me. She helped me take off my soaked clothing. Uncle Tyler had to go back to the café to close up, but I heard him tell her not to yell at me. Again he said, "She saved that boy's life."

Nothing felt as good as the warm bath when I lowered myself into it. Aunt Zipporah brought me a hot tea with a little whiskey in it to sip as I soaked.

"I'm sorry about your car," I told her.

She stared down at me.

"That's the least of it, Alice."

"Are you going to call Grandpa and Grandma to tell them?"

"Do you want me to?"

"No," I replied quickly.

She smiled. "You mean, you don't want to tell them the truth? You aren't tired of a little deception?"

I lowered my head. She was making me swallow my own words, but I deserved it.

"It's all right," she said. "It's all right that you aren't as tough as you thought you were. We'll tell them what has to be told to them when the time is right. No need to spoil their holiday."

"Okay," I said. "Thanks."

"How did you know to go there?" she asked me.

I shook my head. "It just came to me. As if it was supposed to come," I added.

"Maybe it was," she said. "I'm proud of you, honey, as proud as your mother would be," she added, and the dam that had been holding back my tears since the policeman found me on the road finally broke.

Later, I sank into sleep as easily as Duncan would have sunk into the river.

I didn't even dream.

I was that exhausted.

19

Another Trip
to the Hospital

I didn't visit Duncan in the hospital until late the following afternoon. First, I didn't get up until it was nearly noon, and second, Aunt Zipporah wanted to be sure Duncan's mother wanted him to have visitors. Anyone brought into the hospital after an attempted suicide was referred to the psychiatric department, and Aunt Zipporah wasn't sure they wanted him to have visitors—or me in particular—yet. She said she would find out for me, and she called me early in the afternoon to tell me.

"Duncan's mother called us at the café just a little while ago, Alice. The doctors say it's all right for you to visit him. I'll take you there at about four, okay?"

"Thank you, Zipporah."

"I'd rather be taking you to Disneyland," she joked. I laughed.

"Maybe you will next," I said and prepared myself for the hospital visit.

Although she went along with me, Aunt Zipporah remained in the lobby. I told her she didn't have to take me. I could have gone myself, but she was insistent. When I pressed her, she confessed to being worried that "a second shoe might drop." Who knew how I would react to Duncan and what I might do as a result? I was too unpredictable as it was, and I knew that she and Uncle Tyler were still reeling from the shock of what had happened and all that I had done.

I couldn't blame her for being concerned. She and I both knew it wasn't going to be easy explaining all this to my grandparents when they returned from their vacation. We had decided there was no reason to call them yet.

"Your grandmother will be angry at me for not calling her right away, but you and I both know she would ruin your grandfather's holiday. Hopefully, the remaining weeks of this summer will be relatively un-eventful," she said. She said it more like a prayer than anything.

I took the elevator to the psychiatric wing and made my way down the corridor toward Duncan's room. Before I entered, I stopped at the nurse's station to announce myself. The head nurse saw me and nodded her permission. I had expected some special instruc-tions, but no one told me anything. I took a deep breath and entered his room.

Duncan was lying back in his bed. His head was bandaged and his eyes were closed. For a few mo-ments I just stood there looking at him. I didn't want to disturb him if he was asleep. After a few moments, his eyes opened slowly. He stared at me without ex-pression, as if he was trying to decide if I were real or not.

"Hi," I said. "How do you feel?"

"I don't think I've ever felt this tired. I have a debate with myself when I want to raise my arm. The effort seems enormous," he said.

I had so many questions to ask him. Why did he make his mother out to be such an ogre? Why did he tell me all those false things? Why did he want to get to his father and berate him before his father died? Why did he decide to drown himself?

I was silent. I was afraid that if I brought up anything, it would cause greater problems. Now that I was here in his room, I truly felt as if I were walking on thin ice. Should I go forward, remain where I was, retreat? What should I do?

"So I understand you saved my life," he said. "Don't expect me to be grateful," he added before I could even think of smiling.

"I didn't come here to hear you thank me. I can't imagine why you would be any more cordial now than you were when I first met you in the café," I added, and his lips softened.

"I'm afraid to laugh," he said. "It hurts too much."

"How bad was your head injury?"

"They told me it needed nearly fifty stitches. You bleed a lot when you injure your head, but apparently I don't have a concussion. I'm on some pain medication, so I drift in and out."

"I remember that sort of thing after I came out of my operation," I said and went to the chair beside his bed. "I hated it and almost would rather suffer with the pain, but the doctor told me it was better that I wasn't under stress. I would heal faster."

"Yeah," he said somewhat bitterly. "I'm on my way to healing myself."

"Do you remember any of it?"

"Not much, no."

"Am I permitted to ask you why you did it?"

"Why not? Everyone else around here is. I don't know why anyone expects me to provide a satisfactory answer."

"The answer that satisfies you is the one you want," I said.

"Wow. That's deep. Maybe you should put on a lab robe and be the doctor here."

"Maybe I will, smart-ass," I said, and this time he couldn't help but laugh and then grimace, bringing his hand to the back of his head.

"Ouch."

He looked at me, the smile quickly fading, and then he looked away.

"I'm not a psychiatrist, Duncan. I'm not even an amateur psychiatrist, and I'm certainly not anyone who should give anyone else advice. I can't deny that there were times I considered doing what you tried to do. I fell into pools of depression and darkness from which I never thought I'd emerge. I got to the point where I ran out of tears and sobbed dryly. I never stopped asking myself why I was born if my birth brought so much unhappiness to the people who were supposed to love me."

"Maybe you should check into the next room," he said without turning back.

"Maybe I should, but that's not the point now, is it? You and I shared some intimacy, trusted each other with our pain and sorrow and hunger for happiness. I deserve better than what you gave me," I said. "Than what you're giving me now."

I held my breath and waited. Would he just explode

at me, go into some mad rage, or would he continue to sulk and be agonizingly silent, forcing me to give up and leave? Slowly, he turned back to me.

"You're right," he said. "I'm sorry. I shouldn't be taking anything out on you, especially on you."

"Then give me some answers," I said firmly, casting all caution to the wind. "Why did you lie about your mother? Why did you say she destroyed every picture of your father? Why did you pretend to be unwanted, to lead me to believe your mother saw you as what you called a child of sin? All those quotes from the Bible, that stuff about inheriting sin . . . why?"

"Because I liked you. I liked you very much. You're the first girl I felt comfortable being with, talking to."

"Liked me?" I shook my head. "How does that explain why you lied to me?"

"I saw how important it was to you for me to be like you. You had the same distrust of people I did. When you called us birds of a feather, I wanted to keep that special relationship. I wanted to hold onto that idea about us helping each other, being there for each other. We said so many things like that to each other.

"Besides, it wasn't all a lie. I never stopped resenting my father for deserting us. I did believe that he didn't want the responsibility of having a family."

"He was an alcoholic, wasn't he?"

"Yes, and I did like drinking, too. My mother doesn't know to this day how much I did drink when I could. Remember I told you about my finding his stash of whiskey in our basement?"

"That didn't mean you'd be like him, Duncan."

"It seemed to me I would. I have no real friends and I didn't pine over it. I know everyone at school thinks

I'm weird and I let them think it, maybe encouraged it. When you told me that same sort of thing had happened to you, I thought again that you liked me because I was like you, because we were experiencing the same sort of things."

"But you had me believing that your mother thought I was evil. She was just worrying about you the way any parent would worry about her child. Why did you pretend to be afraid of sinning with me, treating a kiss like a blasphemy or something?"

"I was shy," he said sharply. "I was never that close to any girl. You seemed so much more sophisticated. I didn't want to look so innocent, inexperienced."

"You answered the phone that time and pretended you were your mother, didn't you? You were the one who called me Satan, not her."

"It was all part of it," he said. "I'm sorry I did that, but I thought if you continued to pity me, you might grow more fond of me, maybe even fall in love with me."

"Real love doesn't come out of pity, Duncan. Sympathy isn't love. Compassion isn't the kind of love you wanted to have with me. It's not enough. If that's all you have with someone, then when he or she gets better, you move on. There's no commitment, no more reason to care."

"You're right. I'm sorry," he said. "If you came for an apology, you have it."

He turned away again.

"I didn't come for an apology, Duncan. I came for understanding. Yes, I was upset when I visited with your mother and learned the truth. No one likes to be duped, Duncan. I felt betrayed."

He nodded, his face turned away from me, then slowly turned back.

"I knew you would. I figured you would hate me now, think I was as weird as everyone else thinks, and you wouldn't want to have anything more to do with me."

"Don't tell me that was why you tried to drown yourself in the river," I said. "Don't lie there and tell me I'm indirectly responsible. You know how I feel about that, how I still feel about it."

"It was a part of it, I guess, another nail in my coffin, but not your fault, no. I was just tired of it, and I didn't want to face you afterward."

"Now you are facing me," I said, "and being honest, too. Would you rather be dead?"

"I don't know. I haven't had the chance to compare."

"Yeah, well I can tell you this, Duncan, my uncle's great pasta sauce is not being served in cemeteries."

He laughed again.

"Ouch, but a good ouch," he said.

"Look," I said. "I'm not going to say I wasn't very upset with you, but when I hear your reason for doing all that, I'm also happy, even flattered, you would go to such extremes to win my favor."

"You are?"

"Yes, but I still think you're weird," I said.

He nodded. "You think I'm weird. Believe me, when what I did gets out, it's going to be even worse for me around here."

"So? Are you running for class president?"

He smiled and shook his head. "You're right. I would have missed you and your uncle's sauce. Mostly you though."

"I have no idea what the road back is going to be like for either of us, Duncan, but you have to work on it sincerely, and you have to help your mother understand it all as well. You have her to apologize to as well. No mother wants to go through what she just went through."

"Right." He sighed deeply. "I guess I do have to thank you for saving my life," he said. "How did you come to get there in time?"

"I don't know. It just came to me to go there when I didn't find you in the studio."

He nodded at the bandage on my arm.

"You got beat up a bit, too. You have a lot of courage and strength, Alice."

"Maybe, but I can think of about seven million other things I would rather have done and places I'd rather have been," I said.

"What do your aunt and uncle say about it? Are they very upset?"

"My aunt and uncle were very concerned about us both. My aunt spoke with your mother and found out I could visit. She brought me here to see you."

"She did?"

"Again, I'm the last person to give you advice, Duncan, but you have to permit yourself to have a little faith in other people."

"Can you have any faith in me anymore?"

"It's the only way I can have faith in myself," I replied, and his eyes brightened as he pushed back the medication and the pain.

"Then you're not going to go back to live with your grandparents?"

"There's only one direction for me, for you, Duncan, and that's forward, so pull yourself together and get out of here. I expect to walk into school the first day of class holding your hand."

He smiled again and then looked serious again, even a bit angry.

"I was disappointed in my father dying before I had a chance to confront him."

"You don't know what you would have done, but I think I can guess," I said. "You wouldn't have been so tough and hard on him. You would have seen him as deeply wounded, in his own pain, and as regretful about his life and his end as you could have been for him. He might even have asked for your forgiveness. What would you have done?"

"I don't know."

"I used to resent my father until he revealed his own weakness and failing to me. I couldn't hate him for that."

"What about your mother?"

"I don't know. I never had the chance to find out."

"Maybe you will."

"Yes," I said. "Maybe I will."

I rose and went to his bedside. He looked up at me, and I took his hand and just held it for a moment.

"Don't stay here too much longer," I said. "I saw a small leak in the studio kitchen sink faucet."

"Okay. I'll be over as soon as I can."

"Make it sooner," I told him. I kissed him on the cheek and started out.

"Hey," he said.

"What?"

"I still have to help paint your bedroom."

"Frankly, I don't see how you have much time for anything else," I said and left.

I heard him cry, "Ouch," as a result of another laugh.

Aunt Zipporah looked up instantly when I entered the lobby.

"It was okay," I said. "He's going to be all right."

"That's great, Alice. I know you have every reason to look toward the dark side of things, but is it all right for me to say that maybe everything will be fine, after all?" she asked.

"No," I said.

She turned at the door.

"No? Why not?"

"Because there's one more thing first that I have to do before I can stop looking at the dark side, if you'll do it with me."

"And what is that?" she asked.

"Take me to the clinic to see my mother," I said.

She started to shake her head.

"Your grandparents, especially your grandmother, would—"

"It's time we both did, Zipporah, and you know it. In your heart, you know it."

She pressed her lips together. I kept my eyes fixed on her.

"You can't keep pretending you didn't do what you did, Zipporah. My grandparents have to forgive you, too. You have to make peace with the past."

"You do have that third eye," she said and thought for a moment.

"I'm not sure whether it's a curse or a blessing," I replied.

"It's a blessing, Alice. Okay," she said. "You're probably right. It's time for me to go to see her, too."

My heart was pounding at her agreement.

Grandpa used to always say, *"Be careful what you wish for, because you might get it."*

I was sure he would be saying it now.

And even if he wouldn't, I would.

20

Meeting My Mother

Days passed without my aunt Zipporah mentioning my mother again. I began to think she had agreed to go see her just to keep me quiet, to satisfy me, and that when asked again, she would come up with some excuse as to why we shouldn't go. I was about to ask when she announced to Tyler that she and I were taking the following day off.

"Where you going, shopping?" he asked her.

She looked at me and winked.

"No, we're going to visit someone."

I was surprised she hadn't discussed it with him beforehand, but this was truly going to be our secret, our own special experience. Whether or not we would ever tell anyone, especially my grandparents, was something we would decide later. So many years had passed that neither of us could predict how this would turn out. We didn't know if it would be a blessing or a terrible blunder.

For Aunt Zipporah, it was truly the opening of old wounds. For me, it was risking some terrible disappointment that would or could reinforce all the terrible things I had thought about myself. Both of us could return in a deep depression and do great damage to not only ourselves but also the people we loved.

I couldn't imagine being more nervous about anything than I was about visiting and finally meeting my own mother. In the morning I changed three times, unable to decide what I should wear. Did I want to look as pretty as I could, as old as I could? Should I wear a lot of makeup, no makeup? Should I look at the pictures of my mother Aunt Zipporah had and try to highlight the resemblances?

And when we got there and I was face-to-face with her, should I come right out and tell her who I am? Would Zipporah? Would that be psychologically damaging to my mother and cause new problems? What if that drove her to try suicide, too? *That's all I need,* I thought, *another reason to believe I can bring only bad things to people.*

I finally settled on a blue skirt and light blue blouse. I styled my hair the way Rachel had shown me and put on just a little lipstick. Aunt Zipporah wore one of her newer skirt and blouse outfits, too, and brushed and pinned her hair. She wore no hair bands or any of her Indian jewelry either. The two of us were as simply dressed as we could be.

"Ready?" she asked me when I walked out of my room. She was waiting in the kitchen, sipping some coffee and looking out the window.

I nodded. "Do I look all right?"

"You're fine," she said. She put her coffee cup in the sink and smiled at me. Then I followed her out to her car.

It was a perfect day for a drive—sunny, with only a few scattered clouds looking permanently pasted against a deep turquoise sky. The brightness brought out the vibrant mint green in the leaves, giving the forest and the tall grass a richness that suggested nature was bursting with new life. Even the shadows looked intimidated and retreated.

We drove in silence for a while. The trip would take us the better part of two hours.

"I don't want you to think I've never inquired about your mother over the past dozen or so years. I was very interested in her condition right after . . . after it all was settled, but I didn't want to get too involved because I didn't want to upset my parents any more than they had been."

"I understand," I said.

She looked at me. "Do you? I felt so terribly guilty about everything. I knew I had hurt my parents deeply, especially my father, because he had defended me when the police were being very inquisitive. After the truth came out, I had done great damage to his legal reputation. Your grandfather was, and is, too sweet a man to have made me feel any more terrible than I did, but all I had to do was look at his face and I could see the pain I had caused, both Jesse and I had caused. Your mother's name was almost a curse word after that. To show any interest in her was truly like throwing salt on a wound, so I found new friends as quickly as I could, especially at college, and tried to keep myself involved in everything I could, any activity I could.

"It got so I didn't enjoy returning home because I would start thinking about Karen, about your mother, and remember every detail about that time with her hidden in the attic. I would even break out in cold sweats thinking about it.

"Sometimes, I wonder if I didn't get married quickly just so I could avoid going home. Don't ever suggest such a thing to Tyler," she added quickly. "I mean I do love him very much and he's brought me so much joy, but there are lots of reasons, deep reasons sometimes why we do serious things in our lives. Nothing is simply black and white. But," she said, smiling at me, "I don't think I have to tell you that."

I just nodded. I didn't want her to stop talking. First, it was soothing for me, and second, she was telling me more about a time that had been forbidden to me.

"Anyway, from time to time, I did try to learn how your mother was doing. Not being a member of her immediate family or anything it was difficult, but one day, years later . . . in fact, I was already married and living here . . . your grandfather told me about her. Unbeknown to me or even to Jesse, he had periodically inquired about her discreetly. Your grandmother never knew about it and doesn't to this day, I believe. I mean, she knew some of the basic things we all did in the beginning, but as far as I know, she didn't make inquiries even though, being a nurse, she might have had an easier time finding out things than any of the rest of us."

"It was always hard to get Grandma to tell me anything about her, and it still is."

"Yes, I know. I didn't know until years later that part of what my father agreed to do when he and your grandmother took you in to live with them was to pay for your mother's stay at the clinic and treatment there. This better place was part of the arrangement your grandfather made with the district attorney in a plea bargain. Karen would have had a much harder time of it if your grandfather didn't take on her case.

"I've never been there, of course, but from what I know, it's a very nice place and doesn't look like any insane asylum or anything. The patients are people from well-to-do families, some suffering from addictions and others from different psychological conditions, so your grandfather was a great deal more involved in it all than people knew, than even I knew at the time."

"I always suspected something like that," I said.

"From what I know," she continued after a short pause, "Karen hasn't made much progress. She is stuck in time and resists all efforts to cause her to accept where she is and what's happened to her. She's kind of like Baby Jane. You ever see that old movie with Bette Davis and Joan Crawford?"

"I think so," I said.

"Naw, you wouldn't just think so if you had seen it," she said, smiling. "Bette Davis is sort of stuck in time when she was a child star.

"I guess in a real sense your mother was a child star. When I think about us back there, about her, I realize she was always performing in one sense or another. I told you how we would make up our own world in the attic and how we did similar things in the village and in school. She rarely let go of that. She rarely walked off the stage, and when she did, when she was up in our attic hiding, she remained in the wings and pushed me out on the stage to be her surrogate so she could live vicariously through me while she was in hiding.

"She's still in hiding, Alice. In a sense, she's never left the attic."

"Maybe that's why she doesn't remember me, won't remember me," I said.

Aunt Zipporah tilted her head.

"What do you mean? How does that follow?"

"If she remembers me, remembers having me, re-members all that came afterward, she leaves the attic," I said.

Aunt Zipporah nodded.

"Yes, maybe. You always surprise me, Alice. Just like she always did," she added, and we rode on for a long while, swimming in the pools of our own thoughts, focused and concentrating like two devoted athletes determined to cross the English Channel.

I didn't know we were approaching the psychiatric hospital when it came into view. Aunt Zipporah had the address and directions, so she knew we were just about there, but she was right when she described it as anything but an insane asylum. The main building was located on what looked like prime sprawling acres in a scenic region of upstate New York. The property was well maintained, and we could see a number of grounds people at work on the lawns, bushes and gardens.

The house itself was a Tudor-style old mansion with brick wall cladding and two large, elaborate chimneys. As we turned into the driveway, I could see small tabs of cut stone embedded in the surrounding brickwork. The doorway was arched.

"Impressive," I said.

"Some very wealthy person donated this house to be a psychiatric clinic," Aunt Zipporah explained, "because of her own son's mental illness."

"How did Grandpa find it?"

"Like always . . . he knew someone who knew someone. That's about the extent of my knowledge about it," she said. "I called and made our appointment with a Dr. Simons, a woman who is also the chief administrator."

"I wonder if Darlene Pearson ever visited," I said.

"I don't know. Dr. Simons did imply that no one had visited your mother for some time. However, I have this suspicion your grandfather finds a way to come here from time to time. He cares about the mother of his grandchild."

Was this the time to tell her about my father's visit? I wondered. He did confess it in private to me, and it was his secret. *What difference would it make for Aunt Zipporah if she knew?* I thought, and besides, he did say that maybe keeping it a secret didn't matter anymore.

"My father was here once," I said.

"What? When?"

"Not long after it all happened. He told me so during his last visit."

She pulled into a parking space and looked to me before turning off the engine.

"He never told me that."

"He never told anyone. He said she acted as if nothing had happened and she told him she was here more to do the doctors a favor. He said she looked very good, but he also told me she didn't mention having given birth to me. In the end, he said the visit made him feel better, but he never came back."

"I'm glad he did that," Aunt Zipporah said. "I thought it was selfish and even cowardly of him not to care about her anymore. Thanks for telling me. Next time I see him, I'll punch him in the nose."

She shut off the engine.

"Here we go," she said, and we got out.

Inside, the clinic looked no more like a psychiatric hospital than it did from the outside. The lobby was small, but it had a set of matching, comfortable-looking sofas, chairs and tables with lamps, vases filled with flowers, and framed pictures with pleasant rural scenery on the faux painted coffee white walls, which gave the room warmth. Limestone was cut into the light brown carpet.

A tall, stout woman in a blue one-piece dress was dusting and polishing. She glanced at us but continued her work, her face so unmoving that it looked like a mask. I wondered if she was on the staff or one of the patients.

Seconds later, an elegant-looking woman who looked to be in her mid to late forties, came out of a doorway almost immediately, suggesting that some sort of bell or buzzer had gone off to indicate someone had entered the building. She crossed to us quickly, smiling. Her short reddish hair had a shade of amber running through it as well. She was a little taller than I was and wore a dark-blue skirt suit with a white blouse.

"Zipporah James?" she asked, her hand extended.

"Yes."

"Well, you're right on time. I'm Dr. Simons," she said and looked at me:

"This is Alice Stein," Aunt Zipporah said. Dr. Simons looked at me and nodded.

"I do see the resemblances," she said, which started my heart pounding. "Karen is outside," she continued, turning back to Aunt Zipporah. "She paints, you know, and she enjoys doing it outside."

"Paints?" I asked quickly.

"We encourage our patients to get involved in some form of art, creation, or another. Karen's gone beyond what we normally expect, and she's become quite good. I actually had someone interested in buying one of her paintings, a relative of one of my other patients, but Karen wouldn't part with any of her work. She nearly cried at the mere suggestion."

Aunt Zipporah smiled at me.

"That sounds familiar," she told Dr. Simons.

"I have to get back to start a session very soon, but I'll be glad to see you before you leave. You can take lunch with Karen if you like." She glanced at her watch. "We serve in about an hour."

"Thank you," Aunt Zipporah said.

"Let me show you the way. We'll go through the corridor to a side door."

She started back toward the door from which she had emerged, and we followed.

"How many patients do you have here?" Aunt Zipporah asked.

"It varies, of course, but right now we have twelve. However, none has been here as long as Karen has," she added, pausing at the door. "But I take it you know that."

"Yes, of course," Aunt Zipporah said.

"She's a delightful young woman. I don't think there's a mean bone in her body." She leaned toward us. "Can't say that for everyone here."

"Is there anything we should or shouldn't say?" Aunt Zipporah asked.

"Well, I would prefer you didn't discuss the events that brought Karen here."

"There's no chance she would bring any of that up?" Aunt Zipporah asked, finally exhibiting some nervousness of her own.

"Nothing is for certain, but that's highly unlikely. As I explained on the phone, Karen is like someone stuck in time, someone for whom the clock has stopped, if you will, and it stopped before the tragic events occurred. She lives in her own reality when it comes to all that. You'll see for yourself. Don't press her or contradict her. Of course, I'll be very interested in the effect your visit has on her. We might not see that effect for a while after you leave, maybe days later, if at all."

We followed her through the doorway but walked only a little ways through the corridor before she took us out a door and onto the grounds. A few hundred yards or so ahead there were two huge weeping willow trees, and between them, in the shade, we could see my mother seated before an easel, painting. She had her back to us.

"I'll send someone out to fetch you all for lunch, probably my head nurse, Lila Mills," she said as we walked toward the trees.

"It's very peaceful here, beautiful actually," Aunt Zipporah said.

"Yes. Meditative, conducive to mental health," she added with a playful smile. She winked at me, and then she paused and we stopped.

"Something wrong?" Aunt Zipporah asked.

"No. I just wanted to direct myself to you, Alice, for a moment. It will be difficult for you to understand, but she might not pay much attention to you. Whatever does block her memory might block her awareness of you. Don't get upset if she ignores you entirely."

"Okay," I said, and then after a moment I added, perhaps too harshly, "she's ignored me all my life. Why should I get upset now?"

Dr. Simons didn't smile. She nodded and continued walking.

"Karen, dear," she called as we drew closer. "You have visitors."

My mother turned very slowly and looked our way. It was truly as if her mind, which had stopped time for her, had been able to stop aging for her as well. She looked more like my sister than my mother. I thought she could be stepping out of one of the pictures I had seen of her and Aunt Zipporah. She held her paintbrush up and then put it down and rose, smiling.

"Zipporah? Is that you?" she asked.

Dr. Simons smiled at us.

"You'll be fine," she said. "Enjoy your visit."

She touched my arm as she started back toward the building and left the three of us alone.

"Yes, Karen. How are you?" Aunt Zipporah asked her.

"I'm great. You look tired though, Zipporah. Have you been up all night studying for some stupid test?"

She turned to me, holding her smile. She ran her gaze over my face and then turned back to Karen.

"You've got to tell me everything that's been going on. Don't leave out a detail, no matter how small it might seem or insignificant. You never saw the importance of the little things like I did anyway. Oh, I have no more chairs here. Do you mind if we all sat on the grass? It's beautiful grass. They take such care of the property, don't you think? Well?" she followed before Aunt Zipporah could respond. My mother's burst of verbal energy was too overwhelming. We both simply stared at her.

I recalled a conversation I once had with my science teacher last year. We were talking about what was known about memory, and he spoke about dogs and how their owners could leave them for days, even years, and when they returned to them, how the dog would behave as if they had been gone only minutes. "They don't have the sense of time passage we have," he said.

Was that what my mother had lost, her sense of time passage? Couldn't she see how much older Aunt Zipporah looked? How could she think she had just come from school? And what about me? Where did that put me?

"Sure, Karen. I'd like to introduce you to someone. This is Alice," Aunt Zipporah said, and my mother nodded at me, not so much with suspicion, I thought, as resentment.

Did she think I had replaced her as Aunt Zipporah's best friend?

"I don't remember you painting, Karen," Zipporah said as we all sat on the grass.

My mother leaned back, propping herself on her hands, and closed her eyes to welcome the sunshine on her face. She had a wonderful complexion, rich peach with not a wrinkle or blemish in sight.

We have the same mouth, I thought, and for the first time in my life I considered the real possibility that I was pretty.

Her eyes suddenly opened and she turned to me.

"How long have you lived here?" she asked me sharply.

"All my life," I said.

She stared at me so long that I had to shift my eyes from hers and look to Aunt Zipporah for help.

"Alice paints, too, Karen."

"Oh? Yes, I think I recall you," she said. "Maybe. You sat in the back of the room in art class. You were shy. What do we call the girls who are shy, Zipporah?" she asked my aunt.

"Turtles."

"That's right. Turtles. They pull their heads back into their shells and hope the world will go away."

That was the way I was, I thought. She had no idea how right she was about me.

"Alice isn't shy anymore, Karen," Aunt Zipporah said. "That's why I could get her to come with me to see you."

"Oh, well, that's good. How do you like my estate?" she asked us. "I told you I would live in a mansion someday, didn't I? Remember? A mansion twice the size of the Doral House with ten times the grounds. And there are no ghosts here," she said. "They vacuum daily," she added and laughed.

Aunt Zipporah laughed, too.

I saw the way my mother was constantly sneaking glances at me, and I tried not to look back and frighten her off.

"How are your parents, Zipporah?"

"They're fine. Everyone's doing fine, Karen."

"Good. I like your parents. I know I told you a hundred times that I wish they were my parents." She sat forward abruptly. "What do you like to paint?" she asked me.

"Scenes in nature, animals, birds, things like that."

"Sometimes I paint those things," she said. "I'm doing something different this time."

I gazed toward her easel. "Can I look at your picture?"

She thought a moment, then nodded. "It's not done," she said when I stood up.

I walked over to the easel and looked at the canvas. My heart nearly stopped, and I gasped. Aunt Zipporah was looking at me. I brought my hand to my heart and stared.

"What is it, Alice?" she asked.

I shook my head.

"It's very nice," I said. "It's very good."

My mother rose and walked over to stand beside me. We both looked at the picture.

It was a picture of her standing by the window in the attic looking out, a picture very much like the last one I had done up there.

Aunt Zipporah joined us.

"That's interesting, Karen," she said.

My mother nodded. "I don't know why, but it just came to me. We've spent so much time up there, haven't we, Zipporah?"

"Yes."

I took a deep breath and said, "The girl in the picture looks like she wants to be outside."

"Yes," my mother said. "She does."

"She doesn't want to be a turtle anymore," I added. For a moment neither of them spoke, and then my mother laughed and Aunt Zipporah laughed. We all laughed.

Aunt Zipporah put her arm around my mother's shoulders and squeezed her and kissed her cheek.

"It's so good to see you, Karen."

"It's good to see you. And you, Alice," she said, suddenly reaching to take my hand. "You come over here and you tell me all about yourself."

She tugged for me to follow her back to the place on the lawn.

"Go on," she urged after we sat. "Tell me all the things you like and tell me all the things you hate," she said, scrunching up her nose. "Especially the zeros. We have lots of zeros in our school, right, Zipporah?"

"Right," Aunt Zipporah said, then she added, "why don't you two talk and get to know each other? I want to take a walk and look over the grounds. Is that all right, Karen?"

My mother looked at me and then back at her and nodded.

"Well?" she asked me. "Don't you want to talk about yourself?"

"Yes," I said. "If you want me to, if you'll listen."

She laughed. "I have nowhere else to go," she said.

"Neither do I," I told her.

And the journey back began.

Epilogue

Before we left the clinic that day, we did have lunch with my mother. She showed us her room and her other paintings, which were mainly scenes in nature and animals, much like the work I had done. She was even more buoyant, talking constantly and eager to show us everything she could, doing just what my father had described—making it seem as if the entire institution was devoted to her every wish and need. Interspersed with all that were her references to things she and my aunt Zipporah had done at school, the comments made as if they were still in high school. As Dr. Simons had told us, she didn't make any reference to any of the tragic events. When she made any mention of her mother, she made it casually, offhanded, almost an afterthought. Neither I nor Aunt Zipporah asked her if her mother had visited her.

Lila Mills, the head nurse who had come to tell us it was time for lunch, came to get my mother and take her to some therapy session. Her reluctance to leave us surprised Lila, but she was gently insistent, and after we promised to return very soon, my mother said good-bye.

"I hope you'll come back, too," she told me.

"I will," I said. This was a promise I wasn't afraid to make.

Her face brightened even more. She started away, stopped and then returned to hug me.

Aunt Zipporah's eyes were ready to explode with tears, but she held back, and we both went to see Dr. Simons, who gave me the greatest gift of all.

First, we described our visit, especially my exchanges with my mother. When I told her about the painting and why I thought it was interesting, her face reflected great interest. She asked me questions about my life with my grandparents, deep, prodding questions that I was reluctant to answer, but I could see from the expression on Aunt Zipporah's face that I should. After a while, however, I felt as if I was being treated as a patient. Dr. Simons could either see that or hear it in my voice.

"Forgive me for being so personal," she said, "but it's all part of the puzzle I'm here to put together."

She leaned back in her chair and was silent for a few moments, clearly deciding whether or not to say what she was about to say.

"You're both so clearly tied to everything that happens to Karen, that has happened to her, that I have no trouble connecting the dots. I know as much as can be known about her youth, her relationship with her mother and with you, Mrs. James. I don't know all that much yet about her relationship with your brother, but I feel it's coming more and more.

"As you aptly put it when you described the painting to me, Alice, your mother is emerging from the attic. The first step is to want to, to look longingly at the outside world. It's terrifying for her."

"Just as it has been for me," I said.

She smiled. "Yes, I can understand." She pressed her fingertips together and leaned forward. "I have no evidence that would absolutely guarantee a change in any legal decision made about Karen, but it is my firm belief that she was indeed a victim of some sexual abuse and that her expanded fantasies, if you will, were part of her defense mechanisms to deal with it all and especially the dramatic, violent action she was forced to take. She was already someone who was comfortable in her own imaginary world. It wasn't all that difficult for her to continue and go even deeper and deeper until she was totally in that attic."

I felt the lightness come into my body, my heart race with excitement.

"Why didn't this all come out in the legal proceedings?" Aunt Zipporah asked. It was a question on the tip of my tongue as well.

Dr. Simons shrugged. "It's hard to second-guess another forensic psychiatrist. Maybe it wasn't possible to reach these conclusions that early on. Maybe it's because of the time that's passed and the intense and extended opportunities I've had to delve into it all that gave me the advantage. As I said, this is my conclusion from my sessions and psychiatric evaluations. I do intend to submit them. I can't tell you what the result might be.

"Karen still has a ways to go, but I'm encouraged by what you've told me about your visit and what you've seen. Sometimes, it takes someone out of the box to see more clearly. Sometimes, we're all just too close. So thank you for that."

"No, thank you for sharing this with us," Aunt Zipporah told her.

Neither of us could speak for quite a while after we left for home that day. We were both so deeply entrenched in our own thoughts, our own personal recoveries. I could almost feel the dark cloud lift away from us both. I had dreamed and prayed for this day, this conclusion. There was no evil for me to inherit. I had no power or inclination to contaminate anyone. I was the echo of a scream my mother had voiced before I was born. It was time for that echo to die away.

It was time only for laughter and music.

Whatever guilt and burden my aunt had felt disappeared as well. She still felt she had hurt her parents with the secret she had kept from them, but she also felt less evil. She had never told me what really kept her from having her own child, but it wasn't too long after this first visit with my mother that she announced her pregnancy to my grandparents. We had decided to tell them everything, of course. My grandmother was at first frightened by it all, but in time she accepted everything and in fact accompanied us on one of our future visits with my mother. Each visit brought me closer and closer to her. I could feel the oncoming awareness, the revelation, and most important, the acceptance. It was imminent. It would be like being reborn.

In the meantime Duncan and I had a successful senior year. We both went out for the school play and won big parts. He was a much better student than I was and helped me with homework often. We were an item on and off but never committed to anything much more. He surprised his mother, as well as me, by deciding to apply to Michigan State and become an English major with the intention of eventually becoming a journalist. He would always write poetry, and he talked about his great novel to come.

Uncle Tyler gave him a part-time job at the café to help him earn money for college. He worked as a waiter, but he often used his culinary skills to fill in as a short-order cook, too. The café was busier than ever, and with our weekends working, our schoolwork and my frequent visits to see my mother, the year seemed to fly by. It was the happiest year of my life.

My grandparents visited as often as they could. I was reluctant to return, even for Thanksgiving, but I did. My grandfather decided to take us on a holiday during the Christmas recess, so I went with them to Florida, but during the spring break I remained at the café, working. It was a very busy time, because tourists were coming around since the weather was so much nicer.

In mid-June Aunt Zipporah gave birth to a girl she and Tyler decided to name Patience because, according to my aunt's doctor, the baby was two weeks late. Of course, everyone kidded them about it, but I thought it was a pretty name and quite clever.

A week before graduation, my father surprised me by calling to say he and Rachel were going to fly east to attend. They would come with my grandparents. Rooms were booked for them at a nearby motel. When they arrived, I introduced Duncan to them, and they all got along well. My aunt and I talked about my mother with my father, while Rachel went on a shopping spree with my grandmother, looking for graduation gifts for me.

He had great interest in all that we had to tell him. He explained to us why it had been and still was difficult for Rachel, but he also said she was accepting it more and they would soon be telling the twins the truth about me. He said it was Rachel's idea to start that revelation gradually but early enough for them eventually to completely understand as they grew older. My father said he realized that he would have a difficult burden explaining how and why it all had happened.

"You know, your kids always see you as invulnerable, a hero, perfect," he said.

Afterward, he and I spent some private time together. He knew I had decided to stay close to home my first college year and attend the State University of New York at New Paltz, but he surprised me by suggesting that I consider transferring to the University of Southern California after the first year. He said he and Rachel had discussed it and decided they would welcome me to their home and contribute to my college education. I told him I would keep it in mind. It was exciting to think about. I had already decided I wanted to go into psychology and do something in that field.

A few weeks after graduation, I returned to the Doral House with Aunt Zipporah to celebrate my grandfather's birthday. Despite all that had happened and was happening, I was still nervous about spending time there. After dinner and our singing "Happy Birthday" to him over his cake, I went up to the attic. It was strange, but when I looked at it now, it seemed so much smaller to me—even claustrophobic. I didn't want to stay there long and went back downstairs quickly.

My grandfather winked at me and suggested we

take what used to be one of our famous walks while
my aunt and my grandmother visited together.

We couldn't have had a better summer evening for
the walk. The sharp, cool night air made the stars look
even brighter, so that even though there was no moon,
we could clearly see the old country road ahead of us.

"Are you going to show me the land you're going to
buy and develop again, Grandpa?" I kidded.

"Well for your information, young lady," he said,
"I did buy the land. With a group of investors," he
added.

"I'm impressed," I said.

"You should be. Your grandfather is a real wheeler-
dealer."

I laughed and we walked silently for a while. It really wasn't silence for me, however. Just being beside
him, feeling his love and strength, spoke volumes to
me. He was really what had made me feel safe here
despite it all.

"So," he said, pausing and looking out at his potential housing development, "have you killed all your
demons? Have you found what you were looking for
by leaving here?"

"I think so, Grandpa. There's nothing to frighten
me here anymore. A shadow is a shadow and nothing
else."

"And the attic?"

"Is just an attic," I said.

"Good. Because I'm keeping the house," he said.
"With all you grandchildren popping up, I'm going to
need it."

"You were never afraid, were you, Grandpa?" I asked.

"Afraid? Sure. Many times, but the trick is to make

that fear work for you. I think that's what you did, Alice. You used it to make yourself stronger."

"Then I learned it from you," I said.

He was silent. The darkness hovered around us, simmering but staying back.

We were too bright.

We were lanterns who would lead those we loved for as long as the flame within us burned.

There was no greater gift to give.

SIMON &
SCHUSTER

Virginia Andrews

Delia's Crossing

. . . the first in a spellbinding new series.

After her parents are killed in a road accident, Delia Yebarra's
life is turned upside-down. At fifteen, she leaves the rural
Mexican village where she grew up to embark on a new life in
America. Arriving at her wealthy Aunt Isabella's huge estate
in Palm Springs, California, should be a dream come true for
a simple country girl like Delia – so why does it feel like a
nightmare?

Her aunt refuses to acknowledge Delia's heritage, relegating
her to the servants' quarters with a lecherous language tutor
who is intent on exploiting the beautiful young foreigner.
Her cousin Edward is kind, but cousin Sophia is cruel,
manipulative and resentful of Delia's sultry Latin looks. And
just when Delia tries to embrace the life of an all-American
girl, a heartbreaking chain of events sends her spiralling back
to a Mexico she hardly recognises . . .

ISBN 978-1-84737-471-4
PRICE £12.99

**POCKET
BOOKS**

This book and other **Virginia Andrews**® titles are available from
your local bookshop or can be ordered direct from the publisher.

The Delia Series

| 978-1-84737-471-4 | Delia's Crossing | £12.99 |

The Secret Series

| 978-1-84739-225-1 | Secrets in the Attic | £6.99 |

The Early Spring Series

| 978-1-84739-191-9 | Broken Flower | £6.99 |
| 978-1-84739-190-2 | Scattered Leaves | £6.99 |

The Shadows Series

| 978-1-84739-028-8 | April Shadows | £6.99 |
| 978-1-84739-027-1 | Girl in the Shadows | £6.99 |

The Gemini Series

978-0-74349-538-7	Celeste	£6.99
978-0-74349-539-4	Black Cat	£6.99
978-0-74349-540-0	Child of Darkness	£6.99

Please send cheque or postal order for the value of the book,
free postage and packing within the UK, to
SIMON & SCHUSTER CASH SALES
PO Box 29, Douglas Isle of Man, IM99 1BQ
Tel: 01624 677237, Fax: 01624 670923
Email: bookshop@enterprise.net
www.bookpost.co.uk

Please allow 14 days for delivery. Prices and availability
subject to change without notice